JAMES NORTH, a magna cum laude graduate of Harvard and former president of the *Harvard Crimson*, has spent six years reporting from the Third World in such publications as *The New Republic* and *The Nation*.

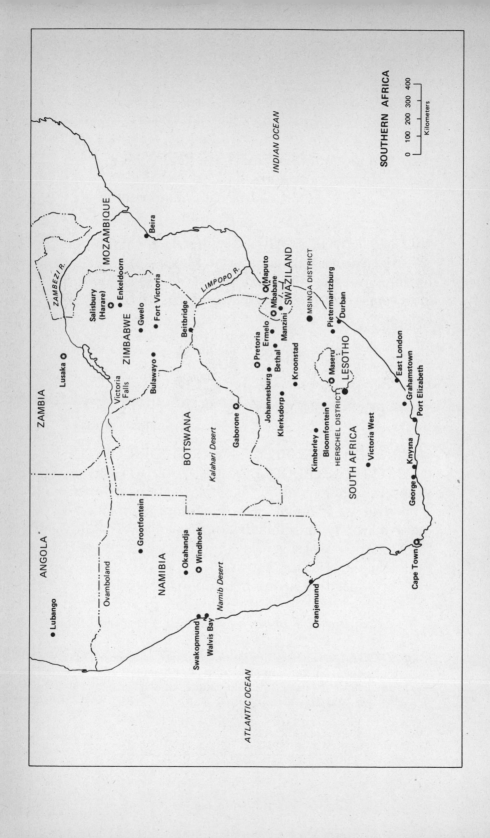

SOUTHERN AFRICA

0 100 200 300 400
Kilometers

INDIAN OCEAN

ATLANTIC OCEAN

ANGOLA

ZAMBIA

Lubango

Lusaka

ZAMBEZI R.

MOZAMBIQUE

Beira

NAMIBIA

Ovamboland

Grootfontein

Okahandja

Windhoek

Swakopmund
Walvis Bay

Namib Desert

Oranjemund

BOTSWANA

Kalahari Desert

Gaborone

ZIMBABWE

Salisbury
(Harare)

Enkeldoorn

Gwelo

Fort Victoria

Victoria
Falls

Bulawayo

Beitbridge

LIMPOPO R.

Maputo

Mbabane

Manzini

SWAZILAND

Bethal

Ermelo

Pretoria

Johannesburg

Klerksdorp

Kroonstad

Bloemfontein

Kimberley

HERSCHEL DISTRICT

Victoria West

SOUTH AFRICA

MSINGA DISTRICT

Pietermaritzburg

Durban

Maseru

LESOTHO

East London

Grahamstown

Port Elizabeth

Knysna

George

Cape Town

JAMES NORTH

Freedom Rising

With a New Epilogue

A PLUME BOOK

NEW AMERICAN LIBRARY

NEW YORK AND SCARBOROUGH, ONTARIO

Published by arrangement with Macmillan Publishing Company

 PLUME TRADEMARK REG. U.S. PAT. OFF. AND FOREIGN COUNTRIES
REG. TRADEMARK—MARCA REGISTRADA
HECHO EN HARRISONBURG, VA., U.S.A.

SIGNET, SIGNET CLASSIC, MENTOR, PLUME, MERIDIAN and NAL
BOOKS are published *in the United States* by New American Library,
1633 Broadway, New York, New York 10019,
in Canada by The New American Library of Canada Limited,
81 Mack Avenue, Scarborough, Ontario M1L 1M8

Library of Congress Cataloging-in-Publication Data

North, James.
  Freedom rising.

  Includes index.
    1. South Africa—Race relations.   2. National
liberation movements—South Africa.   3. Civil rights—
South Africa.   4. Guerrillas–South Africa.
5. Zimbabwe—Politics and government—1979–1980.
6. Zimbabwe—Politics and government—1980–
I. Title.
DT763.N67   1986   320.968   86-698
ISBN 0-452-25805-7

First Plume Printing, April, 1986

1 2 3 4 5 6 7 8 9

PRINTED IN THE UNITED STATES OF AMERICA

Contents

"Injustice anywhere is a threat to justice everywhere."

—DR. MARTIN LUTHER KING, JR.

"Dr. Rieux resolved to compile this chronicle, so that he should not be one of those who hold their peace but should bear witness in favor of those plague-stricken people; so that some memorial of the injustice and outrage done them might endure; and to state quite simply what we learn in a time of pestilence: that there are more things to admire in men than to despise."

—ALBERT CAMUS, *The Plague*

"With confidence we lay our case before the whole world. Whether we win, whether we die, freedom will rise in Africa like the sun through the morning clouds."

—BREYTEN BREYTENBACH, in court
before starting his prison sentence

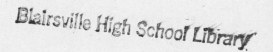

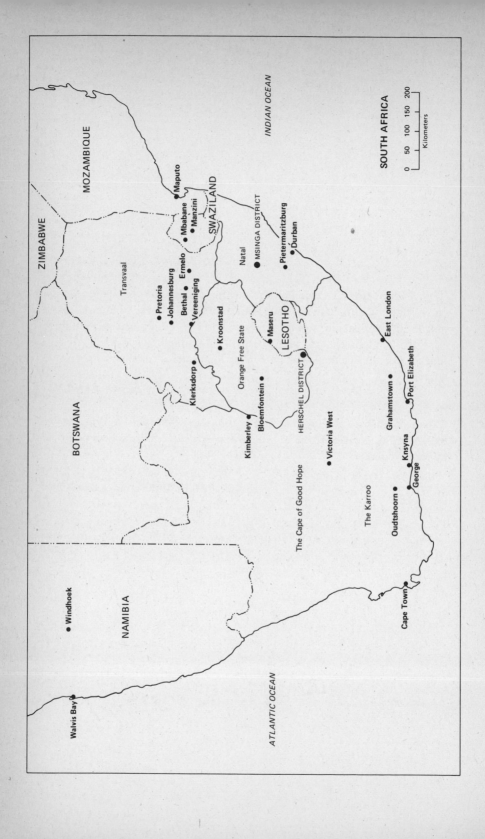

Preface to the Second Edition

MY FRIENDS HAVE OFTEN ACCUSED me of being too optimistic, but not even during my most lyrical flights of fancy could I have imagined how fast the anti-apartheid movement would grow in America and elsewhere in the two short years since I completed the first edition of this book. When I returned to southern Africa for a first-hand look to bring this edition up-to-date, I found a new feeling of gratitude toward the thousands upon thousands of Americans who have worked selflessly to turn the U.S. government's policy around. There is also a great respect for the success of our movement in sending an increasingly louder message to South Africa—we are moving to end double standards. We will no longer support non-racial democracy at home while denying it overseas.

For this edition, I have added an epilogue to describe the tragic and turbulent events of the past two years. I have also included a Glossary and a list of participants to aid readers who may be confused by unfamiliar words and names. My warmest thanks to those readers who have helped me with their observations, their criticisms, and above all with their encouragement.

—Harare, Zimbabwe
October 1985

Preface

I WENT TO SOUTHERN AFRICA in 1978 because I wanted to see for myself. I planned to stay there for a short time, perhaps a year, writing articles for newspapers and magazines back in America. In the end, I became so caught up in the unfolding of history that I remained four and one-half years. I travelled twenty-five thousand miles throughout the region, most of it by land, the equivalent of a circuit of the globe. I visited the small towns, the rural areas, and the great cities between Cape Town and the Zambezi River. I saw Rhodesia become Zimbabwe, and South Africa slide deeper into war. I talked with hundreds of people, of all colors and from every conceivable background. I made dozens of close friends. I went to some of their funerals.

This book is fact. Certain of the better-known people I spoke with, like novelist Nadine Gordimer and photographer Peter Magubane, appear under their real names. But to protect some of the others from the South African police state, I have changed their names, and altered certain small details. It is evident from my book that I engaged in some minor but still illegal activities when I was inside South Africa. I should stress that none of the people I identify accurately were aware of that side of my life.

My greatest regret is that I did not have more time and space to write about the extraordinary people I met. A few paragraphs barely do justice to Hugh Lewin, a white man who spent seven years as a political prisoner in South Africa, and I had no space at all for Indres Naidoo, a black man who did ten years and would cheerfully do another ten if he thought it would help bring his country closer to freedom. At every turn, people like these two, brave and trusting, went out of their way to help me, talking about their own lives for hours and then guiding me on to others. I owe them a great debt. In return, I can only hope that my book serves as some small help to them in their long fight.

This is not an academic book. But I have been strongly influenced by more formal scholarly work, particularly by the bold new revisionist school in southern African history that began to take shape in the early 1970s. I have learned much from the work of Charles van Onselen, Dan O'Meara, Martin Legassick, Robert Davies, Phil Bonner, Q. N. Parsons, Alan Booth, Colin Bundy, and others. My understanding of the long resistance to *apartheid* would have been impossible without many decades of work by Gwendolen Carter, Thomas Karis, Gail Gerhart, and Mary Benson. Other scholars I found important were Terence O. Ranger, John Kane-Berman, Francis Wilson, and the authors of the essential series of booklets published by the International Defense and Aid Fund. Also, as anyone who studies the region soon learns, the annual *Surveys* of the South African Institute of Race Relations are indispensable.

On a more personal level, many people helped and counselled me during my years in southern Africa. I specifically want to thank Arthur James, a white African who shares his continent's devotion to teaching, and Mr. and Mrs. T. Raines, who look after the land. My deepest thanks also to Jan Pager, Quentin dePriest, Mary Cassatt, and Robert Fletcher.

In America, I should mention my appreciation to those who worked at the various publications I wrote for, including Lee Aitken, Sheryl Larson, and Jim Weinstein at *In These Times,* the tenacious Socialist weekly, and Mike Kinsley and Dorothy Wickenden at the *New Republic.* They, and others, were a vital link during my time overseas. Another such sustaining connection was my agent, Wendy Weil.

I thank my editor, Edward T. Chase, for his help and encouragement over the years. Others who reviewed the manuscript and suggested major improvements include: George O. Shadwell, Richard W. Shepro, Elisabeth Scharlatt, and Steven M. Luxenberg. Those who typed the manuscript as it moved through its many incarnations on two continents were a veritable United Nations: June Stevens, Mrs. John Kabalgambi, Kevinne Moran, Mary Montag, and Helen K. Bailey. The finishing touches depended on the help of my friends Dominick Anfuso of Macmillan, Tom Geoghegan, and Miriam Rabban.

My last and greatest debt is to my mother and my late father. They raised me to oppose racism and they taught me how to fight it.

—Manzini, Swaziland
Chicago

Glossary

Amandla awethu	Power to the people
baas	boss, master
bakke	a pick-up truck
Boer	farmer in Afrikaans; used by blacks as an insult
braaivleis	a barbecue
coolie	an insulting term for an Indian South African
dagga	marijuana
dominee	a minister in Afrikaans
dorp	a small town
highveld	the vast inland plateau; includes much of the Transvaal
houtkop	"wooden-head," an insulting term for colored people
iBhunu	"Boer" in Zulu
induna	originally Zulu, now widely used for "foreman"
inyanga	traditional healer, witchdoctor
"join"	widely used as a noun meaning a migrant labor contract
kaffir	originally derived from Arabic for "infidel," now equivalent to "nigger"
knobkerrie	a wooden club
kombi	a small van

kopjes	distinctive, flat-topped hillocks in the Free State
kraal	a circular enclosure for cattle
laager	the circle of covered wagons Afrikaners used as a tactic in their nineteenth-century wars against blacks
lekker	"tasty," attractive, nice
makgotla	Soweto vigilante groups
mielie	maize, corn
numzaan	householder
oke	guy, "fella"
pamberi	"forward" in Shona
panga	a long knife
platteland	"flatland," any rural area
sadza	"maize meal" in Zimbabwe
sangoma	traditional healer
shebeen	semi-legal drinking spot in the townships
sjambok	whip of animal hide; pronounced sham-BOK
skelms	criminals, ruffians
staffriding	the dangerous practice, favored by some Soweto youths, of traveling atop moving trains
tsotsi	a street criminal; said to be a corruption of the American "zoot suiter"
Umkhonto we Sizwe	"The Spear of the Nation," the military wing of the African National Congress
umlungu	white man
vakomana	"the boys," the guerrillas in Zimbabwe
verkrampte	"cramped, narrow," the more conservative wing of the National Party
verligte	"enlightened," the National Party's supposedly more moderate wing
voortrekkers	the Afrikaner pioneers of the nineteenth century

Participants

NEIL AGGETT—White trade unionist and doctor; died in detention.

NEIL ALCOCK—The *Numzaan,* guiding spirit of the experimental farm across the Tugela River from the Kwa-Zulu Bantustan.

ALLAN BOESAK—Black preacher in the Dutch Reformed Church, a leader of the United Democratic Front.

THOZAMILE BOTHA—Leader of a civic association in the Port Elizabeth area, now in exile.

ANDRÉ BRINK—Afrikaans novelist, strongly anti-apartheid.

BREYTEN BREYTENBACH—The leading Afrikaans poet, served seven years in prison for "terrorism."

DENNIS BRUTUS—Exiled black poet, tireless anti-apartheid campaigner in America.

BILL CHINSAMY—A waiter at the Royal Hotel in Durban, like his father and grandfather.

STEVE COHEN—Teacher in Johannesburg.

FRIKKIE CONRADIE—Afrikaans *dominee* who broke with his church.

MODIKWE DIKOBE—Gentle, elderly black writer, former union activist.

MBOMA DLADLA—A man of fourteen, lives in the Kwa-Zulu Bantustan.

STEVE DLAMINI—A veteran black mineworker in Swaziland.

KOOS DU PREEZ—An Afrikaner veterinarian in the northern Cape.

PHILLIP DU PREEZ—One of the last white truck drivers in South Africa.

NADINE GORDIMER—The world-famous English-speaking novelist.

SUBRY GOVENDER—Indian South African journalist.

THOZAMILE GQWETA—Labor leader from East London, detained many times.

LAWRENCE HODZA—A Zimbabwean waiter, actually a blacklisted teacher.

MOSES HODZA—Lawrence Hodza's uncle.

JOE JOKONYA—A Zimbabwean academic and longtime ZANU activist.

ERNEST KADUNGURE—Former guerrilla commander in Zimbabwe, a ranking official in ZANU.

OBED KUNENE—A newspaperman, editor of *Ilanga*, in Durban.

HUGH LEWIN—A white South African, served seven years as a political prisoner.

ALBERT JOHN LUTULI—President-general of the African National Congress, awarded the Nobel Peace prize in 1961.

NOKUKANYA LUTULI—The widow of Albert Lutuli.

PHILEMON MABIKA—Storeowner and ZANU branch chairman in Enkeldoorn, Zimbabwe.

PETER MAGUBANE—The well-known South African photographer.

SOLOMON MAHLANGU—An ANC guerrilla, hanged in 1979.

ELIJAH "TAP TAP" MAKATHINI—A Natal boxer who once challenged for the world middleweight crown.

MAGNUS MALAN—General and South African Minister of Defense.

NELSON MANDELA—The leader of the African National Congress, imprisoned for the past twenty-three years.

MOSUBYE MATLALA—Thoughtful Soweto student activist.

MTUTUZELI MATSHOBA—One of the best-known young black South African writers.

MANDLA MAZIBUKO—Soweto student leader, once a pacifist.

ERIC MCCABE—A white one-time gold miner.

FATIMA MEER—An Indian South African woman who teaches sociology.

SHADRACH MKELE—A young farmer, former migrant laborer, in the Transkei Bantustan.

HELEN MORRISON—A white woman activist in Durban.

DR. NTHATO MOTLANA—A leader in Soweto.

MARGARET MPANZA—A Durban housemaid.

BANDI MPETHA—A woman farmer in the Transkei.

EZEKIEL MPHAHLELE—One of the best-known South African novelists and critics.

ROBERT MUGABE—Independent Zimbabwe's first prime minister.

GRIFFITHS MXENGE—A Durban civil rights lawyer, murdered in 1981.

VICTORIA MXENGE—She took up the law practice of Griffiths, her late husband, and was murdered in 1985.

REVEREND BEYERS NAUDÉ—Once a leader in the Afrikaans establishment, now a prominent opponent of apartheid.

VUSI NDLAZI—An ex-pickpocket who now works in a slaughterhouse.

EZEKIEL NJONGWE—An elderly civic leader in the Transkei.

JOSHUA NKOMO—The leader of ZAPU, the smaller party in Zimbabwe's Patriotic Front alliance.

JABU NZIMA—An exiled official in SACTU, the ANC's trade-union wing.

PETRUS NZIMA—Jabu's husband, a former garment worker from Natal who was active in the ANC in Swaziland.

JILL PARKER—A student at the University of the Witwatersrand in Johannesburg.

SIVA PATEL—A banned Indian South African activist.

FANIE PRETORIUS—A steelworker in Pretoria.

ABEL RABOTATA—A blind bookkeeper in the Kwa-Zulu Bantustan.

RONALD SANDILE—One of the highest-ranking ANC officials in Swaziland.

HENRY SHONIWA—An underground electoral strategist in Zimbabwe.

WALTER SISULU—A leader in the African National Congress, in prison since 1964.

ZWELAKHE SISULU—The son of Walter Sisulu, a prominent journalist.

HANNES SMITH—The eccentric newspaper reporter-in-chief in Windhoek, Namibia.

ROBERT SOBUKWE—The first president of the Pan-Africanist Congress; died in 1978.

HAROLD STRACHAN—Painter, raconteur, marathon runner, political prisoner.

LUCKY STYLIANOU—The first white man to play for the Kaizer Chiefs.

OLIVER TAMBO—The president of the African National Congress, in exile.

COLIN THORPE—Garage owner and civic booster in Enkeldoorn, Zimbabwe.

JAMES THRUSH—Politician and press spokesman for Ian Smith's Rhodesia Front.

HERMAN TOIVO—A leader of SWAPO, the Namibian independence movement, jailed for 17 years.

BISHOP DESMOND TUTU—Outspoken cleric; won the 1984 Nobel Peace Prize.

DÉSIRÉE VAN RENSBURG—Young Afrikaans teacher, opposed to apartheid.

VAN WYCK—Farmer in the northern Transvaal, staunch National Party
supporter.

HENDRIK VERWOERD—Minister of Native Affairs, later Prime Minister;
elaborated the ideological justification for apartheid.

JOHN VORSTER—Prime Minister of South Africa from 1965 to 1978.

DICK WATSON—White farmer in a "hot area" during the war in Zimbabwe.

PART ONE

The Land of Apartheid

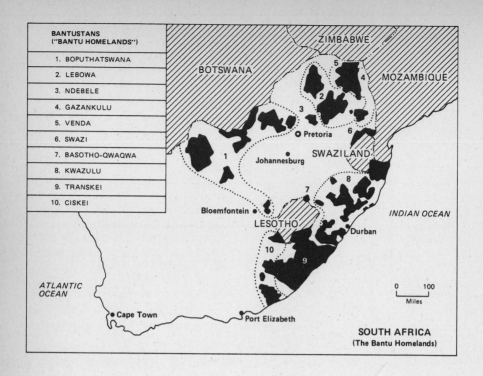

BANTUSTANS ("BANTU HOMELANDS")

1. BOPUTHATSWANA
2. LEBOWA
3. NDEBELE
4. GAZANKULU
5. VENDA
6. SWAZI
7. BASOTHO-QWAQWA
8. KWAZULU
9. TRANSKEI
10. CISKEI

ZIMBABWE

BOTSWANA

MOZAMBIQUE

Pretoria

SWAZILAND

Johannesburg

INDIAN OCEAN

Bloemfontein

LESOTHO

Durban

ATLANTIC OCEAN

0   100
Miles

Cape Town

Port Elizabeth

SOUTH AFRICA
(The Bantu Homelands)

1

Winter Inside South Africa

POLICE STATES SEEM TO ENGENDER a certain revealing grammatical usage.
You go to and from England or France, but you go into and out of a
place like South Africa. One bright winter day in June 1981, I approached the Oshoek border post, which is the main crossing between
South Africa and Swaziland, the small, independent country to the east
where I had been living. I plastered a smile on my face and sauntered
up to the immigration office. The South African regime had removed
some of the more blatant forms of segregation while retaining the substance behind a masquerade of euphemism. There were three separate
windows, divided by glass partitions, marked "Foreign Passports,"
"Republic of South Africa Passports," and "Travel Documents." A long
line of blacks waited quietly outside the "Travel Documents" window.
The other two were free. In previous years, the signs would have been
more explicitly racial.

I filled out the familiar blue form, glancing discreetly inside to see if
any of the uniformed police were taking special notice of me. During
my previous trips inside I had not broken the most serious security laws,
but I still had some reason to be concerned. I watched the policeman
intently as he leafed through my documents, hoping he would not look
upward at the row of photographs hidden on his side of the window, or
move toward either the Rolodex file or the computer terminal in the rear.
I glanced out toward the road, where white soldiers in camouflage uni-

forms stood by the lowered steel barrier. He silently ticked off the items on the form. I nervously ventured an observation about rugby. He showed no interest. Finally, he stamped the passport, and went back to the other window where he had left the line of blacks to wait until he had attended to me. I walked briskly away.

The security police maintain a permanent office at the Oshoek border post. Friends of mine had been thoroughly searched there many times; the police in some instances had apparently been expecting them. I had also heard that the outlawed African National Congress sometimes sent its young guerrillas into the country through this border, unarmed and carrying false travel documents. I looked over at the black people, who were still waiting in line patiently, as I got back into the car.

At that stage, I had already been in southern Africa for three years. I was living in Swaziland and travelling throughout the region as a freelance writer, chronicling the steady and apparently unrelenting drift toward war. In order to move freely into South Africa, I had passed myself off as a graduate student in the innocent-sounding field of geography.

Over the years, I had learned to live with the caution that is essential inside. To avoid compromising the people I met, I avoided the telephone and the mails; I never conducted even marginally sensitive conversations indoors; I was exceedingly careful with my written notes. I confided my real views only to people I felt I could trust. I still feared I could not continue indefinitely; I had no illusion that I could keep on eluding the regime's imposing security apparatus.

On this particular trip, I planned to hitchhike the thousand miles down to Cape Town, gathering material for several articles. I wanted to be there by June 16, the anniversary of the date in 1976 when the huge wave of protest broke out in Soweto, the gigantic black ghetto outside Johannesburg, and spread to the rest of the country. Every year, protests and prayer meetings commemorate the uprising. In Cape Town the previous year, the police had opened fire, killing some fifty people. On my way back to Swaziland, I was to stop in Johannesburg to meet with a member of the underground. I was to carry some messages to his organization outside the country.

My first ride—he had stopped for me on the Swaziland side of the border—was with a young white man named Sean Burke. He was part of the 40 percent of the white population who speak English as a first language; the majority speak Afrikaans, the language descended primarily from Dutch. I had decided on a little experiment; I would deliberately avoid bringing up race or politics and see how long before he did. We went through the preliminaries. I dissembled briefly about geography; he had a degree in commerce, but he disliked the regimentation of large enterprises. He had therefore set up his own small subcontractor, which did roofing jobs in the whole southern Africa region. He was thirty, and about to be married.

We swerved slightly to skirt a black cyclist who was peddling slowly on the side of the highway, and Burke said, "I'll be frank with you—I don't care much for the black man." I carefully said nothing. Fifteen minutes had elapsed. "Or at least for his culture. I don't want it imposed on mine." He said he was planning to emigrate, to Australia, America, or somewhere else. "There's going to be a war here," he explained matter-of-factly. "Everyone knows it. Just like in Zimbabwe. My fiancée's from up there. And even if it all comes right in the end, there's going to be years of violence in between. I'm at an age where I want to settle down, start a family. South Africa isn't going to be a good environment for that."

We left the pine forests, and climbed into barren sheep country, which was brown with winter. We were now on the *highveld,* the vast inland plateau. We approached the tiny town, or *dorp,* of Chrissiemeer. "There was a concentration camp here during the Anglo-Boer War," Burke said. "The English held the Boer women and children to try and get their men to surrender." Then he pointed toward the black township, a quarter mile outside the dorp. It was a cluster of bleak, tumbledown brick structures and mud-walled huts, smoky in the winter air. "There's today's concentration camp," he said. His tone was cynical, with a slight trace of guilt.

We continued on to Ermelo—which had been founded one hundred years before and named for a town in Holland—and dropped into the bar at the Holiday Inn. I relaxed. If the police at the border had found anything in their computer, they would already have radioed ahead to stop us. Sean Burke spoke softly, so that the mostly Afrikaner clientele would be unable to overhear. "I detest this government," he said, launching himself into what was clearly a familiar theme. "These Afrikaners are such rocks. Hard-headed. Stupid. They impose their morality on you, like not allowing films or sport on Sunday. Their bureaucracy is just hopeless—just try getting a driver's license sometime. I think they're so aggressive because they doubt themselves. Deep down inside they think they're inferior to us. A black government wouldn't even be any worse than this one is."

Past Ermelo, the maize country began. It was very reminiscent of certain parts of the American Middle West; rolling, expansive, dotted infrequently with farmhouses and windmills. The sky is darker here due to the six-thousand-foot altitude, a deeper, almost icy blue. Another difference is the mud huts of the black farm workers, which are in some areas brightly decorated with geometric designs. Cattle grazed through the brown, crumpled maize, or *mielie,* stalks, with snowy white tickbirds—the more elegant name is "cattle egrets"—always close at hand, ready to dart at insects stirred up by the beasts. One tickbird was even perched insolently right atop a cow. Stands of towering, perfectly straight eucalyptus gum trees lined the road at intervals. There was little traffic.

In the next small town, Bethal, we met a rarity, an English speaker outside the large cities. The overwhelming majority of white people in the rural *platteland* are Afrikaners. The barman had come recently from Joburg (Johannesburg). "One thing is for certain," he told us, "there's almost nothing to do here. You can't see films; there isn't even a bioscope [movie theater]." He spent much of his spare time in the public library. "I'm glad the blacks aren't allowed in there, like they are in the Joburg library," he said. "They steal all the good books, or bugger them up."

Sean Burke bought him a brandy and asked how he got on with his customers. "It's lucky I speak Afrikaans," he answered. "These bloody Dutchmen don't stand for any nonsense—they say that if you are in their country, you must speak their language." Burke nodded sympathetically.

Forty miles further on, at the little junction of Ogies, we made another stop. The talk in this bar was rugby. The Springboks, the national team, were about to leave for New Zealand and America on a controversial tour that would provoke massive demonstrations in both countries. To deter critics, the national selectors had picked Errol Tobias for the team. He was the first black Springbok in history. The aficionados in the whites-only bar tried to outdo each other with praise for Tobias. They all fervently hoped the presence of a black player would reduce the size of the expected protests.

The rugby fans drifted out. Sean Burke, displaying a prodigious capacity for alcohol, signalled for another round. He hunched forward over the bar and said to me, completely unexpectedly, "I know this black guy over in Botswana. He handles my business there, does it very well. But I find I've got nothing to say to him socially." He stopped for a moment. "I haven't yet met the old black guy that I could sit down with and have the old drink." He looked up, with a flash of wistfulness. Then we left for Johannesburg.

In the metropolis, I kept my appointment with Clive, a truck driver with whom I would make the next leg of my trip. We left at dawn the next morning, hauling a load of electric cables down to Bloemfontein. We left the Transvaal and entered the Orange Free State about an hour later. The temperature was just above freezing, the sky overcast. It drizzled from time to time. A cold wind was blowing.

Clive and I had been friends for several years. He was a so-called colored, classified by the Registration of Population Act as part of the group of 2.7 million South Africans of mixed African, Asian, and European descent. In the early 1980s, the South African population was divided as follows:

White	4.5 million
Colored	2.7 million
Indian	.8 million
African	20 million

Clive, like many other "colored" people, especially the young, found the term insulting; he insisted on being called "black." In so speaking, he meant to stress his common hatred for the apartheid system with the eight hundred thousand South Africans classified as Indians and the twenty million of wholly African descent. Clive's pride was not the least hostile or aggressive; he had many white friends.

As we roared through the small Free State towns, he pointed out the different segregated townships on the outskirts of each one. "There's the black one," he would say, shaking his huge mane of unkempt hair. "And that's the one for coloreds—separate, and a little better. Some of the coloreds are satisfied. They still have other people to look down on." There were no Indian townships. It is illegal for Indians to remain in the inappropriately named Free State for more than twenty-four hours.

Near Kroonstad, we stopped for three black hitchhikers. They stood in the back of the truck (there was no room in the cab), hunched over stoically in the intermittent drizzle. They wore floppy stocking caps and old coats that they pulled tightly around themselves in the cold. Clive said acidly, "Think of these poor guys—travelling hundreds of miles to look for a job that *might* pay them five rand a day." The rand, the unit of South African currency, was approximately equivalent to the American dollar.

We reached Bloemfontein and headed for the building site, where a middle-income Levittown-type development for whites was taking shape. One entry road was too muddy, so we had to back the rig out laboriously and approach from the other side. "This is very typically South African," Clive grumbled, savagely wrenching his gearshift. "They could have made that access road properly, thrown a little stone in the low parts. But they want to make money quickly. While they can."

At the site, Clive negotiated in Afrikaans with the white supervisors, who kept warm inside the office. One of them signalled toward a nearby shed, where a group of shivering black laborers stood around an oily fire. The laborers wore several layers of tattered clothing beneath their distinctive blue overalls. Their battered shoes were caked with reddish mud. Clive helped them unload the truck, while one of the foremen watched desultorily from his pick-up truck, or *bakke.*

In the city, we drove over to the industrial area to fill up with fuel. South Africa has no oil reserves of its own, and no oil-producing country will sell to it openly. The gasoline price was set at well over three dollars a gallon, in part to discourage waste of the precious smuggled supply. As we waited, Clive waved his arm and said sarcastically, "Look at this. The black townships are all downwind from the power plant and these other factories. All the stinking smoke goes right out there."

We lunched on take-out fish and chips in the cab of his truck. Without even discussing the matter we knew that there was nowhere we could sit and eat together, with the possible exception of a five-star "international" hotel, the sort of place that would be ruled out by our dress, our finances, and our attitudes. Clive then headed back to Joburg.

Bloemfontein (Flower Fountain) is a spiritual center of white South Africa. It is the most conservative of the country's major cities. The whites, who are somewhat less than half the total population of about two hundred thousand, are overwhelmingly Afrikaans-speaking. The city was the capital of one of the two Boer Republics that fought to preserve their independence from the British late in the nineteenth century, and it still retains a certain politico-theocratic air, something like Salt Lake City. Prominent landmarks are the Supreme Court building, a huge white Dutch Reformed Church (in Afrikaans, Nederduitse Gereformeerde Kerk, or NGK) which is floodlit at night, and a railway station, with a preserved old steam locomotive in front. A couple of the characteristic Free State *kopjes,* distinctive, flat-topped hillocks, are right in the middle of town; otherwise the city is flat.

Newsbills carried headlines of the latest unrest up in Joburg. Riot police wielding truncheons had invaded a colored area, chasing high school demonstrators right into their homes and beating them. The whites in Bloemfontein showed no sense of urgency. They bustled about, many of them soldiers or government officials, scrubbed, cheerful, and serene. The black waiters, street-cleaners, and laborers remained unobtrusively in the background, part of the scenery.

The next day, I waited out by the highway for a lift further south and watched part of the South African Army pass. Two long convoys of jeeps and personnel carriers went by, followed by trucks pulling artillery pieces. Then, headed the other way, an imposing row of tanks rumbled along.

The chocolate-brown uniforms of the soldiers matched the color of their vehicles. Some of the men, evidently from the parabat commandos and other elite units, wore purple berets. All the soldiers were white.

A huge furniture van shuddered to a stop. The driver, a young white man named Phillip Du Preez, was going straight through to Cape Town. He was one of the last white truck drivers in the country, and therefore a person of special interest to me.

In South Africa, there are "white jobs" and there are "black jobs." The distinction is losing the force of law, except in the mines. But it persists in real life due to rules enforced by the segregated white unions, unequal degrees of skill training, and simple custom. But the boundary line is moving slowly upward, in the direction of greater skill, as the growing shortage of white workers is forcing companies to train blacks. Ten or more years ago, the majority of long-haul truckers were still whites; the commonsense view was that blacks were incapable of doing the job. Now, few whites remain. Employers have discovered, as one of them once told me with grudging surprise, that blacks seem to "have a thing for driving." I was to have many hours on the road to learn how Du Preez felt about being in what had become a black man's job.

Du Preez had turned his heater up to bake level, so he drove along wearing shorts despite the cold outside. One of his arms was tattooed with a dagger intertwined with a flower. He admonished me against getting one; "Once he's there, you can't take him off." Some confusion about pronouns is a common mistake among Afrikaners who have an imperfect command of English.

Sitting alongside Du Preez was his assistant, a short colored man with a two-day growth of beard and a golf cap pulled so low over his eyes that he had to tilt his head back to see. We stopped for lunch, and Du Preez ordered him to check the water and the condition of the load. I innocently asked Du Preez the assistant's name. He grew irritated. "Awww, he's Michael," he said, shaking his head contemptuously and grimacing. "But awww, I must tell you—I don't like these black bastards. I'll stick him back in the trailer when we start up again. He can't drive in any case."

We detoured slightly to the west, to Kimberley, where diamonds were first discovered in the 1860s. Several miles up the highway, a truck was stopped by the opposite side of the road next to a field of maize stubble. The black driver was changing one of his tires. Du Preez enthusiastically leaned on his horn and waved eagerly. The driver stared. Then his face lit up with recognition. He waved back. Du Preez explained with a smile as we thundered by, "He's been on the road as long as I have—seven years."

A little further along, we passed a black bicyclist who was teetering on the edge of the narrow highway. "I hit one of these *kaffirs* a few years back," Du Preez said. *Kaffir* is the South African word for "nigger." "It was late at night—he fell in front of me on his bicycle. They found a half of him on one side of the road, and the other half on the other side. They never found the middle half." He laughed gleefully.

In Kimberly, Michael emerged from his exile in the trailer, accompanied by a bearded black man called Percy. Du Preez loudly ordered them to start unloading, and he apologized to the white man who was waiting for his furniture for the low complement of laborers. "You can't take more than two—they stink too much." He promised the client he would scour the vicinity for some more "boys" to help with the unloading; we instead made for the nearest bar.

After a few Castle beers, we went to a roadhouse, where Du Preez bought curry-and-rice to take out: two large ones for us, two small ones for "the boys." He insisted on holding on to theirs until they finished the job. "Kaffirs work harder when there's fucking food waiting," he explained.

Following dinner, we sped south for a few hours before pulling off the road to sleep; we were back underway before dawn. At sunrise, Du Preez stopped for a stranded colored trucker, and they amiably talked shop in Afrikaans the rest of the way into Victoria West. We were now in the vast desert called the Karroo, having left the maize country behind during the night. The landscape was barren, except for scattered scrub plants never more than a couple of feet high. It was mostly flat, although there was an occasional rise, like an unexpected wave in an otherwise becalmed ocean, from which you could see to the horizon. There were a few brownish sheep browsing through the bush, but neither people nor evidence of human habitation for stretches of ten to fifteen miles at a time. A sign with an arrow pointed toward a solitary windmill said simply: "Water."

Du Preez and his colleague listened to pop music on bilingual Radio Good Hope as the truck barrelled along. The disc jockey shifted back and forth between English and Afrikaans. Du Preez sounded his horn and waved at the occasional trucks coming the other way, all of which were driven by blacks. Both men chain-smoked Gunston cigarettes while they talked. Gunstons are a strong, fairly new brand. A clever marketing executive took Gun- and its macho implications, and added -ston, borrowed from Winston and intended to furnish American glamour. The brand has become very popular among a certain sort of rough customer throughout southern Africa.

We pulled into Victoria West, a neat little whitewashed town. Its name was painted in huge letters on an overlooking hill. Du Preez dropped the colored driver by a telephone, across the street from several Indian shops, and waited to be sure he did not need further help.

Back on the road, I feigned indifference and asked Du Preez how well blacks drove trucks. I had been waiting to pose the question for nearly twenty-four hours. "Badly," he answered without hesitating. "Very badly. They're not safe. They take the money. And they doesn't know how to fill out all the papers." He almost lost sight of the road as he fished about on his dashboard, eagerly produced a sheaf of forms, and went over them line by line to emphasize their complexity. "The kaffir drivers are going to be replaced by Europeans," he concluded.

After Beaufort West, as we slowed through the occasional sleepy town or crossing, we started to see fewer blacks and more colored people—children playing, farm laborers trudging along. Colored people live all over South Africa, but the majority are found in the Western Cape, which was the first area where white settlers, Asian slaves, and Africans mixed. Du Preez said idly, "Some of these colored birds are *lekker* [tasty]." I gingerly mentioned the Immorality Act, which outlaws any sexual contact between black and white. He got excited. "That law's keeping a fucking war from happening here," he said. I didn't understand. "Well, I might go with one of these birds, but then a colored would try to go with my sister—whewww, we'd start killing all the coloreds and kaffirs."

We climbed slightly, then unexpectedly dropped into a totally new environment—a lush, green narrow valley, surrounded by steep mountains. Vineyards in shades of amber, yellow, and dark green were laid out on both sides. After several hundred miles of emptiness, people, most of them colored, stood talking in groups or walked along the roadside. One colored girl in a blue dress who looked about thirteen years old squinted up at the truck and saw Du Preez and me. Something registered in her face. She gestured as if she were throwing a stone. Du Preez didn't notice.

We started climbing again, switching laboriously back and forth up toward the Dutoitskloof Pass, at three thousand feet above sea level. The truck inched through the last gap, and there was the entire Cape, spread out below us. The afternoon sun glinted off dozens of ponds in all directions, creating a glimmering golden sheen. Du Preez, with proprietary pride, pointed out the major landmarks. The town of Paarl was to the lower left, seemingly under us; Cape Town a smudge in the distance, among some mountains.

Du Preez stopped the truck, and summoned Michael back from the trailer. The two then earnestly discussed, in Afrikaans, the logistics of their arrival. Du Preez's truculence had completely disappeared. They decided to drop me next to a certain commuter train station; in half an hour, I was in the center of the city.

Du Preez's contradictory set of attitudes was characteristic of many, probably the majority, of the white people I met over the years. He was clearly not some kind of freebooter, a mercenary interloper in a foreign country. He was an indigenous South African, a man who regarded his surroundings as his only home. But his relations with the four-fifths of his countrymen who are not white were extremely erratic and volatile to the point of something like schizophrenia. He was capable of genuine human feelings toward them, followed moments later by the crudest and most disgusting sort of racism.

Whether his vicious outbursts were a pathetic kind of compensation for his own secondary status in the white community, or a twisted form of irritated guilt at his unwarranted position of superiority over blacks, his views were not part of the realm of the logical. He wilfully misinterpreted the evidence of his own senses, even on simple matters. His contention that blacks were not capable of driving trucks was disproven nearly every time a large rig thundered by going the other way. Perhaps such contradictions explain his volatility. In any case, he is ready to fight desperately to keep South Africa as it is.

Cape Town is situated in one of the world's most beautiful natural settings. The older part of the city nestles between the Atlantic Ocean and Table Mountain, the striking, flat-topped massif that soars three thousand feet upward. A hair-raising cableway goes to the top; at times, the ascent seems nearly vertical. On a clear day, the view is stupendous. Below, the city curves around the base of the mountain, and trickles further down the Cape peninsula. Luxuriant rainfall has created a lush, Mediterranean climate. In every direction there is a dizzy, arresting juxtaposition of evergreens, mountains, and the sea.

Almost due north, five miles offshore, is Robben Island, the prison fortress where some five hundred black political prisoners are held, including Nelson Mandela, the leader of the underground African National Congress resistance movement. The island is a malevolent blur on the horizon, a reminder that not everyone in paradise is free.

I went to meet two black women who were planning a visit to the island. I had arranged the meeting with them through the underground. One of the women was the aunt of the prisoner, the other was his sister. Only the sister, a delicate young woman down from Johannesburg, was actually visiting, but the two were coordinating their efforts in order to convey to him as much information as possible.

Brother and sister would be separated by a glass partition during the one-hour visit. They would talk over an intercom. A white prison official who understood the various African languages would listen the entire time, and cut short any explicit attempt to discuss politics. So the two women—along with other members of the prisoner's family—had devised a code during the two years he had already spent on the island. The aunt, who had been allowed to visit several months before, said mischievously, "I told him Diliza is getting better at long-distance running. He knows Diliza never ran farther than to catch a taxi, so he knows he's skipped the country."

The sister nodded. "Does he know Nomsa went up to Zimbabwe for the independence anniversary? She was very encouraged by the situation there."

"No, I don't think so. How do we tell him?"

"Last year, I used 'Wilfred's home' to mean Zimbabwe. His friend Wilfred comes from that side. Why don't I just say Nomsa had a nice holiday at Wilfred's place?"

"Do they know Nomsa? Do they have anything on her?"

"No. They picked her up in '77, but they only held her for a week under Section Ten. They haven't bothered her since."

"Fine. Knowing more about the change up in Zimbabwe should encourage him. How much longer does he have to go?" The aunt had a hopeful look.

"Only four years. He's almost half finished." They smiled at each other.

A different sort of search for euphemism has characterized the changes in name of the prevailing racial philosophy. The ruling National Party came to power in 1948 espousing a policy it proudly called *apartheid*, literally "apartness," which party leaders promised would strengthen the already existing system of white supremacy, known as "segregation." But the word *apartheid* acquired such disagreeable connotations in the world, perhaps partly because it is pronounced "apart-hate," that it has not been used officially for nearly twenty years. "Separate development," which replaced it, remained in fashion quite a while, but then it too became synonymous with the oppression it was meant to hide. There has been no generally accepted heir, though Prime Minister P. W. Botha has tried "vertical differentiation," "friendly nationalism," even "good neighborliness." The system's opponents continue to call it apartheid.

There has also been disagreement over racial terminology. For several decades, the official designation for people of wholly African descent was "natives." Then, as now, large numbers of black migrant workers arrived each year from neighboring countries to work in the gold mines. They were termed, officially, "foreign natives"—a usage that requires you to have at least some mental agility to render coherent. Government propagandists eventually realized the use of "native" undercut their own claim to indigenousness, which is a central part of their guiding philosophy. They selected the word *bantu,* a corruption of the Zulu word *abantu,* which means simply "people." In reserving the word for blacks, they inadvertently relinquished their own claim on membership in the human race.

Blacks never accepted either word, using them only as a way to scornfully describe the handful of quislings who collaborated with the regime. They instead called themselves "Africans." In the early 1970s, as the philosophy known as black consciousness spread through the urban areas, people began calling themselves "black." The change was similar to and to some extent influenced by the similar change in black America a few years earlier. The regime, meanwhile, had never accepted "Africans," mostly because the word in Afrikaans is *Afrikaners.* There would have been endless confusion. It was therefore with some relief that the government finally abandoned its efforts at linguistic dictatorship and started using "black" as well.

There has been no such consensus about either the 2.7 million colored people or the 800,000 Indian South Africans. The regime's word for Indians was "Asiatics," which was an insulting effort to deny their right to permanence in South Africa despite more than a century of residence. The black consciousness movement fought with increasing success to expand the definition of "black" to include people from both groups. Black consciousness leaders, who included Indian and colored people, argued convincingly that the old collective term *non-white* was a subtly racist way of defining people against some supposedly ideal standard; whites would certainly object to being called *non-blacks.* Yet the use of the old words is at times inevitable. To avoid insult, they are often used with certain modifiers—"so-called," or "classified" colored. You will even see people drawing imaginary quotation marks in the air to emphasize their distaste when they are forced to use the words.

Cape Town, like nearly every South African city, is less than half white. The largest group of its 1.5 million people are colored. Their mixed ancestry is reflected in a wide range of physical appearances. Some are nearly indistinguishable from whites, while others could pass for black. In general, colored people resemble Puerto Ricans and some other people from the Caribbean, though they often have a pronounced Asian aspect as well.

In cultural terms, colored people differ from blacks most significantly in language. They tend to speak their own distinctive brand of Afrikaans, although English is achieving greater popularity, particularly among the better educated. They talk with a musical, almost Cockney lilt, frequently dropping their *h*'s. Black people of completely African descent speak one of the ten or so African languages at home (in Cape Town, it is primarily Xhosa). English and Afrikaans are for work, or beyond a certain grade level, school.

To these moderate cultural differences the regime has applied the rigidity of law. The Registration of Population Act of 1950, one of the main pillars of the apartheid system, "classifies" every South African by "race." In borderline cases, officials use demeaning physical exams. One such infamous exercise in applied racial science is called the pencil test. A white official tries to insert a pencil into the person's hair. If it penetrates, they are colored, if their hair is curled too tightly, they are black. Each year, the minister of the interior solemnly informs Parliament, as he did in 1979, that 150 coloreds "became" white, 10 whites "became" coloreds, 3 coloreds "became" Indians, and so on.

Laws also require blacks, whites and coloreds to live in separate areas, and to attend separate schools and universities. In other South African cities, whites have the choice locations nearer the center; blacks and coloreds are forced to live far out on the periphery. Cape Town is somewhat different. Due to the rugged topography, the city has spilled along the peninsula haphazardly, and the segregated "Group Areas" are jumbled together like a crazy quilt. The black townships are called Langa, Nyanga, and Guguletu—"the Sun," "the Moon," and "Our Pride." The names of some of the colored ghettos are just as comically inappropriate; Lavender Hills, Grassy Park, Valhalla Park. They are in fact impoverished, cheerless patches of tiny homes shaped like matchboxes or several-story housing projects. Even more dismal are the squatter camps, where shacks of corrugated metal sit abjectly among the windblown sand dunes.

A colored electrician took me on a motor tour through some of these areas. In Grassy Park, which naturally has very little grass, we stopped for two cheerful, curly-haired boys about seven years old, who were hitchhiking home together after school. We took them a couple of miles south to the Lavender Hills complex. They thumb every day because their local school, with ninety students in the single first grade class, had no room for them. Their home looked remarkably like a first-generation American inner-city housing project: two-story drab brick buildings, in a setting of bare ground littered with broken glass. Washing flapped outside in the sea breezes. The local street gangs had spray-painted their names about: Wizards. Scorpions. And the biggest: BFK, the dreaded Born Free Kids.

There was also a newer generation of slogans, sloppily done; their authors had obviously hurried in order to avoid police patrols. "This IS a police state." "Free the Detainees." "Down With Gutter Educa-tion." "Azanians—Fight for Your Rights." "The Truth IS: Biko Was Murdered." Steve Biko, the black consciousness leader, had died mys-teriously in police detention in 1977; his death had provoked national and world protest. The electrician pointed out, "Excellent. To see a slo-gan about Biko, a black, in a so-called colored area." Another graffito, apparently a collaborative effort between two people with differing com-mands of English, read: "They Killing US" followed, in a different script, by "i.e., the SA Police."

We continued down to Muizenberg, in a white Group Area. The town, an Atlantic City kind of coastal resort, was nearly depopulated in the off-season. A few intrepid white surfers, wearing rubber wet-suit tops, were braving the cold. The electrician had made friends over the years with a black waiter at one of the shorefront hotels. We stood together in the lukewarm sun, watching the surfers. The waiter was one of the millions of black migrant laborers in the country. He came from the Transkei, some six hundred miles away. He lived in the hotel's servant quarters. His wife and their three children were at home. He buttoned up his dark blue waiter's jacket against the cold breezes and said he had not had a single "off-day" since November 22, seven months earlier. He was emphatic about the exact date. In July, he planned to return home for two months. He said the separation was not so bad; his wife came sometimes to visit. In case of an emergency at home, or a major deci-sion that required his agreement, she could always reach him by tele-phone. The three of us stood there awhile as the surfers rode the waves.

That night, the electrician took me to District Six, the fabled colored area right in the center of town. "The District" was once a bustling slum neighborhood. It was celebrated for its gangsters and confidence men, but most of its residents were solid, poor working-class people, who over many years had created a thriving neighborhood with a strong community life. It was mostly colored, but with blacks and even some white residents. The District had its drawbacks, but most of its residents found it vibrant, and a convenient place to live on their low incomes.

The apartheid government had other plans. Areas like District Six were potentially choice spots for development. Also, their polyglot character persisted in defiance of the rigid apartheid ideal. Under the terms of the Group Areas Act, the regime simply "declared" District Six and similar neighborhoods all over the country to be "white" and razed them. Since 1950, some six hundred thousand people, nearly all of them colored or Indian, were forced to move. The agency responsible, in another masterstroke of euphemism, is called the Department of Community Development.

Now, District Six is even more devastated than the South Bronx and other ghost neighborhoods in America. Only perhaps 5 percent of the houses and apartment blocks were still standing, and even some of them were darkened and evidently evacuated. A single forlorn "babi shop," or tiny grocery, remained functioning on one levelled street. The owner, fearful of robbery, served his few remaining customers through a protective wire grill. The electrician drove his Volkswagen slowly and intently through the deserted streets, picking his way along like a prospector or an archaeologist. He backtracked, got his bearings, and then triumphantly pointed to a heap of rubble. "My mother grew up here," he said.

Most of the twenty-seven thousand District residents were forced to move to Mitchell's Plain, a rectangular, featureless, wholly colored development twelve miles out in the Cape Flats. The electrician took me there the next day, to visit his brother. On the way, he said morosely, "I must know hundreds of people who stay out there now. I can only think of one or two of them who actually like the place." Mitchell's Plain gives an impression of monotony and bleakness rather than poverty. Purplish mountains in each direction are a lofty contrast to the miles of cold red brick.

It was Saturday afternoon. We found a small party already in progress at the electrician's brother's place. About a dozen people, all of them colored, were sitting around in the small, tidy living room. A stereo played Earth, Wind and Fire. Albums by other black American groups were scattered about. A bottle of brandy and a bottle of Coke stood in the middle of an oval table, ready to mix the national drink. On one wall, a stylized poster showed an anonymous black man looking imploringly upward. The caption was: "I Have a Dream." A raucous gaggle of children gave me a brief, curious glance, and then returned to their play. I learned later one of them was named Elvis.

Whites in South Africa enter black areas even less than white Americans visit Harlem or Watts. Most white people in Cape Town are absolutely certain they would be physically attacked the instant they set foot in a place like Mitchell's Plain. In fact, I had always met with generous hospitality on my dozens of visits to black areas. My American accent helped a bit at first, although after the Reagan administration came to power it stopped being much of an asset. Even without its effect, though, black people simply did not often show the reflexive racial hostility characteristic of many whites.

A young teacher named Robert regaled the party with his account of a recent near-clash between two rival youth gangs at a school party. "The Wizards pitched up at the scene, man, even though it's Stalag 17 territory. TrueasGod, there were twenty of them. Jesus, those gangsters were carrying garden forks [rakes] and *pangas* [long knives]. Somebody was gonna get killed, man. I got so nervous I went and rang up the fuzz!"

The rest of the company seemed surprised. A brief debate took place about the ethics of calling in the police. I broke in to ask whether the gang members had any political inclinations. The denial was unanimous. Robert explained, "They are a consequence of the situation in the ghetto. The father's not around; mommy leaves for work at six, when it's still dark; the kids are by themselves most of the time. They are looking for some kind of adult guidance."

Someone changed the record, putting on "Mannenberg." Cape Town's own Dollar Brand, now in exile, had named his album after one of the city's ghettos. Driving piano jazz rhythms filled the room.

Robert was complaining about his salary. As an "unqualified" teacher, he earned only 150 rand a month. He outlined his dilemma: should he return to school for the diploma that would increase his salary, or should he immediately take a job as a clerk—he pronounced it the English way, "clark"—at three times his present pay? "If I go back to school," he said, "I'll need money from the old man. I'll be on his back again. I'm getting too old for that. (He was twenty-five.) My trouble, man, is no self-discipline. I can't decide what to do, and then *do* it." He shook his head. "I need to get married—*that* will give me self-discipline." His older sister, an active feminist, shot him a nasty look.

He brightened a bit, and to great amusement described his recent meanderings through an Afrikaans dictionary. "One expression, *in the dictionary,* is 'as drunk as a colored teacher.' " The electrician commented morosely, "Just like you might say, 'as strong as a lion.' " Robert added that the definition of *meid*—the closest English approximation would probably be *wench*—is simply "a colored woman."

The conversation veered inevitably toward the upcoming protest to commemorate the Soweto uprising. Organizers had declared a two-day "stay-away" for June 16 and 17, a general strike intended to close the city down. Such strikes had succeeded in the past in Cape Town and in other places. Employers were threatening to fire employees who failed to show up without a valid excuse.

Veronica, a sales clerk in a big department store, said some of her black and colored coworkers would "get around the boss" by claiming militants at the bus stops had prevented them from coming to work. "He's not too likely to come out here and search for us," she said, with a deadpan expression that evoked peals of laughter. "Even *with* that gun he carries everywhere. But, man, I tell you he would most definitely see a lot of his missing merchandise in their homes if he did!"

Someone posed the perennial question: how long until the apartheid regime was overthrown? A few people said ten years, but the majority insisted on fifteen, twenty or more. The electrician demurred. "Even longer than that," he said. "Look at Mitchell's Plain here, man. No one wanted to leave the District. Everyone complained. But now Oppenheimer and those other so-called liberal businessmen—they built the new shopping center here. People are happier; they don't have to go all the way into town any more to shop. They extended the rail line out here, so it doesn't take so long now to get to work in town. People are starting to get used to Mitchell's Plain. They don't like it, but they're getting used to it."

"Don't be so pessimistic," said Robert, the teacher. "You're not fucking happy about the situation here."

"No, I'm not fucking happy, man. But let's be realistic. People will put up with a lot."

"You're not satisfied with your life, even though you get a good pay. Why not?"

"No, I'm not fucking satisfied." He fidgeted awkwardly with his glass. Then he burst out, "I don't fucking like the fact that I'm sitting here nicely, drinking brandy and Coke while people are fucking starving in this country."

He looked up glumly. Someone got up to change the record. The teacher nodded, and gave a weak smile of understanding and agreement.

On June 16, the electrician and I drove around town to try to measure the success of the stay-away. We did find most of the shops closed in black and colored areas. The police were out in force; in fact, with their camouflage uniforms and large armored vehicles they resembled more of an army of occupation. But the double-decker commuter buses, particularly in the colored neighborhoods, were at least half full. The electrician was more than usually morose. "Last year, the buses were empty," he grumbled. "The coloreds seem to have let the blacks down."

The electrician said wearily he was used to disappointment. Five years earlier, he had enrolled at the single university for colored people. The institution is officially called the University of the Western Cape, but disparaged by its students as "Bush College" due to its remote location.

He intended to study science. After six months, he joined one of the periodic student walkouts to protest various features of the second-rate education. The strike failed. Some of the other boycotters trickled back, and eventually earned their degrees. He stood firm, and ultimately landed, without enthusiasm, in an electrician's course.

Even someone as gloomy as the electrician had to acknowledge that unity between black and colored people was growing. "They used to call us *malaous*," he remembered. "It's a very insulting word. I think it comes from 'mulatto' or something. In any case, you don't hear it so much anymore. And some of the coloreds used to 'play white.' They boasted of their white ancestors. They used to say things like, 'The white man is our cousin. Give him time. He'll come right and give us our rights.' To those ones, the blacks were 'kaffirs.' " The electrician winced slightly in embarrassment. "That's also finishing."

He paused. "I also think the apartheid won't stay forever. I just think we can't be too optimistic."

In a police state, a democratically organized protest is a very difficult proposition. The Riotous Assemblies Act, in effect continually since the 1976 upheaval, is another triumph of euphemism; it in fact outlaws *any* open-air political gathering, no matter how peaceful and staid. The network of security police informers is adept at keeping their paymasters aware of indoor gatherings. Those who dare to meet, even about innocent matters, risk arrest and harsh jail sentences under wide legal definitions of "sabotage," "terrorism," and "treason."

It was therefore extraordinary that widespread, democratically run protest campaigns continued to take place in South Africa. They have been especially strong in Cape Town. Students throughout the area boycotted schools to protest what they routinely called gutter education. Commuters refused to ride buses after unwarranted fare hikes. People aided striking workers in several enterprises by boycotting certain products.

Anonymous groups (the Committee of 81), never meeting in the same place twice, coordinated these protests. When police detained some members of the steering committees, others were swiftly elected to replace them. The whole process was fiercely democratic. There is something enormously moving and compelling about people in an up-to-date computerized police state, people who because of their skin color are denied any voice in political affairs, constructing their own, alternative form of democracy and maintaining it at the risk of their personal liberty.

These community and labor protests have been chronicled in *Grassroots*, a combative monthly newspaper. Various organizations jointly produce articles about their activities, and then insist on approving the final edited version before publication. They are reluctant to relinquish any control over the printed word. There is no hierarchy, only an elected twelve-member committee.

Grassroots is a lively, argumentative paper, which completely and happily fails any standard of objectivity. One article, describing an unfortunate encounter between a high school principal and a radical student, said, "[The principal] started to hit the student. The student tried to defend himself with his case—which struck the principal's face and knocked off his glasses." In another instance, the paper said an unidentified white man taking photos of an illegal demonstration spoke with "a heavy security branch accent." Individual issues of *Grassroots,* understandably, are frequently banned.

I picked up a copy that described a recent campaign by the Mitchell's Plain community organization to demand that the City Council push back the due date on electricity bills. The municipality had required payment the third week of the month, before most people receive their monthly paychecks. Many inevitably incurred the 10 percent penalty surcharge for late payment. Some seventy-five hundred people signed a petition asking that the due date be postponed two weeks. The authorities only responded that people should learn to budget their income better. Some two hundred Mitchell's Plain residents decided to hand in the monster petition in person at the City Council offices.

Grassroots described the events: "Should a four or five person delegation be elected to present the memorandum unanimously adopted at the meeting to the Council?

"No! The People would be their own leaders. They would ALL go to Cape Town and hand in copies of the memorandum. . . .

"It was decided not to have a spokesperson or persons.

"The People would speak for themselves. Each and every one was fully acquainted with the issues at stake.

"It didn't matter which individuals eventually spoke.

"The People were One."

The City Council gave in. It granted a one-month grace period on electricity accounts, more than the protestors had demanded. And it applied the concession to its entire jurisdiction, not just Mitchell's Plain.

On my last evening in Cape Town, I dropped into one of the whites-only bars, an establishment popular among younger, English-speaking businessmen. I encountered Jerry, who owned a nearby camera shop. He looked and to some extent tried to growl like a scaled-down version of the actor Anthony Quinn. He started to run through the tiresome anti-American catechism common to many white South Africans until I praised the Reagan administration repeatedly and effusively. That mollified him somewhat, although he continued to gibe at the United States, as he made some typically white observations.

On District Six: "That place was becoming a slum. We had to tear it down. I can tell you—there are no slums in South Africa, like you have in America." Like many whites, he pronounced the name of his country "Sao Theffrica."

On his interpretation of South Africa's diversity: "This place is like America forty or fifty years ago—you've got everything here. Bloody English, Afrikaners, Germans, everything. We're not one yet, but we're growing together."

On black/white economic inequality: "In this country, there are maybe two million whites in the work force. We carry the twenty million blacks. They couldn't survive a week's time without us. We are the managers, the professionals, the artisans. We've got to bring them up, and that takes time. They aren't like your Negroes, who have been civilized by being in America. Our blacks have just come out of the bush."

His general observations on racism: "It's everywhere in the world. Look at India and Pakistan, look at Northern Ireland. You've got the same thing in America. Look at what you did to the Red Indians! Did you know you can't buy a Red Indian a drink in America? It's against the law. . . ."

I left the city the next day. The road east passed through vine country. Every mile or so, lanes shaded by evergreens led off the highway toward white mansions with curved Cape Dutch gables. The road continued climbing through Sir Lowry's Pass, affording a spectacular view of False Bay spread out below on the right, and then entered a temperate wheat- and apple-growing region. Saw-toothed mountains rimmed checkerboard fields, which were pale green with the first shoots of the winter planting.

I covered less than a hundred miles; I learned later that hitchhikers had committed several vicious murders in the area, which explained my slow progress.

A brooding, futuristic Dutch Reformed Church was the major landmark in Caledon, my stopover. Several Greek- and Portuguese-owned cafés did a desultory evening business. Some years back, the proprietors would have been Jewish. There were no Indian traders. As in other towns in the platteland, Indians would have been forceably moved to the outskirts, to their own separate Group Area.

Early the next day I made it to Swellendam, where I waited for several hours. I watched ostriches cavort on a farm across the road. A wheeling yellow biplane sprayed some fields in the distance. An engineering student from the Afrikaans Stellenbosch University eventually stopped for me. He was a huge, hearty rugby player who admitted freely he lacked a certain application to his studies. "I'm in the sixth year of a four-year course," he chuckled, with a strong Afrikaans accent.

The student shared the belief, widespread among many white South Africans, that the government was carrying out sweeping and fundamental reforms in the apartheid system. He said brightly his experience at university had helped broaden his own racial views. "Before," he said, "I wouldn't pick up a colored hitchhiker. Now, I do." He added earnestly, "They are people, just like you and me." I asked his view of the far right Herstigte (Reconstituted) National Party. The HNP, a growing organization, argued heatedly that the ruling National Party was selling out the interests of white people. The engineer dismissed the HNP with a shake of his head. "Ach, man, those ones—they're just like the Ku Klux Klan."

The engineer-to-be deposited me in the tiny dorp of Heidelburg, where I waited through the long afternoon. Very few vehicles passed. There was an infrequent bus service for blacks only. There were no buses for whites, all of whom own, or are presumed to own, vehicles. White farmers also gave blacks, probably their own laborers, lifts to and from town in their bakkes. The convention, adhered to like a taboo, is that a black must always ride in the back of the truck, like a piece of cargo, even if the farmer is driving alone. There were also occasional black taxis, battered, big third-hand American cars, with fur-rimmed steering wheels and dashboards and gaudy tinsel ornaments outside. Some of these vehicles had seen so much action that their bodies and their wheelbases were grotesquely out of line, giving them an odd, crablike appearance as they moved askew down the highway. Black taxis were usually overflowing, a state of affairs that has inspired an Afrikaans expression for a woman with many lovers: "Her heart is like a black taxi—there's always room for one more."

At dusk, I finally got a lift. A white couple named Sally and Gavin were heading east to the coastal resort of Knysna for a short holiday. I at first stuck to my usual identity as a geographer, until Sally asked me about Cape Town. I made a noncommittal reference to its natural beauty. "That city is truly a stunning paradox," she said, with a sneer in her voice. "Absolutely magnificent scenic beauty. Which surrounds so much hatred, so much oppression, so much seething resentment."

By no means do all white South Africans support the apartheid system. But those who say they oppose it differ greatly in the degree and sincerity of their opposition, and in what they would like to see in its place. Many white South Africans who would describe themselves as "moderate" or even "liberal" and who vote for the opposition Progressive Federal Party really prefer the continuance of much of the present system, with some moderation of only its most blatant features. Others, a small but by no means insignificant number of people, want more sweeping and genuine changes and work with energy and courage toward bringing them about. Gavin and Sally were part of this more radical band.

Sally, the more talkative half of the couple, had started working in advertising, and then, after divorcing her first husband, a businessman, switched to public relations work for a Cape Town charity. "I know 'charity' sounds paternalistic," she apologized, "but it's at least something to help. My advertising experience helps me with the promotions."

We continued driving through the coastal evening mists, passing Mossel Bay and George. The car radio started broadcasting "The Boys on the Border," a program in which a female announcer played music requested by listeners who dedicated their selections to friends or relatives in the South African Army. The woman spoke with a forced heartiness, as if trying to present herself to the listening soldiers as a favorite younger aunt.

Sally switched the radio off abruptly. "My son is sixteen," she explained. "He stays in Joburg with his father. Next year he gets called up for his first two years in the army. Then of course he has his three months every year after that. His father is pressurizing him, but I hope he decides not to go. I've told him that I'll send him to Zimbabwe, or anywhere else out of the country. I'll miss him terribly. But I don't want him in *this* army."

The next morning, a middle-aged white couple offered me a ride all the way to East London, my next destination. I perched in the back of their bakke as we climbed through the Knysna forests in the early morning mists. Wild elephants still survive back among the lofty fir trees. Halfway up to Nature's Valley, overlooking the sea to the south, we stopped for a young, uniformed soldier. He was heading home on a weekend pass from the big military base at Oudtshoorn. He joined me in the back of the truck, buttoning up his brown jacket against the chill. He said he was a tracker in a canine unit. He had just been in the combat zone in the north. The regime's propagandists refer to the area as "the border." In fact, it is not in South Africa at all, but rather part of Namibia, the vast desert territory that Pretoria continues to call South

West Africa and rule in defiance of the United Nations. A giant South African expeditionary force of nearly a hundred thousand men has been fighting an increasingly bloody and ugly war against SWAPO, the Namibia independence movement.

I asked the soldier—he looked about nineteen—who was winning. "No one," he said indifferently. "We once tracked a SWAPO terrorist detachment for twenty-seven straight days. Then we lost them. Their tribes help them hide. They can't beat us, but we can't win either. Eventually, it will be just like Mozambique, Angola, and Rhodesia. We'll pull out of South West, and then the fighting will start here." I probed for his feelings, but he seemed totally uninterested, detached. He preferred to talk about his girl friend until we got to his destination.

The bakke continued east, through scratchy bush country, with rugged mountains on the far horizon. We skirted the big industrial city of Port Elizabeth, a pale skyline off to one side, and entered a white ranching area. A healthy odor of manure wafted through the warmth of the early afternoon. Plump cattle, watched over by a few black herdboys, grazed everywhere.

We stopped in Port Alfred, a trim little town at the mouth of one of the many narrow rivers that flow south through the Eastern Cape to the sea. An almost totally black crowd swarmed around the river bank, fishing or gossiping in the warm sun. A few whites mingled in, either also fishing or visiting the small shops that lined the street next to the river.

Suddenly, a white police van rolled up to the bottle (liquor) store. Two white policemen in their early twenties leaped out, made their way through the crowd, and disappeared inside. They emerged minutes later, escorting a handcuffed black man who looked to be about their age. They put him in the back of the van. He peered out dully through the wire mesh grill. No one paid any attention as the van drove off.

At lunch, Mike, the bakke driver, launched into an enthusiastic overview of local lore. His bubbly wife helped by supplying or corroborating certain details. He explained that the first English settlers in the area, who included his ancestors, had laboriously changed the course of the river back in the 1820s. "The poor buggers wasted their time," he said. "Within a year, two ships sank right in the middle of the new channel." He discoursed at length on the local vegetation—he was a woodworker—and on animal life. His eyes brightened as he promised he would later show me a "superb" deposit of fossilized bird dung. He discussed the Xhosa language, which is spoken by black people in the Eastern Cape, and gave what sounded like a good rendition of its difficult "click" sounds. (In general, African words are pronounced phonetically. *Umfundisi* (teacher, parson) is therefore approximately Oomfoon-*dee*-see; *ubhuhle* (beauty) is Oo-*boo*-hlay. In "th" and "ph," however, the *h* is almost silent. The click sounds, written *x, gc, qh,* or similarly, are almost impossible without practice; whites pronounce most of them very approximately as "k.")

Mike's tone in talking about black people was very characteristically white South African—warmly paternal, as though he were describing some favorite pets. "They're good people, high quality," he said. "It's because they never suffered from the slave trade. In central Africa, slavery took the best people and caused a reduction in the breed's qualities." He shrugged. "It's the same whether you are talking of cows or whatever."

We continued on to the east, reaching the Ciskei Bantustan at dusk. The Bantustans are the centerpiece of the apartheid system, an extraordinary complex and evil system of territorial segregation unique in the entire world. They are an archipelago of ten territories that extend in an arc around the eastern, northern, and northwestern periphery of South Africa. They are the only areas in the country where blacks are legally entitled to live permanently and own land. (The policy does not apply to coloreds and Indians.) They constitute only 13 percent of the land area, but contain more than half the black population—disproportionately the old, the young, and the infirm. Those healthy enough to work travel as migrant laborers to the cities and farms in the other 87 percent of the country designated as white South Africa, sending back money their desperately poor relatives in the Bantustans need to survive.

The South African government uses the Bantustans to justify the whole apartheid system. All blacks, even those who live semipermanently in the urban areas, are assigned by law to one of the ten territories. The regime, starting in 1976, has been forcing the areas to take "independence." As each Bantustan becomes a new "nation," all the black people assigned to it lose their South African citizenship. The Ciskei was scheduled later that year to be the fourth of the impoverished territories to become "independent." Cabinet ministers have stated openly that the ultimate goal is "no black South Africans." It would be as if the United States government declared Harlem, Watts, and certain counties in Appalachia to be independent nations, apportioned all poor people to one of them no matter where they actually lived, and then proudly announced to the world that it had ended poverty in America.

The change on entering the Ciskei was dramatic. In the "white" area, the pastures and fields swept right to the horizon; there were few people about. In the Ciskei, there were occasional stunted patches of brown maize stalks, clusters of round, beehive huts scattered everywhere in the hills, and throngs of black people walking along the roadside or talking in groups.

Mike had picked up a young black hitchhiker in Port Alfred, who was returning home to the Ciskei for the weekend. He sat next to me in the back of the bakke. One of his eyes was glazed over with a whitish film and apparently sightless. He was very deferential and included in his answers to my questions the word *baas*, Afrikaans for "master." It is still a very common way blacks address whites, especially in the rural area.

The hitchhiker said he was nineteen years old. He worked as a bricklayer, earning forty-five rand a week. (It would be about the same in dollars.) He gestured proudly toward the pocket of his tattered trousers, indicating the pay packet he was bringing home to his parents. He caught me staring at his dilapidated shoes; both soles were on the verge of falling off. He made a sheepish, self-deprecating gesture. "They are old, baas," he said. Halfway through the Ciskei, he got off. He greeted some of the people by the roadside, and then started to make his way up through the dark toward a group of huts. He turned to wave to me before disappearing into the underbrush.

East London is an ordinary, medium-sized port with a population of two hundred thousand—about the size of Corpus Christi, Texas. It has an appreciable industrial sector, but it is not regarded as a factory town in the same way as, say, Port Elizabeth, Vereeniging, or the East Rand near Johannesburg. The port's emergence during 1980 as one of the leading centers of the new wave of radical black trade unionism was therefore somewhat unexpected.

That year, the South African Allied Workers' Union, starting from scratch, enrolled twenty thousand members. SAAWU's growth, which was continuing without pause into 1981, was part of a nationwide upsurge by black workers. A half-dozen militant new labor groupings were conducting successful organizing drives all over the country.

Organizing a union in South Africa is not easy. The government has not tried to crush the new movements completely, in part because it fears the reaction overseas. But the Riotous Assemblies Act, the various detention-without-trial statutes, and other repressive legislation serve to hamper the organizing efforts. In the case of SAAWU, the regime had been so disturbed by the union's success despite the obstacles that the Minister of Manpower Fanie Botha had personally visited the city to encourage business resistance.

I naturally made no effort to contact the union by telephone. I instead strolled into headquarters, located in an aging office block in the center of town. I was immediately and courteously ushered through the bustling office to meet SAAWU's national president, twenty-nine-year-old Thozamile Gqweta. He was bearded, athletic, and dressed informally in a golf cap and T-shirt. His office was bare except for his desk and a telephone. Black South Africans tend to be short in stature; at five feet nine, he was taller than average.

Thozi—everyone in the office seemed to call him by his nickname— had completed high school, a rare accomplishment given the awful state of the segregated black educational system. He then worked as a salesman in a furniture store. "It was there that I became aware of the problems of the workers," he said. "A guy would come in and buy a dining room set on hire purchase. Then he would come back the next month and say that he'd been sacked, he couldn't make the payments."

He was himself eventually fired for protesting the low sales commissions at the store. He went straight to the East London library, to borrow books on trade unions. He "linked up" with black labor organizers elsewhere, including the legendary Oscar Mpetha, the seventy-one-year-old who was then on trial for his life in Cape Town, charged with "terrorism."

Thozi started labor organizing with a significant advantage. He was already well known in Mdantsane, East London's black township, as a star rugby player, the captain of his amateur team. "I guess I never made any enemies," he said. "In rugby, in the township . . . I always tried to treat people straight."

He described his proselytizing efforts with exuberance. Some of the workers were wholly unfamiliar with the concept of a union; to them, it sounded at first like some insurance scheme, possibly bogus. Thozi passed out leaflets at factory gates before and after work. "I got so I could make three from one piece of paper, to save money," he said. "I would be handing them out, and looking for the police at the same time." He grinned, and pantomimed a medley of furtive gestures. He also rode the local segregated buses. "I'd sit up in the front, right behind the driver. Once the bus got started, I'd jump up, turn around and start giving my speech."

Thozi Gqweta's prominence had quickly attracted the attention of the security police. They had detained him three times in 1980, though they never brought him to trial. The longest stretch lasted a month. He insisted the repression would not stop SAAWU. With a summarizing flourish, he recited one of the formulations he had undoubtedly used at hundreds of his impromptu sessions: "As long as there is work to be done, there will be workers; as long as there are workers, they will be aggrieved; as long as they are aggrieved, they will want trade unions to look after their grievances.''

The time for my rendezvous with the underground up in Johannesburg was near. Rather than rely on the vagaries of hitchhiking, I bought a second-class ticket the next day on the state-owned railway. First and second class are for whites, third and fourth for blacks. As the train left town and crawled through Mdantsane township, I spotted a young white soldier patrolling alongside the tracks. The African National Congress guerrilla movement had blown up sections of this line several times, so the regime had evidently called in the army—although the press, probably restrained by certain recent legislation, had carried no mention of the move. A number of other white soldiers were on the train itself, identifiable despite their civilian clothes by their closely cropped hair and their boisterousness.

As the train began the slow climb to the Free State and the inland plateau, a waiter moved through the car, selling sandwiches and cold drinks. He was white. The railroads are just about the only institution in the country where you can see whites doing actual physical work. In fact, one of the very first things South Africans, whether black or white, notice on their trips to Europe or America are whites working on road crews. The white waiters were a legacy of the 1920s and '30s, when the railways and other state-owned enterprises deliberately employed whites in even menial jobs at subsidized rates of pay in order to end white unemployment. It was called, euphemistically, "the civilized labor policy"—whites, as "civilized" people, merited a guaranteed job at a high standard of living. The policy survives today in the white psyche as the comfortable realization that they will never be without some sort of a job. Never in more than four years in southern Africa did I ever hear a white person express fear of unemployment. Of course the waiters back in third and fourth class were blacks, who were earning probably one-third as much as their white counterparts.

The train continued into the night. The six-hundred-mile trip takes a full twenty-four hours. In the Free State the next morning, groups of black people were rummaging through the brown mielie stalks next to the tracks, gleaning maize cobs to burn as fuel. Further along, at Sasolburg, the train passed one of the three gigantic oil-from-coal refineries built so far to reduce the regime's dependence on imported oil. This, known as Sasol One, was an immense conglomeration of futuristic steel pipes, machinery, and smokestacks. The contrast between its up-to-date technology and the maize cob gleaners was very typically South African. A year earlier, African National Congress saboteurs had bombed a section of Sasol One, sending pillars of smoke thousands of feet into the air and inflicting more than seven million dollars in damage.

We arrived in Joburg just after noon. I decided to try and meet my contact right away. This man—I'll call him Simon Khumalo—worked as a copydesk editor at one of the city's newspapers. I had contacted him about a year earlier, carrying a verbal message from outside, from an exiled friend he had not seen for ten years. I had doubted my visit would be worthwhile; how was he going to trust an unknown white man? My skepticism proved groundless. Within minutes of meeting me, he had led the way to a nearby international restaurant (in case his workplace was bugged). He was talking away freely. He could have gotten years in prison for what he was revealing to me.

This visit, I strolled into the newspaper offices, and gave the receptionist my pseudonym. Khumalo appeared, dressed in a three-piece suit. He was beaming. "Hello, man." He shook my hand heartily, and we rushed off to our now familiar meeting place. "How's Joe?" he asked eagerly, referring to our exiled mutual friend. He then began a familiar speech: Joe and he were friends and political allies for more than twenty years; Joe was godfather to one of his children; he missed Joe terribly. He squinted and drew in his breath sharply. "Ahh, that one. He's never flinched. He's a very, very brave man indeed."

You could say much the same about Khumalo. In the early 1970s, he had been held in solitary confinement for an entire year, and then tried and sentenced to three years for "furthering the aims" of the African National Congress. He was sent to Robben Island. He had once told me off-handedly that prison had been a relief after the year in detention. "At least I now had other people to talk to." On his release, he seems to have hesitated not at all before rejoining the ANC underground. He seemed to be mixed up in enough activity to get him returned to the Island permanently.

Khumalo was enthusiastic at the guerrilla movement's recent successes. Three weeks earlier, saboteurs had struck simultaneously in East London, Durban, and Johannesburg, hundreds of miles apart. "Our boys are starting to hit them hard, man," Khumalo said. "And they're following orders to hit military targets—railway lines, police stations, that army recruiting office in Durban."

He suddenly grew somber. "I've got some bad news for Joe. They've caught Maphiri. He's being held under Section Six. It looks like they got him to talk—they probably used that electricity machine. Now, the link to him was Nomathemba. Maphiri told them he gave her some money. They put her inside, but she said nothing. She said she never met Maphiri. They let her out, but it's getting too dangerous for her here now. Tell Joe it's time she skipped. If they approve, we'll do it the usual way.''

A couple of white men in business suits walked into the restaurant. One of them exchanged greetings with Khumalo. "He's from advertising," he explained. "He votes for the Progressives. A nice guy." He shrugged.

He continued, "Joe must be getting tired of hearing this—but we need money. The boys in one of the East Rand sections *must* get a car. Then we've got the legal fees to pay. And have him send us more *Sechaba* magazines—the one with O. R. Tambo's latest speech in it. He must send them the usual way.''

Traffic whizzed by on the busy street outside. A black waiter came over to bring more coffee. Khumalo and he conversed briefly in Zulu. The waiter smiled and nodded. After he left, Khumalo explained, "I was asking him about our attacks. Of course he's happy. Everyone is. They celebrate in the beer halls and the shebeens when we make a big raid. That one is a Gatsha Buthelezi supporter. He's a migrant from Zululand, and he thinks he must stay loyal to his chief. But I've been talking to him. I think he's starting to move in our direction.''

Khumalo then gave me a stream of further messages. About half of them were about political matters; the rest concerned personal affairs—so-and-so's father greeted his son in a guerrilla training camp, someone else regretted that she had been unable to attend a funeral held outside; another person who was looking after the teenage daughter of an exile needed advice about disciplinary problems he was having. By the end, my head was swimming with the long list of mellifluous African names I was going to have to commit to memory.

We left the restaurant, and parted on a busy nearby street corner. Khumalo looked around furtively, winked, and quickly jerked his thumb into the air. It was the ANC salute. He grinned and turned back toward his office.

I started hitchhiking back to Swaziland the next day. My first ride was with a uniformed Afrikaner soldier, a burly, mustachioed fellow who spoke English badly. I edged into my stock line of questioning about the war in Namibia, expecting a bravado response. I was surprised as he winced. He shook his head emphatically and said he was glad his unit had been recalled. Then, unexpectedly, he started talking, frowning to himself as he spoke:

"The army went into Angola and took some Germans. East Germans, prisoners, two of them. The army say to one, where is the weapons hidden? He says no, he won't tell. They give him to the reccies. Those are blokes who are sick in the mind or something, they doesn't like people.

"The reccies takes the first German up in a helicopter. It goes up fifty feet. They push him out. He breaks his legs, but he still doesn't talk. Then they takes him up a hundred feet and pushes him out again. It kills him. Then the other German tells the reccies where the weapons is buried under ground."

I had my doubts, but he insisted he had actually seen the man pushed out by the reccies—members of the reconnaissance commando, an elite unit suspected of many war crimes in Namibia. "Those reccies," he said with disbelief, as if discussing members of another species, "They doesn't have wives, they stay there in the bush *all* the time. They like war."

My next two lifts were both with supporters of the far right Herstigte National Party, who were pleased at the HNP's improved showing in the elections the previous April. The party, for a decade only a marginal force in all-white politics, had increased its vote total to 14 percent, and it showed signs of even further growth. Whites disturbed at the ruling National Party's talk of reform had deserted to the far right in record numbers. The first HNP supporter, a muscular refrigerator repairman, maintained the government was "giving too much to the kaffirs." But, he added, "Maybe I'm talking too much. I don't say push all the kaffirs into the sea—where would we be without them?"

The next driver, an insurance salesman in his early forties, could have answered that. He spent the first half hour, from Bethal to Ermelo, talking enthusiastically and in enormous detail about fishing. He even praised the revolutionary government in neighboring Mozambique; it had apparently outlawed certain extreme fishing practices on its side of the border, causing the reappearance of certain kinds of fish upstream in South Africa. Only gradually did he reveal his far-right views. "I was raised to say 'kaffir,' " he said peevishly. "I don't mean anything derogatory by it. But the government now says we mustn't use it."

The essence of his larger philosophy was that whites had to reduce their dependence on blacks, in order to clear the way for absolute and total territorial segregation. "They complain we don't pay them enough—well, the thing to do is just get rid of them. I have friends, farmers, who've sacked all their laborers and bought machinery. Now they and their sons do everything themselves! There's not a single black staying on the farm!"

He glanced over to see if I was suitably impressed by this radical new departure. Then he added wearily, "The government will carry on giving everything to the blacks, until we have a black government. I expect I'll have to leave. I'll go to America, Australia, somewhere.''

The fisherman turned off at Chrissiemeer. I waited several more hours in the cold wind for the last ride of my two-thousand-mile journey. Black people walked along the roadside, between town and distant white farms where they lived. A lucky few pedalled bicycles. One woman drifted by, and approached a dead tree a hundred yards further up the road. She passed the other way a half hour later, with an enormous and unwieldy bundle of firewood balanced effortlessly on top of her head.

From time to time, I idly bent over for small stones to hurl at a nearby utility pole. Once I reached down just as three little black schoolgirls skipped by, neat in their black-and-white uniforms. They darted away quickly, amid nervous laughter. I realized they had thought I was going to throw stones at them.

Back at my home in Swaziland a few days later, I picked up the Johannesburg *Rand Daily Mail* to learn that the East London police had once again detained labor leader Thozamile Gqweta. This time, they held him for six weeks. Within days of his release, he was back at work negotiating union recognition agreements with East London companies.

A few months later, a mysterious fire swept through the home of Thozi's mother and uncle, over in King William's Town. Both were killed. Police opened fire on mourners returning to East London after the funeral, killing one woman union member. The woman had been Thozi's fiancée. He himself was detained again shortly afterwards.

There was even worse news just before Christmas. The wife of the underground leader Simon Khumalo reported him missing. Witnesses said he was last seen talking to two white men in a car outside his Johannesburg office. The ANC said he had not gone into exile, and they presumed him murdered. His wife said he had been getting anonymous death threats for more than a year. I wondered why he had mentioned nothing to me at our last meeting. He probably thought he had more important things to worry about.

2

City of Darkness

I HAD ALREADY FORMED a mental picture of the apartheid system before I arrived in southern Africa. I visualized apartheid as being very much like my image of the racial system that prevailed in the American South before the 1960s. I imagined bizarre, absurd, almost comical features, like separate drinking fountains and separate Bibles in courtrooms for witnesses of different races. South Africa's rulers sounded familiar, like odd primitives, Afrikaans-speaking variants of old southern backwoodsmen like the former Georgia governor Lestor Maddox, who had once handed out axe handles to white patrons of a restaurant he owned so they could help him keep out prospective black customers. I imagined that similar crude savagery helped to maintain white supremacy in South Africa.

In my years in southern Africa, I learned, at first hand, that my vision of apartheid had been very largely inaccurate. There was certainly no lack of segregation, which in South Africa is sometimes called petty apartheid. There was plenty of vicious, primitive racism as well. You could open your Johannesburg *Star* to the letters page and read, "If it weren't for the whites who started education in this country, the blacks would still be running around in their tribal dressing, destroying everything they can get hold of, or killing all the wildlife they see." The writer, like most whites a self-styled expert on the intimacies of black life, added that before whites had arrived blacks were "satisfied to drink themselves to a standstill, sleep with a different girl every night and gamble their money away without thinking of the hungry stomachs at home."

This hysteria over race, sometimes ridiculous, was also sometimes tragic. There was the well-known case of the white Laing family, whose daughter Sandra started to show certain "black" physical features as she grew older. She was forced to leave her all-white school and otherwise ostracized until she had no choice but to live as a black among blacks.

Another even more horrifying episode took place in 1980. A white police constable named H. du Toit told a court he did not intervene when he saw another white man beating a black man because he "didn't want to get involved." He did allow that he felt "a bit guilty" because he was in a government car at the time. The black man, Mojukwena James Oliphant, died later from his injuries.

But apartheid is much, much more than the sum total of such racist episodes, depressingly common as they are. Apartheid is in fact an enormously complex, sophisticated, and modern system of racial and economic domination. It employs the most advanced technology, much of it obtained from the West, to regulate the life and work of millions of people. I was to learn that the computer is as characteristic a tool of apartheid as the *sjambok* (pronounced sham-*bok*), the animal hide whip the police still use and venerate.

The apartheid government has carried out massive changes in South Africa. It has forced, sometimes at gunpoint, nearly four million black, colored, and Indian people to resettle, often hundreds of miles from their original homes, in places in which poverty and disease approach genocidal proportions. Apartheid forces millions of black workers to live as migrants, apart from their families most of the year, in conditions of servitude that are nearly the equivalent of forced labor. It enforces these regulations on where blacks can live and work by requiring all of them to carry the hated pass; police arrest several hundred thousand people a year for failing to produce the document. The violence of apartheid is not expressed primarily in the form of random street incidents, but officially, in one of the highest rates of imprisonment and judicially sanctioned executions in the entire world. Violence is also expressed in another way, in a huge army and police force, equipped with modern arms, probably including atomic weapons, that is already at war in Namibia and in a state of chronic, tense hostility with its other neighbors and with the majority of its own population.

The central institution of apartheid is the Bantustan system, the horseshoe-shaped archipelago of territories around the nation's rim. These areas, which constitute only 13 percent of the total country, are the only places where blacks have the permanent right to live and own land.

Everywhere else, in the other 87 percent of the country, which includes all the cities, blacks are present only as "temporary sojourners." Several million are migrants, who leave their families behind in the Bantustans most of the year throughout their entire working lives. Others are laborers on the huge white farms, who live and work under conditions not far removed from serfdom.

Still others, about one-fourth of all black South Africans, live on a semi-permanent basis in the "white" urban areas. Their right to live in the cities with their families is not due to a fit of government altruism. The official Stallard Commission, back in 1922, stated bluntly that a black man "should only be allowed to enter the urban areas, which are essentially the white man's creation, when he is willing to enter and to minister to the needs of the white man, and should depart therefrom when he ceases so to minister." The "urban blacks" are in the cities primarily because they work in semiskilled, or more rarely, in skilled jobs. It would be more costly and less efficient to train new migrants every year to do their work. So they are allowed to remain, on sufferance, in the great cities that they built in their own country.

The urban blacks are reminded of their insecurity of tenure every time the regime declares another of the Bantustans "independent." They have all been assigned to one of the ten fragmented territories. With the stroke of a pen, hundreds of thousands of them find themselves "citizens" of distant areas they may never even have visited, while they are now "foreigners," required to turn in their passes for "passports," in the very places they may have spent their entire lives. In theory, and sometimes in practice, they can be deported overnight.

Urban blacks are not allowed to live just anywhere they choose. They are confined, by law, to segregated ghettos that were once called locations, but which the government has renamed townships to make them sound more hospitable. Every white city, town, and hamlet in South Africa has its black twin or twins, its shadow city separated from the white area by a sanitary cordon of open space. Pretoria has its Mamelodi and Atteridgeville; Durban its Umlazi and Kwa-Mashu; Cape Town its Langa, Nyanga, and Guguletu; Bloemfontein its Bochabella; Benoni its Daveyton; Krugersdorp its Kagiso. The biggest township of all, outside Johannesburg, is called Soweto. It has a population of one and one-half million people, making it by itself one of the largest cities in all Africa.

You can get lost more easily in Soweto than probably anywhere else in the world. There are no signs to identify either the handful of paved roads that crisscross the sprawling township, or the confusing maze of dusty side streets. The houses, one hundred thousand of them, look almost exactly the same: one-story, tiny, rectangular brick structures, universally called matchboxes, each about twenty feet wide and twenty-five feet long. Row upon row of them stretch out over the bare rolling hills, lined up in military fashion, their corrugated roofs in yellow, green, or red providing sparkles of color against the light brown background.

The township is even more difficult to get around in at night. There are few street lights, and only about one-fifth of the homes are electrified. Most of the limited illumination is provided by flickering wood, coal, or kerosene stoves. On winter nights especially, a heavy cloud of acrid smoke from the burning stoves hangs over the townships, scattering the dim light into an eerie phosphorescent fog.

There are few distinguishing landmarks in Soweto. There are no large shopping complexes, only the occasional small grocery or liquor store, often housed in a converted matchbox. There are gas stations, grimy, concrete train depots, three run-down soccer stadiums, and not much else. If a Soweto resident wants to buy a hat or a soccer ball, go to a drugstore, or stroll through a tree-lined park, he or she must go to Johannesburg, which is close to one hour away. There are seven swimming pools and three movie houses for Soweto's estimated one and one-half million people.

The primitive conditions, the absence of the most elementary amenities associated with urban living, are not merely due to the township's poverty. They are also a consequence of the apartheid fiction that blacks are only "temporary sojourners" in "white" South Africa, with permanent living rights only in the Bantustans. Thus, no one in Soweto is allowed to own either his home or the land on which it is built; everyone rents from the government. Other laws prohibit blacks from setting up establishments that provide more than the basic necessities. There must be no chance that anyone gets the confused idea that they have a permanent right to remain.

Soweto is divided into about twenty sections. The areas have slightly distinctive characters, although they are almost indistinguishable in appearance. Long-term residents tend to live in Orlando, which is nearest to Johannesburg and which was first settled in the 1930s. Orlando has second- and even third-generation residents. In the 1940s and 50s, the township grew rapidly as the regime forced more black people out of Johannesburg proper. Orlando was joined by Diepkloof, the improbable sounding Meadowlands, and Dube, where the handful of better-off Sowetans have added second stories and fancy wooden siding to their matchboxes, and surrounded them with tidy, landscaped lawns—incongruous splashes of suburbia amid the bleakness. Further out are Mofolo, Klipspruit and White City–Jabavu, a poorer section, with an added measure of street crime. The main roads and the two railway lines then branch out to "deep Soweto," Moroka, Chiawelo, Emdeni, and Naledi, which are fully ten miles from the township's nearer frontier.

As the huge complex mushroomed, there were efforts to find a name, including several contests sponsored by newspapers. Finally, in the middle 1960s residents somewhat reluctantly settled on Soweto, which is often pronounced So-*way*-two. Despite the African ring to the name, it is actually merely a contraction of the words "South Western Townships." The name was never wholly satisfactory and there were sporadic efforts to choose another. But since the 1976 uprising the name has entered history and Sowetans feel a new pride in it, which probably ensures its permanence.

Despite the sprawl, Soweto is densely populated. Each four-roomed matchbox has an average of about fourteen people living in it, and some have twenty or more. The extremely cramped living conditions, another consequence of the regime's policy to discourage permanent black settlement, means that people must do much of their fraternizing outside, in the streets. You commonly will see a group of neighbors animatedly discussing the latest soccer match, an upcoming marriage, or, in lower tones, recent political developments, while they keep a watchful eye on the groups of children cavorting in the dust. A battered, overflowing taxi may roll up and deposit a relative or friend from another part of the township. In the evenings the group thins out, and by 9:00 P.M. there is no one on the street aside from an occasional pedestrian, nervously hurrying along, on the alert for knife-wielding muggers.

Inside most of the tiny homes, candles flicker as children finish their schoolwork and parents review the events of the day. Soweto is extraordinary, a quasi city of one and one-half million inhabitants in which candles are the major source of light, in which evening activities take place in half-darkness, with dancing shapes and long shadows. The regime has finally agreed to electrify Soweto totally. The township should have light by the mid- to late eighties, four decades after it was founded. Several generations of Sowetans will have grown up by candlelight, stumbling about in their darkened matchboxes, conscious that the faint glow on the eastern night horizon emanates from a fully electrified Joburg.

Soweto goes to bed early, except on weekends, in order to be ready for the long trip into work the next day. By 5:00 A.M. people are lurching out of bed, stumbling through the darkness to the detached privies, sponge bathing with water at the outside taps, and then streaming toward the train stations and bus stops. A lucky few can afford the quicker taxi ride into town, as everyone calls Johannesburg, and even fewer drive their own cars along the motorway, through a barren stretch of grassy veld, between the yellowish mine dump hills, and then into the city's outskirts.

Townships elsewhere in South Africa are similar in appearance and style of life. But there is a unique quality in Soweto. In most of the other urban centers, people from only one or two of the ten or so black ethnic groups, drawn from the closest rural area, form the vast majority of the residents: the Zulus predominate in Durban, Xhosas in Cape Town, Tswanas and Sothos in Bloemfontein.

Johannesburg has always attracted people from all over South Africa. The government has tried to promote tribalism in Soweto, by segregating sections of the township along ethnic lines and by establishing separate schools for the different groups. But Soweto has resisted. It is the black melting pot, the place where ethnic consciousness is disappearing fastest. Friendships are formed without a thought to ethnic origin. Intermarriage is growing. The remarkable linguistic skills of Sowetans—some have mastered as many as eight or nine languages—promote further understanding. Typically, a Sowetan will address a stranger in one African language, guessing at his ethnic origin, then, depending on the response, perhaps slide easily into another. Among young people particularly, the languages have merged into a kind of Interlingua, which includes English and Afrikaans expressions as well. Certain Afrikaans expletives are especially common. Afrikaners, like many religious peoples, tend in their profanity toward the blasphemous, the curt guttural sounds of *God, Here, Yell* (God, Lord, Hell). It can be quite startling at first to hear musical black English with its long open vowel sounds punctuated regularly by these Teutonic verbal explosions. Black South Africans can also be extraordinarily inventive linguistically. I once overheard a man tell his female drinking companion, "Stop speaking in hieroglyphics."

Soweto's sheer size and diversity have long established it as a South African Harlem: a bubbling, rollicking informal capital and cultural center. It attracts musicians and artists from all over the country. Theater groups are constantly at work, one step ahead of the censors, producing original plays in ramshackle school halls or churches. The leading black soccer teams, with fans in the millions, are based in Soweto. Even the township's lawbreakers are considered somehow epic, larger than life; in the past, notorious criminal bands like "The Torch Gang," "The Russians" and, more recently, "The Wire Gang," a group of thugs who tied up their robbery victims with clothes hangers, were spoken of with fear and awe elsewhere in the country.

The overall crime rate is phenomenal. Soweto has about one thousand murders a year, several hundred more than Chicago, which has twice its population. Strict gun control regulations for blacks means most of the homicides are committed with knives; the death toll would surely increase even further if firearms were more accessible. One of the world's highest capital punishment rates is apparently no deterrent; in 1980, a typical year, 130 people, all but one of them black, were hanged.

Since June 16, 1976, Soweto is a name recognized worldwide, a fact that its residents realize and in which they take a certain pride. The events which began that day are often described as ''riots,'' a word that lends a mistaken sense of random turmoil to what originated as a disciplined student protest against the regime's educational policy.

On that winter morning, young organizers moved among the several dozen Soweto high schools, encouraging students to abandon their classrooms and join a march snaking through the township to the northeast, to Orlando Stadium, where they planned to hold a protest rally. The students, who begin school at the age of seven, were two or three years older than American students of a similar level, but almost all were still in their teens. No one expected violence.

The young people were protesting against the threatened introduction of Afrikaans as the medium of instruction in a number of Soweto schools. They were not objecting to studying the language itself, which they already grumbled their way through during a single class period each day. What they vigorously resisted was the regime's effort to force them to learn their other subjects in Afrikaans. The students argued they were not proficient in the language, nor were their teachers, and they wondered cynically whether the regime's proposal was not intended to increase the failure rate and force even more of them out of school.

That kind of cynicism was at the heart of student protest against the entire system of ''Bantu Education,'' of which the dispute about Afrikaans was only a part. Black schooling in South Africa, not surprisingly, is characterized by financial starvation, prodigious teacher/pupil ratios of fifty, sixty, or more to one, makeshift classrooms, rudimentary, inferior facilities, whether for science experiments or for sports, unqualified teachers, high dropout rates, and so on. Even so, black parents are required to pay school fees, while white education is free.

But Bantu Education means something even more sinister. The students believed that the system was designed to thwart their efforts to learn, to teach them only the simple skills that they would need to perform inferior jobs, and to promote divisions among the various ethnic groups. The student view is not some paranoid fantasy, but based on an explicit statement by Hendrik Verwoerd, the cold ideologue who, as minister of native affairs, designed the system back in the early 1950s before he moved up to be prime minister.

Verwoerd, in a famous speech to Parliament that many black students could quote three decades later, said: "There is no place for him [the black student] in the European community above the level of certain forms of labor. . . . For that reason, it is of no avail for him to receive a training which has as its aim absorption in the European community. . . . Until now he has been subject to a school system which drew him away from his own community and misled him by showing him the green pastures of European society in which he is not allowed to graze."

Many black schools back then had been run by some of the churches, and the regime regarded them as dangerous centers of liberal influence. Verwoerd brought them all under state control, forcing them to follow a course of study that advanced the Nationalist view of South African life. To pass the standardized exams, for instance, black pupils were required to regurgitate the old fiction that the Europeans arrived at the Cape in 1652 at the same time as their ancestors were migrating southward into the region. (The archeological evidence has been clear for years. Iron Age black peoples from central Africa were migrating into what is presently South Africa in the third or fourth century A.D. at the very latest. The Khoisan peoples, those who were once known as Hottentots and Bushmen, who are also the ancestors of black South Africans, had been in the area much longer.)

Even worse, Bantu Education reversed the previous pedagogical trend toward using English as the medium of instruction among younger children. In many cases, students were now to be taught in their home languages until high school. The policy was partly intended to promote tribalism, especially in a place like Soweto, where next-door neighbors might find themselves attending different medium schools. It also worked to reduce the standard of English among blacks, cutting them off from the outside world precisely as Verwoerd had intended. Black parents were certainly proud of their own languages, but they had insisted their children learn English as well. They protested vigorously from the start, even planning massive boycotts. But the government responded with a threat to expel students who missed school, and the resistance fizzled out.

The thousands of students marching toward Orlando that cold June morning had spent their entire lives under Verwoerd's calculated system. Their crudely lettered, often misspelled placards, which would later be followed by similarly grammatically faulty leaflets, gave the initial impression his plan to perpetuate ignorance had succeeded. They marched along, chanting, into an open patch of veld near the soccer stadium. The mood was cheerful and nonviolent; one poster read, "If we must do Afrikaans, Vorster [then the prime minister] must do Zulu." It was a totally peaceful demonstration.

The South African police waited with automatic weapons. The students, many of whom were wearing their school uniforms, pulled up, uncertain. Someone started to sing the hymn, "Give Us Strength, O Lord." The rest of the nervous multitude joined in. As the harmonies wafted across the grassy veld, brown in midwinter, the police opened fire.

The first victim, thirteen-year-old Hector Petersen, fell dead. The students raced for the safety of the familiar dusty streets, their stupefaction turning quickly to rage. In the days and months to follow they were to demonstrate very clearly that Verwoerd's deliberate effort to mutilate them had not broken their spirit.

They set up a remarkable organization, the Soweto Students Representative Council, to coordinate a sophisticated protest campaign. The SSRC carried out an indefinite school boycott, which won support from teachers and some administrators. One of the proliferating number of protest leaflets said: "Parents, you should rejoice for having given birth to this type of child . . . a child who prefers to die from a bullet rather than to swallow a poisonous education which relegates him and his parents to a position of perpetual subordination." Many parents, proud of their children and somewhat embarrassed by their own compliance with apartheid, became politically active themselves.

The students won adult support for several successful stay-aways, or general strikes, which brought Johannesburg to one-day halts. They also requested that adults stop patronizing state-owned beer halls and liquor outlets, arguing that alcohol weakened the will to resist apartheid, and that the government should not enjoy the profits from such dubious enterprises. The SSRC sponsored marches to town, to bring their protest to the attention of whites. Within two months, the uprising had spread, first to Cape Town and then to many other urban centers.

The SSRC, a democratic organization, established by young people who had never known democracy, held regular clandestine meetings; members referred to each other by code names and sought replacements for those who had to flee into exile. The organization itself rejected violence explicitly, though students or others did burn down beer halls and other government-owned buildings, and, in the first outbreak of rage after the police started shooting, killed several whites they encountered in the township.

By far the major responsibility for the death toll, which eventually surpassed a thousand, rested with the police, or with mysterious whites, police, or vigilantes, who cruised the township firing indiscriminately from unmarked cars. For more than a year, Soweto frequently suffocated in blankets of tear gas and heard the chatter of automatic weapons fire into the night.

The uprising could not last forever. Too many unarmed people were simply being shot dead in the streets. Several thousands of students left the country, many of them looking for guns of their own; others were arrested and imprisoned. The majority of the students trickled bitterly back to school. Soweto returned to an uneasy calm.

The uprising did not accomplish much in practical terms. The regime did drop its plan to enforce Afrikaans as a medium, but it maintained Bantu Education largely intact. There was much talk of upgrading Soweto more generally, but more than seven years later there has been little discernible change, aside from the still unfinished electrification project.

Among Sowetans—and black people generally—the uprising almost completely ended whatever lingering hopes they had for peaceful evolutionary change. The savagery of the regime's response to a reasonable protest over a relatively minor issue was accompanied in the white population at large by a panicked rush to buy firearms.

At the same time, blacks drew from the uprising the lesson that they were fully capable of mounting a coordinated, nationwide protest, of shaking the regime. The Soweto uprising was easily the most profound and widespread upheaval in South African history. "How far have we actually come along Freedom Road?" asked the writer Mothobi Mutloatse. "At least we know now that we shall not transfer another legacy of fear to the coming generation." The years of sullen doubt were replaced by a kind of grim optimism. Few black people doubt any longer they will eventually achieve power. Few deny the human cost will be tremendous.

Signboards on the major roads to Soweto remind you that it is against the law to enter the township without a special government permit. Police in camouflage uniforms often mount roadblocks to enforce the law. On my many trips out to Soweto, I usually took my chances without the permit. Despite the risks, I calculated that as an innocuous geography student I could not demonstrate an overpowering interest in township life without attracting government suspicion.

In past years, the limited social contact between black and white usually took place in Johannesburg, often at awkward gatherings in white homes. Some whites smugly preened themselves for their daring in attending such soirees, while some blacks resented the opulence and the atmosphere of self-congratulation. In fairness, the ever-present pressures

of apartheid tended to distort even the best-intentioned attempts at relaxed contact. It was illegal, for instance, for whites to serve liquor to
blacks, so black guests sometimes brought their own booze, labelled
prominently with their names, in case vengeful white neighbors called
the police to raid the party.

More recently, blacks have tended to insist that whites also make the
trip out to Soweto. There seems to be a desire to try and redress the old
imbalance, to try to socialize a little less unnaturally. There is also the
somewhat contradictory wish to confront white people more directly with
one of the ugly realities of apartheid. At the same time, though, blacks
can be embarrassed by their bleak surroundings and upset at the voy-
euristic stance the whole situation imposes on whites. Also, informers
in the township may view the gathering as an interracial conspiracy. Despite these drawbacks, though, black people do prefer to be visited, and
they treat their guests with extraordinary and bustling hospitality.

My first guide to Soweto was the young writer, Mtutuzeli Matshoba.
I first met Mtutu early in 1979, early in his writing career. He had published a couple of stories in *Staffrider,* an exuberant new literary magazine that took its name from the daredevil practice, favored by some
Soweto youths, of riding atop moving trains. Mtutu wrote more stories,
which were gathered into a collection, *Call Me Not a Man,* that was
widely acclaimed before it was banned. He also published a moving play,
Seeds of War. Mtutu, who is now in his early thirties, is one of the best
known of an entire new generation of black writers—young daredevils
of another sort who try to keep one jump ahead of the censors.

In the introduction to his stories, Mtutu describes his youth in Soweto,
"the dog-kennel city." He explains how he compiled a strong academic
record that carried him through college; how, although his written com-
positions had always received special praise, he only started writing seriously after "June 16, 1976 exploded in my face."

He continued, "My life was so full that I knew that if I did not spill
some of its contents out I would go berserk. I started scribbling and
burning the scraps of paper on which I wrote, torn between writing or
heading for the beckoning horizons, my country become my enemy. . . .
I want to reflect through my works life on my side of the fence, the
black side: so that whatever may happen in the future, I may not be set
down as 'a bloodthirsty terrorist.' "

Mtutuzeli Matshoba's stories are straightforwardly realistic accounts
of daily life in Soweto. He need not exaggerate for effect, because the

routine there has more than sufficient drama. He writes about people who are jailed for not carrying the hated pass, or for other trivial offenses: a 1980 study revealed that one in four adult Sowetans is arrested every year. He describes a visit to Robben Island, the prison fortress; his own brother did a year there on a political charge.

Mtutu is a listener, a quiet, unobtrusive, watchful man with a dry, controlled air. He is a walking archivist of Soweto's folkways; he knows the career trajectories of famous soccer stars, of the handful of small businessmen who are called, somewhat grandiloquently, tycoons, and of the sinister leading *tsotsis*. The word, several decades old, means "gangsters" or "thugs." It is said to be a derivation of the American "zoot-suiters."

Mtutu has detected a number of changes that have taken place since the 1976 uprisings. He says ethnic consciousness—"tribalism"—has declined markedly: "When I was young, we used to look down on the Shangaan people, the 'dirty Shangaans.' They dressed differently, and they kept their rural customs. We Xhosa-speaking people were supposed to be dishonest, thieves. That used to bother me a lot. The Tswanas were said to be cheap; the Zulus were said to be big, tough and violent; they contemptuously called the rest of us *izilwane,* or animals. Since '76, which we all went through together, you hardly ever hear those kinds of insults."

"For much the same reason," he continued, "the class system here is starting to ease up. There is the small group of the educated, and then there is everybody else. The educated guys used to wear suits all the time, carry newspapers ostentatiously, and look down on the rest. But since '76, that kind of feeling is going down. Before, if a guy from Jabavu–White City went out with a girl from Dube, the girl's parents would disapprove because he was poor. But you don't hear that so much anymore."

The uprising accelerated another change which had already been underway—name changing on a vast scale. Black children generally are given two first names, one in English, or less often Afrikaans, the other in one of the African languages. The English version is sometimes called the school name. The regime requires it to be used in school, and on passes and other official documents. The authorities simply refuse to recognize other names. In English, black names tend strongly toward the Biblical: there are Isaacs, Zephanias, Ezekiels, Polycarps, Cains and Abels, Abednigos; there are Marys, Miriams, and Esthers. Mtutu's school name is Ignatius.

Despite the official hostility, most parents contrived to give their children African names—in part, probably, as a form of quiet resistance against the regime's inhuman policy. The names often have fascinating meanings: Thokozile (Happiness) is a girl who delighted her parents, who already had four sons; Sipho's parents regarded him as (A Gift); Phindile (Again) is the third girl in a row; her little sister Zanele is (Enough).

Nkosinathi (God is with us) was born healthy despite his mother's protracted and painful labor pains; Bonisile (Evidence) proved her mother had actually been pregnant, despite remaining quite thin. Politically involved parents might name their sons Tokologo (Freedom), or their daughters Masechaba (Mother of the Nation). Mapule (Rain) was born during the spring planting season, and Mangaliso (Surprise) is a boy who came along unexpectedly; the putative father in such a case might be the victim of stifled guffaws.

Mtutu (The Comforter) is still slightly embarrassed that he once preferred to use his English name. In the late 1960s, the black consciousness movement started to emerge, led by the martyred Steve Biko. The movement, which borrowed some of its philosophy from black America, promoted pride and awareness. As one consequence, young people started dropping their school names. The '76 uprising largely completed the change, so that there are today few Samsons and Obediahs under the age of about thirty.

Mtutu explained that other Soweto customs had remained unchanged. The *makgotla,* informal bands of controversial vigilantes, tried to enforce their brand of discipline in the disorderly township. "They come and get you and put you on 'trial' for various offenses," he said, laughing. "They came for my neighbor once because they said he had gotten a girl pregnant and not offered to either marry her or support the child. They sometimes use the lash to carry out their judgments." Mtutu added that although Sowetans share some of the makgotla concern for order, many dislike the vigilantes for being self-appointed and brutal.

Another custom that Mtutu investigated and used in his stories was the *stokvel.* The host or hostess holds a big party and sells beer and food to the guests at several times the normal price. In a circle of friends, each takes turns hosting a stokvel. "People have been known to even buy a car from what they earn at a stokvel," he explained. "It's basically a cooperative scheme . . . and characteristic of the way many of us live here."

Mtutuzeli was slightly apologetic about the persistence in an urban setting of another cultural feature, the *inyanga.* The word can be translated either as "witch doctor" or "traditional healer." He says, "The whites make fun of us for going to them, but they have very good records in treating mad people. There was a guy down the street from me who got so bad he was not able to even speak. The inyanga moved in with him, and within a few months he was recovering." He estimated 90 percent of the people in Soweto have faith in the inyangas, especially in their abilities to cure mental and emotional ailments.

He was bitter about the utter lack of facilities in the township. "I don't call this place a city," he said. "I call it a labor camp. The main nighttime activity, particularly for older people, is drinking. They drink to forget their suffering and because there is nothing else to do here. If you want to go to the cinema, you have to buy the ticket way in advance, and you won't always be able to get in. If you go out with a girl, about all you can do is stand around on a dark street corner and hold hands." He laughed. "One form of recreation is to go to visit The Fort, the prison in town. Any time you go, there's always someone you know in there, for a pass offense or something else."

Despite Mtutuzeli's strong feelings, he is determined to judge white people as individuals—after a long period, beginning in his childhood, when he disliked nearly all of them. "I used to go into the shops in town," he remembered, "and speak to the white supervisor in, say, Zulu. He would answer in English, and I would pretend not to understand. He would get a black guy from the back of the store to translate. When he arrived I would speak in perfect English."

He now says, "I've started to see our situation here as not only caused by race. I think the rich use apartheid as a barrier to keep the white workers from joining with us. Anyway, I'm very concerned that I don't become a black racist. We have a word, *iBhunu,* which used to just mean 'Boer.' It was a great insult. Now, we still use the word, but we are starting to apply it to anyone who acts badly, whether he is black or white. Not all whites are amaBhunu and some blacks are. When I write my stories, I try to put in at least one sympathetic white character to balance out the bad ones. I don't call the situation here race relations . . . I call it human relations."

In Soweto, people of different backgrounds are thrown together, living under similar conditions along the same dusty streets. Unusual friendships can and do flourish. Mtutu is a college graduate; Vusi Ndlazi, his good friend, is an ex-pickpocket, who did his higher learning during three stretches in prison totalling seven years.

A favorite spot for the thieves is Hoek Street, a busy thoroughfare near Park Station in the center of town. The pavement artists catch the "Kontrak" in from Soweto at noon: the train got the nickname because many of its passengers, tsotsis and prostitutes, have an informal "contract" to live from crime. The tsotsis wear distinctive clothing. At times, they have favored woolen shirts of certain plaid patterns; stocking caps pulled low over the eyes; or spectacles without glass.

The pickpockets then position themselves. One or two of them bump into a victim, who, especially if white, can fly into such a rage at being even touched by blacks that he does not notice his wallet disappearing.

Vusi is actually embarrassed about his past, and dislikes discussing it. He is thirty-five, and just under six feet, which is very tall for a South African black man. He has a long, rubbery face that he twists frequently into a grin, a slightly lopsided grin as he is missing one of his two front teeth.

"Now I work," he says with wry regret. "I don't want to work, but my father is dead and the old lady is sick. She and the little ones depend on me. I work at an abbatoir way the other side of town, where I cut up the meat. I have to get up at four-thirty to get there by seven. On Mondays I sometimes don't get there. I've been out until half past three boozing the night before—how am I supposed to get *up* one hour later?"

Vusi was earning forty rand a week when I met him. He said excitedly, "The iBhunu doing the same job gets one hundred thirty rand. Last week I went up to the white *induna* [a Zulu word, which means "foreman"]. I said to him, 'Do you like it when we call you baas? Does it make you feel proud of yourself?' He just answered, 'Ach, man, don't give me that bloody rubbish'—and walked away."

Vusi got paid every Friday. "I go home, give the old lady what she needs for the week, and then I'm off, moving around Soweto, having some beers at the shebeen, meeting friends. By Monday, I have no money, so I have to go and see these guys at work. In our language we call them [he groped for the translation, then, triumphantly] 'the sinkers,' because they can *sink* you. I borrow five rand from them, knowing that on Friday I'll have to pay them back six rand, twenty-five. They don't drink, they don't smoke, all they do is keep their money so they can lend it out." He shook his head with disgust at such puritanical behavior. *"Hawu,"* he snorted. "The sinkers."

"A car," he continued, "is something I don't even think about. Not even a Volkswagen. I never even learned to drive. All I can do is pay my mother's rent, keep food in the house, pay transport, and have something left over for booze and smokes."

Vusi did allow that his venture into the labor force had one happy consequence. "Now, my pass is in order. Before, when I had no job, the police would look at it and say, 'What's this?' " He mimicked the police, as a guffaw started bubbling up inside him. "You're not working! Listen, man, you're not being *used.*"

Vusi Ndlazi is proud of his friendship with Mtutu, the university man. He added, "I have another friend who's also educated, a social worker. But there are very few like this in Soweto. Sometimes I think to myself, I would like to go away from this place, to where I could continue my education, get a job that interests me . . . Ach, but I'm dreaming, I can say it won't happen."

One warm Saturday in February, toward the end of summer, I toured Soweto with Mtutu and Vusi. We met at midday at Mtutu's house in Orlando. He lived in a typical matchbox. We arranged ourselves in the tiny living room while his younger sister served us tea and biscuits. She had to edge her way about cautiously because the tiny room was overflowing with furniture: two sofas, chairs, a low glass table and a battery-powered phonograph in one corner together with a collection of American jazz records. Six people lived in the house—five family members and, Mtutu explained, "one woman from the Transkei who had nowhere to stay, so my mother invited her in." His brother was absent, imprisoned on Robben Island.

Our first stop, Mtutu explained, would be the notorious Mzimhlophe Hostel, which was located just up the street. Hostel is the regime's deceptive name for the single-sex residential compounds, scattered across Soweto, in which about forty-five thousand people live. Hostels are the regime's mechanism to limit the number of what it coldly calls superfluous black people in the urban areas. The unskilled migrant workers, most of them men, sign labor contracts in their rural Bantustans and come to the cities, where they live alone in the hostels, usually for eleven months a year. They return home to their families for only a single month, usually around Christmas.

"The people in the hostels have all of the worst jobs," Mtutu explained. "Road construction, refuse collection, things like that. Before '76, we in the township had little contact with them. They have no children in school here, so they didn't understand our grievance about Bantu Education. We called the stay-aways and said no one must work. They didn't understand why they couldn't go to work."

Some of the hostel residents became extremely angry. There is evidence they were urged on by the police. At any rate, they stormed out of Mzimhlophe Hostel during a two-week period in August 1976, armed with *pangas* and the wooden clubs called *knobkerries*. The township residents banded together and fought back. More than seventy people were killed.

"After the fighting," Mtutu went on, "we were afraid for a time to go in there. But we realized we must get to know them. We've started to visit.''

On the way, I navigated the car carefully through groups of children playing in the dusty streets. Vusi laughed uproariously at my official map of Soweto, a fanciful document that included many splashes of emerald green to denote the location of parks. He gestured, ''There are *many* parks here . . . ten, twenty, more than fifty.'' He looked out of the window. ''There's one.'' He was pointing toward an empty field covered with rocks and scrubgrass. ''The map says there's another one . . . just here,'' as we turned a corner and sighted a smouldering garbage dump.

Vusi assumed his most somber expression and concluded, ''The white man has given us ma-a-a-ny fine parks.''

We reached the hostel, which is surrounded by a barbed wire fence ten feet high. Vusi's mood darkened. ''It is a zoo,'' he said savagely. ''They are supposed to be animals. They must be kept in the zoo.'' We drove in a hundred yards past the hulk of a building burned in the rebellion, and parked between two long rows of shedlike structures. Some twenty men were seated around the dirt courtyard, many talking loudly in an advanced state of intoxication. One man sat apart, laboriously stitching a sole to a shoe.

As I emerged from the car, there was general consternation. ''A white man in Soweto,'' Mtutu grinned, happily quoting from one of his stories, ''is about as common as an Eskimo in the Sahara.'' He explained quickly in Zulu that I was not a policeman. One man asked, half-seriously, ''Why did you bring an *umlungu* here? We see too many in town during the week.''

''Mfowethu,'' Mtutu answered. ''My brother. He is from America. He is coming to see how we live.''

The man smiled with understanding. ''Welcome.'' He gave me an American black-power handshake and guided us up the courtyard to one of the sheds, which had been converted into a shebeen, one of the semilegal speakeasies.

We entered the dingy room filled with the aroma of wood smoke from the stoves on which the men do their cooking. A Donna Summer record was playing on a battery-powered phonograph. Two dozen men were standing around drinking quart bottles of beer, or taking turns dancing with three women. Strictly speaking, no women, or any outsiders, are permitted in the hostels, but the police had relaxed their vigilance—possibly bought off by bribes.

In three dimly lit side rooms we saw straw pallets placed over concrete slabs—these were the sleeping quarters. ''Their wives *do* sometimes come for short visits,'' Mtutu explained as we entered one of the cheerless rooms, "but as you can see there is no privacy here. When they have guests, they look for a spare room out in the township."

The "shebeen king," evidently pleased at having exotic visitors, hustled over with bottles of Lion and Castle beer. Vusi joined a heated discussion about Soweto's three major soccer teams, Orlando Pirates, Moroka Swallows, and Kaizer Chiefs. He beamed approvingly at another man's pro-Pirate views, nodding and saying "sharp" several times at each of his new ally's verbal thrusts. Team pictures of the clubs, together with a multiracial collection of pinups, decorated the dirty, streaked walls.

A wobbling young man seated across from us tentatively passed across his beer bottle and gestured that I take a drink. As I did, he smiled vacantly and muttered something vaguely in Xhosa. Mtutu translated, "He says he thinks not all *abelungu* are bad." Mtutu paused, then added, "See, we are not black racists."

We then drove off toward Dobsonville, in northwestern Soweto, where we were going to visit a relative of Mtutu's. On the way, we passed a funeral motorcade, the second we had seen that day. "A funeral is very big here," Mtutu said. "Even if you don't know the guy it's enough that you are a friend of a friend—you go. Such a waste, people should be cremated."

The discussion stirred Vusi's memory, and he started to laugh. "Back in '67, I worked for some months in a cemetery. People came every day and put things on the graves—flowers, coins. I *took* those things. *He's* down there [Vusi pointed earthward] but *I'm* up here. I need the things more than he does. At the end of a day I might have two rand—enough to buy some few beers!"

Mtutu's relatives lived in the same standard matchbox, but they were among the minority in Soweto blessed with electricity. They could therefore have a refrigerator, which they had placed in the living room due to a lack of space in the kitchen. They also enjoyed another luxury, a flush toilet; most Soweto homes have an outside latrine.

After the introductions, Mtutu's cousins conducted a ritual I experienced numerous times in my years in southern Africa—the showing of the photo albums. Black people acquire truly prodigious numbers of photographs of themselves, their families, and their friends, which they mount in albums, often adding explanatory or humorous captions. Some of the photos are of the normal sorts of occasions, like weddings—I once counted seven photographers clicking away at a friend's nuptials. But no pretext is even needed. The bleakness of Soweto in fact stimulates photo-taking expeditions to the green parks in town, in search of more attractive settings in which to pose. Photos are often kept in duplicate, ready for exchanging with friends. Visitors are invited to pore through literally hundreds of the snapshots, listening to a running commentary, in an exercise that can easily last an hour.

I never figured out the reason for the popularity of photo albums. Was the custom an effort by people who are only supposed to huddle in the shadows to furnish themselves and each other with visible, tangible proofs of their existence? Or was it rather simply a mode of artistic and poetic expression? Some of the albums are cleverly arranged chronicles, with witty captions. I was never sure.

Just as we completed the ritual, Mtutu's uncle returned home. He was a middle-aged, burly, jovial man, who worked as a clerk for an insurance company in town. "That's the highest they'll let us go," he explained. "When I first got the job, they put me out on the floor like everyone else. But then some white customers started to complain, so they put a partition around me so the customers couldn't see me." Everyone laughed heartily. "We also have separate teacups. The whites use the blue ones, and I use the yellow."

Mtutu mentioned it was getting late, and I should start driving back to town before the permit I had obtained for this visit expired. It was only valid during daylight.

As we headed through the dusk toward the main road, drivers were honking their horns and pedestrians were moving through the twilight at a happy, bouncing gait. Someone shouted at us, "The Bucs won," and we understood. The Orlando Pirates had defeated a white club in a major soccer match, and Soweto was celebrating.

Earlier, I had asked Mtutu and Vusi for some African proverbs. As I parked on the edge of the darkening township to let them out, Vusi said something in Tswana, and Mtutu nodded. "There must be room for all the dancers," he translated. "It means if some people are in the center they must move over and give the other people an opportunity to also dance."

We parted, and I started off toward the lights of Johannesburg, gleaming in the distance beyond the shadowy mine dumps. The stream of cars going the other way honked continually to celebrate the Pirate victory.

Many white South Africans mistakenly believe that apartheid is disappearing. This belief is based more on the pronouncements of white leaders than on demonstrable fact. Even as the ashes of the burned government buildings in Soweto were still cooling, there was already extravagant talk in the white community of "reform." Business leaders and politicians from both the National Party and the small moderate opposition tried to outdo one another with promises to improve the township.

The government offered certain Sowetans a chance to purchase a ninety-nine-year lease to their matchbox homes. The proposal preserved the fiction that blacks were "temporary sojourners" in the cities, while in practice allowing them more security of tenure. Telephone service was expanded. The electrification scheme went forward slowly. Prominent philanthropists ostentatiously announced the expansion of education and community health programs. The regime proposed giving black municipal councils some control over local affairs (although it steadfastly continued to repeat that urban blacks would exercise their political rights in "their" Bantustans, and never in the South African Parliament). In 1979, P. W. Botha even helicoptered into Soweto, the first prime minister in history to visit the place where one and one-half million of his fellow South Africans live.

Despite an endless cacophony of favorable publicity, few of the proposed reforms were getting far past the talking stage. Only a handful of Sowetans had acquired the ninety-nine-year leases; most were too poor to come up with even the modest necessary down payments. Nonetheless, the white businessmen and politicians remained bravely optimistic.

Their aim, which they made no secret of, was to create and nurture a black middle class as a bulwark against revolutionary change. One white politician had once argued that such a "responsible class . . . could be a stabilizing influence and could cooperate in the maintenance of law and order." By giving some urban blacks at least some stake in the prevailing system, the white leaders hoped to separate them from the millions of black people who are even poorer—the migrant laborers and those suffering in the Bantustans.

In theory, Peter Magubane is the sort of man the government would like to try to co-opt. He is a successful professional man, one of South Africa's best-known photographers. In 1979, when I met him, he had a good job at the Johannesburg *Rand Daily Mail.* He has published four books, two of them in the United States. He travels widely overseas; in South Africa, he also moves in circles the average Sowetan will never frequent. But despite his success in life, he continues to be staunchly active in the fight against apartheid. The regime is not going to find it easy to win over people like him.

Magubane's photography combines technical skill with a great deal of courage. Many of his shots of the 1976 uprising are world famous. One particularly harrowing picture shows two young women demonstrators instants after a police bullet had gouged an ugly wound in the stomach of one of them.

"I was standing about twenty feet away," he recalled matter-of-factly.

"They were just in front of me, chanting 'power.' I heard the bullets whistling over my shoulder. She didn't realize at first she'd been hit. Then she lifted up her shirt. I don't know whether I would do it again, but I felt that there had to be a record."

Magubane is short and stocky, with salt-and-pepper hair. His nose is bent sharply to one side, the result of a police pistol-butt during a 1977 disturbance. He is a cheerful extrovert who greeted friends on every corner in central Johannesburg as we walked to lunch one day. He carries his camera with him everywhere.

He grew up in Sophiatown (pronounced Sof-*eye*-a-town), a legendary polyglot neighborhood in western Johannesburg much like Cape Town's District Six. The government razed the neighborhood in the middle 1950s after forcing the black residents to move out to Soweto. Then, with a sneer, it renamed the area, now for whites only, Triomf—Triumph in English. "Sophiatown was a very pleasant place to live," he remembered. "It was not at all a slum like the government claimed. It was very cosmopolitan; there were blacks, coloreds, Chinese, Indians, even some whites. It had gangsters with flashy cars, bootleggers, boxers, musicians. The Odeon Cinema—if you were a singer you had to sing there, you had to please that audience in order to make it."

Magubane's father, who hawked vegetables in the street, gave him a box camera when he was a boy. He used it to take pictures of his school friends for fifteen cents each.

In the early 1950s he admired the work in *Drum* magazine, a famous crusading black-oriented monthly at which many leading writers and photographers worked. "The only vacancy was a driving job, but I took it. I had to get near a darkroom."

The chief photographer, a German, loaned him the money for his own camera. "After work, I would walk around town doing night shots, using the available light. I sometimes had to sleep in the darkroom because the last bus to Sophiatown left at ten. Then, after a while, a photography job opened up and I got it."

Peter Magubane was present at the 1960 Sharpeville Massacre, when police fired on a demonstration against the pass laws and killed sixty-nine people. It was an epochal event in South African history. "I was so shocked when they started shooting that I just stopped dead. I really flopped the assignment. I got too involved in what was happening. I learned from Sharpeville that you have to be a pro if you want to get the story. I never made that mistake again."

In 1969, Magubane was arrested on a political charge, eventually tried with twenty-one others, acquitted, rearrested, tried and acquitted once again. He spent a total of 586 days in solitary confinement. "You cease to be a person under those conditions. You just better forget about the outside life. You try to sing, walk, exercise in the cell. You feel happy when you hear the clinking of keys along the passage. You try to speak to the warder. Usually they answer, 'I'm not allowed to talk to you.' But you feel happy. At least you opened your mouth."

In 1971, the regime "banned" Magubane for five years. A banning order is a cruel restriction, in which a person is forced to become his own jailer. The minister of justice, without giving any reason or allowing any appeal, simply ordered Magubane to stay in the Johannesburg magisterial area. The order prohibited him from entering any school or newspaper office, thus forcing him out of journalism. It also specified he could not attend any "social gathering," which meant he could never be present with more than one other person, even in his own home. The security police regularly monitor banned people and launch unexpected raids to catch them in sinister group activities like dinner parties. Magubane was apprehended once, for which he served a six-month prison sentence.

"I even had to stop taking pictures," he said, still incredulous. "You see, there usually is more than one person in my pictures, so I would have been present at an illegal social gathering." He supported his family by conducting a one-man merchandising business until the ban expired—just before the Soweto uprising.

Magubane is not at all optimistic about a peaceful solution in South Africa. He dismisses the reform talk with contempt. "The whites here must sit and negotiate seriously with black people. But I don't know if they are capable of it. They are used to waking up, the servant has prepared the tea for them, then they get driven to work. They don't know how to do anything on their own. They would find it very hard to assimilate to a hard way of living. Here's an example: some of their young people have formed communes, just like you have in America, but there is a big difference—the commune has a *servant!*

"Even among the liberals, there is a lot of racism. They invite *me* to their homes, but my brother, who they don't know, can't use their front door."

Magubane is cosmopolitan and urbane. His bitterness is genuine and deeply felt, not at all a pose or the petulant outbursts of a weak man. But even he felt hostility toward many whites who worked with him at the *Rand Daily Mail,* the newspaper with the worldwide progressive reputation.

"Ninety percent of them are racist and patronizing. They are just here to earn a living. They have no commitment. When they join another paper, they just drop their liberal ideas. In the office, they speak to you, but out on the street they shun you, they don't know you.''

Magubane got even angrier as he explained that certain of his white colleagues still lack respect for black photographers. ''We did all the work during Soweto, because they couldn't get in there. We proved ourselves. But there is still discrimination in assignments. They give us only the small head-and-shoulder jobs, while the big photos on page one, two, and three go to whitey. I try to do my own thing, not let it get me down, but why must I be given only easy assignments?''

His flare-up passed quickly, replaced by a more reflective mood. ''Many people, including my old colleagues at *Drum,* have left and now work overseas. But I never felt the urge to leave.''

He broke off, and then spoke again, quietly, ''I am very much in love with my camera. I make it speak. I do what I like. I never allow myself to be frustrated by anybody. This is how I keep sane.

''Even when I was banned, I was still able to eat, to feed my children. South Africa is my country. Only if I could not support myself here would I consider leaving.''

In the years following the Soweto uprising, as the talk of reform continued to come to nothing, several thousand young people did decide to flee into exile. They crossed illegally into the neighboring independent states of Botswana, Lesotho, and Swaziland. A variety of motives prompted this exodus. Some of the young people left to escape certain arrest and probable imprisonment. Others wanted to join one of the liberation organizations based in exile, to volunteer for training as guerrillas. Still others sought only to continue their schooling, away from the detested Bantu Education system. Some ''skipped,'' as the word for flight became, for the same reasons young people anywhere leave home: a search for adventure, a desire for independence. Most young people left for a combination of these reasons.

The urge to remain at home was also strong, in part due to the natural bonds to family, friends, and place. Reports filtered back that life in exile could be a struggle in unfamiliar surroundings. Many young people argued quietly but persuasively that liberation would not only come from outside South Africa: some would have to remain behind and work inside the country.

Quite a few people spent months, even years, weighing these many factors. They agonized guardedly, confiding only in close friends, as it is a prison offense to try to leave the country without permission. Once gone, there was no coming back; after the first flush of excitement in

'76, most people soberly realized the apartheid regime would survive for a long time to come. I watched two of my friends spend several years trying to make up their minds.

Mandla Mazibuko spoke slowly and deliberately, in a soft, hypnotic tone of voice. He dressed very casually—a pair of jeans, a T-shirt, and *tackies,* or sneakers. He was very muscular, the result of daily exercises and runs of up to marathon distance. "We must be strong," he said. "We must not succumb to the temptation of material things." He was twenty-two years old when I first met him, in 1979.

Mandla was raised by his grandparents, whom he calls his parents, in the Naledi section of "deep Soweto." His grandfather, the epitome of elderly dignity, was more than ninety years old. He was a laborer who experienced a religious conversion after what Mandla suspects was a hell-raising youth. He was a preacher in the African Methodist Episcopal Church, which had been started by black American missionaries. The old man still worked, helping out as a shop assistant. Mandla explained, "He qualifies for his pension of twenty-five rand a month but he can only receive it in 'his' Bantustan—which is a place where he has never lived. He wants to stay here, so he must work."

The dominant influence of grandfather Mazibuko produced a very religious grandson. "I started preaching myself when I was only thirteen. At home, we still sing two or three spirituals and pray together before going to bed. As a child, I used to often read the Bible and other religious books instead of going out to play. Because of my religion, I always avoided the fights that the other small boys would sometimes have with each other."

At Orlando High School, Mandla Mazibuko was one of the students looked up to as leaders by the others. "I always," he said, "spoke in favor of nonviolence and Christianity. During '76 and '77 some of the fellows would say we should go and burn down the government bottle stores, or burn the houses of police and other sell-outs. I debated with them, and quite often I was able to talk them out of these acts."

In late 1977, Mazibuko was leading a prayer meeting at the school, reading and interpreting certain Bible verses. The principal, T. W. Kambule, an educator highly respected by both parents and students, was on hand. Suddenly, police in riot gear burst in with snarling dogs. "The one closest to me had a dog called Bobby," Mandla remembered. "He kept saying 'Get them, Bobby' as the dog jumped at us. The police started to beat the girl students with their batons. Mr. Kambule tried to stop them, but they just pushed him out of the way. I have never in my life seen anyone so humiliated."

Mandla and twenty other students were taken away to Protea police station, where they were methodically beaten. "I still believed in non-violence, but I questioned myself. I got books by Frantz Fanon and Mao Tse-Tung; I borrowed them even though they are all banned. I gradually came to think that if you endure evil, if you do not resist evil, you are assisting evil. You are becoming part of evil."

After white vigilantes shot to death his favorite cousin in the street one morning, he changed further. "I started to have what I think was a kind of neurosis. I looked in some books that said the symptoms are brooding, insomnia, all of which I had. Sometimes I had to press my temples as hard as I could to keep the pain away."

Mandla decided to leave the country, to study mechanical engineering. He had done well in high school science. "They don't let us study anything advanced here; there is probably not a single black mechanical engineer in the whole country."

He paused, and asked me, "How can it be that in a time when man's capacity and man's mind are expanding that such creatures who believe in racism can still exist?"

The police caught him just short of the Botswana border. "I was so foolish," he said, grimacing. "I was carrying a book by Mao Tse-Tung in a paper bag, and I was wearing blue jeans and boots. People don't dress that way in the rural areas."

The police in Swartruggens, a small town in the Western Transvaal, interrogated him. They asked why he was leaving. "I told them, 'to study mechanical engineering.' That really made them angry. One of them laughed and said, 'So now these black things are getting clever, hey!' "

Mandla continued speaking, as if in a trance, "They called for the commander. He started asking questions politely. I answered those about myself, but I refused to tell him names of some other people in the struggle. He became angry, left the room, and came back with four huge Boers."

Mandla recreated the scene, repeating the police statements in Afrikaans and then translating. " 'So you won't talk, hey? Take off your clothes. We're going to cut your penis off.' Then they started laughing about someone they had tortured before. . . .

"I still wasn't going to tell them anything. I can't explain . . . you have to be in that position yourself. I had *nothing* to lose. All I wanted was my dignity as a human being. I would keep that. I told them so. 'If I die, I die,' I said. Also, I knew I had my own foolishness to blame for getting caught. I felt I had to endure.

"I waited in that chair as they walked around me asking more questions. Then they pushed me over to a closet and told me to look inside.

There I saw all kinds of canes—long ones, short ones, thick ones. They told me to pick one out. I refused. They sat me down again."

"Then, one of them looked at his watch and started to complain. They wanted to leave work for the day. They said, 'Don't worry, we will come and get you in the morning.'

"Back in the cell, I didn't sleep all night. I refused the food, because I had already learned you can take the cuffs better if you haven't eaten. About 5 A.M. I heard a woman singing a beautiful spiritual somewhere else in the prison. I started to sing along with her. When they came for me later, they handcuffed us together and took us down to the office."

Mandla started to smile. "I waited. Then they took me inside. It was not as bad as I expected. They cuffed me some few times, and used one of the canes."

He bit off the words, obviously recalling the scene vividly. "I—told—them—nothing."

Two months later, the police released Mandla without charging him. He joked that he regretted missing a major soccer match while he was in jail, in which his team, the Orlando Pirates, had trounced the arch-rival Kaizer Chiefs. He lingered around Johannesburg, unsure of his next step. He felt the press of family obligations. His grandparents had been deeply upset by his detention.

He resolved to stay until they passed away. "I don't want to hurt them anymore," he said. "My grandfather was once very much in the struggle, but he is now old and tired." Meanwhile, he signed up with a correspondence school to study various subjects on his own, a step taken by many students who refused to return to Bantu Education. He still suffered from headaches. He looked forward to when he would eventually leave and join the guerrilla army. He said he had largely abandoned religion, though he was interested in Islam because he had heard "it does not say to turn the other cheek."

"I would not like to kill," he told me in mid-1979. "But I am not afraid to die. I read a book once by a revolutionary from East Africa, which said we must not be afraid of religion. We must be prepared to be like Jesus and die for the people. We must resist evil to avoid becoming part of it."

Mosubye Matlala also dresses informally, like his friend Mandla, but he has a flair for the unusual—a bead necklace, a stocking cap even in summer. He is constantly thinking, questioning, weighing, with an intensity that is perceptible from his expressions. He squints often, furrowing his brow, twisting himself awkwardly as he chooses his words with extreme care. His mood changes from day to day; he is sometimes irritable and withdrawn, on other occasions open and relaxed. He was twenty-three years old and living with his family in Orlando when I first met him. He had also been a leader in the Soweto student movement, and he was detained for seven months. He did not talk about his time in jail, but he occasionally let slip random comments that indicated he was beaten up badly.

Mosubye's father first arrived in Soweto in 1963. The Matlala family was from the Lebowa Bantustan, in the north. "It's nice there in the mountains and you can sometimes even hear lions roaring at night. But there is no work there."

He says he had a troubled childhood, due to his tyrannical father, a large and humorless man. "He didn't let me go out and play on the mine dumps with the other kids. On weekends he stayed in the house and did his carpentry. He built tables and chairs. We had to sit quietly with him, and hand him a nail or a screw when he wanted it. Whenever I disobeyed and went out to play, he would give me the lash and send me to bed without any food. My mother tried to take my side, but he never listened to her. It became a pattern since I was young—I would disobey and get the lash.

"My father is a traditionalist. He demands we speak our own language, Pedi, at home instead of the mixture we use in Soweto. He didn't approve when my eldest brother married a Xhosa, so they had to have a small, civil wedding without the white gown and all that. He doesn't like Soweto; he says he will go back to Lebowa after he stops working. He doesn't have many friends. His health is not good. So he put up a sign in the house that says 'No Smoking.' We have to put out our fags in the street. [He laughed.] He's always telling me to comb my hair, and until recently I had to take off my beads in the house.

"My father's idea of politics is to accept. He doesn't approve of apartheid, but he accepts. He thinks the blacks are too stupid to run the country. And he says that people who fight the system always lose. He says, 'Look at Mandela and the others—they're still on Robben Island and will stay there for all their lives.' When I got involved in the struggle, he always told me to stay away from 'that bloody rubbish.' After I got out of jail he told me, 'See what your nonsense got you. Why can't you be sensible—finish school, get a good job as a clerk or something, dress nicely, get on the waiting list for a house, marry, start to raise a family? Why can't you do that?'

"He's my father, sure, and I respect him. But he could make you run mad. I don't know why none of us did. My eldest brother had to leave high school after two years; my father just said he had spent too much money on him already. My next brother ran away from home once and now he spends most of his time at Slow's shebeen. [The owner "walks slow, talks slow, generally is slow." Few people know his real name.] My father sometimes made us stay at home all evening while he lectured us, accused us of not respecting him and following his rules.

"After I got out of jail, I went to work at a television factory. I refused to call the Afrikaner induna baas, or speak to him in Afrikaans. I never say baas and it hurts me inside to see older people saying it. I always spoke to him politely, but in English. He didn't like that, so he started calling me a monkey. I complained to the personnel office, but he kept on doing it. I quit after two months."

"My father was pleased when I got the job. He didn't believe I was working at first, but then I showed him my monthly train ticket. When I quit, I explained to him that I could no more put up with them calling me a monkey. He looked at me and said, 'And how long have they been calling me a monkey so that I can feed you and your brothers?' "

Mosubye shrugged wordlessly. Then he continued, "I can't do what he wants, though, get a job as a clerk and that. I might become another 'cat,' one of those stuck-up guys that imitate everything the black Americans do. The 'cats' sit around in the shebeen talking shit, using big words, English phrases they've memorized that have nothing to do with the way people actually talk. They wear their suits and talk about 'the poor black masses' as if they were better. And they're just clerks, messengers, nothing special."

Mosubye, like many of the Soweto student leaders, had been strongly influenced by black consciousness. But he was starting to have serious doubts by 1979, the year we became friends. "Black consciousness can make you into a damn racist, going around with these hard guys preaching against 'whitey.' Alone, black consciousness just leads to chaos. All it tells us is to have pride and awareness. It doesn't tell us how to get rid of this system, and it doesn't prepare us with the kind of skills we will need after the white conservatives piss off and we have to reconstruct the country."

He was also skeptical of the guerrilla movement. He had once had a heated argument with two ANC sympathizers about the eventual fate of John Vorster Square, the main Johannesburg police station at which so many political detainees have died suspiciously. "I told them the building must be destroyed. It is symbolic of so much evil that it must be destroyed. They said I was too sentimental. A democratic government could use the building for some good purpose."

In 1979, Mosubye Matlala planned to remain in South Africa. He also wanted to work with whites, even though he still suffered dizzy spells due to police beatings during his stretch in detention. "I think what exists here among whites is more statutory racism than real racism. The laws keep them apart from us, not their own feelings. Especially the younger people—I don't think they're racists. We should set up contact groups between black and white students. We need something like a multiracial debating society, or a high school newspaper for all the schools, in both Soweto and town.

"But this regime is very clever. You can't do fuck-all here without them knowing. They have eyes everywhere. When they detained me, they knew details about meetings I had been to that I could hardly remember myself. They've banned moderate programs like this before, and they could do it again. But we must give it a try.

"I meet with some white liberals here to try and get these contact groups organized. Liberals here give you money before you even ask for it. [He laughed.] I'm worried about being around them. Maybe I'll become more moderate and soft. . . ."

"The Albert Street pass office," Mosubye had explained, "is absolutely the worst place. At the other places where we have contact with the regime, there are usually blacks who do the work. But at the pass office we confront the whites directly."

Survey after survey has shown that the chief grievance of urban black South Africans is the pass laws. The actual document is a rather innocuous-looking brown plastic booklet with green pages, about the size of a passport. In it, though, is stamped information that governs where a black person is allowed to live and work, and sometimes even what work he or she is allowed to do. Failure to produce the pass on demand is a crime.

Mandla and Mosubye had let their passes expire. They therefore ran the constant risk of being caught in one of the police raids that often take place in town, particularly at train and bus stations. In 1978, about 275,000 people had been arrested on pass offenses—one out of every 60 black South Africans. The two young men were streetwise and circumspect, but they still moved around with the nagging fear they might be caught off guard. The penalty is a fine or even a prison term. So Mike, a white friend of theirs, offered to provide false documentation saying they worked in his business. He accompanied them to Albert Street one afternoon to get their passes in order.

The building is located in a run-down area just south of central Johannesburg. Several hundred black men and some women sat outside, on the curb or leaning against the wire fence. As we arrived, some of them rushed up to Mike and beseeched him for a job. "These men are on 'Specials,' " Mosubye explained. "That's a certain pass that allows them to remain in the Joburg area for 14 days to look for work. With unemployment as high as it is, some of them must be on their sixth or seventh 'Special.' "

Inside, we got into a line over which a sign said, "Registration of Male Bantu." Mandla headed over to another section. A young, brown-haired Afrikaner woman was behind the counter. Just in front of us, an elderly black man inched forward, alone. The woman, who had been continually making harried gestures, spotted him. "Where is your baas?" she snapped. He muttered something meekly. "Leave," she ordered. Later he returned with a middle-aged white man, to whom she said politely, "I'm sorry, they can't wait in line by themselves."

We reached the front, and Mike started to fill out the green form. The woman slammed down the phone, noticed Mosubye, and said abruptly, "You go and please sit down." (In our postmortem, Mosubye said, "The 'please' was because you two whites were there.")

Mike handed over the form. We inwardly stiffened. Would she see through the ruse? She grumpily approved the documentation and brought down the huge stamp in Mosubye's book. Christopher Matlala, Male Bantu, was "permitted to remain" in the prescribed "white area" as long as he held his present job.

We moved down the corridor to check on Mandla, who was languishing in a section for blacks unaccompanied by their baases. There were a dozen lines of about twenty people each, mostly men, who waited quietly and stoically. We observed from one side.

The second clerk away from us, a small young man with curly hair and a scruffy beard, shouted something in Afrikaans at the black man facing him across the counter. Mike translated quietly, "Are you deaf? Open up your ears." Both the bearded clerk, and the man nearer us, who was larger and modishly dressed, frowned continually and threw papers back over the counter at the black people. From time to time, a smartly dressed black man, wearing a picture ID badge clipped to his shirt, spoke harshly in Sotho, ordering the lines to reform, then turned and exchanged friendly, complicit laughs with the bearded clerk.

A short black man came around the side, next to us, and asked the modish clerk a question in polite, but halting Afrikaans. The clerk turned away, irritated, and said, "I don't give a fuck." Moments later, the bearded one yelled at another client, "Don't go to sleep—where is your pass?"

Mandla finally made it to the front. He remained calm, spoke in Afrikaans and was rewarded with the coveted stamp unaccompanied by insults. On the way out of Albert Street—almost precisely two hours after we had entered—Mandla mumbled, "This section is not nearly so bad as the other section down the way, which everyone calls the cattle kraal. There, they really treat you badly.'' And, while a dozen workseekers again besieged Mike in the street outside, Mosubye, the sentimentalist, added, ''Someday, we will burn this place to the ground.''

I maintained my friendship with the two young men in the years that followed. In 1981, the security police arrested several of Mandla's friends and started looking for him as well. He faced a potential lengthy prison term for his underground activities, so he had little difficulty in deciding to flee. To his surprise, his grandfather supported his choice. ''A month before, another old man had stopped me in the township and said, *'Wena!* You? The grandson of Mazibuko? They put up our rents again, without warning. Your grandfather used to fight against such things. What does he think we must do?' ''

''I went home and cornered the old man. I asked him, 'Are your beliefs still the same?' He said, 'I'm old. I fought, but always alone. Now I'm weary.'

'' *'Baba,'* I said to him. 'Father. You taught me the truth remains forever.'

'' 'All right,' he answered. 'Yes, my beliefs are still the same. I will go and see what we can do to stop the rent increase.''

A month later, grandfather Mazibuko went into action swiftly when he learned his grandson was on the run. He consulted his wide range of contacts. Within twelve hours, a truck carrying gold miners home to a neighboring country had an additional passenger—a young man intending to train as a guerrilla soldier, and, later, as a mechanical engineer. Grandfather and grandson parted, probably for the last time.

That same year, Mosubye Matlala had a horrifying experience. ''I caught the last bus from town at eleven. I was walking down my street in the pitch dark, when I saw this tsotsi stabbing another guy with a 'seven.' That's a big knife that they can give you seven years in prison for having.''

''He was 'weeding' this guy with the knife. That's the only word I can use to describe it—he was just carefully stabbing the guy like you might pull weeds from a garden. Another group of guys was just standing around, smoking *dagga* [marijuana] and laughing.

''What could I do? I had nothing. They would have come for me as well. The police were not around, and it was already too late. I just ran home. I didn't sleep all night. I read in the *Post* the next day a guy's body had been found there.''

Mosubye, characteristically avid for knowledge, had acquainted himself with the works of Paulo Freire, the renowned Brazilian educator who teaches poor people to read while simultaneously promoting their self-respect and political awareness. Mosubye planned to try and set up a program along similar lines in the hostels, among the sort of people he had seen 'weeding' their victim on the darkened street. "I don't mean we should go and tell them what to do. We should smoke dagga with them, get to know them as friends first. They are *people*, oppressed people. Then maybe we can try to get them to start seeing why they shouldn't be killing each other."

He had finally resolved to stay inside South Africa. "In '76, I got myself so worked up that I was ready to just go after the enemy with my bare hands. I'm more patient now. The guerrillas are coming, but people here must do more than just cheer for them. If we win the struggle and people are still stabbing each other on the street, what good will the fighting have accomplished? What kind of country will we live in?"

3

City of Gold

THE STORY GOES that the surveyors who laid out Johannesburg in the late 1800s calculated that corner lots would bring more on the booming land market, so they put the cross streets absurdly close to each other, to create the maximum conceivable number of corners. Their legacy has been twofold—a hopelessly clogged central business district, and an early contribution to the Joburg ethos: making money.

The city is located at six thousand feet above sea level, directly atop the richest gold-bearing geologic formation in the world, the Witwatersrand (Ridge of White Waters). There is no other reason for this metropolis of 1.5 million people sitting incongruously in the middle of the platteland; no lake port, or confluence of rivers, or strategic trade routes; nothing. Black people have long called it Egoli—The City of Gold. In the years since World War II, the major mining activity has moved southwestward down the Rand all the way to the Free State, in pursuit of more lucrative deposits, but it has left behind remnants in the form of the heaping, yellowish hills that surround the city. It has also left behind what is arguably the largest agglomeration of wealthy people anywhere in the world.

Joburg is a spacious, sprawling city, often likened by American visitors to Houston or Dallas, with perhaps a touch of Denver thrown in. It is an extremely clean, tidy city. Black laborers in dark blue overalls empty the trash containers regularly, sweep the streets, and keep the grass in the parks the length of a golf green. The city is not a cultural landmark. The wealth from gold, and from the manufacturing plants scattered to the south and east, has not been converted into first-rate art museums or exciting architectural innovations. It is an angular, matter-of-fact industrial and commercial center, with several skyscrapers, the tallest of them fifty stories.

Johannesburg is a suburbia writ large. Just north of the city center are Hillbrow and Berea, congested regions of multistory-tower blocks with names like Golden Oaks, inhabited by singles and young couples. But immediately thereafter the sprawl begins. Parktown, Houghton, Highlands North, and Kew fan outward to the north: mile after mile of large, modern homes, often with distinctive red tile roofs. Some twenty-five thousand of them have their own swimming pools (there are seven pools in Soweto) and many have private tennis courts as well.

Pleasant parks, playing grounds and countless country clubs are interspersed along the winding, shady streets. The residential areas are rarely interrupted by shopping strips: commercial activities are centered in mammoth, multipurpose complexes called hypermarkets, which are several times the size of American shopping centers. It is a society based almost exclusively on the automobile. The whites-only buses stop running at 7:00 P.M., and there are surprisingly few white taxis, so people move around in cars, including an astonishing number of Mercedes-Benzes. Most socializing is done in the homes, as there are relatively few bars, clubs, or restaurants outside the central area. People are anyway increasingly frightened to go into town at night, due to the well-publicized increase in muggings.

Johannesburg does have a few older neighborhoods tucked out of the way, places like Doornfontein and Fordsburg, or Vrededorp, but the dominant sensation is of a city engulfed in an overwhelming suburbia, a lopsided tilt toward wealth without the intervening inner-city slums or working-class areas, without even a proper bohemia. It is Westchester without the Bronx or Greenwich Village, Lake Forest with no Back-of-the-Yards.

Wealth has not purchased serenity in the northern suburbs. The opulence is behind barriers: stone or red-brick walls, high wooden fences, or thick hedgerows. On virtually every front gate is a metal sign that warns: "Protected by the ———— Burglar Alarm Systems." Many of the houses also have watchdogs, ferocious German shepherds, known as Alsatians here, or Dobermans. Inside, as the ultimate defense, their owners have guns—one for every four white South Africans, which must be the highest civilian armament ratio in the world.

The objects of this fear and hatred have little real contact with the subjects. Each morning, the tens of thousands of black people stream in from Soweto, wedged into the overflowing segregated buses and trains; they perform their assigned tasks, and return home. At the same time, white people drive south along Jan Smuts and Louis Botha Avenues, or along the tree-lined Motorways, and drive home again in the evenings. In between, there is little interaction other than the giving and receiving of orders.

In part, the persistence of petty apartheid keeps the races separate. The regime has loudly announced its intention to end "unnecessary and hurtful discrimination" (which prompts a certain curiosity about the necessary and painless sort). In reality, reform has usually only meant removing the much-photographed signs, while usually retaining the practice. Buses, taxis, commuter trains, and public toilets are still segregated, as are most hotels, bars and restaurants, and movie theaters. Liquor stores still have separate entrances, labelled with the touchingly helpful bilingual signs: "Whites—Blankes. Non-whites—Nie-Blankes." This is still an improvement on the pre-1960 period, when blacks were forbidden to buy booze at all. (That reform, allowing blacks into the bottle stores, deprived white hoboes of a valuable source of income as middlemen.)

There have been other changes. Park benches are no longer segregated, nor are lines at the post office. The number of "international" hotels and restaurants is increasing slowly. Certain foreign blacks, such as U.S. embassy employees, are officially designated as "honorary whites" and allowed to eat and stay anywhere. Outside one group of lavatories in the Carleton Centre, there is a new sign that says: "These toilets are open to all WELL-BEHAVED PERSONS." Then, to reassure those frightened at the fast pace of change, "Whites-only toilets are located on the second-level above." In a nice twist, there was even a short-lived restaurant called Sit 'N' Eat, which, though owned by whites, could only serve blacks. I was ejected from it one evening when I dropped in with my friend Mosubye Matlala. The black waiter, with a malicious gleam in his eye, explained, "Black, colored, Indian man, yes—baasman, no!"

Custom has changed more slowly. Blacks still tend to avoid the park benches and sit directly on the grass. At lunchtime in central Johannesburg, blacks dressed in the ubiquitous blue overalls of a laborer, the blue or pink maid's dress, in the casual attire of a messenger or clerk, or in the uniform of a watchman, gather together and converse animatedly in one of the African languages as they eat half-loaves of unsliced bread and sip sugary fruit drinks. In town, they almost never use English or Afrikaans among themselves, as though to maintain distance and privacy. The white people—the men in business or safari suits, the women immaculately dressed and made-up, both a few years behind Western fashions, but doggedly trying to keep up—spend their lunch hours in restaurants, as the black waiters circle silently. Back out in the streets, black and white people never walk together. They pass each other in silence, avoiding eye contact, denying any recognition that the other exists. There is an eerie sense about that if all the people of one race were to instantly disappear, a not inconsiderable amount of time would pass before the others even noticed.

This indifference is to some extent an illusion. Blacks and whites are more aware of each other's existence than they seem to let on. Black people throughout southern Africa invent nicknames for people with whom they are in regular contact, such as their white superiors.

Some of the names are perfectly straightforward: "Black Hair," "Big Stomach," "Four Eyes." Others venture toward the poetic; "Blue Sky" is a woman with eyes of an arresting shade. Still other names are concerned with posture. A young man who stoops constantly is "Question Mark"; another who has a bobbing, loping walk is the "Wildebeest." An elderly woman who smokes heavily is "Sitemela" or "Train"; she always moves under a cloud.

Some of the nicknames sound somewhat hurtful. "Grasshopper" is a young woman with spindly legs and a barrel-like thorax. "Testicles" is a farmer accustomed to wearing shorts that are probably too short. A college teacher who watches his caloric intake is called the "Backside-less Wonder." A middle-aged man with a rare profile is known, literally, as the "Map of Swaziland." Another, an elderly Johannesburg lawyer who paces his office corridor, looking downward, lost in momentous thought, is "He-who-walks-with-his-head-to-the-ground-like-an-anteater."

These nicknames are given in one of the ten or so African languages. They are applied to black and white people alike. Blacks naturally understand the names they acquire. But in many cases whites remain ignorant as their servants or employees regularly describe them so graphically, within earshot.

Whites tend to be less creative and individual in their selection of terminology, and less circumspect in its use. Blacks are still openly called kaffirs, which is derived from an Arabic word that means merely "infidels" but which translates accurately as "niggers." To many whites, there are no "men" or "women" among blacks. Even grandparents are "boys" and "girls," although sometimes, as a generous concession, the prefix "old" is added. Alternately, whites use the word "coon," which must be an import from America. Colored people are sometimes *hout-*

kops (wooden heads), or *Boesmen* (Bushmen). Indians are "coolies." In response, blacks have also used imports from the United States, occasionally among themselves describing whites as "honkeys" and "whiteys."

"Boers," which is pronounced *Boo*-ers and means simply "farmers," is somewhat of an oddity; blacks use the word as an insult, but some Afrikaners take pride in it as a reminder of their rural, pioneer past. There is plenty of invective within the white community. English-speaking whites insult Afrikaners as "hairybacks," "rocks," due to their alleged lack of brain power and their political intractability, or the more evocative "rock spiders." Afrikaners retort with "rednecks"—the soft English-speaker's neck burns easily in the hot African sun—or *soutie* (salty). The English-speaker does not feel himself a part of the nation; he has one foot in England, the other in South Africa—and a portion of his anatomy dangling in the salt water in between.

Johannesburg is predominantly an English-speaking city. Before I arrived in southern Africa, I had assumed that the 40 percent of the whites who speak English constituted in the main a force for moderation and reason; that unfortunately for the cause of racial harmony, bigoted Afrikaners outnumbered and outvoted them. Many English speakers, I found right away, encourage this view. They will force a tired smile and in a tone of complicity, as one enlightened person to another, they will tell you of the exasperating racism of "those bloody thick Dutchmen."

It is certainly true that English-speaking whites tend to treat blacks with less direct brutality and more formal civility. Many blacks prefer to work under English-speaking supervisors or employers. It is true as well that the apartheid regime's most notorious figures, from cabinet ministers down to security police torturers, are predominantly Afrikaans-speaking. It is also true that English-speakers sustain the opposition Progressive Federal Party, even though that organization is far more conservative than is supposed overseas.

Yet the prevailing view of the heroic and embattled English-speaking moderate is less easy to maintain when you sit among them, sipping gin and tonics at sundown in the gardens of their large homes, while their servants move discreetly in the background. Their racial attitudes are really not much different from those of the most right-wing Afrikaners; they simply express themselves less crudely. And not always: at one such gathering, a blond woman in her late twenties leisurely told me, "I don't think I could shoot a colored or an Indian; I think of them as people. But an African is different."

Rarely does the English-speaking moderate's fight against apartheid amount to more than a perfunctory contribution to mainstream charities or to the white political opposition. The business community, which is still largely English-speaking, is quick to denounce government economic regulation; it is less vocal about deaths in detention and other crimes against human rights. Perceptive Afrikaners used to say sardonically that the English-speaker says he is a Prog, votes secretly for the United Party (a now-defunct centrist group), and thanks the Lord every night the Nats (National Party) are still in power.

In part, though, what seems to be English-speaking hypocrisy is actually a genuine misunderstanding of the meaning of apartheid. English-speaking moderates often interpret the word to mean only segregation in certain areas of life, rather than the much more profound system of Bantustans and migratory labor. The English-speaker is perfectly content to call for an end to segregation in housing, employment, and amenities, knowing that few blacks could ever move into his neighborhood, compete with him for a job, or even afford to eat often in the restaurants he frequents. The English-speaker tends to be more reticent about apartheid's more fundamental features, which have helped him achieve one of the highest standards of living in the entire world.

There are, however, genuine radicals and liberals among English- (and Afrikaans-speaking) whites. One of them is Jill Parker, who was a student in literature at the English-language University of the Witwatersrand when I met her in 1979. Jill was active in several political groups on the campus of Wits, as the school is known popularly. She was also working a couple of evenings a week as a waitress, an unusual activity for the pampered, wealthy white students. "I wanted to actually do physical work," she explained, a little embarrassed. "Few whites here ever do."

Jill told me a story about her niece Lisa, who had just turned nine. "My sister had a birthday party for her, and a black woman from her father's business came over to help with the arrangements. Lisa and this woman got on very well.

"After the party, we drove the black woman back to Soweto. Lisa had never seen such a place. . . . The tiny houses, the smoke, the little children her own age playing in the dust. She was just stunned. To go from my sister's big house . . . to that. As we drove back, she was quiet. Then she said to my sister, 'Mummy, we better move overseas. I can't stay here where I feel so embarrassed.'

"I grew up, like Lisa, in Houghton in a big house with servants. The whole *toot*. But in spite of the wealth, it was often very lonely there as a child. Sometimes the maid (we called her Monica but I'm ashamed to admit I never learned what her proper name was) took me out to the park, but I had to play by myself. There were no other children around.

"In high school, we had another maid, Sibongile. *Her* name I learned. [Jill laughed self-consciously.] She and I got to be friends, even though she was an older woman, in her forties, and we didn't have much in common, to say the least. But we discovered we both liked classical music, and one Christmas they were giving Handel's *Messiah* at a theatre in town. I rang up, found it was multiracial and invited her to come. She invited her sister along. When we arrived, there were *such* stares. The ticket seller said we'd made a mistake, that *coloreds* and *Indians* were allowed to attend, but not Africans. I was so embarrassed. As I explained to Sibongile and her sister what had happened, I started to cry. But they said not to worry. We left quietly. I'll never forget how they walked out with such dignity."

Jill, in common with other English-speaking radicals, feels such incidents cannot be blamed conveniently on Afrikaners alone or on the National Party regime. "The typical English-speaker says if *we* were in power, everything would be better. But that's not true. We *are* in power, in the sense that English-speaking people still dominate in business, in commerce. Most of those businessmen do nothing to change the apartheid system. They're happy just to sit back and let the money come in—money from cheap black labor.

"There are white people, though, who really do want to change this system. There are more of us than the outside world realizes, I think. We feel our first duty is to remain here—*not* to emigrate like some English-speaking people are doing. After '76 especially, people are getting their university degrees and heading straight for America, the U.K., Australia. There's even supposed to be a neighborhood in Houston with so many ex-South Africans it's called Houghton West."

Jill said English-speaking whites emigrate partly because they have never felt fully at home in Africa. She quoted from a recent issue of the *Wits Student*. "The white student's very culture and outlook is a hybrid of American commodity culture and a Western European intellectual heritage. So it's not unusual that he can be highly articulate on New York's urban violence, England's trade unions, and Israel's borders, while he's reduced to a stutter when asked about migrant labor, security legislation or homeland under-development."

The National Union of South African Students, of which Jill Parker was an active member, officially opposes emigration. Instead, NUSAS, which is based on the five English-speaking university campuses, started a program in the late 1970s called Education for an African Future. She explained, "We want to remain here and contribute to the life of the country, to *all* of its people. We don't see ourselves as participating in a paternalistic way, trying to lead blacks to liberation or anything like that. Blacks have quite rightly criticized us for that kind of arrogance in the past. We *have* been privileged, but we can't do anything about that now. At least we can put what we've learned to use for all of our people, instead of just making money like most of our parents. The universities don't teach us what we need. They train highly specialized doctors while there is a desperate need for primary health care. They train more mining engineers when what South Africa needs are labor lawyers. We try to get students to question their education, to refocus, to think.''

In 1979, Jill Parker was pessimistic about persuading large numbers of white students. She estimated the Wits student body was 20 percent radical, 60 percent moderate and apathetic, and 20 percent conservative. ''We control the student organization and the newspaper because we're more active, but we must be always alert. It's the racist environment here. In our homes it's always the master-and-servant relationship. It's not easy for us to leave behind our racist ideas.''

She also said the two-year army requirement made NUSAS work even more difficult. Young men entering university after fighting in Namibia can be bitter at the radicals, who almost openly support the SWAPO guerrillas they have just faced in combat.

The draft also put radical young men themselves in a terrible dilemma. One of Jill's friends accepted his ''African future,'' so he went into the army when he got his call-up papers rather than emigrate. (There is an extremely limited provision for conscientious objection, for which only a few members of particular religious sects qualify.) Her friend's predicament troubled Jill enormously. ''He was back on leave recently. He said he'd managed so far not to fire his gun on patrol, or to fire it into the ground or something. He supports SWAPO. He thinks they should be governing Namibia. But he must fight them. What can he do?''

In the next four years, it became increasingly clear Jill's pessimism about white students had been somewhat exaggerated. The radicals retained control of the student government apparatus and continued to spread their views. The number of black students at Wits increased, to roughly 10 percent, and they and the white radicals cooperated to an unprecedented degree in staging joint, effective protests on campus.

At the same time, the African future campaign attracted a steady growing number of adherents who, moreover, maintained their commitment after graduation. An appreciably sized group of young radical lawyers, journalists, teachers, academics, trade union advisers, and others continues to grow. Even part of the growing trickle of draft resisters is choosing to remain in the region, working in the neighboring, black-ruled countries rather than head for the West; Jill's friend went to Swaziland after he could no longer fire his rifle into the ground.

Jill herself took her literature degree and started to work in a literacy program. Quite a few of her friends have been detained without trial, in some cases nearly for a year, while others have been convicted and imprisoned. But she has no plans to leave South Africa. "I want to go through the coming trauma with my people," she says simply.

The city of Johannesburg is not entirely divided along racial lines. One of the oldest neighborhoods, the legendary and picturesque Doornfontein, stubbornly survives as a pocket of some integration. Doorie, as its residents fondly call it, is the other side of Nugget Street, just east of the central city. In the late 1800s, it was the first redoubt of the wealthy in the burgeoning mining town, and a few of the big mansions are still standing.

Then, the newer suburbs sprang up to the north. By the end of World War I, Doorie was the home to white workers, many of them just-arrived Jewish immigrants. It is said that one fiercely secular Jewish worker organization publicly roasted and ate a pig during the most solemn religious holidays. The whites were soon joined by blacks, who moved into incredibly congested slum dwellings known as yards.

During the 1950s, the last black people were forced out to Soweto, and many of the buildings were torn down and replaced by small factories, warehouses, or vacant rubble-strewn lots. In 1980, the area was further disfigured by the renovations to Ellis Park, a white elephant of a rugby stadium.

Starting in the 1960s, Doorie experienced a modest revival. By law, colored and Indian people are required to live in separate townships out near Soweto, places like Coronationville, El Dorado Park, and Lenasia. But there were enormous housing shortages in those areas. Families were forced to settle illegally in Doorie, which had been zoned for whites only under the Group Areas Act. A semiofficial history of Johannesburg fancifully and insultingly described this in-migration of desperate people in search of housing as an influx of "hoboes, prostitutes and dagga-men."

Today, in what is left of the neighborhood, white and colored children play together along the shady streets. Their parents live amiably side by side in small, tidy stucco houses, painted in pastel colors, or in two- and three-story apartment buildings. There are even a few mixed marriages, in open contravention of the Immorality Act, which outlaws any sexual contact between the races.

Not surprisingly, Doorie and similar neighborhoods, backwaters of relative racial tolerance where the apartheid laws are flouted, have attracted the government's attention. Weasel agents of the misnamed Department of Community Development sneak around Doorie, looking for telltale Indian saris on washing lines and other evidence, and then serve eviction notices on colored and Indian families. The tenants who face eviction have nowhere to go due to the lengthy waiting list for housing out in the townships. A coalition of Doorie residents and sympathizers from elsewhere formed an organization, called Act Stop, to fight the evictions.

Monica Kelly and Colleen Wheeler were sisters. They lived next door to each other in small, fourth-floor apartments on Beit Street, Doorie's main thoroughfare. From their balconies, an Indian clothing store, Goldenberg's Kosher Market, and the Apollo Theatre were visible down the street.

One bright morning in the summer of 1979, they welcomed twenty other Act Stop members of all races into Monica's apartment. The group planned to try to resist the eviction nonviolently; Community Development had served Monica with a notice, due that morning. Colleen had demanded one as well. "When the man came—his name was Marais— I said to him, 'Just try to evict me—my husband is a white man.' " She pirouetted coquettishly, recreating the scene with Marais, as she shrieked with laughter.

Both women were classified colored; they were of course prohibited from marrying whites. They had olive skin and wavy black hair. They were forceful, boisterous, and interrupted each other constantly.

They bustled about, serving tea, starting conversations, or nervously stepping out on the balcony to scan the street for police vans. Their husbands remained in the background, swapping jokes about Van der Merwe, pronounced Fahn der *Mehr*-va, the obtuse Afrikaner Everyman who is the central figure in South African humor. "Marais was here again this week," Colleen informed the gathering. "I made him sit right down in that chair over there and take some tea. I asked him, in Afrikaans mind you, where we're supposed to go since there are no houses in the township. He kept saying, 'No comment. No comment.' I said to him, 'Shame, Mr. Marais, you've been watching television *too much*—that's where you get those 'no comments' from.' "

Monica broke in, "We've been arguing where we should pitch our tent when they put us out in the street. Sam [her husband] wants to go on Davis Street, because we can keep out of the rain under the balconies. But I say *no way* I'm going there—I'm staying just here on Beit

Street, right next to the bus stop so I won't have far to walk!'' Sam paused in his joke-telling and glanced fondly over at his noisy wife.

After about an hour, several women who were prominent in moderate white politics swept into the small flat. They had come from other nearby apartments where similar anxious vigils were taking place. ''We've done it *all wrong,*'' one of them said sharply, before greeting anyone. The convivial gathering fell silent at her tone. Colleen and Monica gave her a friendly but quizzical look. ''We didn't make it clear we *wouldn't* accept houses in the township.'' The government, she explained, disturbed by the prospect of bad publicity, had apparently offered to disregard its waiting list and offer the defiers housing immediately in one of the outlying colored ghettos. The scowling white woman shook her head in exasperation. ''We should have emphasized that our demand is to remain right here.'' She rushed outside again.

By eleven, it had become clear that Community Development and the police would not strike that day. Colleen explained gleefully, ''They were just *afraid* to come here. We beat them . . . at least for today.'' The sisters then guided their guests out. They tidied up a bit and then sat back to relax, indicating their exhaustion with sighs. They had not slept at all the night before.

Monica, the older sister, began abruptly, ''I don't agree with the government on the evictions, but there *are* some things that I *do* agree with. Like keeping down the Africans. I always say, give the coon a finger and he'll take the *whole* arm. They can be nice as possible, but when they get angry the savage comes out in them. Just last week five of them attacked Sam's friend, right on the street in Fordsburg, beat him up and stole his car. We can never bring them up to our level, and it's good that the government keeps them in their place.''

Colleen, who had been following her sister with increasing disbelief, responded in the form of a shout. ''Nonsense, just rubbish. They haven't had the education, the chance, to better themselves. This government doesn't even have a law that they must go to school—that's why you see so many of the little ones running around selling papers on the street. I've read *Ebony* magazine; the Negroes in America are doctors, businessmen, everything. If the African children got a good education they would do the same!''

''I don't think so,'' Monica answered a bit awkwardly, subdued by her sister's outburst. ''I don't know. I never used to think this way. I used to go to parties out in Soweto all the time. I guess I've changed.''

''These bastards who run the government,'' Colleen continued, still at a high pitch, ''they haven't changed. I never realized how bad things were here until I took that holiday in Europe . . . back in '74 before I got married. Well I met a German guy there, in Austria. . . . How can the law say who you can fall in love with?''

"In any case, I flew back to Durban, where I was staying, a day early. No one came to meet me at the airport. I went out to stop a taxi . . . and then I *remembered*. I told myself, 'Here there are whites-only taxis.' I mean, in Europe I had gotten used to stopping any taxi in the street. I was so damn angry . . . I just jumped into a white taxi and *made* him take me home!''

She was completely on fire by now. "They are so blind here, so stupid. South Africa is like that Van der Merwe joke my husband told me the other day. Van is in Europe, on holiday, and he sees these six guys putting a big telephone pole into the ground. 'Ach, man,' he says [she imitated a strong Afrikaner accent] 'what a bloody waste of manpower. Look at all those blokes. Give me twenty kaffirs and I could easily do that job myself.' '' The sisters laughed, partly reconciled. "He is so stupid he doesn't think the Africans are *people*.''

The defiers went through another two weeks of jumping at every knock at the door. Then, Marais returned with a compromise. He offered to house both families out in the township of Coronationville. They felt badly as they discussed the proposal at full-scale family meetings. They had already paid appreciable fines for living illegally in the "white area,'' and they faced the certainty of many more days in court. Colleen's husband was out of work. In the end, the pressure won, and, somewhat ashamed, they consented to move.

A couple of years later, I walked through Doornfontein again. I ambled along Beit Street, past the building where Monica and Colleen had lived. It was still standing, completely vacant. As the white politicians continued their talk of reform, Johannesburg was more segregated than ever.

The more politically ambitious of Steve Cohen's university classmates were always afraid he might decide to run for student government. He was so popular that it was accepted he would easily win any election. After Steve finished school, he continued to extend his circle of friendships. There are many Afrikaners who affectionately call him *die Afrikaner-Jood,* (the Afrikaner-Jew) due to his fluency in the language, rare among English-speakers, and his lack of prejudice.

He is a history teacher, now nearing forty, at a school in the northern Johannesburg suburbs. On some evenings he tutors in Alexandra, a black township to the northeast. Visiting him at his school was an exhausting experience. He would move through the halls at a slow pace, exchanging greetings and sharing jokes with everyone, students, colleagues, and custodians.

In his office, he was still cheerful, but circumspect. With knowing winks, he would pull out pen and paper, and indicate that sensitive information should not be spoken aloud. He had been under police surveillance in the past, and it may not have ended. We used to visit random restaurants and bars around town for our more serious talks.

Steve's parents came to South Africa in the 1920s. "My father," he told me as we took our seats at a little Greek place one evening, "was from Latvia. My mother was from Poland. In both cases, they were escaping from police states. I wonder if they ever thought, back then, that their own children would live under another police state." He smiled maliciously and peered over his spectacles.

Steve's father settled in a small town in the northern Free State. "There were ten other Jewish families. Two of them had come from his village in Latvia, as sort of a bridgehead. The rest of the town was all black or Afrikaner. My mother, who had worked in Joburg as a bookkeeper, moved to the Free State after they got married.

"I'm told I was sent to school early, at four, to prevent me from playing too much with the black kids in our part of town. Also, they say that at the same age I saw a cop loading a drunken black man into a truck, really knocking him around. I'm supposed to have remarked, 'They wouldn't treat a white like that.' I don't remember at all, but I think my family repeats these stories to show I was rebellious from an early age."

Steve laughed. "My father ran a trading store. He struggled at first, but then he built it into a sizeable enterprise, and he made quite a bit of money. I never saw him, because he was always working. In fact, we were taught to continue with our educations so we wouldn't have to work that hard.

"I think, back then, my father may have been a Communist, part of his baggage from Europe. At least he was Left, although I don't know what flavor. After he made it in business, he completely forswore politics. I can understand why he did it. The area was dominated completely by the Nat Party. He came here with fuck-all, and he felt he had to make it. What I don't understand, or accept, is people of the second-generation—my generation, who go along with this system."

At Steve's school, there was one classroom for the English-speaking children. As a youth, Steve had played with black children, a common experience for whites in small towns and on farms. "But as we got older the social distance started to appear. I remember one black kid, Clement, he used to help me with my homework. He was particularly good in maths. Now, I'm a teacher, and he's a delivery man back there, riding around on a bicycle. When I go home to visit, we both feel bloody un-comfortable.''

Steve shrugged and grimaced. His mood clouded over further. ''Just down the street from us the principal of the black primary school was staying. I used to play in his back garden, with a pellet gun he let me use. Years later, I was away at boarding school in Joburg. . . . I must have been fifteen or sixteen. I went back there on holiday . . . and I met him in the town's main street.''

His cheerful mood was now entirely gone. He unexpectedly choked. His eyes misted up. ''I said to him, 'If we weren't here, if we were in the city . . . I would greet you by the hand.' I'm so . . . ashamed. I was too afraid of the other white people there to shake hands in public with a black man . . . who had been my friend.''

Steve paused for a few seconds. Then he changed the subject. ''I was at boarding school, here in Joburg, for seven years. In our town, all the English-speaking children were sent away. Our parents didn't feel the local school was good enough. I was apolitical then. I do remember in '60, after the Sharpeville Massacre, the fear. We weren't allowed to leave the school grounds, even though the shooting had happened many miles away. The uncle of one of my schoolmates was banned, and we talked about that in hushed tones. But the school was so isolated from South African life, it never really added a political dimension to anything.''

He entered the army in 1964. The requirement was only nine months, as there was no fighting yet. ''One of the instructors, an Afrikaner guy, told me, 'Look Cohen, you're a Prog, and I'm a Nat. But when the war starts we'll be sitting behind the same rock, shooting kaffirs.' ''

Steve then entered Wits, intending to study medicine. Within three months, he transferred to history. ''I started moving leftward. The fights with my parents got more intense. I was also going out with a woman who wasn't Jewish.''

One summer, he took part in a systematic survey of one of the col-ored townships for a sociology project. ''It brought me face to face with a reality I had tried unconsciously to ignore. I got farther away from my parents and stopped going there for holidays. Finally, I broke with them. I took my bar mitzvah money, got a part-time job tutoring, and moved in with some other rads.''

Steve Cohen completed his degree, did a year of postgraduate work, and then started teaching. He befriended one of the banned people in Joburg, an older man. ''We used to jog together. Only the two of us, because a third person would have constituted a 'social gathering,' and violated his ban. We discussed politics while we ran, because it would have been harder for them to bug us out in the open like that.''

Not surprisingly, Steve very much likes his work. ''Though it may sound strange,'' he said, ''I also like South Africa. Not for what it is now, but for what it will become. South Africa has unbelievable potential. It is a wealthy country, with a strong economic foundation. It is materially great. What we must now do is see to a proper disposal of the benefits of that wealth to the whole population, to make our country spiritually great. I see us not as a black state, although blacks should certainly constitute the majority in the government as they do in the population. But I see us rather as a nonracial, democratic state, an incredible mixture of people and cultures, an important part of the Third World. We need to detune the sophistication of the economy, and devolve power to all of our people.''

Steve continued, with complete assurance, ''There is definitely war on the way. I sometimes try to picture what the big buildings in town will look like with bazooka holes in the walls. There are two kinds of whites who will remain through it, the reactionaries—those who will save the last bullet for themselves—and us. The diehards and the radicals.''

He laughed. ''The others, especially the wealthy, they already have the bags packed, the numbered accounts in Switzerland. They're ready to roll. As for the blacks, the agents of the change are not entirely clear. We aren't sure yet who will be the parties to the conflagration. Hilary [his wife] and I have talked it over. If the situation becomes very complicated, we may have to leave in order to come back.'' He diagrammed round-trip motions in the air. ''We definitely want to live in the Socialist South Africa.''

Steve then spoke, half to himself. ''But if there is a role for me in the struggle, I will fill it. Ex-sergeant Cohen is skilled in the use of ten weapons. I'm glad of those skills.''

His tone relaxed. ''Nothing is going to happen overnight. The regime has enormous room for compromise. They can give a helluva lot—international hotels is just a first step—and it still won't change anything. And this regime is bloody clever. In Namibia, they are giving the people free FM radios, plastering the country with them. Why? Because SWAPO broadcasts on shortwave. The regime thinks that if people have FM they will be less inclined to listen to SWAPO.''

His family never accepted his ideas, even though they were at least partly reconciled on the personal level. ''My father died in the early 1970s, worrying about me to the last. My mother, who still stays in the Free State, doesn't understand me at all. I was telling her on the phone the other day about tutoring in Alexandra, and she burst out, 'Why do you waste your time teaching those pigmented heathens?' ''

He shook his head. ''That hurt me. It really did. And it's so completely irrational. My father's store, most of his customers were black. My family made their living off black people for years. . . .''

There are, in Johannesburg, a couple of curious cases of genuine multiracialism. Both are giant scale public chess games, which have twenty-foot boards and plastic pieces one to three feet high. One is in Joubert Park, a seedy area just northeast of the heart of the city. The other is inside the Carlton Centre, a lush fifty-story office and shopping complex. At each place, blacks and whites regularly play each other, trundling the enormous pieces around the board, while a mixed crowd of onlookers eagerly discusses the progress of the game. Nowhere else in the city can you see sights like a middle-aged white man nodding thoughtfully as a young black man in jeans expounds on the pitfalls of a certain defensive strategy.

One late afternoon at the Joubert Park game, I got to talking to James, a well-dressed black man in his forties who was on cordial terms with the other regular players. He comes to play four or five times a week after finishing work in a clothing shop. He is a migrant worker with little else to do in the evenings; his family lives in far-off Natal. He said he was too shy at first to ask the rules of chess; he simply learned by observing play for several consecutive days. He brought his wife along on one of her occasional visits to town; she approved of his recreation, though she found it "very complicated." He would get his own, more conventionally sized chess set, but no one in his hostel knows how to play. A few games later, James checkmated a slightly intoxicated but good-natured Afrikaner, whose merry wife spurred James on by repeatedly calling her husband "useless." The only white people James is on any kind of equal basis with are his acquaintances from chess.

Far more representative of Joburg, however, is the twenty-five-foot statue erected by the Chamber of Mines on Rissik Street, just below the Civic Centre. The statue is of three figures, all gold miners. Two crouching black men, muscles bulging, hold a drill, directing it slightly upward. To their side stands the white foreman, holding a flashlight and pointing to the imaginary rock face. The baas is in firm command. The Chamber has provided a concise depiction of the central feature of Johannesburg's history and, perhaps unwittingly, also indicated the current state of its human relations.

4

Gandhi's Heirs

IN THE FALL OF 1893, a young lawyer named Mohandas K. Gandhi disembarked in the port city of Durban. He was wearing a black turban, a starched white shirt, a black tie, a black frock coat, striped trousers, and glistening black patent leather shoes. He was twenty-three, and he had studied law for three years in England. Two leading Indian merchants in South Africa had retained him to mediate a major financial dispute. He intended to remain in the country for one year. He observed the Hindu prohibition against eating meat, but otherwise he was not a social or political activist of any kind.

A week after Gandhi arrived, he boarded a night train to Pretoria, 350 miles away, where one of the quarrelling merchants lived. The dapper young lawyer naturally travelled first class. A white passenger demanded that he move back to the non-white car. Gandhi refused, and produced his first-class ticket. His appeal was ignored. A policeman ejected him from the train at Pietermaritzburg, a smaller city up toward the Drakensberg Mountains. He spent the entire night shivering in the station, too embarrassed to ask for his baggage, which contained warmer clothing. In his autobiography, he described the long cold night as a turning point in his life. He wrote, "The hardship to which I was subjected was superficial—only a symptom of the deep disease of color prejudice. I should try, if possible, to root out the disease and suffer hardships in the process."

After further indignities en route, Gandhi arrived in Pretoria, where he promptly called the city's Indians to a series of meetings to discuss ways to fight racial discrimination. Thus began his extraordinary career. He remained in South Africa for twenty years, during which he led huge cross-country protest marches, founded a newspaper, and established an experimental farm. He developed, step by step, his social and political philosophy. He gradually shed the garments in which he had arrived, and became the Gandhi recognized by history, clad in a simple white cloth *dhoti* and sandals. By the time he returned to India in 1914, he had established in South Africa an already strong tradition of nonviolent protest, a movement that would win an increasing number of adherents both within and outside the Indian community in the half-century to come.

Today, the majority of the eight hundred thousand Indian South Africans still live in Durban or nearby, in the smaller towns scattered through the steamy sugarcane country along the coast of the Indian Ocean. The Grey Street shopping area near central Durban, which is clustered about a prominent mosque, is a congested eastern bazaar, bustling with hundreds of shops, restaurants, and importuning sidewalk vendors who hawk all manner of trinkets along the crowded, narrow passageways.

Grey Street, to which Indian businessmen are confined by the Group Areas Act, is in fact the only part of the city with any charm whatsoever. Durban is otherwise a hideous monument to garish poor taste, a gritty industrial town and middle-class seaside resort that combines the worst features of both. The potentially splendid beach front, already marred by an injudiciously placed railroad line, has been further disfigured by a string of luxury hotels. Each has a black doorkeeper in a demeaning costume: men in turbans, top hats, even a Zulu warrior in battle dress are on hand to open the doors for the white holidaymakers from Joburg as they step out of their Mercedes-Benzes and Chevrolets. The beaches are still segregated. The one closest to town is reserved for whites, while the more remote have huge ugly yellow signs: "Coloureds," "Asiatics," and, most distant, "African Bathing Beach." In the little park facing City Hall are several statues honoring white colonial heroes and veterans of the world wars. Nowhere in Durban is there a monument to Mohandas Gandhi.

Inland, a ridge, called the Berea, sweeps upward from the ocean, affording those who live on its slopes a spectacular view. Naturally the residents in the large homes and modern apartment blocks are whites, predominantly English-speaking. The province of Natal has been termed the last outpost of the British Empire, a description that is becoming even more appropriate with the arrival of embittered whites after Rhodesia became Zimbabwe in 1980. Many do not even make the pretense at moderation that is characteristic of English-speakers elsewhere in South Africa. You find it impossible to regard vicious racism as an exclusively Afrikaner characteristic after you spend a couple of hours in one of the bars at the Royal Hotel, listening to a monotonous litany of English-accented abuse against kaffirs, coolies, Jimmy Carter, British trade unions, and the modern world generally. I once watched one of these fellows spend an entire weekday afternoon perched atop his bar stool, disparaging blacks for laziness, while his sidekick chimed in regularly, like a metronome, with "Bloody kaffirs; I hate them." Durban is already well known as a recruiting center for mercenaries who take part in the attacks on independent African states. Other white reactionaries have tried to murder local people active in the movement against apartheid; in 1978, one of them shot to death a highly respected white academic, Dr. Rick Turner.

The third major ethnic group in Durban are the Zulu-speaking black people who originally lived in the area. During the nineteenth century, they resisted efforts by both Afrikaners and English-speaking whites to subjugate them, retaining a semblance of independence. The sugarcane planters who had found the humid Natal coast ideal for their crops therefore had to lure indentured workers from India, beginning in 1860. The whites finally defeated the Zulu in 1879, and drove them into the labor force as well.

There has been tension between blacks and Indians over the years. There are undeniable differences in culture and language between the two groups. Indians only earn one-quarter the income of whites, and an estimated 65 percent of Indian households in the Durban area live below the poverty line. Nonetheless, they are still better off than blacks. They, like the colored people, are also somewhat less oppressed in legal terms; they are not, for instance, required to carry a pass. Another important source of friction is the sensitive position many Indian small shopkeepers are in with respect to their poorer black customers.

In 1949, rioting erupted after an Indian assaulted a black youth. Blacks retaliated by attacking Indians; the police and the army eventually opened fire on blacks. In all, 147 people died, and more than 1,000 were injured. The apartheid regime has been pleased over the years to use the 1949 riots as one of the major pieces of evidence it uses to justify its system of rule.

The primary assumption of apartheid is that there is no single South African nation. There are, rather, many "nations," which, due to accidents of history, occupy much the same geographical territory. What confused outsiders mistakenly regard as "South Africa" is actually "a human mosaic," "a world in microcosm." The official 1982 *Yearbook* explains, "The population of South Africa does not comprise a conglomerate of individuals, some of whom merely happen to be White and others Black. History—British imperialism—brought together, within the confines of the same geo-political entity, various peoples, each with its own culture, language, traditions, political and social systems and area of hegemony."

The theorists of apartheid hasten to add gravely that they do not imply one "nation" is superior to another. National Party leaders have not made raw racial appeals since the 1950s. It is even against the law to publish anything that is "harmful to the relations between sections of the inhabitants of the Republic." Instead, government publications are stuffed with tributes to the "multinational" diversity in South Africa. There is exaggerated detail to the differences in culture, with especial loving attention to practices that will seem exotic to Westerners. All is presented in solemn tones of unimpeachable respect, of touching solicitude for the venerated "traditions" of the various "nations."

Unfortunately, the apologists for apartheid will concede, these different "nations" do not always get along. They point out with a forced sadness that the problem is worldwide. Conflict in the Indian subcontinent at independence forced the partition into Pakistan and India; ethnic and religious turmoil continue in Northern Ireland, in Africa, and elsewhere.

In South Africa, the advocates of apartheid insist there is a similar potential for conflict between certain black groups. They distort the historical record with audacity by claiming, as in another government publication, "The black nations of South Africa are as different from each other as Greeks from Turks, Dutch from Germans, or Jews from Arabs." And of course even greater differences exist between blacks on one hand and whites, Indians, and coloreds on the other.

The only possible solution is apartheid. A system of one man, one vote, in a unitary state is unacceptable. The *Yearbook* insists such an arrangement "would inevitably mean domination by the numerically strong Black peoples not only of the Whites, but also of the Coloreds and Indians, as well as the numerically lesser Black peoples." "Citizens" of each black "nation" must exercise their political rights in their own particular Bantustan.

The dispensation for Indian and colored people has been less clear. The regime created certain interim separate political institutions for both groups, while deferring a long-term decision. Then, as the internal resistance and the external threat of economic sanctions grew from the mid-1970s onward, the government realized it had to act with more speed.

Its legislative draftsmen started to elaborate various complicated formulas that would allow coloreds and Indians token representation in the central government without fundamentally threatening white domination. The objectives of these "reforms" were clear—to win over at least some colored and Indian people as allies in the coming war, and to respond to the critics overseas.

The apartheid theory of nations is clearly dishonest. It has obviously absurd inconsistencies; Afrikaners and English-speakers, who fought bitterly only eighty years ago, are somehow regarded as a single white "nation." But Tswana-, Xhosa-, and Zulu-speaking South Africans, three black groups who have been at peace with each other for twice as long, are supposed to be on the brink of conflict. Furthermore, none of the theory's advocates, aside from a few powerless eccentrics, envisions a genuine separation of these "nations," one that would deprive the whites of the services of the poorly paid black, colored, and Indian workers on whom they have built their high standard of living. Finally, the whole fraud is based solely on force. If the people of these fictitious "nations" felt genuinely distinct, there would be no need for all the harsh laws, enforced by a computerized police state, that keep them apart.

Still, there is no doubt the apartheid laws, as intended, have helped to reinforce existing cultural distinctions, in ways that have sustained some degree of tension. This unease is probably greater in Durban than elsewhere in the country. There have been no recurrences of the 1949 riots, but there is still a certain edginess among certain Indian and black people. Some Indians, recalling 1949 vividly, are convinced they will be crushed in any black revolutionary upheaval, and they can speak with racist distaste of those they fear. Some blacks, who may have had unpleasant encounters with Indian shopkeepers, can also resort to crude racism. The leader of the Bantustan for Zulus, the well-known Chief Gatsha Buthelezi, has contributed to the unease with some speeches that veer ambiguously close to indulging in the prejudice against Indians.

It has been the anti-apartheid movement that has campaigned bravely over the years to unite South Africans. Mahatma Gandhi himself worked mainly within the Indian community, which was itself, especially at first, greatly divided by religion, caste, and language. But the organization he left behind, the Natal Indian Congress, was by the middle 1940s already building alliances with blacks to resist the increasingly harsh apartheid system. As white politicians snickered sanctimoniously at the 1949 carnage, black and Indian leaders met even before the riots ended, moving courageously together through the embattled city in a joint plea for peace. The unity forged during this disaster deepened in the 1950s, when the

NIC and the African National Congress, then still a legal organization, joined with other groups in the Congress Alliance. Among those in the forefront of the wave of protest in that decade was the Mahatma's third son, Manilal, who had remained in South Africa.

Mrs. Fatima Meer, a lecturer in sociology who is now in her early fifties, has been at the center of the Durban anti-apartheid movement since she was a teenager. She has attracted the attention and hatred of the right-wing vigilantes who inhabit the city. There is a bullet scar in the front door of her home, an ugly deep splintering in the wood. The assailants were never caught. Mrs. Meer's family remains defenseless. Her husband, Ismail, a lawyer who has long been active in protests inspired by Gandhi's philosophy, refuses on principle to have a gun in the house.

When I met Mrs. Meer in 1979, she was a banned person. As such, she could not be quoted anywhere, not even outside South Africa. I have therefore not interviewed her. I have spoken instead with someone who is very close to her, and familiar with nearly all aspects of her thinking.

At our first meeting, Mrs. Meer, a plump, pretty woman who wears both saris and Western dress, invited me to join her in eating a trifle, a dessert from a party she had been unable to attend the previous evening due to her restriction. Her close friend explained, "If she went, she would have tempted the police to raid and break up the party. But even if they didn't burst in, her presence would have been dramatic enough to have detracted attention from the real reason for the party. She wanted her friends to celebrate their wedding anniversary without distractions."

Mrs. Meer gave her first political speech at the age of sixteen, at the instigation of her father, a crusading journalist. Her friend explained, "In 1946, the Natal Indian Congress started a big passive resistance campaign against the Land Act. The resisters pitched tents illegally on a piece of land on Gale Street, a place where Indians were not allowed to reside. Her father was not at all a conventional man; although he was a Muslim, for instance, he never wore the fez. He also had unconventional ideas about women. He didn't think they should remain silent and out of sight. He wrote out the speech for her. She learned it by heart and spouted it out. One of the lines was, 'The government is giving us nothing but wormwood.'

"So she became a very sought-after speaker. Every Sunday the resisters held a mass meeting, and she was standing up there not mincing words. It was all reported in the daily press. [By now she was giving her own speeches.] The principal at the Indian Girls High School hauled her into his office and ordered her to stop. She refused, and her father backed her stand. She was expelled. She had to study on her own to pass her final exams.''

Mrs. Meer continued on to take a degree in social work at Natal University's special ''non-European'' classes, graduating in 1951. She and Ismail, whom she married the following year, were energetic in the effort to work with black people. The black and Indian women concentrated on the mixed, poor neighborhood of Cato Manor, which had been the site of some of the bloodiest internecine fighting. They set up a nursery school, a program to provide milk to poor children, and other welfare measures.

She was banned for the first time back then. She thinks she may have been the first woman to receive a banning order, although she is indifferent to the distinction. She does think she was banned because she was working with black women; if she had just worked in the Indian community, the regime would have left her alone.

As Mrs. Meer reflects on her past, she sometimes bursts out with irritation against certain well-known white moderates and liberals, some of the sort of people who are regarded overseas as stubbornly heroic. Her friend explained, ''She feels they don't suffer at all—physically, financially, or spiritually. If the apartheid system changed, they would lose their positions as prominent moral spokesmen.'' By contrast, Mrs. Meer herself was banned; her husband was ''listed,'' a related form of restriction; her son was banned and in exile; her son-in-law was banned. Her family had to apply for special dispensation so its members could talk to each other.

In 1956, the regime arrested Ismail Meer and charged him, along with 155 other people, in the infamous five-year Treason Trial. The charges against him were eventually dropped, but his almost continual court appearances up in Johannesburg prevented him from working. Mrs. Meer, with her three small children in tow, bustled about making the arrangements to keep his legal practice going. She also returned to school, completed her masters degree in sociology, and started teaching.

Next, Mrs. Meer tried to enroll in a Ph.D. program. A ranking official in her department told her she ''couldn't write English.'' She was discouraged. She also put together a book about Indian South Africans; one publisher rejected it because the people she quoted used incorrect English, while another wanted to censor it. She is still hurt and somewhat defensive about these setbacks.

In the late 1960s, she became sympathetic to the philosophy of black consciousness, of which the late Steve Biko was the best-known advocate. Black consciousness exhorted its followers to ignore wounding racial episodes, to instead feel pride in themselves and in their abilities. It also expanded the definition of "black" to include colored and Indian people; Mrs. Meer calls herself "black." Black consciousness had, for a time, an especially strong appeal to the black intellectual and professional group.

Mrs. Meer stifled her self-doubts and decided to publish her book herself. She and younger student friends brought out *Portrait of Indian South Africans* to critical acclaim. She also published her masters thesis, on suicide. She became a sought-after lecturer, invited to overseas conferences. It was her growing prominence, and her calls for black unity after the 1976 uprising, that prompted the regime to ban her a second time.

She now would describe herself as a "late starter." Her friend explained that she would compare herself, and black people generally, to "our own 'Tap Tap' Makathini," the Natal boxer who lost a challenge bout for the world middleweight title in 1979, at the age of thirty-seven. She would laugh at the strange relevance of the seemingly far-fetched comparison. Many South Africans felt that the apartheid system had held back Elijah Makathini—his fans conferred the nickname in recognition that he floored opponents with merely a tap—until he was too old to mount his strongest challenge.

As South Africa moves into deeper crisis, Mrs. Meer pinpoints two related but still distinct problems: racism, and class inequality. Her confidante explained, "She would say that we have to overcome the race problem first. We must establish a nonracial society. But that, by itself, will not solve the tremendous problem of inequality. We will have to reorganize our whole economic system. Any such decisions will have to be made democratically, by the whole people. Black people here have been deprived of knowledge about other political systems, like socialism. They will have to learn before they will be in a position to decide."

Mrs. Meer, as an heiress of the tradition of nonviolent protest bequeathed by Mohandas Gandhi, would prefer to see peaceful change in South Africa. She has participated, since the age of sixteen, in passive resistance campaigns. One of her friends who was also banned, Mrs. Ela Ramgobin, is Gandhi's granddaughter. But Mrs. Meer is not optimistic. Her alter ego explained, "Peaceful change is not a realistic hope anymore. Black people are being attacked and violated all the time. It is an emotional violation of the spirit as well as physical. If Gandhi still lived in South Africa, he might well have retained his nonviolent beliefs. But he would not be effective today. He would have lost his following."

Before my first visit to Durban, I had heard that a banned Indian man ran a superb bookstore in the center of town, off West Street. I stopped into the shop, and found the owner, who was in his mid-thirties, fidgeting behind his desk. The shop, which featured books about African history and culture, had an air of seriousness totally out of place in the surrounding tinselly shopping mall. I edged over, determined to be discreet in case he was reluctant to talk. I asked an oblique and relatively innocent question about the government list of banned books. He answered courteously and then stared straight at me. "By the way," he said, "this criminal regime has also banned me."

After the owner, who was named Siva Patel, and I became friends, he showed me a scrapbook he had haphazardly kept through the early seventies. It contained newspaper accounts of his many strongly worded speeches, and included his polemical battles with certain conservative Indian politicians in the letters columns of the local papers. The clippings described his arrest during the July 1976 crackdown, and his release and immediate banning that December 31. Then, there was nothing.

Siva's ban weighed heavily on him. He was like a person trapped in a small, invisible cage, constantly pacing back and forth with exasperation. He, like nearly all banned people, did manage to elude the intermittent police surveillance; more than once he even left the magisterial area for vacations. But the security police did eventually catch him, in the subversive act of hosting a dinner party in his own apartment. He was convicted of breaking his ban and sentenced to six months in prison, suspended on condition that he not be caught again.

His interest in politics had started innocently, due to his youthful passion for the sport of cricket. He was a bowler, a position roughly equivalent to a pitcher in baseball. He was a young phenom. In one match, he took seven wickets for three runs, which in baseball would be something akin to pitching back-to-back no-hitters. "For us blacks, the facilities were atrocious," he remembered. "There was no grass to speak of on the pitch. We had old pads and no gloves. We never had a day's coaching. I sometimes went to see the whites play in their areas, on their beautiful green fields. They even had umpires. The gap was big and wide. I was denied the same opportunities because of my pigmentation." His banning order, which barred him from meeting more than one person at a time in a social situation, limited his participation in sports to singles at tennis.

At home, Siva's parents spoke Telegu, one of the Indian languages, but they never taught it to their children. Most younger Indian South Africans speak only English. The caste system, which had been imported from India, has also been dying. Siva smiled wickedly as he explained, "The only good aspect of the Group Areas Act is that it uprooted people from all over the city and dumped them all together into the Indian ghetto of Chatsworth. The caste system is not going to survive that upheaval.'' Many decades earlier, Mohandas Gandhi had said that the experience of working among Indian South Africans who differed in caste, religion, class, and language had been a catalyst that had started him along the road to his universal and egalitarian philosophy.

In addition to Siva Patel's athletic prowess, he also performed well in the classroom. He continued on to the single Indians-only university, where he specialized in African history. After graduation, he taught at a private school for "African" girls. "It was marvelous," he said, smiling at the memory. "I was the first Indian teacher there. We had always been isolated by law from Africans, and now I was living with them. There was a little prejudice at first from the older staff, but it withered after three or four months. By law, I had to teach what the regime included in the syllabus for Bantu Education. But I would do both—teach them the truth first and then tell them what they needed to pass the government exam." After Siva was banned, one of his former students wrote him an encouraging letter to say that he, along with novelist Alan Paton and Afrikaner dissident clergyman Beyers Naudé, had been the major influence in her life. "I was most moved," he said with a tired smile. Siva also helped run a multiracial summer camp. His codirector was the revered white philosophy lecturer Rick Turner who was assassinated in 1978.

Siva Patel was detained just after the Soweto uprising. "I had given a speech to the Indian university students, in which I said, 'Soweto has set the pattern, and now you must follow.' '' Photographer Peter Magubane was one of the several hundred other detainees he was imprisoned with near Johannesburg. Magubane and Siva became friends. "He is a man without any iota of racial prejudice," Siva remembered with admiration. The regime warned the detainees they would be held until the nationwide unrest simmered down. "In a way we were hostages," Siva said, chuckling, "and we observed the outside situation with a little ambivalence. We would complain jokingly, 'They are bloody into the streets again.' ''

Siva's banning order forced him to give up his job at the Institute of Race Relations, where he had been organizing and doing research. He settled by elimination on bookselling, as one of the few worthwhile jobs he could do without breaking his ban by teaching, writing, or merely being in regular social situations. Banned people often find it nearly impossible to earn a living. Siva built up a comprehensive and useful enterprise, but he chafed at the boredom of the work.

When I met him, he was debating inwardly whether to leave the country. He listed the arguments on both sides:

In favor of staying: "One. I can be more useful inside, even in a limited role; there are already many exiles. Two. You should stay for symbolic significance, to encourage others by your presence. Three. They may not renew the order."

In favor of leaving: "One. I have trouble making a living from the bookshop. Two. I feel stifled and frustrated—I can't do what I want, which is make speeches and be openly active in politics. Three. I'm not really contributing to the struggle; the bookshop is too peripheral. There is still a possible role for me overseas, or elsewhere in Africa. Four. There is the constant air of uncertainty. Is it really worth it to risk a jail sentence just for going to a party? Five. A selfish reason. I like to travel, and I want to visit other places."

By now, he was pacing quickly back and forth in his tiny bookshop. "There is a strong pull in both directions. I change my mind from week to week."

He was sadly more definite about another fact—that Gandhi's non-violence is helpless against the police state of South Africa today. Siva had been raised in the Gandhian tradition; he and other young activists had been instrumental in reviving Gandhi's old organization, the Natal Indian Congress, early in the 1970s. "In the past," he said, "there were hundreds, no thousands, of Gandhians here. I understood and respected them. They lived very much on hope. But there are very few of them left now. Those who maintain their views are, I think, simply unrealistic."

The legal impediments that deter people of the various "nations" from mixing cannot be exaggerated. One Sunday afternoon, as I innocently walked with a black woman to visit friends in a colored area, an unmarked Toyota with two white men in it screeched to a halt beside us.

"Where the hell are you going?" the younger one snarled. I was relieved at the authoritarian tone in his voice. It indicated the two were police rather than possibly violent vigilantes. I answered his question politely.

"Don't you know about the Immorality Act?" He shot an insulting glance toward my friend Anne, who was trying to restrain her anger.

I said I doubted walking down a thoroughfare on Sunday afternoon constituted conspiracy to commit immorality.

"Well, there's the Group Areas Act." He was very angry. Anne and I assured him that nothing prevented us from being in a colored area, though we knew we would have needed a permit to be in an African one.

The older cop, who had by now realized that I was a foreigner, did not want to risk "an international incident." "Look," he said in a conciliatory tone, "It's for your own protection. There's a lot of crime up here."

They drove off. Anne, still in a rage, pointed out they might battle crime more effectively if they stopped harassing people for acts that were illegal nowhere else in the world.

Those kind of hindrances are what made the mixed party I attended hosted by the Indian waiter Bill Chinsamy such an extraordinary accomplishment. Chinsamy had been at the Royal Hotel for twenty-five years, and both his father and grandfather had worked there before him. His party, held at his small, tidy home on the far side of the Berea, attracted the widest crosssection of people I ever saw in one place during more than four years in southern Africa. Indian Congress activists, Afrikaner women clerks, blond English-speaking surfers, black dishwashers, all danced late into the night, brought together by their friendship for the irrepressible and kindly Bill Chinsamy. The mood of harmonious exaltation, together with a certain amount of liquor, prompted some of the guests to let their imaginations roam. One black waiter, with a slightly drunken grin, pulled me aside to confide that he was "planning" to "hit an 84,000-rand jackpot" at the racetrack later that week and move to America with his winnings. He did admit to some ambivalence about putting his plan into effect; he said sadly that he would miss Chinsamy and his other coworkers at the Royal.

In the early hours of dawn, Chinsamy, who had been the consummate host, finally managed to sit down and rest. He was elegant and stylishly dressed. During his fifty-four-hour work week, his taste is obscured by the white turban and flowing robes the Royal Hotel owners think appear appealingly exotic on their staff.

Bill Chinsamy's fondest hopes are centered in his only child, a thirteen-year-old boy, who had had the time of his life at the party. "He's a good kid," Bill said, the shimmer in his eyes belying his understated tone. "He has his friends, but he doesn't go out all the time. He chooses his TV; he doesn't watch all the rubbish programs. He studies. Sometimes I see him still up at twelve when I get off working late."

A few guests wobbled over to say good-bye. Bill continued, "He loves animals. He has a puppy and a kitten. They sleep with him. I see his cat and beckon to it, but it will always go straight to him.

"He thinks he wants to be a vet. I still have to tell him that it's not quite possible for a non-white to study that in this country. Kids don't understand these things. You take them to the beach; they see other children swimming there; they want to know why can't they go? I'll have to try and send him overseas to study.'' Bill looked at me with some embarrassment. He was sorry to bring up an unpleasant topic.

No Western government dares to defend the present state of affairs in South Africa. But certain of them continue to insist that peaceful reform is underway; they deplore violence, and in effect they urge black South Africans to have patience. How long can a people wait? Bill Chinsamy's son, who will probably never get the chance to become a veterinarian, will become an adult around 1992—one hundred years after Mohandas Gandhi was thrown off the train from Durban.

I later described the scene at Bill Chinsamy's party to the well-known black newspaper editor Obed Kunene. His delighted smile widened at each step of my account. "This is one of the many faces of South Africa,'' he summarized after I had finished. ''Life is so confusing here. I might walk into a shop, to be treated by the white woman counterhand with astounding conviviality, an easy manner, no trace of bitterness. I walk out feeling elated, with cause for hope.

"But no sooner do I have this highly elevating experience than I run into something entirely different. A white man brushes against me on the pavement and mutters, 'Bloody kaffir.' Now what happens to my hope?

"That is the tragedy of South Africa, a country marked by such stark contrasts, conflict, and contradiction. The sad irony is that with the fantastic mix of people here it could be the most exciting country in the world.''

Obed Kunene worked his way up from poverty to become one of the most talented and prominent newspapermen in South Africa. He edits *Ilanga Lase Natal,* a Zulu-language paper with a biweekly circulation of one hundred thousand. He also contributes frequently to the English-language press. He is a small compact, graceful man who is deadly in earnest, precise, even fastidious as he tries to employ the correct, exact word or phrase. He is in his mid-forties, married with four children.

Obed Kunene grew up in the slum district of Cato Manor, in a tin shanty with an earthen floor. To supplement the meager income of his father, a laborer, his mother illegally sold highly combustible home-brewed liquor. Obed, her eldest son, helped out. "I bought the ingredients, assisted her to make it, and supervised the hiding of it from the police raiding parties. The penalty if they found even a dreg was a very high fine—five pounds or ten days in jail.

"We also went out to sell cigarettes, tobacco, fruits, and vegetables. I would get up early in the morning, and go down to the bus stations to be in time for the first group of workers. Or we went pilfering, taking fruits from the Indian orchards. Another Indian hired me as a barker; I used to stand outside his shop, touting for business.

"We knew there was a better world on the other side of the Berea. But then we thought whites were the blessed of God; they should be looked up to; they were superior to us.

"Many of my friends from that time went off the track. One has become an incredibly inept bankrobber. Others are more successful pickpockets. The strict Christianity of my mother kept me from such an end. She didn't let me ditch school, or hang out, or mix with the 'bad' boys."

Obed did well at primary school, and continued to a highly regarded boarding school in the rural area. His uncle and his Indian employer helped pay his fees. Among his classmates were Lewis Nkosi, now a respected academic who lives in exile, and Nat Nakasa, a brilliant young journalist who committed suicide in 1964.

After graduation, Obed went straight to work to put his younger brothers and sister through school. Then, as now, blacks had to pay fees, even for public school, though white education was free. He worked at gardening, as a laborer on construction sites, and as a janitor. "I was always an avid reader. Even on the job, I would collect scraps of paper obsessively and in the quieter moments slink away into a corner to read them. I got the idea to write from reading. I visited the library, and studied a book called *How to Write an Article*.

"Now, boxing was my hobby. (I had always been a failure at soccer.) I took notes on boxing, then did a practice piece following the advice in the book. It was all self-taught."

Kunene sold his first article in 1956, to *Ilanga*, the paper he now heads. Soon, he was working full-time as a journalist. His high school friends, Nkosi and Nakasa, broke into the field at about the same time. All three attracted notice—and eventual job offers—from bigger papers up in Joburg.

Obed's father had passed away in the late 1950s, leaving him the main breadwinner. "My mother is a simple woman. She said to me after my father's funeral, 'I will never know another man.' She couldn't countenance the idea of my leaving Durban. It has been a helluva burden on me.

"Nkosi, Nakasa, they went off to Joburg. I told my mother I was planning to take a job there as well. She burst into tears. She said that Joburg was a city of sin, and that I couldn't leave her alone. I couldn't talk back to my mother, so I would just fume inwardly and go away.

"I thought over the whole matter. She'd rarely known happiness. My brothers and sisters were in no position to help. It was up to me. So I remained old-fashioned, tied to the family. Here I stay today."

Despite the disorders of life in the townships, blacks have been able to keep the family a surprisingly strong institution. That is the reason, for instance, that the chronically high unemployment rate is not more painfully noticeable. Social services are rudimentary at best, but black people continue to look out for their relatives.

In theory Obed Kunene is another of the kind of successful, established, stable black family men the government thinks it can win over. In 1979, it even made an explicit gesture toward him, appointing him to a special committee to "study" constitutional change.

But the regime still has a long way to go before it persuades Obed Kunene. He refused the appointment, angrily: "I was not invited in the normal manner," he said. "My 'appointment' was simply announced, released to the press."

We were sitting in a restaurant in the Royal Hotel, which was one of the few places we could eat together. His anger clashed with the plush surroundings. He was the only black diner present. "We read how white politicians talk about the 'moderate' blacks," he went on. "I have never met a moderate black. We have what we might call moderate-radicals. Moderate on the outside, and radical on the inside."

He paused, and pretended to whistle to attract the attention of the white waitress. "I never was a herdboy, but I do have a shrill whistle," he said with a short laugh. "What a sensation it would be in here!"

Obed returned to his theme. "I still attend these dialogue sessions with white liberals. I'm asked, 'What are your negotiable demands?' How can we negotiate about part of our freedom? I just want to break out. I feel like a fly in butter, just swimming around."

Just because a section of the city is zoned for the "white population group" does not mean that only white people live there. The hypocrisy of the apartheid theory of separate "nations" is evident instantly in all the white neighborhoods. The area along Ridge Road, at the top of the Berea, typically always has black people about. The majority of them are women, dressed in light blue or pink smocks, the telltale sign of the housemaid. Particularly during lunch hour or in the twilight of early evening, they will be sitting on the grass or in front of a neighborhood café, or shop, exchanging the neighborhood gossip in Zulu. Or they may be taking white toddlers on a stroll to the park. At times they will be pressed into service walking fancy exotic poodles or Afghan hounds. It would seem that contact between the separate "nations" is permissible provided blacks continue to minister to white needs.

There are about 800,000 maids in South Africa. Some of the 4.5 million whites refuse, for one reason or another, to employ a maid. But they are not many. Every home and apartment block provides space for servant "quarters." Kitchens are consciously designed to be large, to allow both "madam" and the maid to maneuver about simultaneously. Special cheap cuts of meat are openly labelled either "dogs' meat," or "servants' meat." When you enter a white home, the maid is invisible at first, but she will soon appear, as a gliding background presence.

The relationship between the white family, particularly the madam, and the black maid is a central one in South African life. Often, the madam believes she has established a remarkable rapport with her maid, a true breakthrough across the barriers of color and class. Madam discusses cooking and clothes, and she may even confide her strategies for dealing with the husband or other intimate matters.

In return, madam believes that the maid also confides in her, and that she is therefore privy to remarkable insights into black life. Naturally, she is convinced her maid is happy at work, satisfied with the wages and working conditions, and more than pleased with the strong bond of friendship between the two women. The maid will be cited often to other whites as evidence that blacks generally are happy with their lot.

Mrs. Margaret Mpanza, who lives in the Ridge Road area, has a truly memorable voice: rich, carefully modulated, resonant. She also carries herself with an imposing sense of dignity. You could easily imagine her an actress, a queen of the stage. Instead, she has worked as a maid for thirty of her forty-six years. She is presently employed by an elderly couple who live in an apartment.

I met her just as she was about to leave town for her two-week annual vacation. "I was supposed to go on holiday about three months ago," she explained. "But then they had two weddings in a row, for two of their children. I had to do all the arranging for the weddings. I suppose they just forgot about my holiday. Finally, I reminded them. It's a paid holiday, but I won't get the money until I get back to work. My family will be short of money in the meantime."

Mrs. Mpanza said she nonetheless preferred her present job to most of the previous ones. "It's a small flat, so I don't have a lot of cleaning and polishing to do. And there are only the two of them, so I don't have any work with children."

She gets up at six-thirty every morning, and makes her own breakfast. "Then, I go up to the flat and prepare theirs. Afterward, I wash up, do the house cleaning, and wash the clothes. By then it's lunchtime, so I go out to the street, or maybe to the park, and talk to some of the other women who work around here. After lunch, the clothes have dried, so I do the ironing. Before you know it's time to make the dinner. After that, at about six-thirty, I'm off for the day. I go back to my room, and cook myself something on the primus [kerosene] stove. Sometimes, I can cook up in the flat, if I want to. They let me keep my own pots and pans up there.'' Her expression suggested it was an uncommonly generous practice.

Mrs. Mpanza rarely goes out at night. She is afraid of *skelms*, or criminals. ''Anyway, I'm tired. I'm too tired after a day of work to even scratch myself. I lie down and listen to the radio. I used to sew a few things for my grandchildren. But now my sewing machine is broken, and I haven't got the money to repair it.''

Her family—her disabled husband and two grandchildren are her present dependents—lives in a segment of the Kwa–Zulu Bantustan about twenty miles from town. She tries to return home at least twice a month. ''I don't have the time to go more often, and the bus fare is too high. But I'm always worrying about the children, if anything has happened to them—there's no way for them to contact me here in town. Sometimes I don't eat because I'm thinking of the children and worrying if they don't have enough to eat.''

Mrs. Mpanza started working when she was ten years old. She looked after an even smaller child. ''I got up, walked over to the little boy's home, woke him up, and made him his little breakfast. I took him off to the school. Then I walked over to my school. After, I fetched him, played with him, cooked him his dinner, put him to bed, then went back to my own place. I worked for three years like that. They were the only years of schooling I've had. That's where I first learned English, both at school and from the little boy.'' She laughed. ''I also taught him some words in Zulu.''

She worked straight through until she married, at the age of twenty-four. She then had two children of her own. Her husband suffered a disability when she was thirty-one, so she was forced to go back to work. The grandchildren belong to her daughter, who is unmarried and has been unable to find work.

She reflected matter-of-factly, without any effort to evoke pity: ''I've had some terrible jobs. Just terrible. At one place, they locked up everything, the cutlery, the liquor. They didn't trust me. I was so insulted that I left after eight months.

''At another place, they used to entertain a lot. They depended on me. I can cook curries. I can bake nice cakes. So those people—the Lewises—had me catering for sixty or seventy people. I had to cook, go around and serve everyone, and then clean up. I would be up until one or two in the morning, and then have to get up at six-thirty for the next day's work. They never gave me anything extra. So I left there.

''I suppose I could say I'm happy now, compared to before. But I still worry about money all the time. I earn thirty-eight rand a month, and all the prices are going up.'' Mrs. Mpanza continued with total resignation: ''I can say that my life has been terrible. Just terrible . . .

''Nothing will get better here. These white people are rock-hard—they will never change. Why is there the separation here? If I touch you, you don't turn brown, do you? It must be better in other countries.''

The next day, I drove Mrs. Mpanza out to her small mud-walled home in a rural area to the north of Durban. It is in a magnificent spot in the Natal hills, perched atop a steep cliff overlooking the confluence of two rivers a thousand feet below. ''In summer, it's much greener here,'' she apologized as we gazed out at the spectacle.

The Mpanzas live next door to a *sangoma,* or traditional healer. He proudly showed me his collection of skins, his herbs and other medicinal paraphernalia, his two wives, and his embossed certificate from the Natal provincial society of *sangomas.* There was a striking contrast between the homes of the two neighbors: his was tumbledown and uncared for, hers was clean and spruced up; his children were dressed in old, worn clothes, her granddaughters, who had run out to greet her, were neat in their school uniforms. Mrs. Mpanza translated the brief conversation between me and the *sangoma,* smiling with pleasure at being able to help us communicate. We parted, and she turned to walk into her house, one granddaughter at each side, to begin her vacation.

In 1979, there appeared in South Africa a remarkable book called *Maids and Madams,* a lengthy study of more than two hundred domestic workers by a white sociologist named Jacklyn Cock. Although the book inclined toward the academic, it nonetheless reached a surprisingly large audience among whites, many of whom evinced shock at its reports that maids feel dissatisfied and bitter.

The study showed the average wage was only twenty-three rand a month, and one maid was earning four rand. Some 77 percent of the women worked more than forty-eight hours a week, while a full quarter were on duty for seventy-two hours. More than 80 percent were required to work on national holidays.

The women also complained about their extreme isolation and loneliness. They said their employers were often rude and interfered with their work. They said they took pride in the quality of their work, but they were seldom thanked. Some mentioned they were required to cook better quality meat for the family dog than they received as part of their own ration.

Helen Morrison and her husband never expected to hire a maid. She explained, ''We didn't employ anyone before we had the children. Then, it was a real soul-search. Some of our friends don't have maids, but then the women don't work. There aren't any adequate crèches [day-care centers] around. We felt we had no choice. We pay high wages, which shock our friends, and we try to teach them certain skills, so they can go on to a better job. We also don't believe in a live-in maid, who's separated from her family. But there again you're caught. Elizabeth was living up north in a squatter settlement. She came to me and said the water was bad, that it was killing her baby. Her husband also had a case of TB. So we arranged, by mutual consensus, that she would bring her family here to live.''

Helen is a lecturer at Natal University who had already won acclaim in her field by her early thirties. She is lively and vivacious, the sort of woman who can dive fully clothed into a swimming pool at 3:00 A.M. and be up a few hours later, making breakfast for her two small sons and getting ready for work with complete equanimity.

Helen and her family were living in Durban North, a pleasant suburb next to the ocean. She felt she had to excuse her surroundings. ''When we were first married, we moved into a white working-class area. We were trying to uphold our principle of avoiding excess. But the white workers were so racist. The kids were coming home talking about 'the kaffirs.' We couldn't have our black friends over; the neighbors would complain and make comments. So we moved here.''

The Morrisons neglected to register their maid with the local Bantu Administration Board. The woman was therefore living in the ''white area'' illegally. Administration Boards (government euphemizers have since dropped ''Bantu'') are huge, powerful institutions that regulate black life. They even have their own police, who conduct regular raids looking for ''illegal'' workers. ''They came at 5 A.M.,'' Helen recalled. ''Their excuse was that they were trying to make certain that terrorists were not being harbored in the homes around here. They found Elizabeth without the proper stamp in her pass, and they served me with a summons.''

In the late seventies, the maximum fine for employing an illegal worker was 100 rand or 100 days in prison. (The regime has since increased it fivefold, and plans even further hikes.) Helen was fined 30 rand or 30 days. ''It's like a traffic court in there—hundreds of people milling around, and they rush you through. I had arrived with a prepared statement. I said I couldn't as a Christian pay the fine, because the money would be used to help finance the Administration Board system. I chose jail.

''Outside the courtroom, a policeman warned me I would see 'bad sociological things' in prison.'' She laughed. ''Then, after I had been locked up for two hours, an anonymous person paid the fine. I was released. I never found out who it was.''

Helen Morrison has considered emigration. "Leaving would give the children an opportunity to grow up in a more sane society. Am I depriving them? Will they just grow up to be frustrated radical/liberals like their parents? But then I think: staying here can be a good, though demanding, experience. They will have to work through the issues of racial equality in a way they wouldn't overseas. To do it here will be a greater triumph for my children.

"Also, I couldn't take my opportunities out of the country. I've benefited from the system here. It's not fair to leave. I must try to share what I know.

"I wouldn't say I'm extremely religious. I don't draw immense strength from my religion. I do try to use it as a guide, and as a way to get at other Christians." She stopped for a moment. "We have a very sound saying here in South Africa. We say a Christian here is either going to jail, or going to hell."

Just over the Berea, in a quiet neighborhood called Overport, is a modest old house that has been converted into a fortress. The windows are bricked up; there are high fences in both front and back and several layers of doors and metal gratings. The yard is patrolled by Dobermans.

The proprietor of the stronghold, a white man named Harold Strachan, is not some sort of embittered misanthrope. Quite the opposite; he is an extremely warm and outgoing man who makes a point of greeting all the clerks in his neighborhood shopping plaza by name. But he is also a man who was not afraid to go to jail for his political beliefs, and the right-wing vigilantes have tried twice since his release to kill him.

In one of the murder attempts, the attackers merely fired through his front windows. But the other time a single gunman rushed through the back door and pointed his automatic rifle at Harold and his ten-year-old son Joe, who were talking at the kitchen table. "He was bloody inexperienced," Harold said. "He aimed right at us. He didn't realize the kick would force the weapon off to one side." Harold made a slight dismissive gesture. "He missed us by several feet."

Afterward Harold strengthened his fortifications and armed himself with a revolver and at times a shotgun. He has not been attacked again, although his friend Rick Turner was murdered by a similar—or the same—assailant. None of the Durban vigilantes have been caught, and they could strike at any time. I asked him why he did not leave the country. "My motto is *Nil carborundum illigitimae,*" he said, laughing. "I won't be ground down by any bastard."

Harold is lean and wiry, with his slimness accentuated by a prominent, sharp nose. He is in his mid-fifties but looks younger. He presently earns his living as a restorer of paintings. Also, though, he is a painter himself, a teacher, mechanic, ex-fighter pilot (an accomplishment of which he is enormously proud), father of two, raconteur, linguist (he is an expert on the slang used by all the people in South Africa), marathon runner, humanist, existentialist, and something of a chemist.

This last facet of his persona earned him his first prison sentence, back in 1962. During the 1950s, he had been active in the Congress of Democrats, a small white organization that worked closely with the African National Congress and other groups. The Congress Alliance, a rainbow coalition of all races, was a brave and defiant answer to the apartheid system and its efforts to divide. After the ANC was banned in 1960, some of its members, together with sympathizers like Harold, carried out a campaign of sabotage. They set off carefully selected explosions, meticulously planned to avoid any loss of life, to try to shock the apartheid regime into negotiations. The legacy of Gandhi was still so powerful that they could not readily adopt full-scale violence.

Harold and two black ANC men, including his good friend Govan Mbeki, who is presently doing a life sentence on Robben Island, were arrested in Port Elizabeth and charged under the Explosives Act. Harold had concocted the devices from freely available materials; he had gotten the idea for one of his formulas from watching a Zulu witch doctor set off tiny explosions to spellbind his clients. Harold had been so worried deadly accidents might occur that he never told the liberation movement the formulas for the most potent ignitable substances.

The heart of the case against the three accused was another ANC man who had turned state's evidence. ''I could guess what testimony he was going to give,'' Harold remembered, ''so I wasn't even paying attention when he came into court. I was just sitting there in the dock, reading the newspaper. Then suddenly, I heard the judge shouting at the witness, 'Get out of my courtroom.' I realized he had changed his testimony completely. He now said he didn't know us from a bar of soap. He said he had lied during the preliminary investigation. Most of the state's case fell apart. The judge immediately had to free my two co-accused. They jumped up and went straight out of the courtroom. Special Branch came right into the court, picked up the witness bodily, and just carried him out of there. He got a year or something for perjury. . . .''

In Harold's own case, there was enough other evidence to convict him. He got three years. He was one of the two first white political prisoners, but others soon joined them in a special section at Pretoria Local. Harold was released and, as Hugh Lewin, a fellow political, wrote later, he "soon joined the amorphous haze of Outside, fondly but infrequently remembered."

Almost immediately though, the prisoners noticed certain improvements. They got hot water. They got new eating bowls. The changes affected other prisoners as well; they noticed that blacks in the other section had, for the first time, been issued with shoes. The prisoners soon pieced together an explanation for the mysterious reforms. Harold had collaborated in a series of three devastating articles in the *Rand Daily Mail* about prison conditions that had created a national scandal.

South Africa since 1959 has had a sinister statute called the Prisons Act, which makes it a criminal offense to publish anything inaccurate about the system. In practice, the Act, as its framers had intended, prevented anything from being written about prisons at all except articles approved by the authorities. Harold was the first to dare. His work created a revolution throughout the huge prison system. He became a hero even to hardened convicts—he calls them "crims"—who otherwise had no interest in politics. South Africa's prisons are still terrible places, but due to Harold they are a little less medieval.

The regime prosecuted Harold under the Prisons Act. He was convicted purely on technicalities. The articles said, for instance, that the wind "whistled" through the broken window panes in a certain prison; the authorities produced witnesses who testified it made no sound. Harold was sent right back to prison for another year and a half.

Late one evening, other friends of his and I were sitting around a fast diminishing bottle of brandy in his kitchen—his wife Maggie matter-of-factly cautions guests to avoid certain seats that could be in "the line of fire"—and I asked him if he knew he was going to be sent back to prison when he wrote the articles. "Yeah, I suppose so," he said. He winced slightly because he did not want to seem to be playing the hero. Then, seeing a way off the pedestal, he grinned and said, *"Nil carborundum illigitimae."*

On his release in 1967, he was banned and house arrested from 6:00 P.M. to 6:00 A.M. every day. He took up marathon running. The Durban magisterial area to which he was confined was long and narrow, affording him adequate distance in which to train.

But his banning order posed a problem when he tried to enter the Comrades, the double-marathon that is South Africa's major distance event. The race starts in Durban, but then heads up into the Drakensberg Mountains. He trained for the entire year, and then applied to the magistrate for a relaxation of his ban. "I said I would report to the police when I started, and again when I finished. If I dropped out of the race,

I would go to whatever cop shop was closest and report there. But he still turned me down." The memory of the disappointment flashed quickly across Harold's face.

Now, with his banning order finally expired, he has resumed a more normal life. You only have to see him at work, lovingly touching and describing an old painting he is restoring, to glimpse how much art means to him. Now, after three decades, he is finally living and painting as he wanted to all along, much as he might have lived had he been born in America or the Scotland of his ancestors. But even though he is no longer active in politics, he cannot fully escape his past. There are still people around who want to kill him.

By early 1981, Siva Patel had made up his mind to leave South Africa. His bookstore had collapsed; his sense of frustration had reached an intolerable level; there were strong indications the regime would re-ban him at the end of the year. He kept his decision a total secret from all of his friends and relatives, to avoid implicating them. It was agonizing for him to make appointments he knew he would never keep. He saw his aged mother, probably for the last time, trying to pretend it was just another routine visit.

Just before he made his move, we met in Durban. I intended to show him how to use the compass we thought he might need to help find his way over the border at night. Our teaching session could have aroused suspicion due to his wish to flout the hated petty apartheid laws one last time. He insisted on practicing with the compass at the beach for whites-only. We must have been an odd and conspicuous sight as we took degree readings and paced off distances while people frolicked in the late afternoon surf.

It turned out Siva did not need to use the compass. He crossed into Swaziland without any trouble, under a helpful bright African moon. He arrived with no passport, no job, and no assured haven. I had never seen him happier. Six months later, he had settled, at least temporarily, in independent Zimbabwe, where he was rewriting textbooks and producing radio programs.

Back in South Africa, the Natal Indian Congress he had helped revive was involved in one of its most crucial fights. The apartheid regime had in the 1960s established the South African Indian Council, which was supposed to manage the "internal affairs" of the Indian people. The Council's members, all appointed by the government, had been obscure conservatives with little popular following. The government had announced it would hold elections for the body in November 1981. A large turnout of Indian voters would legitimate the Council, and give an encouraging boost to the regime's grand strategy of carrying out further changes to lure Indian and colored people to its side.

The Natal Indian Congress and other organizations boldly called on Indian people to defy the regime's threats and to boycott the elections. Indian and other black leaders stood alongside each other on the same platforms, encouraging large audiences to reject the Council as a separate apartheid institution and to instead fight for a nonracial society.

The boycott was a huge success. It outstripped the predictions of even its most hopeful proponents. Fewer than 20 percent of the eligible Indians voted; in some areas, the turnout was a laughable 2 percent. The election that had been staged to divide South Africans further had in fact served to bring them closer together.

The enraged security police arrested a number of Indian Congress leaders, including the brilliant lawyer Yunus Mahomad and Praveen Gordham, who eventually had to check into a hospital psychiatric ward to recover from the torture he apparently suffered in detention. But the apartheid regime's main target was a distinguished black Durban lawyer named Griffiths Mxenge, who had been a lifelong ANC member, a political prisoner, and who continued to work closely with Indian and white people. Two weeks after the Indian Council elections, Mxenge was found brutally stabbed to death, with his throat cut. Those who murdered him were obviously trying to attribute his death to ordinary street criminals. The fifteen thousand people of all races who attended his funeral were not persuaded.

In the face of such barbarism, Gandhi's philosophy of nonviolence seemed even more irrelevant. Through the early 1980s, African National Congress guerrillas were waging their growing nationwide sabotage campaign. They were particularly active in Durban. The organization declared a phase of "armed propaganda," during which it attacked visible and symbolic targets to encourage the spirit of resistance among its increasing number of supporters. The guerrillas bombed power stations, which forced occasional lengthy cuts in electricity; the army recruiting office right in the middle of the city; the showrooms of British-based auto manufacturers, to underscore the opposition to foreign investment; and the offices of government agencies most directly responsible for enforcing the apartheid laws.

In theory, the guerrillas could easily have set off explosions in whites-only theaters and restaurants, or kidnapped and assassinated white people randomly. Ironically, petty apartheid had created conditions of separation that would have made such racial attacks even more feasible. But there was nothing of the kind. The guerrillas were also careful to minimize civilian casualties by triggering the blasts in the early hours of the morning. They were observing the pledge made by their president, Oliver Tambo, who had gone to Switzerland to sign the Geneva conventions on the conduct of war. The ANC's promise was in stark contrast to the apartheid regime, which has continued to hang captured guerrillas instead of properly treating them as prisoners of war.

Mohandas Gandhi's legacy has not been entirely forgotten. Even though most people in the national liberation movement see no alternative to violent resistance, they have resolved to avoid an apocalyptic racial bloodbath. They waited many decades before taking up arms. They neither glorify violence nor use it indiscriminately. They remain willing and eager to negotiate instead. They have never denied people with white skins the right to remain in South Africa. In their principled refusal to answer hatred with more hatred or to make war gladly, they are still in some sense the heirs of Gandhi.

5

The Afrikaner Paradox

VAN WYCK'S NEIGHBORS on the surrounding farms probably regard him as something of an eccentric. He calls his natives "black people," even if he does revert now and then. He lets them ride on the front seat of his bakke, next to him. He also speaks English perfectly.

On the other hand, Van Wyck is in the Nederduitse Gereformeerde Kerk on Sunday; he belongs to the National Party; he does not disturb the local equilibrium by paying his farm workers more than the prevailing wage. He is always ready to help if a spare tractor part is needed in a hurry. His neighbors probably excuse his slight peculiarities as the inevitable consequence of his urban past.

Van Wyck had worked in the cities for an agricultural supply company, so he brought a scientific outlook to farming when he moved back to the platteland in his late fifties. He was originally from the Cape, but the scorching Karroo droughts of his youth convinced him he would never again depend wholly on the whimsical southern African weather. He studied climatological maps before deciding to settle 200 miles north of Johannesburg, in the well-irrigated Loskop Dam area between Groblersdal and Marble Hall. When I met him, he had been farming about six years, and he was still enthusiastic. "I could have retired and just waited for death," he shrugged. "But I didn't choose to."

Van Wyck—his name is pronounced Fahn Vayk—employs ten permanent black farm laborers. He also hires seasonal workers, mostly women, from the nearby Lebowa Bantustan. His farming operation is partly mechanized. Two or three of his laborers operate his green-and-yellow John Deere tractors, which he uses for plowing, planting, and some cultivating of his seed *mielies* and his lucerne, or alfalfa. Harvesting, however, is still done by hand.

He was surprisingly direct about why he had not mechanized totally. "Cheap labor," he said. He caught himself. "But it's not so very cheap, because it's inefficient." Then, inexplicably, he blurted out: "But then, if I were a black man, I don't know how hard I would work either."

He caught himself again, with what seemed to be a slight shiver of amazement. "They," he continued, in the tone whites use that conveys the pronoun's meaning without further elaboration, "have different customs, an entirely different way of life, than we do. My foreman . . . I give him food and a place to stay, and I pay him forty-five rand at the end of every month. So that money is his to spend as he wants. He could buy a wireless, or one of the other comforts of life. He could even buy a motorcar. But he has three wives. So he spends to support them. He drinks. He gambles."

Van Wyck broke off again, perhaps momentarily weighing his extravagant assertion that his foreman could afford even a fourth-hand automobile on forty-five rand a month. Then he rushed on: "Some of the men, I pay them thirty rand the last Saturday of the month, and by the following Monday, they have nothing. They come to me for a loan. They've gambled it away."

He cut off his irritation with a sigh. "We have to civilize and uplift them. Without us, they would have nothing. We are giving them the right to develop in their own way, in their homelands, under our guidance. I tell you frankly and truthfully—ninety-eight percent of the Europeans here would not mind mixing socially with civilized natives, er, black people. But first we must bring them up to our standards. We have been moving away from discrimination, we allow our black people into certain international hotels, restaurants. . . ."

I had not started this discussion at all. Nightfall had halted my efforts to hitchhike north to the Rhodesian border, and Van Wyck had invited me to stay over at his farmhouse. He was dressed in the Afrikaner platteland uniform: safari suit, shorts, and knee socks. His horn-rimmed glasses gave him a slightly austere, high-school-principal look.

He had launched into his earnest justifications as soon as he heard my American accent. He continued to talk throughout the evening, bustling about to offer me fresh farm milk or another cup of coffee.

On the subject of petty apartheid, I asked innocently why certain other facilities, such as public toilets, remained segregated. He became angry.

"Here is the truth—they smell. They don't bathe. They have venereal disease. We don't want to mix with them." He caught himself once again. "But the civilized ones, yes."

But he could not shake off his irritation. "They have this custom, that the man must buy his wife from her father. He must pay several hundred rand. So, they breed like flies. The more girl children they have, the more money it will be worth to them one day. . . ."

Van Wyck shifted back again to his weary, resigned voice. "We have a unique problem here, unique in the whole world. We're not Nazis. We're normal human beings, who are faced with this problem. If your American pioneers (who were very much like our own *voortrekkers*) had not massacred your Red Indians, you would find yourselves in the same position. You gave them blankets infected with smallpox. We defeated the blacks in battle, and we killed very many of them. But we let others live, and that's why, today, we have this unique problem: two completely different civilizations, on vastly different levels of development, in the same area.

"Everything would fall apart without us. We built up this country and we're not going to give it up. Certainly, the black man contributed labor. But always under European guidance, with European brains. It's sad, but true, that the further north you go in Africa, the poorer the black man becomes. That's why so many come here to South Africa for work. Why would thousands of blacks, many thousands, cross our borders every year if our system were so bad?

"We have had other divisions in South Africa, tragic divisions, between the English-speaking people and ourselves, the Afrikaners. We had our Anglo-Boer War here from 1899 to 1902. It was like your Revolution, except that the English won. During the war, our men were off in the veld, fighting, as guerrillas. They wouldn't surrender. So the English, to pressurize the men, herded their women and children into concentration camps. In those camps, the English soldiers (and these are not tales I'm telling you, this is the truth), put ground glass into their food, secretly, in order to kill them. More than twenty-six thousand of our women and children died.

"But those painful differences between Afrikaners and English-speaking are disappearing. In another generation, another twenty-five to thirty years, they will no longer exist. Already, there are Afrikaners who belong to the Progressive Federal Party, the opposition, and there are many, many English-speakers who support the National Party. In fact, there is no ruling party in the entire Western world that commands such an overwhelming majority as the National Party does, which is clear proof that it is following the desires of the people.

"We do have a problem, caused by the English-language press. It doesn't, for some reason, feel itself to be a part of South Africa. So it tells all these lies to the rest of the world about our system here. The press gives people overseas such a mistaken impression about what we are trying to do here, in the face of our unique problem."

By now, Van Wyck was flagging visibly, trying to stifle his yawns with increasing lack of success. He wanted to continue, but I suggested we adjourn for the evening.

The next morning, after a huge farm breakfast, we went out in his bakke to check on the mielie harvesting. Van Wyck said apologetically: "I should be there all the time, to supervise. My experience is that if the European is not supervising, the native, uh, the black man, does half as much work, and he does that half half as efficiently."

A dozen women emerged from among the rustling maize stalks. They were swathed up to their eyes, wrists, and ankles in rough garments made of brown sacking, which protect them against both the sun and sharp edges of the plants. They looked on silently, twelve Bedouins of the fields, as Van Wyck and his foreman huddled to one side. The foreman, who was wearing a floppy stocking cap, punctuated Van Wyck's Afrikaans instructions with an occasional, *"Ja*, baas."

As we bumped back across the fields to the farm house, Van Wyck said he often ignores the rigorous requirements of the pass laws when hiring or firing his laborers. "They can go to another farm if they want, or to the city; I don't stop them. But usually they come back. They have to work. This is essential. We have to feed them; it's our responsibility really, and we can't feed them without having them work."

On the way north to Marble Hall, Van Wyck stopped his bakke for two black hitchhikers. He explained that the early morning bus had already passed, adding: "If the European doesn't pick them up, who will?"

As we parted, Van Wyck shook hands firmly, and invited me to return at any time. "And remember," he said somberly, "we are not Nazis here. We are human beings, faced with a unique problem, unique in the whole world, for which we, with much sacrifice, have developed a solution. We call that solution apartheid."

Television only came to South Africa in 1976. The regime had previously barred it as a dangerous outside influence. Television has caught on among whites; American programs like *Dallas* became popular reference points, causing declines in patronage at restaurants and other evening activities. But television has not been in existence long enough to ruin the old-fashioned art of storytelling.

Koos Du Preez, the veterinarian in a small town in the northern Cape, has gathered his material from his postings all over South Africa. Du Preez, a stocky man, with the trim Clark Gable–type mustache still in favor among older Afrikaners, is a master raconteur, brilliant in his characterizations, florid with his gestures, precise in his timing, extravagant with detail.

His house is an agreeable mess, overflowing with four dogs, five cats, an indeterminate number of chicks, and one tame mongoose. He performs some of his lesser operations, which he describes as "panel-beating" (body and fender work), on his kitchen table. "One Christmas it was a little ridiculous," he admitted. "I was spaying a bitch on one side of the table while my wife was preparing the turkey on the other."

I spent an entire evening sitting at that table, listening to Du Preez talk fondly about the idiosyncracies of the rural Afrikaners he has worked among for three decades. He had been posted at the start of his career to a small town on the edge of the huge Kalahari Desert. The local ranchers, men of limited imagination, had trouble giving him directions around the area. "They would tell you to follow a certain road until you get to 'Stoepshitter' Maritz's place, and then turn to the right. [A *stoep* is a porch.] You drive off happily. Then thirty miles up the road you realize you have to ask for him by that name!"

Many of the ranchers thoroughly distrusted the modern antibiotics Du Preez prescribed for their sick animals. They often preferred folkloric home remedies, which they had "learned" from their neighbors. In one case, Du Preez had to explain to a rancher that the worthless concoction had actually hastened the death of the diseased cow. The rancher nodded glumly at his mistake. "I can see what I did wrong, Doc, of course, man. The stuff needed a pint of kaffir piss. That meant one of the local Tswanas. But the bloody boy I got the piss from turned out to be a bloody Basuto!"

Du Preez himself had grown up in the northern Cape in the 1930s and '40s, when some of the farmers still used a horse and wagon to get around. Often, after a protracted evening session at the town bar, the heavier drinkers would simply be dumped, unconscious from booze, into their wagons. The trusty horse could find its way home, which might be as far as ten miles away.

Du Preez and his friends often waylaid and tricked these snoring passengers. Once they nailed a boozer to the seat of his wagon. In another case, they unhitched the horse, opened a huge iron gate, drove the horse through, closed the gate and rehitched the horse. The victim, awakening at 4:00 A.M. to see a gate bisecting his wagon, simply mumbled to himself that he must be dreaming and rolled over to go back to sleep.

In an even more elaborate hoax, the mischief makers enlisted the help of some colored sheepherders, who they bribed with wine. They hijacked the unconscious victim off his wagon and dropped him among the shepherds. The instant he awoke, the coloreds called him Pa. He growled and threatened to beat them. They remonstrated, "Pa, every time you get out of that hospital for the mad you think you're a white man named Fouché." The completely flabbergasted victim looked at his skin for reassurance. It had been stained a nice brownish color with walnut juice.

Du Preez, in the course of the evening, did poke fun at his fellow Afrikaners, but always in tones of affection. He clearly had a keen and sympathetic insight into other people; misanthropes do not make good raconteurs. But his tone changed sharply when he mentioned blacks. They appeared in his stories only as ludicrous and peripheral characters. He grimaced as he referred to them, routinely using the words *coons* or *savages*. These racial epithets sprinkled through his otherwise genial and humanist monologue were like a burst from a police whistle in the middle of a symphony.

Van Wyck and the veterinarian Du Preez are in many ways typical of the three million Afrikaners. They are confusing, paradoxical people, a mixture of the most extreme and often contradictory qualities. This ambiguity is not new. In the 1830s, the daring voortrekkers left the Cape, where they had been settled for nearly two centuries, to head north, out of the reach of the British authorities who had captured the colony from the Dutch early in the nineteenth century. The trekkers justified their exodus in declarations that rang with noble affirmations of liberty. In the interior, they established fiercely independent republics, rickety creations in which the proud burgers constantly sabotaged the efforts of their own elected leaders to assert authority.

The trekker manifesto, however, also included the statement, "It is our determination to maintain . . . proper relations between master and servant." They had objected to British rule partly because the new authorities outlawed slavery and carried through other reforms. The trekkers moved into the interior accompanied by several thousand black "apprentices," who were little more than slaves.

At the turn of the twentieth century, the Afrikaners fought the first modern anti-imperial war, the first effort by a Third World people to use sophisticated technology to preserve their independence from an aggressive colonial power. The independent burgers formed a people's army, run in a strikingly democratic way, to defend their two cherished republics after the British colonial regime at the Cape had provoked war in order to establish political control over the recently discovered gold mines.

The imperial army, which outnumbered the Afrikaners by 450,000 to 60,000, fought an entire year before defeating them in conventional battles and occupying their towns.

The Boer generals turned to guerrilla warfare. De Wet, de la Rey, Botha, and Smuts led their horsemen on dashes across the veld, striking relentlessly at the occupying army. Lord Kitchener, the imperial commander, introduced savage countermeasures that would see further use in the twentieth century; he burned farms and crops to deprive the guerrillas of food, and he forced their women and children into concentration camps, where twenty thousand to thirty thousand did die—not from ground glass, but from initial British indifference to the appalling medical and hygienic conditions. Kitchener built a string of block houses across the veld, linked together with that recent invention, barbed wire, to try and cut down guerrilla mobility and improve the prospects for the imperial search-and-destroy missions. The undaunted guerrillas fought on. The frustrated Kitchener wrote coldly, "Extermination . . . is a long and very tiring business."

In the end, the superior imperial manpower and resources finally prevailed. The two Republics surrendered and were joined to the Cape and Natal in what became the Union of South Africa in 1910. From the very start, the defeated Boers sought and obtained guarantees that the slightly liberal franchise in the Cape, where a minority of better off coloreds and a few Africans also had the vote, would not be extended to the two northern provinces. White control over the entire country, which would eventually strip the franchise from blacks completely, was thus guaranteed. The stirring Boer resistance to imperial power had been conducted purely on their own behalf.

In the postwar years, the consolidation of larger, more efficient farms pushed a number of Afrikaners who were no longer needed in agriculture into the towns, where they started to constitute what eventually became known as the poor white problem. They clustered in urban slums, little more than shantytowns, where they lived close to and often alongside poor blacks who had also come to search for work. The Afrikaners faced discrimination from the English-dominated government and business establishment; they were often not allowed to use their own language in stores and offices. This cultural oppression, which has something in common with what blacks continue to experience, even induced some Afrikaner parents to give their children English first names. After Nationalism grew, some of the embarrassed children reverted to using only their initials.

The Afrikaners tried to maintain their independence by establishing their own small enterprises, in horse-cab driving and brick manufacturing, but they were eventually forced out of business by larger concerns. The Afrikaners then had to seek work, in the mines and elsewhere. They started to react to their new status as workers, often subject to bouts of desperate unemployment, with protest marches and support for the Labour party, which had been founded by English-speaking skilled artisans. In 1922, they joined with the English-speaking miners in a ferocious strike; the government sent in artillery, tanks, machine guns, even warplanes. In five days of pitched battles around Johannesburg, more than two hundred people died.

This working-class unity did not, however, extend to black people. The 1922 strike was carried out partly to resist the mineowners' efforts to replace whites with lower-paid blacks. The Afrikaners, like the other white miners, appealed to racism to protect their job security. One of the 1922 strike slogans embodied the consummate paradox, "Workers of the World Unite—and Fight for a White South Africa."

Emergent Afrikaner Nationalism, which was dominated by better-off farmers, professionals, and small businessmen, then concluded an alliance with the Labour party. The two won the 1924 elections and ruled together until 1929. This "Pact Government" strengthened the racial Color Bar, which restricted certain jobs to whites, and also started to implement the "civilized labor policy," which reserved certain jobs for whites at a subsidized wage. The poor white problem started to ease.

Afrikanerdom split in the 1930s, and a more virulent form of Nationalism went over to the opposition. These Nationalists moved into the all-white unions, where Afrikaner workers were now in the clear majority, and won their allegiance with appeals to unity among *die volk*— "the folk." In the watershed 1948 election, working-class Afrikaners shifted from Labour to Nationalism in sufficient weight to provide the margin of victory. The workers who had once cherished their autonomy had now fully accepted a subservient role in return for continued protection against black advancement.

The 1920s Pact Government had also started to carry out a remarkable program of economic nationalism, intended to reduce the nation's dependence on overseas investors. The Pact subsidized agriculture, raised tariffs to promote domestic manufacture, and established Iscor, the state's iron-and-steel enterprise. Together with the state-owned railways, electric utility, and other concerns, the Pact's policy increased South Africa's economic independence dramatically. In some ways, the program could be an appealing model to certain other struggling Third World nations.

But the fruits of economic independence were not to be shared among all South Africans. Nationalism has rather used its increased and diversified economic power to strengthen its domination over its fellow countrymen. The regime boasted in 1981 that it had made itself self-sufficient in the production of ammunition. Its other, even more ominous effort at self-reliance, the secret nuclear program, may already have created an apartheid bomb.

By the late 1970s, the unity in Afrikanerdom that had maintained Nationalism in power for three decades with steadily increasing electoral majorities was starting to break up. In 1978, John Vorster was succeeded as prime minister by P. W. Botha, who had held the defense portfolio. The pundits expected that Botha, an old party hack, would provide plodding leadership enlivened occasionally only by his notoriously bad temper. P. W.—he is never called Pieter—turned out to be something of a surprise. At defense, he had apparently come under the influence of certain cunning young army generals who had ambitious notions about how to preserve the apartheid system by making certain adjustments to it.

These cocky officers, led by General Magnus Malan, who later succeeded Botha at defense, viewed southern Africa in long-range strategic terms, rather than with the narrow election-to-election complacency of many of the white politicians. They recognized that the collapse of the protective ring of white-minority regimes in Angola, Mozambique, and later, Zimbabwe, together with the rise of internal resistance after Soweto, had converted the preservation of white power from a police to a military problem. The generals, and their convert, P. W. Botha, told the white public that the Soviet Union was inspiring a "total onslaught" against South Africa. They were clever and well informed enough to know that Soviet aid to the African National Congress and other liberation forces in the region was small; the real threat was posed by their own fellow black South Africans. They used the purported Soviet danger as a way to try and frighten whites into supporting their policies, which did represent something of an unsettling break with the past.

P. W. Botha, in his first year in office, bluntly told white South Africans they had to "adapt or die." He and his supporters in what had come to be known as the *verligte,* or "enlightened" wing of the National Party, began to press for certain changes: the constitutional formula that would allow some colored and Indian representation in the government; the end to some petty apartheid; the more rapid entry of blacks into semiskilled and skilled jobs that had been held by whites in the past but which were now short of manpower.

Botha rarely tried to justify these changes by appealing to morality. He instead said openly his proposals were an opportunistic part of a "to-

tal strategy'' needed to defend South Africa. He told cheering white audiences he wanted to win over coloreds and Indians partly so they could
then be drafted into the army, which white conscripts alone could not
maintain at sufficient strength. The changes in the economy were similarly intended to prepare the country for war.

Support for these verligte policies were strongest among the ''new
Afrikaners,'' the better-off class of business and professional people who
were coming to share the less crude racial attitudes of their English-
speaking counterparts. Nationalism, in its three decades in power, had
helped improve the economic position of some Afrikaners dramatically,
and the distinction between Afrikaans and English business was blur-
ring. Businessmen generally welcomed Botha's initiatives as necessary
to preserve the system over the long term.

But Botha's proposals did provoke a large backlash within other seg-
ments of Afrikanerdom. Even though almost none of the changes Botha
proposed got past the talking stage during his first five years in office,
he was furiously denounced as a traitor to *die volk*. The Herstigte (Reconstituted) National Party, which had stumbled through the 1970s as a
fringe grouplet, increased its vote to a healthy 14 percent in the 1981
general election. The next year, the powerful leader of Nationalism's
verkrampte (cramped, narrow) wing, the dour Dr. Andries Treurnicht,
led a breakaway, taking fifteen other Nat MPs with him. Treurnicht, who
had been dubbed ''Dr. No'' by hostile newspapermen in backhanded
tribute to his stubborn resistance to any change, called his new organization the Conservative party. In another of the bizarre linguistic con-
tortions so characteristic of South Africa, the National Party now came
to be regarded as centrist, or middle-of-the-road. Because only whites
have the ballot, the 165 electoral districts for Parliament have ludicrously low numbers of voters, fewer even than the average ward in an
American city. Politics can therefore be intensely personal. In a series
of hard-fought by-elections in certain rural and urban white working-class
constituencies that had been once overwhelmingly dominated by the National Party, the two far-right-wing groupings steadily gained ground into
the early eighties.

During 1981, Fanie Pretorius was living in a yellow-brick apartment
complex in western Pretoria overlooking the big Iscor steel mill where
he worked, which was a mile away. Smoke of various colors billowed
skyward over the factory. Blast furnaces reared above the tangles of other
machinery. The mill was in continuous operation, so Fanie was required
to change shifts every week. He hated the shift work. His wife was ex-

pecting their first child, and he was certain the night work would impair family life.

Even for an Afrikaner, Fanie (short for Stephanus) was tall, at six feet four. He walked with a slight limp, the result of a serious leg injury he had suffered in the mill a few years earlier. His serious, almost grave manner was odd in a man of only twenty-eight. He was shy, and at times awkwardly overbearing in his efforts at hospitality.

He worked a forty-eight-hour week, and earned twelve hundred rand a month after taxes. It was hard to determine precisely what he did at the mill. He was very definitely a ''white worker'' in the South African context, but it sounded as if he was actually something of a cross between a skilled electrician and a foreman. A two-hundred-rand-a-month black worker he called a toolboy apparently followed him on his rounds through the plant, handing him implements from time to time like a dental assistant.

Fanie Pretorius shared many of the convictions and prejudices of his fellow white South Africans. He was dead certain, for example, that blacks were not intelligent enough to learn the skilled trades. ''The coon,'' he explained sadly, ''can learn to do only one easy thing at a time.'' More virulent versions of this belief assert that blacks cannot see in three dimensions, or judge distances accurately. The most strident whites will point out gleefully that blacks did not invent the wheel, or written language, with a tone of self-congratulation that suggests they themselves had a hand in these innovations.

Fanie and I had preceded our talk with a quick supply mission to the local bottle store. We paused outside the apartment block to admire his gigantic 1300-cc motorcycle and his huge yellow Chevrolet. Gas was priced at the equivalent of more than three dollars a gallon, but the expansive sense of self-worth he got from his big car was obviously worth the cost. Near the liquor establishment, a somewhat tattered middle-aged white man, nearly but not quite yet a hobo, sat on the curb in amiable and slightly tipsy conversation with several blacks. All sipped regularly from canned substances concealed in opaque plastic bags. Fanie stopped to glare in disgust at the inoffensive gathering. ''That's the worst thing I've seen all day,'' he muttered, as he snorted and walked briskly away.

Back in his apartment, he tossed his jeans jacket to one side for the ''coon-girl'' to wash the next day, and continued with his interpretation of South African reality. He shared the commonplace white view that the country was impregnable. He presented one of the usual arguments; the outside world, particularly the West, was so completely dependent on South Africa's strategic minerals that it would never permit a change in government that might interrupt supplies: His confidence in Western backing for South Africa was based partly on his mistaken belief that mining magnate Harry Oppenheimer, the most powerful businessman in the country, was actually an American! He reasoned that the United States would never let "the terrorists" jeopardize the prosperity of one of its own citizens.

He also had faith in South Africa's technological superiority over "the terrorists." He boasted that his steel plant had a contingency plan under which it could completely retool in twenty-four hours to start producing ammunition. He knew nothing about the African National Congress or SWAPO other than that they wanted to install "coon governments."

Fanie Pretorius was convinced the National Party was betraying South Africa. He had been raised as a Nationalist, and he still displayed a certain deference in talking about its leaders. But he was getting increasingly bitter. He no longer trusted the financial integrity of high officials. Some were outright embezzlers; others, though technically not lawbreakers, still benefited unfairly from tax breaks, rent-free homes and other perquisites.

He also disliked the National Party's Bantustan policy. The government was "giving away" part of the country to "the kaffirs," thereby creating more borders for his fellow soldiers and him to defend. He felt the regime was also somehow "giving away" food grains to black African countries, including Angola, even though SWAPO, one of the guerrilla enemies, was based there.

In his disillusionment, he had started to vote for the far-right Herstigte National Party, although he felt that its policies, as he understood them, might be a bit too extreme. "We couldn't do without the kaffirs," he explained. "We can't push them completely out of the country."

Fanie had completed his initial two-year stretch in the army, and five of his eight (since increased to ten) annual three-month call-ups. He was a sergeant in the infantry, and he had fought several times in Namibia and Angola. He said cheerfully he did not mind "border duty." It was necessary to "defend the country," and the extra money he got as a noncommissioned officer would help to support his growing family.

In part, Sergeant Fanie Pretorius is going to war armed with misconceptions that are not his own fault. Government and business leaders who are better placed to know the truth have misled him. He has an unreasonably optimistic interpretation of the balance of forces in the region; a lurid, inaccurate picture of conditions elsewhere in Africa; and no understanding of either the aims or the determination of the liberation fighters he is sent out to kill.

But more information would probably not change his mind. Even if he were required to read a sympathetic history of the liberation movement he would not desert from the army. Racism is not caused mainly by ignorance. There are, after all, black people around who can not only see in three dimensions but who also function more than adequately as medical doctors and university professors. Racial hatred is not simply a mistaken opinion that can be countered with facts and appeals to reason.

For people like Fanie Pretorius, racism is at the very heart of their view of the world; it is a vital part of their identity as they live through every day. They cling to their racial views with the tenacity of a mystical faith. These beliefs incorporate a powerful set of irrational taboos, of which the notorious Immorality Act is only the most extreme. But even shaking hands with a black person, though not technically against the law, can in a small town be cause for social ostracism.

I once met a white mechanic who described how he always drove great distances rather than remain overnight in one of the neighboring black countries he occasionally visited on a job. ''I never sleep in those kaffir places,'' he said proudly. I also heard stories about white South Africans who took their own sheets overseas to be sure the hotels did not give them bedding once slept in by blacks.

South African racism has its rigid rules of conduct. One chief maxim is that a white overseer should be present whenever blacks are at work. He will be in factories, like Fanie Pretorius; on road construction gangs; alongside agricultural workers moving through the fields. He will be wearing shorts, knee stockings with a comb tucked in, and perhaps a hat to deflect the sun. He may puff on a cigarette or a pipe, occasionally gesturing toward ''the boys'' and grunting an order. Despite his rugged, weatherbeaten appearance, he will never do any physical work himself. In most cases, he is superfluous; distinguishing between a maize plant and a weed and using a hoe to remove the latter is not a particularly arcane skill that requires constant supervision.

The baas is present primarily for symbolic value. He is there as a daily living embodiment of white supremacy. Each impatient, commanding gesture tends to demoralize the workers by reminding them of their own powerlessness, both on the job and in the apartheid system generally. Each gruff gesture reassures the baas he is indispensable, both in his specific work and in the country at large. He nods gravely as ''his boys'' work. Despite his low standing in the white community, somewhere he rules.

P. W. Botha's proposals have not threatened people like Fanie Pretorius in any real, material way. Fanie's job and his good life are not in jeopardy. There is no danger his neighborhood or his children's schools will be integrated. At worst, Indian and colored MPs may enter his national parliament (though they will be safely quarantined in separate chambers and comfortably outnumbered by the whites), and he may occasionally find blacks sitting at the next table in certain restaurants. Still, he so heatedly opposes even these minimal changes that he may even be prepared to fight to prevent them.

Fanie Pretorius's tenacity is an ironic tribute to the first theorists of apartheid, especially Hendrik Verwoerd, who battled for the allegiance of Afrikanerdom in the 1930s and '40s before they led Nationalism to power in the historic 1948 election. Verwoerd, who was a propagandizing newspaper editor before he entered Parliament, realized that prospective Nationalists would not be inspired only by negative appeals. Attacking both *die Engelse* (the English) and warning about the *swart gevaar* (the black danger) were important but not sufficient. What was needed was a positive vision, a coherent and convincing blueprint for how the Nationalists were going to reshape South African society.

Some features of the philosophy of apartheid were not new. A less extreme form of Nationalism had already shared political power in the 1920s and '30s, when it had founded the state enterprises that moved the country away from being a complete economic colony of the West. Verwoerd and the other theorists regarded the Afrikaner state as a holy, living entity, intended to achieve much more in the world than simply reflect the pedestrian wants of its individual citizens; this mystical view they borrowed partly from similar Fascist ideas then prevalent in Europe. The Nationalists are understandably quiet today about this portion of their intellectual heritage, but some of their leaders, including former Prime Minister John Vorster, were actually detained during World War II for their pro-Nazi acts of sabotage. Neither did Verwoerd have to invent the Nationalist policy on race, as the three Dutch Reformed Churches had long provided theological justifications for racism.

But Verwoerd understood that South African racism included positive, paternal feelings toward blacks as well as raw hatred. Whites believed deeply that blacks were their inferiors, and responded savagely if that view was challenged. But as long as blacks were meek and subservient, whites claimed to feel a certain responsibility for their welfare.

Paternalism is still to a great extent typical of life on the farms, where the white patriarch treats his ragged workers like children who will never grow up. It is in the first place an arrogant attitude of superiority, but it does include a genuine sense of responsibility as well. Tales of white farmers and their wives nursing their black dependents through illness or injury are a big part of rural folklore. The attitude of white custodianship has naturally diminished in the more impersonal urban areas, but it has not died out entirely.

White paternalism is generally an unconscious attitude, ingrained over the years. I once rode through the northern Natal bush on the back of a bakke with two other hitchhikers, a white soldier in his brown uniform and a shabbily dressed black farmworker who had climbed aboard later. The soldier talked to me at length, smoking a Gunston cigarette, while completely ignoring the other passenger. As his cigarette burned down he reached sideways, and neither glancing nor pausing in his talk, handed the butt to the black man. He had been completely certain that the black man would gratefully accept the gift of the last few puffs of smoke.

Hendrik Verwoerd's genius was that he understood this paternal side of racism, and was careful to blend it with the other ideas of his time in a comprehensive doctrine that claimed to be in the best interests of all in South Africa. One of his colleagues, E. G. Jansen, argued in 1944 that apartheid would be positive for blacks as well; it would reverse the prevailing political system that had been "instrumental in the disruption of the tribal life of tens of thousands of Natives." Jansen noted sadly, "We have robbed them of the opportunity of undergoing their own development. We have tried to make white men of them, which they can never be. We allow all sorts of strange ideas to be propagated amongst them."

There was only some hypocrisy in this kind of statement. No group of people can continue to persist long with the belief that they *wrongfully* subjugate and exploit other people. Even today, after the years of rising unrest, most white South Africans genuinely believe that most blacks are satisfied with their lives, and that "the terrorists" are a minority of the misled.

But whites must have, at odd moments, glimmers of insight into the real injustice of their position. Among Afrikaners, these fleeting glimpses must be encouraged by their memories of how their own ancestors until very recently suffered under the English-speaking. These twinges of conscience probably account partly for the volatile, schizoid, confused, and sometimes violent behavior of many whites, for their otherwise inexplicable outbursts of rage at the innocent objects of their guilt. Apartheid, as elaborated by Verwoerd, has therefore been a welcome, soothing antidote for the occasionally conscience-stricken.

Apartheid, as a philosophy, was obviously fragile and internally inconsistent. And as a way of life, it was under mounting challenge by the majority of South African society. The Nationalists had to reinforce it with a huge and imposing edifice of legislation, which intruded into all aspects of national life. Racial separation that had existed largely as a matter of custom now received the force of law. Some of the changes, at first glance absurd and irrational, in fact had strong symbolic value. Separate toilets and laws against black and white boxers entering the same ring were clearly not vital in any economic or political sense. But such ever-present symbols did serve to bolster the rickety social order.

P. W. Botha and the other verligtes are trying to tamper with a system which, despite its inconsistencies, has become accepted by many Afrikaners and other whites. In theory at least, apartheid is still for them the neat, persuasive ideal of total separation, beneficial to all. By contrast, Botha seems to be offering cavilling, piecemeal changes that will lead to a confusing hybrid system that is satisfactory to no one. His proposals, even though they are still far from reality, are profoundly disturbing. Nationalists cannot discard their ideas as readily as yesterday's newspaper.

The enthusiasm in white politics is now on the far right. The leaders of the two parties complement each other well. The HNP's Jaap Marais is a demagogic, compelling speaker, while the Conservative Andries Treurnicht, who is appropriately a *dominee,* or minister, is a stiff theological purist, a custodian of the Verwoerdian orthodoxy. Meanwhile, the Nationalists are confused and have lost much of their old drive.

Prime Minister Botha did manage in November 1983 to win a referendum among whites approving his proposals to bring colored and Indian people into the national Parliament in separate chambers. But much of his 66 percent margin of victory was provided by English-speaking moderates. Up to half of Afrikanerdom abandoned the National Party over a change that will have no practical significance.

This loss of Afrikaner support has prompted talk of a "De Gaulle" or "Mussolini Option," in which Botha, with army backing, seizes personal dictatorial powers and puts through his changes by fiat. If he, or someone else, dares such a maneuver, they can be assured of stiff white resistance, which might even include violence. White South Africa is entering its deepest crisis deeply divided. In winning so many dedicated adherents to the vision of apartheid, Hendrik Verwoerd ironically did his work too well.

By no means do all Afrikaners believe in apartheid. Women have been prominent among those who have courageously wrenched themselves free. Afrikaans culture is heavily male-dominated, a brawny, blustering, outdoors ethos. Membership in the Broederbond (Brotherhood), the semi-secret twelve-thousand-strong Afrikaner elite, is restricted to men. Of the 115-odd Nationalist MPs in the early '80s, not a single one was a woman.

Not all Afrikaner women have settled demurely into the subservient positions prepared for them. In the 1930s, two extraordinary garment workers named Bettie du Toit and Joanna Cornelius were leading organizers in a nonracial union. The two were undeterred by either social ostracism or police violence. In the 1960s, the young poet Ingrid Jonker included powerful strains of protest in her work before tragically taking her own life. In 1982, Hannchen Koornhof, the niece of a Nationalist cabinet minister, spent six months in detention and another month in prison on political charges.

Another woman rebel was my friend Désirée Van Rensburg, who had left South Africa to teach in independent Zimbabwe. It was there that she met her fiancé, an English-speaking draft resister. Désirée is a very attractive woman who looks something like a younger version of the actress Faye Dunaway. She was raised in two small towns, first in the Cape, and then, after her father, a railway worker, was transferred, in northern Natal.

Her memories of small town Afrikaner life are of powerful pressures to conform. "You had to go to church every Sunday, or else you became a social outcast. After church, you weren't allowed to play sport, or do anything frivolous. You had to keep your Sunday clothes on for the whole day. What if the dominee came around for a visit, hey, and found you carrying on?" She laughed. "The word would get around. People would start to shun you. You might go into a shop in town the next week and find you had trouble getting attended to."

Désirée continued, "Everyone quite normally called black people kaffirs. When I started teaching, the others at the school realized I didn't like that. So they deliberately used an even more insulting word, *houtkop* [wooden head], just to be provocative. You don't have to do much to get labeled a *kaffir-boetie* [literally, kaffir brother; figuratively, nigger-lover]. At one of my schools, I got called it as soon as somebody saw me saying 'good morning' to the black cleaner and asking him if he had a pleasant weekend."

Désirée attended a high school called Voortrekker, which is also the name given to the main street in nearly every small town in the Transvaal and the Free State. "We were not taught to think in school. We weren't encouraged to have any initiative, any independence. We learned the standard version of history; we arrived in South Africa the same time the blacks were coming down from the north. They were an obstacle to us, so we just ran them over. They are a lesser civilization, below our level. One of my younger cousins told me an amazing story from his military training; the sergeant has to teach the new recruits that 'blacks shoot back.' Those young white teenagers in the army, hey, they aren't really sure at first that blacks are smart enough, or brave enough, to use a weapon!''

She paused, shook her head quickly, and changed the subject. "The separation in South Africa is in any case a farce, though. The Immorality Act, hey? We all knew in school that many of the guys on the farms had gone to bed with the black women who worked there. You just never talked about it directly.

"Especially in the Cape, on the farms, the ties between Afrikaners and colored people are strong. We speak the same language; we have the same sense of humor. There's often a real closeness. But when an outsider, any outsider, comes, then you must move apart. You don't want outsiders to see that you have that kind of friendship."

Désirée pondered for a moment. "I had an aunt back there, in the Cape, who eventually committed suicide. She'd been having a secret affair with a colored schoolmaster. It went on for twenty years until they were found out. Then, she killed herself."

Désirée returns home regularly to visit her family. They respect her views even though they continue to disagree with her. She tries, when driving back to South Africa, to select routes on which military roadblocks are least likely. "Many of those soldiers are Afrikaners," she explained. "I don't like to see them there, patrolling. I support the other side. So I feel bad. But even if one of my own relations got shot, I wouldn't change my mind." She sounded only slightly unsure of herself.

The Nederduitse Gereformeerde Kerk, by far the biggest of the three Dutch Reformed Churches, is normally for whites only. The NGK has established three "daughter" churches, one each for Indians, coloreds, and blacks. Over the years, the mother has sent white "missionaries" to preach at the three black daughters, in a paternalist replication in the religious realm of the apartheid theory of separate "nations." More recently, a number of white dominees have joined the black churches for entirely different reasons.

Frikkie Conradie was until his death in an automobile accident in early 1982 a dominee at one of the daughters in Alexandra, a black township in northeast Johannesburg. The regime had long threatened to demolish "Alex," a poor area even by comparison with Soweto. A community movement led by Rev. Sam Buti, a black dominee who was Conradie's senior, forced the government to back down.

Conradie would have preferred to live in Alex, among his parishioners, but the regime refused permission. Instead, he and his wife lived close by, in a small home in "white" Joburg decorated with Vermeer reproductions. I met him there in 1980, nearly two years before his tragic death. He was an intense, bearded man, with blazing eyes.

He grew up on a farm in the western Transvaal. "I'm a real Boer," he said with a laugh. Then he became somber. "On the farm we were taught not to take the black children by the hand. We were taught they were lower than us. We came to our school in buses. We looked out the windows and saw them running along the side of the road to their school. We were told they were trying to catch up with us; we had to work hard to stay ahead. In high school, we learned they were a different breed of people; they had flat noses and so on. God intended us to be separate. Apartheid was in our textbooks, everywhere. . . ."

Frikkie Conradie continued on to Potchefstroom University. He had no strong political feelings, aside from some resentment toward the Broederbond, which he felt was too elite, secret, and undemocratic. He was still loyal to Nationalism itself. He went on to study theology at Pretoria University. "I got bored after one year," he recalled with a quick chuckle. "The first year they talked about heaven. The second year they talked more about heaven. There's only so much you can hear about heaven, so I went to Holland to complete my studies. I hoped to hear something more interesting there."

In the Netherlands, he encountered the Reverend Allan Boesak, a dynamic young colored preacher from the Cape who was also studying overseas. Boesak later became a prominent, outspoken churchman and political leader back in South Africa. "One evening," Frikkie Conradie remembered, "he asked me and my wife what we thought of apartheid. I answered that I had not given it much thought, but it seemed all right, each group developing in its own areas, in its own way, a good system for everyone. . . . He got so angry that he couldn't look at us. He just stared out the window silently for some moments." Frikkie Conradie imitated Boesak. "Then, he started to talk. He told us about the forced removals, about the slum conditions in black areas. We talked all night . . . I had never realized these things were happening. . . ."

Frikkie frowned. "I became an atheist for a time. I asked, 'Where is this Holy Spirit to enlighten me? Why were my eyes closed to this suffering in my own country?' I said, 'No, man, God, you don't exist!'

"Allan and other black church people in Holland started to make a human being out of me. They said, 'Look, man, what else are you going to do back there? You can't leave the ministry; you've been trained all these years. And as a dominee, you will have at least some freedom. The police can't come right into the church and pull you out—it looks bad.' ''

The arguments succeeded. Frikkie Conradie returned to South Africa and joined the Alexandra daughter church. He was spending as much or more of his time on community work as on pastoral duties. He said he had been warned he might lose his family and friends if he became too active. He said with a smile, "I now have a bigger 'family' than ever. We have so many friends that we don't have time for all of them.

"The black people accept you and trust you. They separate the man from the evil deeds of the man. But the first thing you must do if you want to work with blacks is: Shut up. Listen. Before, black people sometimes let some whites speak for them. Now they are so angry they speak for themselves. And this is not always easy for us. A white woman friend said to me, 'I've been trained all my life to speak out, to stand up as a person and say what I think.' I understand what she meant. But we must remain quiet, listening."

He grew suddenly agitated. "No one in South Africa can call themselves a Christian. Terrible things go on in this country. I've seen slavery. My own neighbors, tying farm workers by a rope around the legs and pulling them, as punishment. One farmer, hitting an old black woman. For no reason. She had not disobeyed. She had only answered back.

"Why did I do nothing? I've talked about the indoctrination we receive, but I still should have known." He frowned deeply. "God has abandoned the whites in this country. We may say that we try to live in a Christian way. But we are not Christians.

"When I go back to my father's farm, I take the workers by the hand. My family doesn't like that. I say to the workers, 'I have had a chance to study, to go overseas, because you have suffered.' When something comes to me after my father dies, I'll turn it straight over to them. It should already be theirs in any case."

Frikkie Conradie said he feared that with conflict in the country growing, the forces even further to the right of the National Party could come to power. "If that happens, they will destroy Alexandra Township. In the meantime, we will concentrate on building up the spirit of the people. They will find it hard to destroy us. And even if they do, the spirit of resistance will remain."

Frikkie got to his feet, walked over to his television set, and switched it on. The loud whine accompanying the test pattern filled the room, interfering with possible listening devices. He sat back down and leaned over intently. "There will never again be peace in South Africa until the apartheid regime is destroyed. The violent resistance will continue.

The question in South Africa used to be, 'Which side are you on?' It has now become, 'Which side will you fight for?' ''

In March 1982, Frikkie Conradie crashed while driving back to Johannesburg after visiting his father, who had been ill. He died instantly. Thousands of people, most of them black, attended his funeral. He was buried in Alexandra Township, after the regime granted special permission. One day after his death, his widow, Marietjie, gave birth to a son. She named the little boy Frikkie.

By 1914, four years after the formation of the Union of South Africa, Afrikanerdom had split. One faction, headed by former General Louis Botha, the first prime minister, and his deputy, Jan Smuts, advocated breaking with the past and cooperating with the British Empire. Others, also former guerrilla generals like J. B. M. Hertzog, de la Rey, and de Wet, pushed for the more independent position that became Afrikaner Nationalism. The dispute turned violent at the outbreak of World War I. The proto-Nationalists rejected participation in the fighting at Britain's side, and some of them even rose in a brief, open revolt. One ex-general, Christian F. Beyers, drowned in the Vaal River while trying to escape after the uprising failed. A certain Naudé, who had ridden as a chaplain with Beyers in the Anglo-Boer War, named his newborn son in the late general's honor.

Beyers Naudé was raised as a completely orthodox Afrikaner. He studied to become a dominee. At the time of his ordination, he was also invited to join the Broederbond. He never formally joined the National Party, though he naturally supported it. He rose quickly within the NGK, to become its moderator, or principal official, in the populous southern Transvaal region.

In 1960, an extraordinary church meeting was held at Cottesloe, a section of Johannesburg. It was a joint conference between some of the traditionally more liberal Protestant denominations and major elements of the NGK. In a stunning, unexpected shock, the Afrikaner churchmen joined their colleagues in issuing a strong denunciation of the apartheid system. The conference condemned many features of South African life: migratory labor, the state ban against mixed marriages, low black wages, the erosion of the rule of law, and more. That leading Afrikaner church leaders would sign such an indictment represented a complete reversal from the Kerk's long-standing endorsement of apartheid. They had apparently listened to their consciences and joined in the outburst of honesty.

The Afrikaner establishment started to counterattack immediately against this dangerous and unexpected heresy. Another dominee, Andries

Treurnicht, who would later lead the Conservative party, twisted the Bible further, producing a refurbished theological justification for apartheid. On a more mundane level, huge informal pressure was brought to bear within Afrikanerdom against the rebellious churchmen. Most of them recanted quickly, explaining that their aberrant stand had been due to the shock of the Sharpeville Massacre, where the police had killed sixty-nine black protesters; it had been much on their minds at Cottesloe.

Rev. Beyers Naudé ignored the pressures. He steadfastly refused to step back into line. He had to leave the Kerk, the Broederbond, official Afrikanerdom generally. He became ostracized to the extent that some members of his own family passed him on the street without speaking. His friend, the novelist Alan Paton, has written, "One is forced to conclude—because one does not reach such a conclusion lightly—that this is the work of the Holy Spirit and that Beyers Naudé was struck down on some Damascene road."

Beyers Naudé helped form a new ecumenical organization, the Christian Institute, which denounced apartheid as a "false gospel." Church and lay people of all colors worked together to elaborate a steadily more comprehensive condemnation of the system. This subversive activity brought the Institute in 1973 into the dock before the Schlebusch Commission, a special parliamentary witch-hunt agency. Beyers Naudé was called on to give testimony. He refused, and was convicted of contempt. Though he had steadily advocated nonviolence, the Commission somehow declared he "preached violence."

In 1977, as part of the nationwide crackdown after the death of Steve Biko, the government outlawed the Christian Institute and banned Beyers Naudé for five years. He was not surprised by the banning order. He had told a court years earlier, "In spite of the possibility that such a thing could happen, I am convinced that I should give my Christian witness in this country fearlessly and with love."

He who had been a persuasive public speaker was now silenced. He spent much of his time at home in Greenside, Johannesburg, counseling a steady stream of visitors, black and white, who visit him one by one. He is a warm man, with an inexhaustible inquisitiveness about everyone who passes his way. You drop by to ask him a few questions and find you have spent a half-hour talking about yourself. There is no bitterness about him. Even though he gets regular threatening telephone calls and abusive mail he cannot find it in himself to hate even people like the magistrate who refused to relax his ban to allow him to cross town to attend the funeral of his friend Frikkie Conradie.

Beyers Naudé and his wife attend one of the NG daughter churches nearby. His fellow parishioners are mostly black domestic servants who live and work in the neighborhood. He must be quite a sight as he worships there, a large, powerful man, six feet three inches tall, his hair slicked back in a conservative style, dressed in a safari suit like any other Afrikaner of his generation, standing among the housemaids.

The regime does not know how to deal with him. The cabinet itself discusses aspects of his fate, such as whether to grant him a passport for a single overseas trip (it refused), or whether to renew his banning order (it did at the end of 1982, for another three years). Such cabinet meetings must present a pathetic spectacle, as the group of petty, frightened, blustering men sit around discussing this Afrikaner Prometheus.

The Afrikaner people are entering the greatest crisis in their long historic saga. Their leaders, who claim to represent their best interests, are actually pursuing narrow, ruinous policies that could threaten their permanence in Africa. This is the final paradox. The Afrikaner establishment, as it leads the nation to war, vilifies its dissidents as renegades and traitors. But it is the rebels who recognize that the Afrikaner people can only survive, and flourish, in a nonracial, peaceful, and democratic South Africa. It is the dissidents who are genuinely loyal to Afrikanerdom. The Reverend Beyers Naudé by no means represents all, or even most Afrikaners. But he is certainly the leading custodian for what has over the years been the best in them.

6

Writers Under Apartheid

ONE OF MY FAVORITE PASTIMES during my years in southern Africa was to look through the *Rand Daily Mail* every Saturday morning to see what the regime's Publications Control Board had banned during the previous week. There are two broad, guiding principles that govern the censorship system: politics and puritanism. They provide some remarkable juxtapositions in the weekly banned list. Just after ominous-sounding political pamphlets by North Korean dictator Kim Il Sung will be something called *Cave Man's Sex*. Alongside obscure Trotskyist manifestos from Brazil, in Portuguese, will be various sex aids, primly described as "objects." "Calendars" from the Du Plessis Garage—Brakpan enjoy equivalent illegal status with the latest speech by President Oliver Tambo of the African National Congress.

The censors occasionally produce some amazing howlers. Some years back they briefly banned *Black Beauty,* evidently deciding from the title alone that it was politically or morally subversive. In December 1979, Tolstoy's *Anna Karenina* was also embargoed briefly. A Cape Town bookseller explained: "We can only assume that somebody with a gaping ignorance of literature decided on the basis of the title that, firstly it was Russian, and secondly, it was probably Marxist."

At least somewhat more explicable was the Control Board's decision in May 1980 to ban *The Wall,* a record album by the British rock group, Pink Floyd. The album's title song had become the theme of that year's nationwide black school boycotts. The operative lines, which compare education to thought control, had become, in the Board's view, "a threat to the safety of the state."

The comical features of the censorship system can obscure its overall effectiveness. Each year, the Board outlaws some twelve hundred publications. It says it is merely "declaring" the material "undesirable," but there is nothing mild and euphemistic about the fines and occasional prison terms for those caught with illegal books and pamphlets. Other legislation that governs the daily press is similarly restrictive. As the warfare in the region increases, South Africans are forced to cope with a constricting flow of information and an ever more narrow range of open political debate.

Daily newspapers are not subject to the scrutiny of the Publications Control Board. They instead belong to the Newspaper Press Union, a timid, self-regulatory agency the owners set up themselves in the early 1960s to preempt threatened government action. The dailies also are governed by more than one hundred pieces of restrictive legislation, including the notorious Prisons, Police, and Defense Acts, which effectively prohibit the publication of any news about those agencies without their prior approval. Exposés of prison conditions or of atrocities in the war zones are therefore impossible. Daily papers that too vigorously test the limits of the possible are banned outright, as occurred to the outspoken black *Soweto World* in 1977 and to its successor, *Post,* late in 1981. Individual journalists, particularly blacks, are also harassed, banned, and sometimes jailed.

One such victim was my friend Subry Govender, a self-taught Indian South African in his mid-thirties who had set up his own news agency in Durban. After ten years on daily newspapers there, he had established enough contacts among all the city's people that he could keep a stream of stories moving to the BBC, Radio Zimbabwe, and elsewhere.

The diminutive, stylish Govender, affectionately likened by close friends to a "Jack-in-the-box with a tie," was in perpetual motion between his telephone, his typewriter, and his telex machine, keeping his grandiloquently named Press Trust of South Africa in business. Toward the end of 1980, he confided to me that he was concerned about the upcoming Christmas holidays. News would drop off, and with it his income.

Govender was not entirely wrong. Christmas that year was a quiet holiday, with one noteworthy exception. The regime slapped Govender and another outstanding black journalist, Zwelakhe Sisulu of Johannesburg, with harsh banning orders. The two were house-arrested between 7:00 P.M. and 6:00 A.M. on weekdays, and continually over weekends.

They were prohibited from entering any newspaper office. They could not prepare any material for publication. Subry had no choice but to go back to selling insurance.

Despite the constant threats, certain newspapers have managed to remain independent of the regime, both in their selection of stories and on their editorial pages. These papers—the *Rand Daily Mail* is the best known—have long employed a number of brave, dedicated journalists. The government controls radio and television directly; announcers with sneering, clipped voices read their right-wing editorials with undertones of aggression and violence. The Afrikaans newspapers similarly echo the government line. But the regime has long been irritated by portions of the English and black press. It was annoyed to such an extent that in the late seventies it secretly funded a rival English paper, a nasty little tabloid called the *Citizen*, that advanced its right-wing views with editorials written in an odd sort of blank verse.

The regime's threats, together with the menace posed by the *Citizen*, induced the businessmen who own and manage the dissident papers to back down. Management complained that the *Mail*'s coverage of black affairs was driving away better-off white readers and reducing advertising revenues. (The paper's parent company was happily continuing to make money, arousing suspicion that the whining about finances was exaggerated.) In any case, the businessmen in 1981 fired Allister Sparks, the fairly outspoken editor, and replaced him with more conservative, pliable men, some of whom were rumored to have closer connections with the security police than might be warranted by the demands of newsgathering. The paper immediately became quieter and more frivolous.

What appeared initially as a contrary move toward greater freedom had been taking place at the Publications Control Board, which censors everything except the daily papers. In 1979, the influential head of the Appeal Board, a stodgy *verkrampte* (conservative, literally "narrow") judge named Lammie Snyman, retired. He was replaced by a younger professor, J. C. van Rooyen, and some startling changes started to take place.

The renowned novelist Nadine Gordimer had that year published her masterpiece, *Burger's Daughter*. It was promptly banned. Among other reasons, the book was said to be "offensive and harmful to public morals," and "prejudicial to the safety of the state." One anonymous member of the Publication Control Board's panel added gratuitously: "The book doesn't possess one particular positive quality—of creation, insight, style, language or composition—which can save it as a work of art." Meanwhile, overseas it was receiving one of the most glowing critical receptions of any novel in years—reviewers described it as "magnificent," "superb," and "perfect in all that it attempts."

Nadine Gordimer was enormously frustrated. *Burger's Daughter* had taken her four difficult years to write. She had poured her passion about South Africa into the book, controlled and shaped by an artistry she had honed to brilliance over six previous novels and dozens of short stories. She did know at least that the book would appear overseas. But she realized that only a handful of her fellow South Africans would be able to defy the law and acquire it. She is a fiery woman, who believes strongly that "literature belongs to everyone in the street; it has nothing to do with 'gentility,' with 'exalted feelings.' "

The Publications Act provides for an Appeal Board, before which anyone with a "financial interest" in a book can request a reappraisal. ("A financial interest," she sneered. "To them, principle doesn't count. Money is all that matters.") Still, she, or her publisher, could have appealed. She refused.

A majority of South Africa's leading writers have decided more or less collectively to refuse to participate in the censorship process, even by appealing against its verdicts. It is their view that the system is so unfair, so illegitimate, that they will not dignify it by recognizing its existence in any official way; they will rather continue to battle and discredit it from outside. Nadine Gordimer explained, "Until 1974, the Publications Act at least allowed appeals to be made in a court of law. But censorship is now entirely outside the legal system. The censorship panels are appointed by government. They meet secretly. No one can be sure of their composition. We have decided we will have nothing to do with this process."

A remarkable and unprecedented event then took place. Van Rooyen himself appealed against his own committee's decision. The appeal carried, and *Burger's Daughter* was again available in South Africa.

The same about-face took place later the same year with Afrikaner dissident André Brink's novel *A Dry White Season*. Brink had openly declared "guerrilla warfare" against the censorship system. He prepared for battle by setting up his own small publishing house with the overseas earnings from an earlier book. He finished *A Dry White Season* secretly and printed and mailed off two thousand copies in the week or so before the censors acquired and banned it. Brink also refused to challenge the ban; van Rooyen appealed in his stead, and the original judgment was reversed.

Neither Brink nor Nadine Gordimer were particularly happy over the surprising turn of events. Black writers continued to get their books banned for trivial reasons. *Murial at Metropolitan,* by the talented Miriam Tladi, was suppressed primarily because in one single instance an Afrikaans-speaking woman was described as a "lousy Boer." It is a common, rather mild epithet (which was used by a character who did not necessarily reflect Mrs. Tladi's own views), but the Control Board deemed it "harmful to the relations between sections of the inhabitants of the Republic."

The very same week that Brink's novel was unbanned, *Call Me Not a Man,* the collection of stories by my friend and guide to Soweto, Mtutuzeli Matshoba, was suppressed. The book had sold five thousand copies and gone into a second printing in the short two weeks between publication and banning. Mtutu, like Miriam Tladi, refused to appeal. "I was absolutely sick," André Brink told me afterward. "There is an obvious double standard."

An enraged Nadine Gordimer published a booklet, *"What Happened to Burger's Daughter,"* in which she wrote: "There is the unpleasant suggestion that those among us who are uncompromising opponents of censorship, with wide access to the media at home and abroad, can be bought off by special treatment accorded to our books. There is also a transparent attempt to divide the unity of black and white writers in this country, by favoring the white writers with such special treatment.

"I cannot be bought off and my full involvement in the struggle to abolish the Publications Act continues. As long as the Act is in force, the release of a single book, mine or anyone else's, is not yet a victory for the freedom to write."

Nadine Gordimer lives in a large, two-story home in Parktown, an old, genteel Johannesburg neighborhood. She is a small woman, deceptively fragile; she can be acid and biting in her judgments. During the couple of hours I spent at her home one wet spring afternoon, she got visibly angry several times as she talked about apartheid. In addition to her work, she is active as a patron of nonracial theatre projects and literary magazines. She and her husband, an elegant art dealer, are reliable fixtures at nearly every play and poetry reading, however obscure or experimental, that takes place in the Johannesburg area.

She seemed pleased at the worldwide acclaim for *Burger's Daughter,* which had put her on an even greater number of lists for the Nobel Prize in literature. The book is the story of Rosa Burger, the child of an Afrikaner doctor who is also a leader in the outlawed, underground Communist party. Lionel Burger is arrested, convicted of sabotage, and dies in prison. (He resembles Bram Fischer, an attorney from a prominent Afrikaner family. Fischer received a life sentence in 1966 at the age of 58. He died in 1975.) Burger's friends and associates expect Rosa to carry on in his image, but she resists. She questions some aspects of his beliefs, such as his allegiance, as a Communist, to the Soviet Union.

More important, she is searching for a way of life that does not seem to subordinate everything—human emotions, metaphysical yearnings—to the demands of the political struggle. She takes up briefly with Conrad, a cynical, uncommitted representative of the counterculture. She travels to Europe, falls in love with a Frenchman, and tries to see if she can achieve happiness in a private life. Eventually, after a harrowing telephone conversation with a young black man she had known as a child, she returns to South Africa and reenters the struggle, back in "a land where there are still heroes."

Rosa Burger's dilemma is obviously shared in some sense by a number of white South Africans—including Nadine Gordimer. The white radical community keeps its members under constant, at times oppressive scrutiny, to make sure they do not succumb to the temptations, material or otherwise, that are so readily available to white South Africans. The dilemma can be particularly acute for writers and artists, who work individually, in solitude, and yet seek to contribute toward a collective change. The demands of artistic integrity and social responsibility can seem to tug in opposite directions.

She told me about a recent poetry reading she had attended. "Two young black poets got up on stage and ranted and raved. It was not poetry; it was group shouting, the easy way out. I can't excuse it. Even if they are partisan, they've taken on this job: to write. The experience is here—they must translate it, distill it.

"I'm overcome with terrible reluctance to criticize them. I feel I'm letting the side down. And I know how dreadfully difficult their lives are. But it's for the sake of those who are suffering. After they finished, we all sat and applauded. We should *not* have applauded."

She had been leaning forward, speaking in a raised voice. She relaxed quickly. "If we look at what blacks are going through here now, it is a minor point. But there is this misunderstanding of terms like 'relevance' and 'commitment.' Anything that teaches people to know themselves better is relevant."

When I had first arrived at her home, she seemed somewhat distracted and distant. In part, she may have assumed I was just another foreigner on a three-week familiarization tour, enjoying the vicarious thrill of glimpsing apartheid. It became obvious as we continued talking that I was not a total newcomer in southern Africa. She started to speak with greater warmth. I mentioned how I had recently smuggled in a banned book for a black writer, someone we both knew, who had caressed the thin volume with something approaching reverence. She gave me a quick look of frank recognition. Apartheid, she said with abrupt intensity, could be summarized in a line from the South African novelist William Plomer's work *Turbott Wolfe*. It is, she said, "the sight of horror on the sun. In the reality of the awfulness that we live every day, there comes a point when the sun turns black.

"This simple realization started for me in my teens," she added cautiously, "but it is by no means finished. It is not pity, or empathy, but real horror."

She stopped for a moment. "It is a horror we feel more clearly here than people in Europe or America feel. And that is appropriate. But I wonder . . . in the United States—in Boston, in New York City—I met many people who were quite liberal, indignant at injustice, interested in social issues." She paused again, choosing her words. "These people, they have their homes in the city . . . and a little summer place in the country. Their young people live simply, but they still use the summer place. They don't see the contradiction. . . .

"I've found a sense of wonder in America at our situation here. They haven't had to put their lives on the line. In the antiwar movement there, it was a big deal to be arrested and spend a few days in jail. One had to be brought before a judge. Here, we have unlimited detention without trial. . . ." She stopped short, with a questioning look.

Modikwe Dikobe is a shy, gentle seventy-year-old black trade unionist, poet, and novelist. His personal odyssey is representative of the central experience of black South Africa in this century. He was born in 1913, the same year the white Parliament passed legislation sharply restricting the areas of the country in which blacks could own land. As intended, the Land Act forced them to migrate to the cities and the mines for work; among the uprooted were Dikobe's parents, who moved into the Johannesburg neighborhood of Doornfontein, which was already becoming an overcrowded slum.

He attended school for several years, then dropped out for lack of money. He hawked newspapers and furniture before becoming the vigorous secretary of the Shop and Office Workers Union, which was part of the South African Congress of Trade Unions. SACTU was and is allied with the African National Congress. Dikobe sometimes found the work exasperating: "Clerical workers can be difficult to organize. They are quite bourgeoisie-minded. They want their own wages raised, their own grievances attended to. They don't see that we must act together, for the good of all of us. They get impatient if nothing happens immediately." Throughout this period, he lived in a noisy, crowded single-sex hostel with the inappropriate name of Jabulani (Be Happy). He was forced to do his writing in the union office after hours.

The regime banned him in 1963 and closed down the union. He worked as a night watchman, and then as a clerk for the municipality. In 1977, he retired. He and his second wife Betty returned to the place of his birth, which is now part of the Bophutatswana Bantustan. "After all those years in the compounds, I wanted to have some country around me," he said. It was the first time in two decades of marriage that he and Betty were able to stay under the same roof for more than two consecutive weeks; she had lived in the servants' quarters of the Johannesburg home where she worked, while he stayed in the hostel. They scrape by on his thirty-five rand per month pension, the tiny income from his maize plot, and a trickle of royalties from his first book, *The Marabi Dance*.

The book is in many ways a social history in novel form, the chronicle of an energetic young black woman named Martha making her way through Johannesburg in the 1930s and '40s. The abrupt, bewildering change from rural to urban that people in many societies experience was aggravated by the increasingly repressive racial laws. Dikobe is often asked why he chose a woman as his protagonist, which is a somewhat unusual step for a male author. He gives various answers, but many have to do with the example of his first wife, whom he describes as a robust, intimidating woman. Martha and the other characters, who include a fraudulent preacher, bawdy women selling illegal home-brew liquor, gangsters, and jazz musicians, live in a harsh, confusing world, but they survive with a determined humor.

One of Modikwe Dikobe's own favorite stories from that era concerns his attempt to enlist in the South African Army at the start of World War II. He repeats the tale often, with the same air of bemused disbelief. "The government didn't allow we blacks to carry guns, but I didn't mind going as a laborer. I thought it would be a good chance to see some overseas countries. Just outside the recruiting office, a white policeman stopped me and asked for my pass. I couldn't believe it. I said to him, 'Look, man, I'm going in here to sign up and fight for the country.' He said he didn't care: *'Waar is die dompass?'* I showed it to him, disgusted, and then turned right around and walked away."

During 1980, Dikobe came down to Johannesburg regularly, to help make a historical documentary film. I drove him back to his rural home after one of his visits. He spent the first part of the trip reading to me from a *Star* and commenting. As we passed to the east of Pretoria, visible and faintly foreboding, protected by dun-colored hills, he muttered about the "sell-outs," "puppets," and "bourgeoisie-minded" blacks who run the Bantustans. He said that he was monitoring their machinations in Bophutatswana and he planned to go public with his findings. (He did later publish a piece in the magazine *Frontline*.) He turned back to the newspaper and noticed a small item: a black trade union had won a recognition agreement. "You see," he said happily, "our struggle was not in vain. The movement will just keep growing, little bit, little bit, little bit. . . ."

We stopped off at a small bottle store near the town of Settlers. Petty apartheid in such circumstances can sometimes be ludicrously funny. The front of the store was perhaps twenty feet across, but it nevertheless had separate entrances for Africans and Europeans. Inside, I peered around the partition that divided the two sections and saw Dikobe leaning against the counter with a look of wry forbearance on his face as he waited for the white woman to serve me first. Outside he told me, "I argued with her. I said, 'Look, my white friend and I are travelling together so nicely and now we are faced with this nonsense.' She smiled and said she was sorry, but it was the law. But she could see from my clothing that I was from the city—she wouldn't have treated me so politely if I came from around here."

The paved road naturally ended almost precisely at the "border" of the Bantustan, and we navigated along a treacherous, sandy track. To each side were small, sickly plots of maize; only a few miles back, in the "white" farming area, the fields had stretched right toward the horizon. We arrived at his modest, tidy white house, to see Betty standing in the doorway smiling. Before we went inside, he invited me to help myself from his orange tree. As I bashed inexpertly at the fruit with a rake, he chuckled happily and said: "You're just like me: a petit-bourgeois urban intellectual."

Inside, Betty served us tea and then beer on a table covered with a flowered cloth. A small bookshelf was in one corner. On the wall was a photograph of Dikobe from twenty years earlier; he then looked a firm, determined man of substance. He is much frailer now, due to age and the after-effects of a vicious attack of Soweto tsotsis, who left him for dead.

He had just completed *Martha,* a sequel to *The Marabi Dance,* which takes the story up to the 1970s. He was working on his autobiography. "I can't stop now," he said. "I've got maybe ten years ahead of me. I'll keep on reading and writing as long as I can still see. I've experienced things in my life, and I just have to put them down on paper. Sometimes, I get up in the middle of the night to write something. The story must be told."

Ezekiel Mphahlele, now in his early sixties, has also taken an odyssey, one even more distant than Dikobe's. Mphahlele was part of the first boom in black writing in the early fifties. He contributed frequently to an effervescent black magazine called *Drum*. Toward the end of the decade, he went into exile, along with many others of his literary generation. "I wanted to be free of the bludgeoning effect life here has on one," he told me. "I wanted to see things at a distance."

Exile was not kind to black South African writers. Can Themba, a legendary carouser who wrote moving, bittersweet short stories, drank himself to death in nearby Swaziland. Nat Nakasa, the brilliant twenty-eight-year-old who had been selected as the first black South African to be a Nieman Fellow at Harvard, jumped from the window of a New York City hotel. Mphahlele (pronounced M-pa-*hlay*-lay) also suffered an exile that was often lonely and disjointed. But he survived. He taught all over Africa and in the United States. He wrote more fiction. He became a prominent critic of black literature, both African and American. He was appointed a professor at the University of Pennsylvania.

In 1977, he gave it all up and returned to an uncertain future in South Africa. "Nothing has changed for the better," he said, answering my obvious question. "Soweto—where I had lived before—is bigger, slummier, and more violent. People are less friendly. It's not the passive coldness of the white suburbs, but an aggressiveness, a terrifying kind of hostility. In political meetings, the rhetoric is much sharper than in the fifties. There is more nervousness caused by the greater stringency of the laws. There is a frenzy now.

"Nevertheless, I'm glad to be back."

A major factor in Mphahlele's return was his passion for teaching. As he explained in his touching, beautifully written autobiography, *Down Second Avenue*, he regarded himself as a teacher foremost and only gave writing his full attention after the regime blacklisted him for his opposition to the introduction of Bantu Education. Even today, with several books to his credit, he still rates teaching and writing as equally important. He seems typecast for the part: bespectacled, soft-spoken, painstakingly precise. In the African Studies program at the University of Witwatersrand, in seminars he arranges himself, and in a column in *Staffrider* magazine, he ministers patiently to the needs of younger writers. He is just about their only link to their literary past.

Mphahlele had a number of difficulties readjusting to South Africa after his twenty-year absence. He was technically an immigrant, and he spent long hours getting his documents in order. But perhaps his greatest frustration was that his books were largely unavailable. Some of them were banned. But others, including *Down Second Avenue*, could have been sold legally. He was reluctant to place blame, but he did suggest bookstore owners were being overly timid about stocking his books. "It's like standing on a beach trying to shout to people across the water,'' he said. ''There are atmospheric disturbances. A few words get over but the message is garbled. I can't reach them.''

By the early eighties, Mphahlele's frustration was somewhat alleviated. His books finally started to become available. His autobiography, a compelling narrative of the first part of his long trek from rural herdboy to distinguished professor, now circulated in the land of his birth, twenty years after he had written it.

André Brink and his fellow members of the Afrikaans Writers Guild had approached the Publications Appeal Board on behalf of another of Mphahlele's books, a biting work of criticism called *African Image*. (The Board inexplicably allowed their appeal even though they lacked the requisite ''financial interest.'') They won a partial victory. The book's first edition was unbanned. Unfortunately, the first edition was out of print.

Afrikaners rallying to support a black writer is no longer a flustering notion. Brink is one of the prominent members of a group of dissident Afrikaners called the *Sestigers* (literally, the Sixty-ers), named for the decade in which they emerged. He writes his novels in both Afrikaans and English, translating back and forth as he goes through drafts and then publishing a final version in each language simultaneously. He and his fellow Sestigers are bitter opponents of apartheid, and the regime has turned on them with a special rage it reserves for apostates.

Brink was haunted by the tragedy of his closest friend, the intense, bearded Sestiger poet named Breyten Breytenbach, who was sentenced to nine years in prison for ''terrorism.'' The two had met in Paris in 1963, as footloose young men exploring the world. ''We became so close,'' Brink told me in late 1980. ''We communicated intensely, shared our feelings. Even now, they haven't allowed me to visit him in prison, but I still have the feeling of being in touch all the time.''

Breytenbach had married a Vietnamese woman in France, but was prevented by South Africa's Immorality Act from returning home to live with her. Nevertheless, in 1975, he came back—disguised, with false documents—and travelled about the country attempting to establish a white underground. The secret police, who had been tipped off, arrested him just as he was about to board the plane back to Europe. The regime offered him a deal: if he pleaded guilty, it would give him the minimum five-year sentence and drop charges against five other accused people. It did let the five off, but sentenced him to nine years.

In 1880, Paul Kruger, a leader of one of the Boer republics, had made an impassioned plea for independence from the advancing British colonialism. Breytenbach, with a fine sense of history, had echoed Kruger's words in the courtroom nearly a century later. "With confidence we lay our case before the whole world," Breytenbach said. "Whether we win, whether we die, freedom will rise in Africa like the sun through the morning clouds."

Brink, who had already published five books, channelled his fury at his friend's sentence into three more powerful novels: *An Instant in the Wind, Rumors of Rain,* and *A Dry White Season.* He somehow found time to write them while simultaneously holding a full-time professorship in Afrikaans language and literature at Rhodes University. *A Dry White Season* was clearly influenced by the 1977 murder of black leader Steve Biko. In the book, an apolitical but honest Afrikaner high school teacher, Ben du Toit, is shocked when two blacks, the school custodian and his son, die mysteriously after the security police take them away for questioning. Du Toit hesitantly begins his own investigation. He immediately attracts the hostile attention of the police. They warn him but he perseveres, increasingly determined. The police then threaten him, intercept his mail, search his home, shadow him, and get him fired from his job.

"Everything that happened to Ben has happened to me," Brink said. "Except that the university stood firm against their efforts to get me sacked."

Rhodes University is in Grahamstown, a charming little place near the southern coast. It resembles a Midwest American college town, sleepy and remote. But it is not aloof from the tension of South African society. Several people had died out in its black township in the disturbances that were part of the 1980 nationwide wave of unrest. The security police that year had arrested a black journalism student for possessing literature from the outlawed African National Congress. The week I arrived to visit Brink, the student was sentenced to eight years in prison.

In person, André Brink is tall and lanky. He hunches over, perhaps to avoid intimidating people with his height. He is an open and very likable man.

He was born in the northern Free State, where his father was a magistrate. The family moved frequently and he has lived in small towns all over the Republic. "I was in my third year at Potchefstroom University before I used a lift for the first time," he laughed.

"I had a very traditional, conservative, Christian, Afrikaner upbringing. I occasionally felt qualms of uneasiness, that the blacks were not getting a fair deal. But you must remember: I had never been exposed to blacks outside the master and servant relationship.

"Then, in 1959 I went to Paris to study comparative literature. It was a shattering experience. To give you one example, I actually found myself eating with blacks. At first, this was a terrible experience to someone from my background.

"People still go through this process of awakening. I get a lot of feedback from my work in the form of letters. Some are from young Afrikaner students who write, 'Your books have shown me for the first time in my life that a black person is a human being.' This is terribly, terribly sad, but it is an accurate indication of our reality here.

"Looking ahead, it's hard to conceive of a future without some sort of cataclysm in South Africa. Maybe the real question now is: How much will it be eased, or will it be total violence? In a way, that's my justification for writing: to ease the cataclysm.

"I can completely understand the violent efforts to overthrow the apartheid system. But being a writer means one rejects violence. It is a denial of human dignity. It kills the victim and the perpetrator alike. I'm still writing to try to get through to the human being.

"But I must say, I'm speaking from a white, privileged point of view. If I were a black I might have even less patience."

In late 1982, the South African regime unexpectedly released Brink's friend Breyten Breytenbach, two years before the completion of his sentence. There was said to have been strong pressure from the Socialist government in France. Breytenbach, looking tired and gaunt, flew off to Paris. André Brink, in the short two years since I had visited him, had already completed another novel.

One outstanding feature of André Brink's novels is his keen eye for the language and culture of all South Africans; his respectful and detailed descriptions of black life are the more remarkable in a country where most whites have never been to Soweto a single time. These appreciative insights into other cultures are characteristic of other writers as well. Nadine Gordimer has an amazing ear for Afrikaans dialogue or the sometimes subtle differences in black politics. Black writers also treat whites with understanding, as in my friend Mtutuzeli Matshoba's sensitive story about a lonely young Afrikaner with confused racial attitudes who breaks the Immorality Act.

As a group, South African writers are an exception to the separation that prevails in their country. Although, paradoxically, they spend long hours alone, they are in alliance with each other and collectively more in touch with their fantastically varied country than almost any other group of people. As André Brink explained, "Writers understand the common

humanity here.'' Their efforts will probably not avoid Brink's cataclysm, though they will certainly help to ease it. But their persistent,
collective effort to understand their country and communicate with their
people will be one departure point for any eventual national reconciliation.

7

Sports: The Kaizer Chiefs

THE SPORTING PREFERENCES of South Africa's various ethnic groups seem almost the creation of a mischievous stereotypist, designed to reinforce the prevalent group images. Afrikaners are, or try to be, gigantic, burly, powerful men, who prize strength over subtlety and finesse. Their favorite sport is therefore appropriately rugby, which is basically American football without the forward pass, a rugged ground game played without helmets or other protective equipment. English-speaking whites, who regard themselves as a more refined, diffident lot, prefer cricket, a leisurely gentleman's sport that lasts for days and in which form can be as important as the final result. Black South Africans are fanatics about soccer. Their preference is partly shaped by circumstance, as soccer is the least expensive team sport in terms of equipment or facilities. Also, though, the sport's grace and speed, its blend of individual panache and carefully orchestrated teamwork, has a certain resonance with the life experiences of blacks, particularly in urban areas.

All kinds of South Africans have a phenomenal passion for sports. Among whites the remarkable amount of energy they devote to playing, watching, and discussing sports is partly the simple consequence of ample leisure time in a near-perfect climate. But also, the widespread white participation in sports must have some compensatory association with their lack of gainful physical exercise. Their vigor on the rugby field is partly a way of asserting the physicalness they are not called upon to display during the work week, to demonstrate the strength it is nearly taboo to utilize at any other time.

Until very recently, sports in South Africa were rigidly segregated from the professional down through the school level. No teams could be mixed; all-black teams could not play all-white teams; even individuals, whether boxers or tennis players, could not compete. South Africa repeatedly sent totally white teams to represent the entire country in the Olympics and other international competitions. As protests against this clear violation of the Olympic charter mounted both inside and outside the country, the white sporting authorities promised change. In 1964, they told a black weightlifter with the improbable name of Precious MacKenzie they would allow him to join the team for the Tokyo Olympics if he won the trials. He did qualify, but they went back on their promise. MacKenzie emigrated to England, and later won an Olympic medal for his adopted country. Another black man, cricketer Basil D'Oliveira, also had to choose exile in Britain in order to play internationally.

The South Africa regime even went to the unbelievable extent of dictating to foreign teams who they could bring on competitive tours. New Zealand's national rugby squad, known as the All Blacks due to the color of their uniforms, have historically often included Maoris, New Zealanders of Polynesian descent. In 1965, Prime Minister Hendrik Verwoerd announced in a major speech that New Zealand could not include Maoris in the team scheduled to tour South Africa later that year. One newspaper headlined: "No Black All-Blacks." But there was nothing comical about how the New Zealand rugby generalissimos meekly agreed to bring only white players.

Such outrages naturally generated increasing opposition. The courageous black poet Dennis Brutus was among the leading activists who lobbied with increasing vigor for South Africa's expulsion from world sporting organizations. Brutus was arrested, shot while trying to escape, jailed on Robben Island, and then exiled, but his campaign did not stop. South Africa was expelled from the Olympics and from the world federations in rugby, cricket, soccer, and other sports. Brutus and a young white exile in Britain named Peter Hain, who had led huge demonstrations against a South African rugby tour there, were at one time the most hated men in white South Africa. Blacks, on the other hand, were ecstatic. During the visits by teams from overseas, they had habitually crowded into their sections in the segregated grandstands—and cheered loudly for South Africa's opponents.

The regime's ideologists soon had the white sports-mad populace snapping at their heels. They hurried to concoct some formula that would not violate the doctrine of apartheid but that would allow some interracial sport in order to bolster their pleas for readmission to international competition. They tried something they called multinational sport—under certain circumstances, blacks could constitute teams from different "nations," which then could compete against an all-white "South Africa." The ruse failed to end the country's sporting isolation. The regime then had to tacitly allow the evolution of a more genuine form of integration, which is still hedged in with encumbrances and limited to the highest and most conspicuous professional levels.

Desegregation has proceeded the furthest in soccer. In the mid-'70s, teams from the separate black and white leagues started to play each other in exhibition matches. In 1978, they merged to form the National Professional Soccer League. At first, the teams in the new circuit remained either totally black or white. Gradually, though, player trades have brought about some integration. Teams have tended to retain their original character, but with additional players from the "other" race.

The three most popular black teams are the Kaizer Chiefs, Orlando Pirates, and Moroka Swallows. The Chiefs, also known by their Zulu name, Amakhosi, probably enjoy the edge. All are based in Soweto, but all have legions of followers nationwide. Early in the 1979 season, the Chiefs took a momentous step. They acquired their first white player, an accomplished veteran midfielder named Lucky Stylianou. Instantly, the twenty-eight-year-old Stylianou, by virtue of joining the Chiefs, became one of the best-known whites in black South Africa, with a name recognition literally on a par with the prime minister and other leading political figures.

The Chiefs have established a network of support clubs across the country, in even the most remote hamlets. The network has more than two million signed-up members, making it probably the largest voluntary association in South Africa. Whenever the team plays, thousands upon thousands of radios are tuned in from Cape Town to the Limpopo. Lucky Stylianou came under intense scrutiny from this exacting multitude, which frowned as he made a few mistakes in his first games in the black-and-gold uniform. Then, he scored two goals in a key match—and won instant acceptance. "Black people greet me everywhere," he said when I first met him. "Waiters. Petrol station attendants. Watchmen. Chiefs supporters are fanatically loyal."

The Chiefs play a gruelling regular schedule that can last ten months or more. In addition, the team makes regular barnstorming trips to distant areas to play exhibition games for the benefit of its widely deployed army of supporters. Lucky had been amazed at the enthusiastic turnout at one of his first such "friendlies," held in the northern Transvaal. "The places around there are like old Greek villages with donkeys and stuff—

very poor. Those people had waited twelve months to see Chiefs. It's like Christmas to them. They put on black-and-gold clothing and came a couple of hundred kilometers to the match. We had a crowd of forty thousand. For a friendly.

"It touches you off. You're playing for the people. If you have a bad game, you're letting down millions. Well, we won. They carried us off the pitch on their shoulders after the match. One guy came up to me and dumped all the change he had into my hands. I tried to give it back to him. But then I saw it was better to keep it."

Stylianou, the son of Greek immigrants, is a personable, articulate man who was bemused and excited by his unexpected path-breaking role. He had already been a pro for ten years, including stints in both Britain and South America. He claimed soccer was more popular in South Africa than in the other two areas, neither of which is known for its indifference to the sport. To illustrate his contention, he described another recent away game at Witbank, the "Coal City" on the East Rand: "We were safely ahead toward the end, so the victory celebration started early. Thousands of women dressed in the black-and-gold snake-danced onto the field, singing hymns. No one gets treatment like that overseas, no one. It was like we had just won a war or something."

Stylianou had joined a team that had won its huge national following in only ten short years. In the late 1960s, Kaizer Motaung, a star with the Orlando Pirates, a Soweto institution nearly as old as the township itself, became embroiled in a dispute with the club's management. He, along with allies like the irrepressible Ewert "The Lip" Nene, broke away to form the new team, which he named after himself.

After this earthquake struck, households across the nation divided. Younger people, the mellow "cats" and "hippies," tended to go with the newer team, which adopted the *V* peace symbol as its talisman. The Pirates and Swallows retained their hold on older people, traditionalists, many of whom still regard Motaung's move as consummate treachery and cannot utter his name without tones of pained resentment. The Pirate symbol is an aggressive crossed arms in front of the chest, meant to stand for the Buccaneer crossbones.

Motaung and his energetic high command scoured the townships and rural areas for talent, and came up with winners. Up front, the Chiefs boasted the agile, gentlemanly Abednigo "Shaka" Ngcobo. His nickname, that of the famous Zulu warrior-king of the early nineteenth century, was conferred on him in his youth as a tribute to his courage in leaping against taller, rougher opponents for "headers"—high balls a player tries to control with his head. Through the early eighties, he was supplemented on the offensive front line with other nimble strikers including skinny, lithe Nelson "Teen Age" Dladla, and Leonard "Wagga Wagga" Likoebe, a stumpy little fireplug of a man who moved about the goal mouth with surprising grace. Younger sharpshooters included Marks "Pro" Maponyane, a prodigy who was still in high school, and Zebulon "Sputla" Nhlapo—his monicker, which refers to a type of hard liquor, was an exaggerated allusion to his purportedly freewheeling lifestyle off the field. Another striker with the club for a time was called Zachariah "Computer" Lamola. Computers are not household objects in the electricity-less townships, but people do know they function at impressive speed—much as Lamola used to dribble the soccer ball up the field, darting around and through defenders.

Just behind the front line was the domain of the Chief field general and playmaker, Patrick "Ace" Ntsoelengoe. Ace—his last name is pronounced Nt-sway-*leng*-way—always took off part of the season to play in the more lucrative North American league. Other midfielders included Sylvester "City" Kole, Jan "Malombo" Lechaba, and Stylianou. Later, other whites joined the team, among them the merry veteran Frank "Jingles" Pereira, who helped captain Johannes "Ryder" Mofokeng back in defense, and Pete Bala'c, who ultimately replaced the legendary but aging Joseph "Banks" Sethlodi as the goalkeeper.

Lucky Stylianou had entered a new world. He told me how he and coach Eddie Lewis, then still the only other white associated with the club, had attended the victory party after a 1980 win over the Witbank Black Aces. "The party was out in the township, at the house of one of the members of our local supporters club. I wish whites could see how black people are forced to live in those places. They squeezed about forty people into one of those tiny houses. Another five hundred were outside, singing and dancing.

"They served us mielie meal. I was already used to the stuff. But Eddie Lewis wouldn't eat it. I looked at him out of the corner of my eye. Finally, he started eating, but with a long face." Lucky shrugged. "Give him time."

Lucky Stylianou had grown so immersed and enchanted with his new world that he was eager to explain, and, if necessary, defend, its customs to outsiders. One such tradition is the use of witch doctors to improve the team's prospects. The Chiefs had just put a man from far-off White River on retainer when Lucky joined the team. "He took us through a whole ceremony the night before the game. First, he burned something to drive away the evil spirits, and we all had to step over the burning coals. Then, he had us come back early, early, early the next morning. He had killed a lamb. We bathed in the blood as the sun rose."

Lucky paused, with a slightly defensive air, to make sure I was taking him seriously. "All our guys are well educated. Most of them have passed matric. They don't believe in this *muti*. But after we got that witch doctor, we went fourteen straight without losing. How d'you figure it? Or say a guy's hurt. He goes to physiotherapists, guys who've been through varsity. Nothing happens. Then he tries the witch doctor. He gets cured. I've seen it."

The Chief shaman, lured possibly by a better offer, jumped to the Orlando Pirates the following season—and the slumping Buccaneers started, indisputably, to improve. "He's gotten death threats from Chief supporters," Lucky said, laughing.

In 1979, Lucky's first year with the Chiefs, the team achieved the coveted "double"—finishing first in the league standings and also winning the trophy in the knockout Mainstay Cup. In 1980, the Chiefs slipped to also-rans in both competitions, sending ripples of horror across the subcontinent and causing coaching and player changes. The shame was compounded by an enterprising British film crew, who captured the thrilling Swallow victory in the Mainstay semifinal. Chief fans died inwardly as they trooped into the theaters to see their heroes humbled.

In 1981, the Amakhosi had better fortune. They had sputtered along in second place through the forty-two game season, trailing Highlands Park, a methodical, mostly white team from Johannesburg's northern suburbs. The Chiefs had doggedly kept pace, but Highlands's stolid defensive style of soccer looked impregnable. In the season's last weekend, though, Highlands inexplicably dropped a match to middling Durban City, only their second loss of the year. The Chiefs roared past, beating the Swallows to win the league crown by a single point.

The Chiefs also forged ahead in the simultaneous contest for the Mainstay Cup. Hundreds of teams from all over South Africa, including amateurs, entered the knockout competition. Months later, at the end of November, only two remained: the Chiefs and the Pirates. The classic matchup monopolized attention among blacks across the nation. In shebeens, on buses, and in homes, politics and other topics were forgotten in the heated exchanges about the Cup Final.

The consensus heavily favored the Chiefs. They had just crushed the Pirates decisively in the last league match between the two clubs. Even hard-core Pirate stalwarts like one Robert Sandile Mbatha were evidently moved by the spirit of fairness to make their feelings public. "Through the medium of our paper, the *Sowetan*," Mbatha wrote in the letters column, "I would like to congratulate those gladiators, Kaizer Chiefs, for a five-star performance they gave against my favorite club, Orlando Pirates." But Mbatha's touching generosity of spirit disturbed neither his faith nor his loyalty. He went on: "To Orlando Pirates fans especially, I say don't give up. Have hope, as we still have to defend the Mainstay Trophy."

The Pirates definitely could not be counted out. Their inscrutable, crafty goalkeeper, Patson "Kamuzu" Banda, was always at his best in the big games. Even more important, Ephraim "Jomo" Sono, their superstar goalscorer, had apparently recovered from an injury. Two years earlier, I had watched Sono completely befuddle the Highlands Park goalkeeper with some spectacular acrobatics. He had leaped up, with his back to the goal mouth, to bounce a lateral pass from a winger off his chest. He spun gracefully in the air as the ball hovered, now in front of him. He feinted a shot with his right foot, pulling the keeper to one side. Then, still airborne, he rocketed a shot with his *other* foot to the *other* side of the net, which was now completely unprotected. The crowd, overwhelmingly partisan for the Pirates, gasped in unison for several seconds before bursting into cheering. Here and there in the grandstands, disbelieving fans tried to simulate Sono's aerial maneuvering.

The Chiefs gathered as usual in the Devonshire Hotel in Joburg the night before the big match. First on their agenda was a session with their latest witch doctor, a woman who flew up from Durban for every game. "Think of the expense," Lucky chuckled. "But we keep on winning."

The woman washed the Chiefs' black-and-gold game uniforms in special potent solutions to rinse out the evil spirits. She sprinkled other potions into their soccer boots. Each Chief then bundled himself into a blanket and sat near a boiling pot, bathing in the steamy medicinal vapors. Meanwhile, team agents were heading through the night to Orlando stadium, where they would doctor the field itself. They planned to gain entry either by climbing the walls, or by prior, probably paid arrangement with confederates on the stadium's security staff. Pirate henchmen would also be treating the pitch, Lucky said. (On one occasion, a team in neighboring Swaziland rode onto the field on bicycles at the start of a match, determined to avoid touching the muti they were certain had been sprinkled around its perimeter.)

Much less humorous, he continued, is the poor condition of the stadium itself. In several instances, white municipal authorities had banned mixed soccer from the large comfortable stadiums, forcing the NPSL to play in ramshackle, inferior facilities out in the townships. "The NPSL draws four million spectators to matches. Football is the number-one sport in this country. But we get nothing."

He was getting worked up. "I've always been liberal. But since I've joined the Chiefs, I'm even more so. In some ways, I'm now in the position of the black man. I also have to stay in quarter-star hotels when we play away. I get stopped in Soweto by police demanding my permit. I've seen the terrible slums, the tin shanties. True, I've seen the same things when I played in Brazil. But this country could afford to do something. Why must all the whites have three cars, three servants, three-hundred-thousand-rand homes?''

At noon the next day, the Chiefs started for the stadium, wedged into two large *kombis,* or vans. One was driven by the white goalkeeper Pete Bala'c. He was already tensed up. "They insist I drive," he explained. "We're undefeated since I started driving to the stadium."

In town, only a few clusters of white people were left from the Saturday morning shopping crowds. In general, whites were oblivious to the big match, aside from a vague perception that black people were excited about something. They stared quizzically as the Chiefs, slick in their blue-and-white warmup suits, flashed by. The two kombis moved through the rundown Diagonal Street area and then into the no-man's-land between Joburg and Soweto.

Pete Bala'c was visibly nervous. "Banks" Sethlodi, the star Bala'c had succeeded in the nets who was now an assistant coach, sensed his mood from the rear of the vehicle. "I feel it," Banks said loudly. "Bala'c's going to get a goal himself today. That's every keeper's dream." Bala'c grinned thankfully as he peered ahead at the traffic. A wordless message had passed between the two men. Only they knew the lonely feeling of standing in front of fifty thousand people, the last barrier between a Jomo Sono and a mark on the scoreboard.

Jingles Pereira, the white defenseman who was coming to the end of his fourteen-year career, turned to Banks and said: "Man, a keeper did score. Back in '71." The two veterans, who had then played in the segregated leagues, started to reminisce happily. Each had obviously felt a keen interest in the other's exploits.

Once in Soweto, bystanders started to recognize the Chiefs with car horns and excited waves. All the overpasses had been spray-painted with slogans like: "Up Chiefs," or "Bucs Will Win."

As the vehicles neared the stadium, one of the trainers started to lead the team in singing a spiritual in Zulu. The low rumbling voices of the men echoed in mournful contrast to the festival air outside. The miniscule parking area was already overflowing with buses and cars, some of which had license plates from Pretoria, Durban, and even farther. There was a huge crush at the gates, even though game time was more than two hours away. The Chiefs were ushered through quickly. As always, they were escorted by an army of worshipping acolytes, small boys with shining eyes who jostled each other to carry the equipment bags of their heroes.

In the dilapidated, cramped dressing room, the trainers started bandaging the wounded. The expectant roar of the crowd sounded louder every time the door swung open briefly. Liniment, sweat, and nervousness were in the air. Bala'c tried to find enough room for some limbering-up exercises. He said quietly, "Once you get out there, you don't notice the tension. It's getting there that's the problem."

Ace Ntsoelengoe, the superstar, sat to one side, completely impassive. He nibbled slowly at an orange. Teen-Age Dladla, loose and relaxed, skipped about, keeping a practice ball spinning in the air by using only his head. Jingles Pereira stalked back and forth, joking that he had to make his unruly hair more presentable for the television cameras. He was handed, to some merriment, an Afro comb. Outside, the noise from the crowd rose.

The team grouped together for a prayer, led by their soft-spoken novice coach, Elkim "Pro" Khumalo. The black Chiefs closed their eyes and tilted back their heads as the coach spoke; the white Chiefs bowed theirs.

The team jogged up the passageway, to an immediate baying of boos from Pirates fans on the same side of the field. Their own supporters, across the way, riposted immediately with an explosion of cheering. The stadium, a drab, rickety structure equivalent to a Class C ballpark in America, somehow contained sixty thousand spectators, nearly twice its capacity; a further twenty thousand had been turned away at the gates. Almost all were black. Fans perched precariously everywhere, even atop the scoreboard. Behind them, rows of Soweto matchboxes stretched toward the treeless horizon. The Chiefs crossed over to their side of the field. A row of men in wheelchairs were lined up close to the sidelines, with expressions of complete, utter happiness.

I positioned myself on the edge of the pitch, between Lucky Stylianou, who was not playing due to injury, and a large arch-Chief fanatic, who was dressed in a home-sewn flowing black-and-gold robe. This hearty fellow reinforced his cheering during the game by thumping everyone within reach.

The game started. The dreaded Jomo Sono showed at once his ankle had fully mended. As the Pirate fans across the way roared with mounting approval, a blur of black-and-white Buc jerseys, with Sono somewhere in the middle, streaked up the field, passing back and forth effortlessly. Twenty meters out, one of them unleashed a scorching shot. Pete Bala'c leaped, twisted . . . and gathered the ball in firmly. There was loud, reassured cheering from the Chiefs fans. Their goalkeeper, a popular player, was very definitely on form.

Off the field, two white police officers led a dozen black constables over to guard a potential breach in one of the stadium gates. But the blacks lingered, hypnotized by the action on the field, and simply sat down to watch. The whites good-naturedly reminded them they had work to do. Later, the white officers also would become so engrossed in the match as to also be derelict in their duty.

The game continued scoreless until halftime, with the Pirates continuing to have the edge. The teams trooped off to their dressing rooms for a welcome rest, while hundreds of small boys swarmed onto the field to kick around soccer balls, imitating the parries and thrusts of their idols. Up in the grandstands, the Chief multitudes sang the rhythmic old Xhosa work song, "Shosholoza"—the lyrics and tempo are evocative of a pick-and-shovel crew. The bulky arch-fan next to me muttered darkly about a lack of tenacity in the Chief defense.

The Chiefs struck early in the second half. Nick "Yster" Sikwane—his nickname means "Iron"—passed up to one of the midfielders, who just as rapidly rocketed the ball forward to Teen-Age on the left side. He and Marks Maponyane, the high schooler, exchanged glances and set to work, sprinting in parallel lines ten feet apart. One defender stood between them and the goal mouth.

The two young Chiefs passed back and forth smartly, tying the hapless Pirate in an ungainly knot. Teen-Age, again with the ball, now faced the cunning Pirate keeper Banda one-on-one. He faked a medium shot, drawing Banda out, and then lazily lofted the ball right over the keeper's head—and into the net.

Absolute complete pandemonium broke out on the Chief side of the stadium. Tens of thousands leaped to their feet, screaming with joy. The tubby man next to me did an impromptu dance along the sideline, kicking euphorically at imaginary soccer balls.

Suddenly, the Pirates pulled themselves together. Sono and his henchmen started moving almost at will along the left side. Pete Bala'c made a couple of fine saves, but the Bucs returned to the attack almost immediately. Finally, Jerry Sadike looped a sizzler from fifteen meters out. Pete dived to his left, but not far enough. The ball hit the far goalpost and bounced in.

The deafening roar from the other side contrasted with total, stunned silence in the Chief precincts. The realization set in instantly, with a shared horror: the Pirates could win. If Sono kept penetrating along that vulnerable left side, he was going to score eventually. My portly neighbor grumbled, "Some of our boys are off form." Lucky Stylianou whispered: "Let's hope the crowd doesn't start booing our players. It affects some of them—they pass off when they should keep the ball."

But the Chief defense tightened, and the game ended in a deadlock. The crowd poured onto the field at the end of play, just as the first raindrops fell from the early summer thunderstorm that had been gathering all afternoon. The mood was mixed. Chief partisans were disappointed; my robed associate disappeared, muttering and looking downcast. But the Pirate fans regarded the draw against their favored opponents as some sort of moral victory.

Inside the Chiefs' shabby dressing room, there was somber relief. Kaizer Motaung voiced the widespread feeling: "We were lucky. We deserved to lose." Jingles Pereira, sporting a magnificent black eye, chuckled as he explained that Pirate Oscar "Jazzman" Dlamini had surreptitiously slugged him when they were both sprawled out after a collision. He added, with no animosity and some admiration, "He got away with it. He had a good game." Jingles seemed to hint, though, that he was going to prepare some surprises for the pugnacious Jazzman in the replay.

In the spirited postmortems the following week across southern Africa, two points stood out. Chief star Ace Ntsoelengoe had been bottled up, while Jomo Sono had the run of the field. And the youthful Chief strikers had been rattled somewhat by the combination of big-game tension and rough Buccaneer play.

There was little the Chief high command could do about the first problem, other than to gently encourage their superstar. But a few changes in their starting lineup could restore a little experience up front.

The replay a week later attracted another huge crowd. The new Chief strategy paid off immediately. Within minutes, the veteran Wagga Wagga Likoebe, apparently impervious to pressure, shot through the Buccaneer defense. He passed off to Jan "Malombo" Lechaba, who headed the ball home. Jomo Sono equalized for Pirates early in the second half, but then Ace Ntsoelengoe, completely back on form, headed in a picturebook goal. Another veteran, Shaka Ngcobo, teamed up with Wagga Wagga to put the game on ice, 3–1. Once again, the Chiefs had won the double.

In part the love affair black South Africans have with soccer has the same explanation as sports ardor anywhere in the world: fans have warm feelings of admiration for their idols and enjoy the vicarious thrill of escaping, however fleetingly, from their humdrum existences by watching or listening to the heroes drub the enemy. Black passion for soccer is not restricted to men; many women are knowledgeable fans. Quite a few domestic servants, for instance, have team pictures of the Chiefs, Bucs, or Birds taped up in their "quarters," and they can name all the players down to the substitutes.

In the case of the Kaizer Chiefs, the extent and depth of this hero-worship is so astonishing that it is really quite remarkable that they remain pleasant, unassuming men. An awed Pete Bala'c told me how he and fellow goalkeeper Banks Sethlodi were walking along in a rural area before an exhibition match. "An old man was sitting by the side of the road. He saw us and his eyes started popping out of his head. 'Banks? Banks!' he said. He ran up to greet us and he said, 'Now I can die in peace. I've shaken hands with Banks Sethlodi.' He meant it."

That sort of idol-worshipping is enhanced by the peculiarities of the South African situation. Black people have few if any political leaders who are not imprisoned or exiled who they can admire openly, and few cultural stars who have not chosen or been forced to choose exile as well. Teen-Age, Ace, and Jomo are inadvertently carrying a lot of excess weight on their shoulders.

What's more, to some extent following the soccer heroes is a substitute for other kinds of leisure activity from which blacks are barred by the apartheid laws or simply by lack of money. Lucky Stylianou says, with only slight exaggeration: "Black people can't do anything in this country. They can't go to films. They can't sit in restaurants. Soccer is at least something for them."

The apartheid system affects black soccer in another quite remarkable way. Soccer is one of the few areas where black people can participate in making decisions about things that matter to them. The black clubs are guided by management committees, which select coaches, acquire or transfer players, and even affect strategy on the field. Determined fans can seek to join or influence these committees at regular, often heated meetings.

More commonly, though, the fans assert themselves by a much less circuitous route. They sit en masse in the grandstands and scream until the coach makes the player adjustments they want. Swallow stalwarts may yell in unison: "Phuma Six Mabone"—and sure enough, Andries "Six Taillight" Maseko leaves the game, to be replaced by Jeff "Tornado" Ntsibande. If the coach ignores this stentorian counsel, the crowd screams for his head—and often eventually gets it.

In fact, the Chiefs' string of successes is often partly attributed to the club's ability to minimize the direct pressure of the fanatics. The canny Kaizer Motaung insists he is only a sort of general manager, who gives his coaches an entirely free hand. It is clear, though, that he makes the major decisions himself, such as which new players to acquire. He can therefore hide behind his coach of the moment and try out a newcomer relatively impervious to the baying of the crowd, conscious that such personnel changes usually take time to click. Meanwhile, the management over at the archrival Pirates is marked by massive confusion and dissension, which can result in an incoherent selection of players and a strategy that vacillates during the game in response to the hotheads in the stands. After the Bucs lost that 1981 Mainstay Cup final, the leader of one management committee faction even claimed that mysterious gunmen had opened fire on his home. It was later suspected he might have staged the attack himself to gain sympathy, which he could then parlay into a greater voice in Pirate affairs.

The advent of integrated professional soccer together with the much less significant relaxation of some apartheid barriers at the top level in other sports has prompted increasing pleas from whites, joined by a few blacks, for South Africa's readmission to world sports. Most of the white public accepts as self-evident that the changes of the past few years are sufficient to justify an end to South Africa's isolation. They argue sanctimoniously that sport and politics should be separate, wilfully forgetting that it was their government that mixed the two in the first place.

The organizations both inside and outside South Africa that argue for continued ostracism summarize their argument in the formulation: "No normal sport can exist in an abnormal society." The apartheid laws obstruct the true, unfettered comradeship that is as much a part of genuine sport as formal integration on the field. White athletes who play in black areas are regularly stopped and even arrested if they are without special permits; their black counterparts are often refused entry to white restaurants or bars for postmatch celebrations.

But even sport itself, in the narrow sense, is not genuinely integrated. The regime's position is that mixed sport is only for adults. Black and white high schools, for instance, almost never complete. On the professional level, there is continued gross discrimination in facilities and in coverage by the government-controlled broadcast media.

White businessmen, with the regime's help, have tried to break the world boycott by offering enormous payoffs to lure sportsmen from overseas to play in South Africa. Despite the huge financial offers, the promoters can usually only get makeshift teams of uneven quality that include many has-beens. Some foreign athletes observe the boycott for genuine reasons, while others are deterred from coming by the threat of subsequent blacklisting at home or elsewhere.

In early 1982, there was such an effort to import a world-class soccer team, with stars from England and South America, to tour South Africa. The sponsors were dead sure blacks would pour into the stands to see their heroes pitted against international competition. They knew black South Africans had long had a special interest in English soccer; "Banks" Sethlodi, for example, was even nicknamed for Gordon Banks, the English star goalkeeper in the 1960s.

To the surprise of the sponsors, the black community declared a boycott of the tour. The leading clubs—the Chiefs, Bucs, and Swallows—all refused to play the visitors. Only a handful of spectators turned out for the other matches. The tour was cancelled at the halfway point.

Some whites, sportswriters and others, accused the black clubs and their fans of spiting themselves foolishly by boycotting the tour. There were certainly sighs of longing and temptation in many a shebeen while the foreign stars were in the country. But most black people realized that the international sporting boycott was still justified morally and was still a powerful weapon in the struggle against apartheid. They, like sports fans everywhere, theorize endlessly about the makeup of a national team. They dream about seeing Teen-Age, Ace, and Pete Bala'c playing together in pursuit of a world championship. But they value their freedom more. They are willing to wait.

8

Heroes Underground

THREE BILLION YEARS AGO, a vast inland sea surrounded by rugged mountains covered parts of the Transvaal and the Free State. Over the eons, storms lashed at the landscape, breaking flakes of gold loose. Streams and rivers carried the particles down to the edge of the sea, where they sank to the bottom. The world's most valuable goldfields follow a three-hundred-mile arc along the rim of the ancient, long-dead sea, from Evander on the East Rand, up through Johannesburg, then curving down toward Welkom and Virginia.

The yellow metal built South Africa, and remains the backbone of its economy. Gold sales still account for roughly one-third of export earnings, even more when the world price is high. There are fifty or so working mines, controlled by seven gigantic mining houses. The gold industry is South Africa's major employer, with 575,000 workers, all but 40,000 of whom are black. Each year, South Africa mines about half of the world's gold.

Klerksdorp is a small town in the western Transvaal that is situated on the edge of the prehistoric sea. Outside the town is the Hartebeest-fontein gold mine, known simply as Harties. Aboveground, it seems insignificant: a small group of shedlike structures surrounded by heaps of whitish debris, and two towers, each less than one hundred feet high. There is nothing to suggest that the green wheels atop the towers lower elevator cages more than one and one-half miles down into the earth, into a vast underground city that employs twenty thousand people and uses 1,600 large scraper units, 225 small locomotives, 109 mechanical loaders, 1,800 hoppers, and 1,487 deafening rock drills.

The Chamber of Mines, the coordinating body for the industry, sponsors guided tours of certain mines—partly to respond to public curiosity and partly to present its controversial labor policies in the best possible light. At Harties, we began the tour with a trip underground. The visitors—all of us were white—donned protective clothing, hard hats, and lamps. Elevator cages, clanking in the rush of air, relayed us down through the darkness to one of the working levels. The descent only took a few minutes. A series of guides, all of them white mining officials, directed us through the dimly lit tunnels to one of the "work-places," where the "reef," or gold ore, was barely visible as a thin, jagged line, faintly brownish.

The Chamber's publicists have produced a vivid and often quoted description: "Imagine a solid mass of rock tilted . . . like a fat, 1,200-page dictionary, lying at an angle. The gold-bearing reef would be thinner than a single page, and the amount of gold contained therein would hardly cover a couple of commas in the entire book. . . . The 'page' has been twisted and torn by nature's forces, and pieces of it may have been thrust between other leaves of the book."

The miners, working miles underground, have to trace the elusive reef and remove it with close to surgical precision. Our guide indicated a workplace where several black miners were drilling deep holes next to the reef, following markings in red paint. The workplace was low, which forced the miners to lie flat on their backs, aiming the drill slightly upward. They were impassive despite the ferocious noise. The guide reassured us that the drill was not particularly taxing to operate.

The guide explained that later a white miner, who had a "blasting ticket," a certificate that only whites are allowed to earn, would fill the holes with explosive charges. The mine would be cleared, and blasting would start at the deepest working level and continue upward. Then, more black miners would shovel the broken-up reef into a linked network of mechanical scrapers and narrow-gauge railroad hoppers. It would then be transported to one of the elevator shafts to be hoisted to the extraction plant on the surface. The gold content is surprisingly low; one metric ton of ore yields only eleven to twelve grams, or just over four tenths of an ounce.

As the supervisor guided us through the network of tunnels, groups of black miners, wearing hard hats with headlamps, white overalls, and heavy boots, glanced sideways impassively. Their faces glistened in the faint light from the naked bulbs. The supervisor arrived at two pressure doors, which were part of the ventilation system that keeps air circulating through the mine. *"Vula,"* he grunted at the black doorkeeper, speaking in Fanakalo, the pidgin language of mining. "Open." The door hissed slowly, emitting a strong gust of wind. Our touring party passed through. *"Vala."* It started to close. The doorkeeper turned, revealing that he had stencilled across the back of his white overalls: "Vula-Vala."

Back on the surface, we visited the training school, which was under the aegis of de Villiers, a middle-aged man who talked almost as rapidly as an auctioneer. "First, I teach all the new men Fanakalo," he said. "They come from all over southern Africa. They are Mozambiques, Rhodesians, there are all the ethnic groups of our own Republic people. They speak more than 10 different languages. We have to communicate with them, and they have to be able to talk to each other. With my methods, I can teach them in three or four days."

De Villiers verbally rushed ahead, not pausing to mention that only an extravagant definition would include Fanakalo as a "language." It is a pidgin, suited only for rudimentary commands. You cannot imagine someone using it to discuss, for instance, the subtleties of trade unionism or politics.

He described how he gives tests to divide black recruits into "the leaders, the mechanicals, and the lower class." He vigorously shepherded us over to a "leader" identification test that he had invented himself. A half-dozen black men, each wearing a different colored hard hat, stood around a jumble of large wooden slabs, which de Villiers explained were the pieces of a gigantic puzzle. "There is a way to do this," de Villiers said conspiratorially to us. "But I'm not interested in whether they finish it. I'm going to watch their leadership qualities. I want to see who takes charge. We need good leaders to bring obedience into the others."

He signalled the men to begin. They rushed around attempting with partial success to fit the unwieldly wooden pieces together. After five minutes, he merrily called time and invited us to comment. There followed a brief discussion about the relative degrees of initiative displayed by "red hat," "green hat," and the others. De Villiers said he was proud of this particular group. "They carried on," he explained happily. "Others sometimes give up and say, 'Let's go ask the baas.' " As the tourists talked and gestured, the black men waited, well within earshot. A couple of them gave brief, flickering glares of resentment. Their sidelong glances were just barely detectable.

We continued on to one of the hostels, the single-sex compounds where virtually all black miners live for ten or eleven months a year. This, the newest of four at the mine, was an octagonal complex housing four thousand men, with twenty to a room. The place had the masculine, regimented feel of an army base. Hundreds of men moved along the paths between the various buildings; the day shift had apparently just completed work. There was not a single woman in sight.

The hostel superintendent was a flinty white man called Verster. One of his favorite words was "traditional." He sounded like an amateur anthropologist as he used it frequently in reference to the habits of his charges.

Verster first led us to one of the hostel rooms. It was clean and bright, with ten double bunk-beds lined up along the brick walls. A few curtains had been placed strategically, evidently to provide a little privacy. "All the men in each room are from the same tri—er, ethnic group," Verster caught himself. "They like staying together that way—it's their tradition."

We arrived at the immense dining hall just as a section of the day shift poured in. The men moved through the serving line at a dogtrot, stretching out their enamel plates for the food. They were almost all between eighteen and thirty-five years old. Verster, with a tone of concern like the manager of a livestock feedlot, encouraged the visitors to inspect the provisions. "There's the mielie meal," he said, gesturing toward a metal vat that was big enough to pour molten steel. "That's their traditional food. Further along are vegetables and fruits. They get meat twice a week. We make sure they have two thousand, eight-hundred and fifty calories a day. The kitchen is open twenty-four hours, so they come when they want."

The long line of miners continued jogging along. Servers ladled the food into plates like fast-paced robots. Most of the men ignored the visitors; a couple of older ones genuflected slightly toward Verster. One woman tourist approved eagerly of the cleanliness. "I've seen dirtier boarding schools," she said. Verster nodded in happy agreement.

He led the way to the beer hall. "They get one and one-quarter liters of sorghum beer a day for free. That's their traditional drink. They can of course buy more, at a subsidized price." Then, the medical clinic. "We insist they go, even with just a little scratch," he explained. His solicitude for the men's health is no doubt strengthened by the desire of his superiors to avoid lost man-days and injury compensation payments. He next indicated an open-air cinema. "They have films four times a week. They have several TV sets. They have soccer, athletics. On weekends, they do their tribal dancing—that's traditional to the blacks."

A huge, uniformed black man was stationed at the hostel gate, checking the documents and the parcels of the miners as they entered. "They come and go as they like," Verster emphasized. "The policeboy is just there to protect them, to keep out weapons and unauthorized people."

At the gate, Verster gestured back toward the mammoth complex with a proud, proprietary air. "They like it here," he assured us. "When they come back, or go to work on another mine, the setup isn't strange. It's traditional for them."

Verster had unwittingly used the word properly for the first time. A system of work that requires most of the workers to be away from their families for most of the year may sound unnatural. But after nearly a century in southern Africa, it is, in fact, traditional.

The mine supervisors hosted a luncheon at the nearby Klerksdorp Club. No workers, black or white, were present. One of the tourists, a stockbroker from Britain, apologetically ventured a question about a report he had seen in the morning Johannesburg newspaper. Some ten thousand black workers at the President Steyn mine further south in the Free State had stopped work and rioted against the introduction of a new pension plan. Police had killed at least one miner when they stormed into the compounds to quell the uprising.

The Harties officials had been stupefied by the news. One of them said, in a wounded tone: "The new pension plan is an improvement. I don't see how they can possibly object to this benefit we're giving them."

Some months later, I described my tour to my friend Eric McCabe, a white former miner in his late thirties. He grinned happily at my descriptions: "You were probably on the doctored level for visitors. Nicely painted. Well lit. Plenty of fresh air. Not too hot or cold. On the next level, okes [guys] might be working at a hundred degrees, with dry ice packs strapped to their bodies to keep them cool."

Eric laughed. "We used to trick the tourists, when they were going underground in the lift cage. The guy running it in the control room throws it into fast forward. The emergency brakes lock. But there's give in the cable, so it doesn't snap. It stretches. The miners in the cage expect it to kick up and down, but the tourists don't know what's happening. The cage bounces there in the shaft like a yo-yo for a while. The tourists are as confused as chameleons in a Smartie box [a type of candy that comes in many colors]. They're all sick. They're really fucked. They're not really interested in going anywhere else in the mine."

Eric no longer lives in South Africa. The police harassed him steadily about his black girl friend, so he and she moved to neighboring Swaziland, where there is no Immorality Act. He is a large, powerfully built man, who is covered in tattoos.

One evening, he gave me the official version of life underground. "Here's what's supposed to happen. They start dropping the day shift at five or six, to the bottom level first. The blacks wait down there. They can't even enter the stope (low-roofed chamber) until the white miner arrives, at seven. When you get there, you take your baas-boy, and your picannin, and check everything. You look for loose hanging rocks, or gas. Then, picannins with hose-pipes put down water to keep the dust down. There are signs around that say things like 'Keep Dust Low— with H_2O.'

"Next, you direct your timber-boys to put in the props—a solid pack here, a five-pointer there. You supervise your malaisha-boys, who are shoveling the blast from the previous day. You mark the rock-face, and you tell the machine-boys to start drilling. Then, you charge up. You chase everybody out before you start blasting."

Eric paused, a raconteur with timing. "That's what's supposed to happen."

He winked. "Here's what really happens. You stay in the canteen on the surface until about nine, just talking shit with the other white miners. When you get to the face underground, the black guys are drilling holes already. They've put in the props and marked everything. Your picannin takes your jacket and boots, hangs them up, and brings you a cup of tea. You sit and read the newspaper. You might take a look now and then, just to make sure nobody's fucking up. [You're paid partly on the amount of rock you move.] But really, your baas-boy can take care of everything. About all you do is hand the oke the matches before you blast."

Eric waited for his story to register. Then he added: "I trained twelve months for my blasting ticket. No baas-boy has had any course. But every single baas-boy in the mine, if they tested him right now for a fucking ticket, he'd get it."

He concluded maliciously: "I think they just don't give blasting tickets to blacks because they might start to blow up whites all over the country."

It has been the custom in Swaziland for a man who loves a woman to address her affectionately as though she were one of his most treasured personal objects, his spear, perhaps, or his cowhide shield. These historic words of endearment have become supplemented by another— "my suitcase." To the hundreds of thousands of migrant workers who leave their homes in Swaziland and elsewhere in southern Africa to journey to the mines, their suitcase is often their most valuable possession.

My friend Steve Dlamini was part of this army of workers. He had done four "joins"—the word is widely used as a noun in southern Africa for a migrant labor contract. When I met him, he was tending bar in Swaziland and contemplating returning for a fifth. He had a prominent aquiline nose, which gave him an oddly Arabic appearance, and a soft-spoken, highly observant manner.

When he first described his work to me, he said he had been a "team leader." The wordsmiths had struck again, replacing "baas-boy" with more acceptable terminology. Steve was proud of his expertise in leading his twenty-member team, and he insisted on using the newer job description.

His version of life underground coincided with Eric McCabe's right down to the white miner spending part of the shift reading. "He sometimes even tells us to do the blasting," Steve said. "I could do the whole join properly, all year, without ever seeing him."

He told me he had actually seen a fellow miner killed underground. The accident took place during his first join, before he had passed one of the leadership tests. He was using a hose to clean a section of the money-rock, as he called the gold-bearing reef. "There was a Sotho guy, standing right close to me," he remembered. "He started spraying me with his hosepipe. I sprayed him back. Just when we turned to our work, the rock above him fell. It hit him on his back. He died in hospital."

In the past ten years, between seven hundred and eight hundred men have died in the mines, and thirty thousand have been injured each year. Such dangerous work is at least partly rewarded in some other countries with high wages. But not in South Africa. In real terms, pay for black miners remained about the same for six decades, at only about twenty-five dollars per month as late as 1969. Raises in the early seventies brought some improvement, but black miners in 1982 were still only starting at about a hundred dollars a month. White miners earn more than five and one-half times as much.

Steve Dlamini was understandably annoyed by the wage disparity. But he objected even more to being away from his home for most of the year. He suspects certain of his uncles take advantage of his prolonged absences by selling some of the cattle he has saved up to purchase and then telling him the animals have died. More seriously, he once returned to find his wife, who works as a housemaid in a Swazi town, involved with another man. "She was younger then," he reflected hopefully. "I don't think she'll become a wanderer again if I take another join." Steve says he is usually able to "deny nature," as he put it uncomfortably, during his joins, even though women mill about outside the compound gates every payday, in the market for brief encounters with the lonely men.

The semiofficial explanation for the migratory system is that rural blacks throughout southern Africa, unsophisticated country bumpkins, are lured by the bright lights of the mining towns. They take joins in a search for adventure, for a chance to prove their manhood by working miles underground. This explanation obviously absolves the mineowners of any guilt for the persistence of the migratory system; it is the daring young men themselves, demanding to go through their rites of passage, who have sustained the arrangement.

In fact, Steve Dlamini took his first join for a rather more prosaic reason. He needed a job to support his family, and the opportunities for employment in the Swazi countryside, as in other rural areas in southern Africa, are scarce. He would have preferred to remain in the Luve area where he was born, as a small farmer. "I like living there in the nature, listening to the birds crying," he once told me, chuckling a little sheepishly as if he doubted I would believe him. "But there is no money there."

The insufficiency of rural employment is no quirk of nature. In the late nineteenth and early twentieth centuries, the colonial authorities in southern Africa deliberately levied taxes calibrated high enough to force rural blacks to leave their self-sufficient small farms and travel to the mines to raise the cash to meet their obligations. The colonialists also simply confiscated vast tracts of land from blacks, which also left the former owners no recourse but to go to the mines. This planned and systematic dispossession took place across the entire region.

The South African government used the pass laws to prevent the workers from bringing their families with them. The resulting single-sex migratory system has served the interests of the mineowners well. The migrant's family remains at home, raising at least some of their food. The mineowners are thus relieved of the need to pay wages high enough to support entire families. The owners also cut costs by not constructing adequate family housing at the mines.

The mineowners have a similarly specious rationale for the hostel system of housing. The Hartebeestfontein officials gave us a pamphlet that justified the peculiar arrangement as "a system of life for a large percentage of unsophisticated blacks . . . that enables them to adapt themselves gradually to new conditions without the undesirable effects that might otherwise result from being suddenly uprooted from their tribal environment."

I showed this explanation to Steve Dlamini, one of these unsophisticates. He shook his head sadly, as if he felt a wayward child had been responsible for the statement. "We suffer underground the same as the white man," he said. "It's obvious we should be able to live aboveground like they do."

The real reason the hostels exist is as a means to control the work-force. The miners are confined in the isolated, policed compounds. They work under yearly contracts, so there is little of the continuity that fos-ters the friendships and trust so vital to any organization of workers. Many of the miners do not even speak each other's language. It is there-fore not surprising that there has been no widespread coordinated strike action since 1946. There have been regular, explosive riots, after which the owners simply deported the workers and recruited replacements from among the hundreds of thousands of rural poor throughout southern Africa. Only in 1983 did a new union take the first tentative steps toward or-ganizing in a few mines. It had first obtained permission from the own-ers to enter the hostels.

Despite the awful conditions on the mines, the leading mineowner, Harry Oppenheimer, enjoys a reputation as an opponent of the apartheid system. Oppenheimer, who is in his mid-seventies, headed the gigantic Anglo-American Corporation until he relinquished day-to-day control in 1983; he retained stewardship of the De Beers diamond mining enter-prise. Oppenheimer has long been a major donor to the opposition Pro-gressive Federal Party. He also has a large stake in the relatively independent English-language press. His Chairman's Fund is a highly visible philanthropy that disburses money to a variety of educational projects for blacks. He has repeatedly spoken out in favor of what he calls "political reform," and he warmly welcomed Prime Minister P. W. Botha's proposed changes. He encourages Western corporations to maintain their holdings in South Africa, and to use their position in the economy to help him promote adjustments in the system. In all, he seems far more humane than his late nineteenth-century predecessor Ce-cil Rhodes, who used to amuse himself on Sunday afternoons by sitting outside the labor compound at the Kimberley diamond mine, tossing coins through the fence and chortling as the workers scrambled in the dust for them.

In part, Oppenheimer does stand out in contrast with the other own-ers, who make little pretense at being concerned about anything other than profit. But this lack of competition does not make him an en-lightened reformer by default. His image as an enemy of apartheid is as distorted as a guided tour of one of his gold mines. It is not so much that he is hypocritical, although there is at least something mildly un-settling about a man who advocates continued investment in South Africa while he simultaneously hedges his own commitment to the country; one of his enterprises, the Bermuda-based Minorco, has been estimated as the largest foreign investor in the United States. But Oppenheimer is usually sincere. The confusion about him turns on the ambivalent meaning of the word *reform* in the South African context.

Harry Oppenheimer recognizes that the apartheid system must be modified in order to enhance its chances for survival. He advocates abolishing petty apartheid and improving education and housing to create among blacks a more satisfied and settled skilled working and even middle class with at least some stake in the system. He is not even averse to seeing some blacks share eventually in political power; his enterprises have reached understandings with moderate black governments elsewhere in Africa. Oppenheimer is willing to spend his own money to promote these changes (although the $15-million annual Chairman's Fund budget does not seem quite so bountiful alongside the numbers of the Anglo-American corporation, which made $340 million in a single quarter in 1981).

What Oppenheimer has not challenged is the system of migratory labor, which is the basis of his huge fortune. His apologists argue that he would be helpless; South African law maintains the oscillating migratory system by preventing blacks from bringing their families to the 87 percent of the country designated as white, which includes almost all the mines. But this excuse is less than candid. Oppenheimer is probably the single most powerful man in South Africa; he is the head of an industry that pays taxes annually that amount to a quarter of total government revenue. His economic power might be presumed to give him a certain leverage in Pretoria if he were really deeply disturbed by the essential features of apartheid.

Oppenheimer is in fact much like a U.S. Republican businessman when the Democrats control the White House. He may grumble loudly about the Nationalists and certain aspects of their policy, but he still shares most of their basic outlook. His criticisms are no more fundamental than the alarums once sounded by certain GOP stalwarts about "creeping socialism" when Medicare was first proposed.

The gold mining system is somehow even more shameful and detestable because its final product has not much real use. Gold has few practical applications. It is usually either reburied in bank vaults or hoarded by speculators. Half a million men, bachelors for most of the year, risk their lives in the underground darkness to extract a yellow metal that is rarely of any real value to anyone. The financiers on the London stock exchange have not forgotten the mineworkers though; they have colloquially christened gold mining stocks as "kaffirs."

The migratory labor system has lasted for close to a century. There are absolutely no signs that it will change. The system rests on one essential fact: the majority of the miners, these "temporary sojourners," have continued over many decades to send most of their small wage packets home to the families they see only one month in the year. If they were to forsake their wives, children, and aged parents, widespread starvation would sweep through rural southern Africa. The apartheid regime and the mineowners might be forced to make some adjustments in the system. This is the towering irony; the miners, by heroically fulfilling their responsibilities to the near-strangers who are members of their families in fact sustain the very system that has exploited them, their ancestors, and that will continue, if unchallenged, to exploit their children.

9

Bantustans: The Archipelago of Misery

FAR UP in the Drakensberg Mountains, the Tugela River begins its three-hundred-mile course eastward to the Indian Ocean. Halfway to the sea, before plunging down the escarpment to the coastal sugarcane region, the Tugela passes through the Msinga District, an isolated area roughly thirty miles long that you can reach by only a single dirt road. On the south side of the Tugela, the thick thorny bush is interrupted regularly by spacious farms, which are glistening, emerald-green jewels of irrigated splendor. Tractors churn to and fro across vast fields of cotton, maize, oranges, and alfalfa, here known as lucerne.

On the north side of the Tugela, the panorama is completely different. Clusters of round, mud-walled huts cover a desolate, barren landscape. The thorn bushes have almost all been cut for firewood, and only an occasional bedraggled plot of stunted maize is under cultivation. To the south of the river, the handful of whites live in tidy farmhouses, with the accompanying barracks for the black farmworkers situated off to one side. To the north, thirty thousand black people live along the river itself, while another eighty thousand live up in the rugged hills. To cross the Tugela here is to go from the spacious equivalent of Iowa to the teeming equivalent of Haiti, or Java.

The south side of the Tugela is, by law, part of "white" South Africa, the 87 percent of the country in which black people are not permitted to own land and are allowed to enter only to work, as "temporary sojourners.'' The north side is part of the Kwa–Zulu Bantustan, one of the ten such areas, which cover the remaining 13 percent of the country, in which black people are supposed to ''develop separately.''

One of the farms on the ''white'' south side of the river is markedly different from its prosperous, irrigated neighbors. You have to exercise your imagination strenuously to see it as a farm at all. The stony hillsides are covered only with cactuses and spiky thornbushes. Much of the topsoil has long washed away into the Tugela, so there is little ground cover. The farm is called Mdukatshani, which means, in Zulu, ''The Place of the Lost Grasses.''

A number of paths hacked through the brush lead off the dusty main road to round huts, identical to the dwellings that are visible across the river. There is no electricity. Thin dogs slink about abjectly. The several dozens of black people who live here are almost all either old, women, or children. They are dressed extremely shabbily, in an assortment of aging woolen caps, shredded shirts, patched trousers or skirts, battered cheap tennis shoes, and sandals. A number of the women and children are barefoot. Some of the children have open sores on their legs.

The hairstyles of some of the women are unforgettable. Reddish discs rising gracefully nearly a foot above the head, or flaring winglike structures, also reddish, look at first like exotic, inorganic headdresses. They are actually carefully sculpted combinations of hair and dried mud, and they provide a striking, elegant contrast to the tattered clothing.

Down toward the river, in a small clearing, is an unpretentious crafted stone-walled house with a low thatched roof. This is where the ''the Numzaan,'' a white man called Neil Alcock, lives with his wife and two youngsters.

''It was in the days before the discovery of penicillin. One of my father's farmworkers was in a fight, right around Christmas, and he got the entire side of his head crushed in by a knobkerrie. The witchdoctor was called in. He studied the wound, and then covered it with a plug of cow dung.''

Neil Alcock paused and tilted his head slightly. ''In a few weeks, he removed the dung. The wound was healing properly.'' Alcock stopped again, and shrugged. ''Penicillin is a mold that is found in things like cow dung. Those witchdoctors—their knowledge is so great in a certain sphere that we just don't come near it.''

The Numzaan related this story in a low key but nonetheless proselytizing tone. He is in his early sixties, tall, lean, and gray-bearded, with a spiritual and prophetic manner. His similarity to the Russian novelist Leo Tolstoy is in some respects striking. Like Tolstoy, Neil Alcock started life as a large landowner, the heir to a family estate. Also like Tolstoy, Alcock gradually moved to renounce his privilege, and he has sought to create an ethical community with the very people he used to rule over. To complete the parallel, Alcock even refers to the black farmworkers as "serfs," bitterly biting off the word every time he utters it in another reproach to himself and his kind.

His first language is Zulu. He thinks in Zulu, and at times searches his mind for the English translation. "I was reared by Africans," he explained. "My loyalty to them is not paternalism, but a feeling of family. I became theirs. My own parents were typically lazy white South Africans, who had time for their social activities rather than for their children."

His grandfather came from Yorkshire, England, and bought a farm in Natal. "My father inherited the farm, and because of the work of his serfs, he became even wealthier. I took over the descendants of some serfs who had worked for my grandfather. They were no better off than their ancestors. In some cases, they were worse off. We whites are like the Romans; after a few generations of slaves—there is really no other word for it—we can't exist without them."

As a youth, Alcock preferred to mix with the farmworkers rather than to go to school. "My most worthwhile education came from those black people. I would disappear at dawn with those naturalists, the shepherds, who would take and show me where things like honey could be found. I got a tanning from my parents when I got home at night. But whatever capabilities I have I got from those black people, those philosophers; I got damn-all at school from the white teachers in their high-heeled shoes."

After World War II, Neil Alcock started with some reluctance to farm on his own. He already hated the system, and he searched from the start for ways to alleviate its worst excesses. He started to grow and distribute vegetables, and he gave lectures in his flawless Zulu about the value of a balanced diet in preventing malnutrition and tuberculosis. He began to "turn my serfs into partners" by transferring livestock and lands to them. He spread his budding ideas on agricultural reform by helping to establish a national agency called Kupugani.

Neil Alcock, like many people who work close to the land, has religious feelings. But he was finding himself increasingly in opposition to some representatives of organized religion. "Some of the priests and parsons were more concerned with saving souls than lives," he said, with savage bewilderment. "One of those chaps said to me, 'The way to heaven is through suffering—and you are trying to deprive the Africans of suffering!'"

The Numzaan carried his renunciation further. He sold his family estate and started the Church Agricultural Project in the Dundee district in northern Natal. The project became a successful cattle cooperative. Alcock explained he was trying "to make serfs into individuals." He went on, "I had learned you can't lead from the house on the hill. You have to try to live as nearly identical to the others as possible." He naturally found that the old ways of interacting did not disappear. "They have dependence snatched out from under them, and they find it hard to react sometimes," he said. He insists the other people at Mdukatshani call him Numzaan, which means "householder," rather than baas. They of course observe his request, but many of them infuse the new word with the same old mixture of awe, respect, and deference.

In the end, the Dundee agricultural project was doomed by its location. It was surrounded by "black spots"—scattered fragments of land owned by blacks outside the borders of the ten Bantustans. Enterprising black small farmers had purchased these areas, in some cases generations ago, but they were not consistent with the regime's grand apartheid design. So the government gave itself the power to abrogate the property rights of the "black spot" residents and to move them, by force if necessary, into the Bantustans. This policy, under which three and one-half million people have been forced to move since 1960, is officially called resettlement—a word with a misleadingly pleasant ring to it.

Neil Alcock's oldest son is nicknamed "GG," after the Government Garage vehicles that arrived around the time of his birth to obliterate the spots. Most of the people who had participated in the Dundee project faced deportation into the Kwa–Zulu Bantustan. The Numzaan encouraged his friend Cosmas Desmond, a brave Catholic priest, to travel through rural South Africa gathering material for *The Discarded People,* the first systematic exposé of resettlement. Then Alcock and his fifty-member entourage searched for a new place to continue their agricultural program.

By now, his chief lieutenant was a towering Swazi-speaking man called Robert, whom he had found in a village bound to a tree with barbed wire. "Robert's neighbors feared his destructive outbreaks," the Numzaan explained. "I discovered he was suffering from pellagra dementia. On a proper diet, he started to recover immediately."

The band chose the Msinga District partly because it was the worst agricultural region any of them had ever seen. They wanted to experiment, to see if they could develop a pilot project that could indicate how to start resuscitating the whole area. Also, the Numzaan probably wanted to carry his renunciation of privilege yet another step. Mdukatshani suited their purposes; it was sufficiently rundown, and it was just across the Tugela from the Bantustan.

The cooperative tried to continue raising cattle, but the people in the area rustled nearly all the animals right away. Alcock explained: "They saw us arrive—a group of what were to them rich blacks and whites. They saw no harm in robbing us." The experimenters then turned to large-scale gardening. They fashioned an ingenious mechanical water wheel from an old tractor tire, used it to lift water from the Tugela, and irrigated extensively. They devised a simple grinder to chop up the acacia thornbush into a nutritious feed for their remaining livestock. The Numzaan said approvingly, "A curse, the acacia, becomes a valuable resource." They started using wastes to create methane gas, which they used as fuel in place of the rapidly dwindling supplies of wood. They disseminated their ideas by encouraging their neighbors to form similar cooperatives.

Neil Alcock's ultimate goal was near-total self-sufficiency for Mdukatshani. It was an objective in keeping with his highly apocalyptic vision, his conviction that worldwide ecological catastrophe was very near. He believed the city was doomed, that mankind had to re-create the village, and he could be blunt, even cantankerous, with people who did not share his view. Whatever the accuracy of his prophecy on a planetary scale, it was clearly compelling in the Msinga District. There, the ravaged hillsides were evidence enough that ecological collapse was well underway.

Mboma Dladla is fourteen years old and the closest friend of the Numzaan's two tow-headed youths. They roam through the scrubby brush together, trapping rabbits in snares, flicking berries at each other with switches, arguing whether a baboon or a monkey is superior in battle, playing makeshift guitars made from an empty oil cans.

Mboma, wearing his insouciant purple athletic jacket, agreed to guide me around the farm one morning after he had established that I was not an iBhunu, or Boer. "They take all the money, so we are poor," he explained. He guided me down toward the river, where he introduced me to two old men who were chopping wood. He specified immediately I was not an iBhunu. Some words were exchanged in Zulu. "They say it is good you are not iBhunu," Mboma translated. "They say the maBhunu are horrible. They say the maBhunu carry guns everywhere, call them kaffirs, and make them work for a low pay."

Mboma showed me some of the large garden plots, which were scattered about on the steep cliffs overlooking the river. Carrots, cabbages, onions, lemon trees, and more were growing in neat terraces. Almost all the work was done by hand, including irrigating, fertilizing the fragile, weakened topsoil, and extending the terraces further into the forbidding bush. There was an almost Asian sense of bustling activity as women, children, and old men moved about. Mboma commented: "The maBhunu around here don't like these gardens because we no more have to work for them."

He himself, in the time before Mdukatshani, had spent a year working at a nearby white orange grove. He had been ten years old. He lived the entire week in a barracks with other children, returning to his own home only on Sunday. A bell woke the children at six; they continued until six in the evening, stopping only for meals. He had earned twelve rand each month. The work was "horrible," he said. The maBhunu had driven motorbikes up and down the orange grove, striking out at the children if they slackened in their work. Mboma imitated hitting and kicking gestures.

Back at home, Mboma herded cattle together with his disabled uncle. Both his parents were up in Joburg on migrant labor contracts; he has never been able to live with them. Even under normal circumstances, herding is not a particularly easy task for a small boy, who must know how to place thrown stones with the precision of an artillery commander to get the herd of beasts to move in the desired direction. In Msinga, though, stock thieves, armed with guns and driven by desperation, robbed Mboma and his helpless uncle repeatedly.

The worsening conditions in Msinga District made their lives difficult in other ways. The white farmers no longer needed as many farmworkers, so they simply ordered the surplus people into the Kwa–Zulu Bantustan. The police came and burned down his family's huts to force them to move across the river. At his new home he had to walk two hours each way to school. But after a year he had to drop out.

The increasing overcrowding in the Bantustan has contributed to the scourge of Msinga: bloody fighting between different clans over what are often initially trivial incidents. In one case, Mboma said, a battle started when one clan member spat into the pot of beer of another clan member. Over the years, hundreds of people have died, including Mboma's great-grandfather.

Hunger in the district grew worse. Mboma and the other children took to swimming back across the Tugela, to steal food on the white side. They skulked about, on the lookout for the white farmers who were often armed, tied ears of maize to their arms and legs, and swam back. One farmer even shifted to cotton to end his theft problem.

But the extra food was not enough. Mboma fell ill. His hair started to turn red, and he had sores on his ears. He spent a week in a Joburg hospital, under treatment for malnutrition. He said he didn't like the city; he was awed by the tall buildings and afraid he would encounter dreaded tsotsis.

The arrival of the Numzaan and the rest of his entourage was close to a miracle for Mboma Dladla. Hc carned a small but secure income looking after the project's two horses; he was learning English; he was even collaborating in an effort to turn his "life story" into a short book for children (which indeed appeared later). On the last page, he said: "I was asked what I want to be when I am big. It is difficult to talk about the future. All I can say is that I want to be a MAN."

In official terms, Mboma Dladla's manhood will begin on his sixteenth birthday. He will then be required to register for his pass. (In one indication of the quality of life in Msinga, one youth was initially refused his pass because the fringes on his fingertips were too worn to yield adequate prints.) Mboma's pass will brand him, forever, as a resident of one of the Bantustans. He will never have the right to settle permanently in Johannesburg, Durban, or anywhere else in "white South Africa." If he is lucky, he may be able during times of economic boom to join the stream of migrant laborers. He will live, like his father before him, in a hostel. He will return home only at Christmas.

The Mdukatshani project requires a considerable amount of paperwork. It keeps both its own books, and those of the other co-ops it has spawned in the region. Most of this clerical work takes place at "the office," a simple wooden structure with benches on the front porch. The office is the preserve, at times jealously guarded, of an extraordinary man named Abel Rabotata. He is forty-four years old. He has been totally blind since the age of eight.

"My aim and intention here is twofold," he told me at dusk one evening, as we sat on the bench. "I obviously contribute directly to the project by working in the office. But also, by participating in the world, I intend to show that blind people are no different than their sighted colleagues. I can do anything you can do, with the exception of driving an automobile. I feel that people here, in the rural areas especially, are mesmerized by the white man. They are afraid of the white man's power. I intend to help change that view. The people here see me working in the office, keeping the books, typing, getting around . . . it shows them that we black people are capable of accomplishing things."

Abel is particularly proud of his memory. He lived in Soweto for a number of years, and he can give precise directions to every section of the featureless township. It would be a remarkable achievement for even a sighted person. In his days as a switchboard operator, he was known as "the walking directory," because of his ability to recall hundreds of telephone numbers. As he recounted his personal history, he scrupulously included the exact dates.

He was born in Potgietersrus, a hot, dusty small town in the northern Transvaal. "On May 27, 1945, I journeyed down to the Cape, to attend the school for the blind there. It was there that I started to learn both English and Afrikaans. I was quickly assigned to teach others in the beginners class. I continued at the normal pace until 1953, when the South African government passed the Act establishing Bantu Education. Our school was mixed, coloreds and Africans, and one of the effects of the new law was that we Africans would have to leave because the school was located in a colored area.

"I had to increase the pace of my schooling, before the law came into effect. I completed the entire three-year basket-weaving course in eighteen months. My aim and intention was to work at weaving, but then I was able to obtain a special government permission to remain at the school, to complete my Standard Six [the equivalent of grade eight]. I was at times lazy at reading, but irrespective I came in first in the class. I then left, but I was hastily called back to be the first blind African instructor there. Part of my duty was to encourage the newcomers, to show them how independent a blind person could be. I taught them to make their beds, to clean up. I used to take them for long walks along the main road. There would be more than twenty of us, all blind, walking up, up, up into the hills, and then back again. They would be afraid of the cars at first, but I would show them we could do it. . . . Then, my permit expired, and I had to leave the school. End of Part One.

"On July 21, 1958, I started work as a telephone switchboard operator at the Johannesburg City Council. I stayed there until 1973, when I became ill and I could no more work. Fortunately, my wife had a job. I stayed at home in Soweto, but I never begged. I used my own talents to earn money. I can fix radios, sewing machines, and so forth. I can put a toilet together from the outset, from bottom to top. I don't have diagrams, but I say that if a man made it a man can fix it, so I just keep at it until I learn. I would also do a basket now and then.

"I recovered, and was able to go back to work as a switchboard operator on August 8, 1977. But man, I felt that wasn't enough for the blind. We needed a public relations officer, someone who could show that blind people are not only switchboard operators and basket weavers. Also, I wanted to get back to rural life. So I decided to come to Mdukatshani."

Abel paused, and reached for his Braille Bible. He apologized for not having a printed one handy so I could follow him. "In Johannesburg, the event occurred which changed my life. On February 27, 1961, I became a member of Jehovah's Christian Witnesses. In John, Chapter 16, Verse 31 [he turned unerringly to the proper place], we learn 'Jesus answered then, Do ye not believe?' Further on, 'And yet I am not alone, because the Father is with me.' A too easy life is not a real life. You need the ups and downs to understand."

Abel's voice had by now taken on a rhythmic cadence, almost an incantation. "The Bible teaches us to love one another. That is why this apartheid is a complete abomination in the eyes of the Almighty. One day it will be broken to pieces."

Abel broke off for a moment. He moved through the gloom, found a candle, and lit it. "Some people here believe that the handicapped themselves are responsible for their condition, that they have sinned in the eyes of God and that God has deprived them as punishment. These people keep the handicapped hidden away, locked up even. Jehovah's Witnesses teaches that the sins of all men, the fault of all men, causes the handicapped.

"I was once travelling near my home in the northern Transvaal, preaching from house to house. After I left one home, the people sent a child to bring me back. 'Look, we are astonished about you,' they said. 'We watched as you passed your hands over those dots. We didn't believe you were reading, but then we consulted our own Bibles. Look, our own child is deaf, dumb, and blind. What can we do?'

"They were keeping the child, a thirteen-year-old boy, hidden in a back room, alone. They said the neighbors were laughing at them for having such an afflicted child. Well, I took action immediately. I directed the child to the nearest clinic. I consulted with others as to which school to send this child to. I made all the arrangements, and he is schooling there today."

Abel got up, entered the now totally dark office, and emerged a minute later, gesticulating with some correspondence in his hand. "In our efforts, we are fortunately getting more help in recent years from the white blind. I'm in constant communication with them. We are steadily building a stronger alliance."

In addition to his duties as office manager at Mdukatshani, Abel Rabotata was conducting his own research into poultry raising. He guided me through the moonlit darkness around to the back of the office, where he showed me a wire chicken coop. About ten birds huddled inside. He let himself in, stalked the birds by their sounds, and captured several.

He ran his hands over each one, and discoursed on the characteristics of the different varieties. He said he was even considering writing a monograph of some sort on raising poultry.

"Ultimately," he said, "I might like to return to Potgietersrus, the place of my birth, and devote myself entirely to the raising of fowls. We shall see. In any case, blindness to me means nothing. I challenge life just as it comes."

In spite of the efforts at Mdukatshani farm, the conditions in the Msinga District continued to grow worse. The economic downturn that started in 1981 caused layoffs in the urban centers, which forced the unemployed to return home. Working-age men, once a rarity, became increasingly common in the area, adding to the already intolerable overcrowding. Neil Alcock's prophetic warning—"Hatred is building up with blood interest"—continued unchecked to take the shape of reality.

Faction fighting continued to plague the district. By mid-1981, more than eight hundred people had died violently. Special execution squads in the pay of the rival groups carried the warfare to the far-off hostels in Johannesburg. Periodic lulls seemed to promise peace, only to be interrupted by yet another wave of killing.

The fighting was sometimes cited by white racists as another sign of black savagery, a foretaste of what would sweep the entire country after nonracial rule. That line of reasoning received something of a setback in late 1981, when a white Msinga farmer, Johan Verster, went on trial for participating in the faction fights in the pay of one of the clans. Verster, a husky twenty-nine-year-old reserve paratrooper, was found innocent of fourteen counts of murder on the grounds of insufficient evidence. But he was convicted of "terrorism" and of conspiracy to commit murder. He was sentenced to eight years in prison.

As the fighting continued, Neil Alcock stubbornly kept on trying to mediate between the warring factions. In September 1983, he was driving a minibus with members of one group home from a peace meeting. As the vehicle travelled down one of Msinga's dirt roads, members of another faction opened fire. Six people died, including Neil Alcock. He was buried quietly at the Place of the Lost Grasses.

Msinga is not far, perhaps thirty miles, from National Road Three, the main artery between Johannesburg and Durban. Over vacation periods, traffic on Three can be nearly bumper-to-bumper as white people motor to and from Durban's beaches. None of them ever interrupts their holiday to meander off along the dusty back roads into the other world of the Bantustans. Most whites have only the haziest sort of understanding of the policy, and few have ever visited one of the territories.

Yet the majority of black South Africans live in places exactly like Msinga, and under similar conditions. The populations of the Bantustans are not known exactly; the constantly oscillating migration is just onc of several factors that makes an accurate count difficult. Nonetheless, a tireless researcher named Charles Simkins, at the University of Cape Town, came up with an estimate in 1981. He concluded that 49.6 percent of all black ("African") men lived in the Bantustans, and 54.7 percent of all women, yielding an overall combined figure of more than half. The study estimated further that those figures, for 1980, constituted a striking increase since 1960, when only 35.6 percent of the men and 43.3 percent of the women lived in the territories.

In part, the increase is due to changed "boundaries"; the regime redrew its maps and included in the Bantustans certain urban townships outside Durban, Pretoria, and elsewhere. In part, it could also reflect slightly higher population growth rates in the Bantustans, though this explanation is undercut by the high infant mortality rates in the areas. Primarily, though, the increase is due to the sweeping forced removals from "white" South Africa.

The best estimates are that three and one-half million people were dumped into the territories after 1960. Another approximately one million people are still scheduled to be forceably removed. This upheaval, in a nation which had not reached a thirty-million population figure by 1980, must rank among the major enforced movements of people anywhere in the world since the end of World War II. The mass deportation received relatively little publicity, partly because it took place in remote, inaccessible regions, and partly because it was not a spectacular quick process. But the upheaval has ground onwards year after year, a silent convulsion that has devastatingly altered South Africa.

The ten territories extend in the horseshoe-shaped arc around the eastern, northern, and northwestern periphery of the country. They do not form a solid belt, but rather a hopelessly fragmented archipelago of islands of land. Transkei, which has the best claim to territorial integrity, is in three separate pieces. "Independent" Bophutatswana is in seven parts, separated by up to 150 miles of South Africa; Lebowa is in fourteen. Kwa-Zulu is presently in forty-four separate pieces, although the regime has plans to "consolidate" it down to only ten.

It is an overcrowded archipelago of misery scattered in the ocean of white wealth. Overall population density in the Bantustans is already 119 people per square mile (in Kwa-Zulu it is 173) contrasted with 35 in the rest of South Africa. The degree of poverty is truly astonishing. In the Ciskei, the per capita income is estimated at fifteen rand a month; the figure for Bophutatswana is a princely thirty-six rand. Even a semi-official government agency called Benso has conceded that per capita income is lower in the Bantustans than in all but ten of the forty-five African nations.

That 1981 government report finally discredited a long-standing tedious justification for apartheid, that blacks should not object to their lack of political rights as they instead enjoy economic prosperity by contrast with the rest of the continent.

Health conditions in the Bantustans are appalling. In the Transkei, which was the first to declare for "independence" in 1976 and which the regime intended as something of a showcase, the infant mortality rate is 282 per 1,000. In other words, of every 1,000 babies born there in 1979, the International Year of the Child, 282 had died by the end of 1981, the year in which the territory celebrated five years of "independence." (By contrast, the infant mortality rate for whites is 12 per 1,000, the third lowest in the entire world.)

Diseases that should have no place in a rich, industrialized nation like South Africa flourish in the Bantustans. In 1978, there was not a single case of cholera in the country; by 1981, there were 3,874, most of them in the Bantustans. Typhoid broke out in the Transkei in 1983, killing six people; polio has reappeared in Gazanzulu and Lebowa. Ten million South Africans are estimated to have latent tuberculosis; ten people die each day from it.

You would expect that any government that carried out a policy with such horrifying consequences would be secretive about it. The regime is vague about the specifics of deportations and the deaths of children. But it boldly continues to declare that the overall Bantustan policy is a generous, noble endeavor. In line with the central doctrine of apartheid, that the different ethnic groups in the country constitute separate "nations," the regime argues that in granting "independence" to each Bantustan it is actually carrying out "decolonization." The policy, by providing each "black nation" with its own territory, is chivalrously allowing each to take its rightful sovereign place in the world. One of the government's propaganda pamphlets went so far as to argue that the Bantustans should be called "people's democracies"—except that "the Communists" in Eastern Europe and elsewhere had unfortunately debased the term.

In fact, the Bantustan system started to come into being early in the twentieth century, long before all the high-minded euphemism about "national self-determination." It was not designed in the interests of blacks. It was designed to create a cheap labor force for the white mines and farms.

When white settlers started to arrive in South Africa in 1652, most of the black people who had lived there for centuries were small farmers, who grew for their own consumption. Then, in the later nineteenth century, diamonds and then gold were discovered. The huge influx of white diggers created new markets for agricultural production. Throughout southern Africa, black small farmers increased their own production, brought the surplus to the mining camps and towns, and used their earnings to buy blankets, guns, horses, and other goods. Some of the thriving farmers worked their own land, while others maintained a semi-independent sharecropping arrangement with white large landowners.

These sturdy growers saw no need to leave their prospering plots and their significant degree of independence to become low-paid miners or serfs on white farms. Some of the better-off black farmers were even living, in the words of an early twentieth-century observer, "just like Dutchmen." The colonial authorities first tried to overcome the labor shortage by imposing a high hut or head tax, which was intended to force at least some of the small farmers into the mines to earn enough money to pay it. But the measure was not enough. In the years just after the Anglo-Boer War ended in 1902, the British colonial government was forced to temporarily import sixty thousand Chinese workers to keep the gold mines functioning.

To solve the problem, the Assembly passed the Land Act of 1913. The Act, which was strengthened in 1936, said no black could own or have the independent use of land outside the "native reserves," the 13 percent of the country which is today's Bantustans. Many of the thrifty industrious sharecroppers were forced out of "white" South Africa and into the reserves. These first deportations, back in 1913, started the cycle of overcrowding, erosion, and the drop in agricultural production. As the shortage of mine workers ended there was no fine talk from officialdom about "independent black nations."

The emergent Bantustans had another happy consequence for the owners: the arrangement greatly expanded the migrant labor system. Pass laws, which had existed in some form since the first days of white settlement at the Cape, were strengthened and enforced with growing zeal. Increasingly, blacks could only leave the Bantustans as single migrants, without their families. By the 1970s, more than 70 percent of the "economically active" Bantustan population was involved in the migratory system, and 35 percent of the employable men were away at any one time. In other words, one in three black workers in South Africa was a migrant—a proportion that has surely risen even further since then.

The migrant's family, tenaciously trying to raise crops back in the Bantustan, reduced by whatever they scratched from the soil the amount the family as a whole needed to survive. The mineowners, and later the industrialists, could therefore keep wages artificially low.

The sprawling archipelago of misery has also limited the growth of volatile poor and working-class black communities in the country's strategic heartland, in and around the large cities. The mass deportations of the past two decades have occurred mainly because white agriculture finally mechanized. The farmers no longer wanted to provide for as many laborers for the entire year. But the government, instead of permitting the ex-farmworkers to migrate permanently to the cities, which has been the pattern in most countries, pushed them into the Bantustans. In the urban areas, they would not have achieved instant prosperity, but they would have found or created job opportunities, which are wholly lacking in the Bantustans. And, of course, they would have been able to bring their families. If movement were unrestricted, Johannesburg, which with 2.5 million people is already the second largest city in Africa, would be truly gigantic—possibly another Calcutta or São Paulo. In such a megalopolis, the Soweto uprising would have been an even more shattering event.

With the passing of time, the archipelago has also come to serve as a cheap dumping ground for people who do not participate in the creation of wealth. These people, who have been coldly called surplus Bantu or superfluous appendages, include the sick, the unemployed, the old and the young. Social welfare costs, such as education and pensions, are reduced and pushed out to the periphery.

By the 1960s, the Bantustan system had been functioning for more than half a century, contributing to the wealth of white South Africa in its several ways. There had been vague talk of eventual independence for the territories, but the regime mentioned it as a hazy, distant goal. Then, after the 1961 Sharpeville Massacre, the world outcry against South Africa increased. Prime Minister Hendrik Verwoerd, who usually surrounded his policies with an aura of sanctimony, spoke with brief candor in 1961 when he admitted that granting independence was "a form of fragmentation we would not have liked if we were able to avoid it." He alluded ruefully to "the pressure being exerted on South Africa" and announced the policy would go forward, "thereby buying the white man his freedom and the right to retain domination in what is his country."

Verwoerd's successor, B. J. Vorster, sped up the timetable. The Transkei was declared "independent" in 1976, followed by Bophutatswana the next year, Venda in 1979, and the Ciskei in 1981. The euphemisms kept pace with these changes. The territories, first "native reserves," were called, in succession, "Bantustans," "homelands," and then, in the final bid for respectability, "black states" or "national states."

Before agreeing to even this illusory sort of independence, the regime had to make certain its real control over the territories would continue unhindered. Pretoria feared that the territories might achieve a measure of genuine autonomy, and become Trojan Horses from which subversion could be launched into the rest of the country. The threat was real. Three significant uprisings had broken out in the 1950s in different Bantustans; in the Transkei, the regime was forced to send in the army and arrest nearly five thousand people to quell the rebellion.

South Africa intended to maintain control through the chiefs and other "traditional" leaders, who were already on its payroll. Despite this institutionalized form of bribery, quite a number of chiefs remained faithful to their people and refused to carry out the government's orders. They could not be tried and imprisoned, as they had broken no laws. Banning would not require court approval, but the independent-minded chiefs were so respected they would continue to exercise full authority even while meeting only one person at a time, through whom they could issue counsel. The regime had to devise another cruel punishment—banishment. The recalcitrant chiefs were moved hundreds of miles, into areas in which they sometimes did not even speak the local language. Pretoria then selected pliable replacements, who it put forward as legitimate.

The regime then rigged the Bantustan "constitutions," so that the appointed "legislators"—its docile chiefs and headmen—outnumbered or at least equalled elected members to the "parliaments" in all of the territories. It was a shrewd and necessary move, because in nearly every "election," the rural voters opted for genuine leaders who opposed "independence." The appointed chiefs have kept Pretoria's control from slipping. The regime also dominates the Bantustans financially; the impoverished territories cannot raise much money, so up to 80 percent of their budgets are direct annual grants from the South African Parliament.

The individuals who did manage to gain Pretoria's approval are a ludicrous lot, in the same class as tinpot dictators elsewhere; grandiloquent, brutal, and pompous. They name airports after themselves and extort profitable shares in the local small businesses. Nepotism, not unexpectedly, is common. Lennox Sebe, the Ciskei boss, picked his brother, Charles, a former South African police sergeant, to head the "independent" country's intelligence service. The new spymaster, who favors dark glasses, was promoted rapidly to "Major-General." He seems to regard himself as a sort of renaissance man; he claims to be able to run a marathon eight minutes faster than the world record, to have leaped from a speeding car and driven away ANC guerrillas bent on assassinating him, and to be, in his moments of leisure, something of a literary expert. He has issued orders that all poetry written in the Ciskei be passed directly to him for approval. He is able, he insists, to detect any strophes that concealed subtle political messages. But in mid-1983, the brothers tragically fell out; President Sebe charged that General Sebe had been planning "a coup" and arrested him.

There are in fact quite a number of other humorous features to the odd territories. Their highly fragmented nature has produced jokes: Q. What is the biggest growth profession in the Bantustans? A. Border guards. In a cartoon, a black job applicant, shown an inkblot pattern in a psychological test, says it reminds him of Bophutatswana.

The Bantustans are nonetheless acquiring some of the appurtenances of real countries. "Capitals" are rising in the bare veld; "ministers" issue pronouncements; "ambassadors" and "consuls" are sent out. (They do not have to travel far—only to Pretoria and to other Bantustans—as no other country in the world has recognized them as sovereign states.) In South Africa, the "diplomats," as "foreigners," are allowed to live in white areas and their children can attend white schools. Both facts have provoked some white hostility.

Solemn diplomacy takes place in the region. Venda and Pretoria have even signed a "nonaggression pact." Occasionally, though, there is an unfortunate spat: Transkei "severed diplomatic relations" with South Africa in the late 1970s. (Though the parliamentary grants that kept the territory afloat continued, somehow unhindered, which was surely some sort of first in the history of international relations.)

These comic aspects can obscure an increasingly ugly reality. The Bantustan leaders are so unpopular that they must resort to vicious repression in order to stay in power. Kaizer Matanzima, the Transkei "president," even had to lock up his own son-in-law on one occasion. In many of the territories, harsh security laws have been modelled after South African legislation. Some senior police and army officers are either on loan from South Africa, or are unreconstructed Rhodesian military veterans. Hundreds, perhaps thousands, of people have been detained without trial, for several years in some instances. At least several of them have already died mysteriously.

Not all the Bantustan leaders are hated with the same intensity. Some have a certain following, and one, Chief Gatsha Buthelezi of Kwa-Zulu, is genuinely popular. He is an extremely controversial person, a politician who speaks from the regime's platform while declaring that he supports liberation. Nonetheless, he has managed to build his Inkatha party, which the regime allows to function as long as it calls itself a national cultural liberation movement, into an organization that claims more than three hundred thousand members. His decision to try to change the apartheid system from within has had a limited effect so far; he has been unable, for instance, to stop the deportations of people to Kwa-Zulu. He remains popular, though, largely because he has been able so far to block efforts to move his territory to "independence." A Zulu woman once gushed: "If it weren't for Gatsha, we would be independent by now!" South Africa must be the only place in the Third World where such a statement about a political leader could be offered as praise.

A few years ago, a forty-four-year-old man named Solomon Mpetha hurriedly left his job in a Cape Town brick factory to come to Tshaneni, his home village, which is located in the Herschel District of the Transkei. He was coughing and spitting with tuberculosis. Another Tshaneni man accompanied Mpetha, who was already too weak to travel on his own.

The two men took the train up to Kimberley, where they had a long stopover. They huddled through the cold night in the ramshackle third- and fourth-class waiting room. Mpetha felt himself getting weaker. He asked his friend to pray.

Two more train journeys brought them to Zastron, a town in the "white" Orange Free State about thirty miles from home. Mpetha was gasping now. He said he desperately wished there were at least a single telephone in Tshaneni; he wanted to speak with his wife. The two men prayed again.

His friend helped him on board the bus to Sterkspruit, the major town in Herschel, where they transferred to the local Blue and White Bus Service for the last five miles. It was now the very early morning. They rumbled along the dirt road, through the treeless valleys. Perhaps they noticed the erosion scars were getting deeper. They finally arrived home, at the base of some low, saw-toothed mountains.

Mpetha, with a supreme force of sheer will, staggered out of the bus, greeted his wife and five children, and collapsed. It was about 7:00 A.M. He died at two in the afternoon. He had made it to his island in the archipelago, the only part of South Africa he could call his own.

At his funeral, the men and women of Tshaneni eulogized him as a quiet, reliable person, who had provided for his family conscientiously. Probably they described him as "straight," an English word that has entered Xhosa as a widely used term of approval, agreement, consonance. His neighbors noted that he had signed his first labor contract at the age of seventeen—taken his first join—and married at twenty-four. He continued migrating to Cape Town every year, staying in the hostels there, returning for a month or two each Christmas. Over two decades of marriage, he had spent a total of about three years actually with his family.

His fellow villagers stayed up all night mourning and comforting his widow, Bandi, and her children. Early the next morning, they buried him in an open field across the dirt road from the small house he had built during his brief stints at home. His family had no money for a headstone, so thus far his grave is marked only by a clump of rocks.

There was a problem with Solomon Mpetha's pension. He had changed jobs months before his death. His old employers said he was no longer their concern; the new ones said he had not worked for them long enough. The regime informed his widow that she was too young to qualify for a state pension.

In other Bantustans, such desperate people can often survive for a time by a process known as borrowing, which is a polite euphemism for relying on the charity of their neighbors. Bandi might have been able to scrape by for a while. But then, she would have left the children with relatives, slipped into "white" South Africa and sought work as an "illegal" housemaid somewhere.

She fortunately landed a part-time job behind the counter in one of Tshaneni's two shops. The family continued to cultivate their two-acre strip of land. But it was not enough. The late Solomon Mpetha's firstborn son went to the labor office and took his first join, at a steel mill up in Vereeniging. He was sixteen years old.

Life in Tshaneni, like elsewhere in the Bantustans, is like being part of the rear in a far-off, never-ending war. For nearly a century, the men (and some of the women) have left for the front, the mines, farms, and factories in "white" South Africa. They return only for brief stints of rest and recuperation, or when they are old or injured. Of the village's fifteen hundred people, only perhaps a dozen are healthy men between the ages of eighteen and forty-five. The shops, where teenagers should be hanging out in the early evenings after the day's work, listening to the radio and raucously teasing each other, are empty except for a few handicapped people, probably victims of polio. Half the families in Tshaneni are completely landless, and therefore entirely dependent on regular remittances from the battlefront. The other half cultivate about five hundred acres, which are divided into individual plots of two to four acres each.

The spring rains started on schedule in September 1981, but Bandi

Mpetha was unable to start plowing on time. The oxen she would borrow from an elderly couple were still too weak from the winter hunger, and she could not purchase feed for them. She had to wait until the spring grasses grew enough to provide forage for the beasts. By then, she, and nearly all the other villagers, were a month behind schedule. Maize and sorghum need optimal conditions for the best yields, particularly in the fragile Herschel District. The Tshaneni small farmers had already, due to their poverty, lost part of their crop before they even planted the seeds.

Bandi awakened several hours before dawn to start plowing. After the sun rose, she and the other villagers continued working, pausing occasionally in the shade of small trees, the only ones in sight, which have deliberately been left standing in the fields as a refuge. Meanwhile, her oldest daughter, who is twelve, fixed breakfast, a porridge of sorghum, for the three smaller girls. There is no electricity in Tshaneni; the villagers cook over kerosene stoves or fires of dried cow dung. Two of the girls then lugged plastic pails to fetch water from the spring a half a mile away; they staggered back, giggling and slightly wet, a half hour later. The water would be carefully rationed during the rest of the day.

Three of the girls then headed off to school, leaving the baby with a neighbor. The Tshaneni primary school includes only the first three grades; children who continue must walk several miles to another village just visible in the clear air across the treeless valley. The very few who make it to high school have to board about ten miles away, on the other side of one of the jagged mountains that loom to the southeast.

In the afternoon, the little girls have more tasks. They pick up the baby, and take turns looking after her. They prepare lunch—the sorghum porridge is cold this time, and refreshing in the dusty midday heat—and take some down to their mother at the shop. They clean the smooth, shiny earthen floor of their home. Then, they might go down to the fields to gather wild greens to garnish the maize meal they will cook for supper.

They sometimes play in between their chores, strapping small objects on their backs in imitation of how the village women carry infants. They also learn to balance bulky, unwieldy and heavy objects on their heads; it is a skill they will need when they become women. After supper, they will clean up. There is little garbage in the Western sense; any leftover food is given to the pigs, or tossed at the scrawny brown dogs. Inorganic wastes, like plastic bags or glass jars, are carefully saved for later use.

After dark, the Mpetha family is reunited around the flickering fire. Bandi tells them stories, and listens as they describe their activities at school. The litle girls hesitate to venture out into the dark; they are scared of *engogo,* or goblins. A local woman had claimed recently that she was kidnapped one moonless night by engogo and a large black dog and flown to the top of a mountain for a mysterious ceremony before being deposited back on the edge of the village. Her neighbors tend to think she is exaggerating, though few of them doubt that such evil spirits do intervene in village affairs.

The little girls at times speculate about what they look forward to when they are grown up; they talk about clothes, furniture, eating meat every day. "What about a husband?" their mother once teased. "Oh, a man," answered the eldest. "Yes, but he'll be away working in Joburg." She hesitated, and then added brightly, "Except at Christmas."

The Mpetha family is asleep by nine. The consensus in the village is that Bandi will probably never remarry. A·prospective husband, who would probably be a widower already supporting children of his own, would balk at so many additional stepchildren. She is thirty-six years old.

If Ezekial Njongwe is sitting still, he looks a good ten years older than his real age of sixty-two. His hair is almost completely white and his face is deeply lined. In motion, he becomes younger again—tall, graceful, with a merry glint in his eye. He brandishes his walking stick as he insists, gesturing emphatically, that he can see, hear, and function generally despite his advancing age.

Ezekial Njongwe is best described as a civic leader. He is probably the most respected elder in Tshaneni. He left Herschel in 1932, and settled in Joburg, where he started working as laborer on the railroads and was promoted to supply clerk. His permission to live in "white" South Africa ended with his retirement, and he returned home, just as the Transkei became "independent" in 1976. He jumped into local affairs immediately. He formed a congregation of his denomination, the Church of Christ. He raised a force of volunteers from among the other elderly, the women, and the youths, and they built a new school. He started a farmer's association, which is taking groping steps toward coordinating some agricultural activities, such as plowing and purchasing seed. His efforts in the community have earned him the hatred of both the "traditional" authorities and the established black churchmen.

One gray spring afternoon, the association's governing committee met in a shabby hall to discuss purchasing seed directly from the suppliers. They wanted to circumvent the usurious "cooperative" in nearby Sterkspruit, in which various Transkei "government" officials were rumored to have personal financial interests. As the meeting was getting under-

Jubilant Kaizer Chiefs after winning the 1981 Mainstay Cup in soccer. Jingles Perreira is in the center, with his arm around Captain "Ryder" Mofokeng. Jan "Malombo" Lechaba is behind them, with both arms raised. (*P. Nkomo*)

Ananias Ipondoka, a member of SWAPO, the Namibian liberation movement. In late 1978, South African authorities in Windhoek arrested him, beat him, and extracted his two front teeth with pliers. He later escaped into exile.

Children in front of a shop in Tshaneni, the town in the Transkei Bantustan. As in other Bantustans, women and children are alone most of the year because the able-bodied men are away as migrant workers in the "white" cities.

Comrade Bernard, the Zimbabwean guerrilla officer, sitting atop his AK-47 rifle in Assembly Point Delta, a few days before the 1980 election. "The outside world thinks we are barbarians," he said. "But we are human beings. We fought because of the suffering of our people." (*Paul Weinberg*)

A section of Soweto, showing the identical "matchbox" homes. "It is not a city," said the young writer Mtutuzeli Matshoba. "It is a labor camp." (*Wendy Schwegmann*)

Mtutuzeli Matshoba.
(*Paul Weinberg*)

Ernest Kadungure, the ranking ZANU leader, speaking in rural Zimbabwe during the 1980 election campaign. Joe Jokonya is on his right. (*Paul Weinberg*)

A woman in the Charter District in Zimbabwe cheering Kadungure and other ZANU speakers at a pre-election rally in 1980. (*Paul Weinberg*)

Prime Minister P. W. Botha,
with his hat over his heart, at a
military parade in 1981.
(*Paul Weinberg*)

Monica and Sam, the so-called
colored couple, outside the flat
in Johannesburg from which
they were about to be evicted by
the Department of Community
Development. Under the
Group Areas Act, the flat
was designated as being in a
"white" area. (*Paul Weinberg*)

South African soldiers in the bush near the Zimbabwean border. All white South African males serve two consecutive years in the military, followed by yearly three-month stints.

A group of migrant workers with their belongings in a Johannesburg train station. (*Paul Weinberg*)

Mourners carry the coffin of Dr. Neil Aggett, the white trade union
official who died in police custody in February 1982. (*Paul Weinberg*)

The young *baas* supervises "his
boys." The *baas* will never do
any physical work himself. He is
there as an embodiment of
white supremacy.
(*Wendy Schwegmann*)

A "resettlement area" in the Kwandebele Bantustan. Since 1960, some 3.5 million blacks have been forcibly moved into these impoverished Bantustans, with high rates of disease and child mortality. (*Paul Weinberg*)

Refugees in northern Namibia. The South African occupying army has forced some 60,000 people to flee the war-torn area.

Modikwe Dikobe, the trade unionist and author. (*Paul Weinberg*)

A migrant worker at a mine in Krugersdorp. (*Paul Weinberg*)

Three night watchmen in Johannesburg. They are wearing overalls, typical of black workers, and carrying *knobkerries*, or clubs. (*Lesley Lawson*)

way, various members rose from the wooden benches, walked over to the windows, and gazed gloomily at the overcast sky. The slight drizzle splattering into the dry dust, known in Xhosa as fly-spit, was not enough to begin planting.

The chairman, a short, officious man, was not present; he had hurriedly packed a few possessions into a shopping bag the night before and left for Joburg, where his son had mangled a hand in an industrial accident. The vice-chairman, a woman, therefore presided. She opened the meeting with a brief prayer.

One of the association members, an older man notorious for his long-windedness, then rose to speak. He tucked his thumbs into the lapels of his frayed jacket, and rocked slowly back and forth, like a lawyer about to address the court. Njongwe, sitting in the background, regarded him with warm and patient amusement.

There was a muffled knocking at the door. It was the local induna, or assistant headman, who had apparently been apprised of the meeting by his informal intelligence network. He awkwardly shuffled about in the doorway. He was trapped between his belief that attendance at any village meeting was his hereditary right, and his fear of the association, particularly of Njongwe, whose hallmark, a red plaid coat, he recognized instantly slung over a chair.

A young man, in between joins, rose with dignity. Njongwe looked on from the side, his smile broadening. The younger man spoke politely but plainly. The induna had been neither elected to the committee, nor invited especially by it to the meeting. He therefore had no place there. Furthermore, the tribal "leaders" only collected taxes and gave nothing to Tshaneni in return; the villagers themselves had been forced to improve their school. Was this "straight?"

The induna stumbled out, shaken. As the door closed behind him, Njongwe muttered in a stage whisper, "Jackal." The others laughed in agreement. They turned to congratulate the younger man, who was still angry, on his action. They said they were sorry he was leaving so soon for another join.

Njongwe then described his recent trip down to Umtata, the Transkei "capital," to inquire as to why his thirty-five-rand-a-month pension was delayed. He travelled the 125 miles by bus, only to be kept waiting and shunted back and forth between various "government" offices for several hours. He was finally informed he needed to return to Tshaneni to get a "special paper" from his chief that would establish his very right to petition the "government." "We're going to keep having problems with these people," he predicted, as the committee prepared to turn back to its business. "It's going to be as exciting as at a bioscope [movie theater]." The others laughed.

The meeting continued. The committee decided, with the special reverence of largely unlettered people, that they needed a written constitution to outline their aims and rights and to protect them from "the jackals." They deputized one of their number to consult with the schoolmistress about the writing of constitutions. They made other arrangements, and then the treasurer, a young woman, asked for their monthly dues. They fished about in worn pockets and bags, withdrew knotted handkerchiefs, and carefully counted out bits of change. On a per capita income of twenty-five rand a month, even a five-cent piece is a precious object. The meeting ended with another prayer, followed by the single customary imploring word: *imvula*—"rain."

The committee members laughed happily as they said it. The fly-spit had gradually turned into a wonderful pelting downpour.

As the meeting broke up, Njongwe announced he planned to attend the Transkei Fifth Independence ceremony, scheduled for the coming weekend. He said he realized few other villagers would go, even though it was to be held in nearby Sterkspruit and the "government" was providing free food and drink. "It will be talk, talk, talk, promises, promises, promises," he predicted. "Since 'independence' only the flag has changed. But this time I am going to write it down on a piece of paper. Next time, I can remind them what they said, how they broke those promises." He waved his stick like a marching baton and walked out into the rain, on his way to conduct more civic business on the other side of Tshaneni.

Shadrach Mkele is an anomaly in the village. He is a healthy, strong man in his late twenties, who lives in the village year-round with his wife and two children. He has had to struggle enormously to bring about this state of affairs, which most people elsewhere in the world, even among the poor, would regard as entirely normal.

Shad is an extremely courteous man, even to his adversaries in the "traditional" tribal structure. He is in the habit of repeating the last few words said by whomever he is speaking with, as if to help them along. His politeness, however, is not to be mistaken for weakness.

He grew up in Tshaneni, leaving school after three years to herd sheep and cattle. Despite his lack of formal education, he speaks both English and Afrikaans well; he learned the rudiments on his joins and he is teaching himself more, with the aid of his treasured grammar books. He took his first join at seventeen, as a Cape Town construction worker.

He did three joins there, then signed on at a rubber plant in Vereeniging, where he trained as a maintenance technician.

Shad had bitter memories of his time as a migrant laborer. His reasons give an insight into his proud character. "First, you have to call those rubbishes, those amaBhunu foremen, baas whenever you speak to them," he said heatedly. "No, I will never again say that word to another man."

He warmed to the topic. "You are working there right next to him, the iBhunu. You know the job as well as he does. You see something that can be improved, a better way to do the work. You say it to him nicely. He tells you, "Shut up, kaffir. Do as I say, or you can pack your bags and go.' Then you have to say 'yes, baas' and do as he says.'' Shad imitated bowing and scraping gestures, with an insincere, mock smile plastered on his face.

The other black workers at the rubber plant elected Shad Mkele to the "works committee." "We committee members were from all over the factory. We gathered the complaints from the workers. Then, we had to give the complaints to two white men. They took it to the *makhulu* [big] baas. We never met him. It's like that in the whole nation—our leaders never meet the leaders of the whites."

Shad paused. He had been actually shouting, totally out of character. "Then, I went and got a heavy-duty truck driver's license. I didn't want an iBhunu around telling me what to do. With the truck, you clock in. You take the truck out alone. You come back. Then you clock out."

As a highly skilled worker, Shad Mkele was by then earning about two hundred rand a month. Whites doing the same work were getting eight hundred rand. But only as a sort of afterthought did he complain about the disparity in pay. The lack of respect for himself and for his expertise were obviously far more wounding, and one of the factors that caused him to resolve to free himself from the migratory labor stream.

He continued: "Truck driving was straight, but I was still away on the join, staying in those hostels. I had married when I was twenty-one. I sent money home from every pay packet. But I only saw my family at Christmas. I never thought to bring them with me. If they find you staying in the townships illegally, instead of the hostel where you belong, they send your family home and they send you to the jail."

Shad thought for a moment, then added: "I married when I was too young. I can't say I'm sorry, but I should have waited. The maBhunu put out this Bantu Education, to make us stupid, so we all do what they want. You think you must marry, go on the join, have children, and come back when you are finished working. You keep taking joins, and before you realize you are already old. You could have done something else, but the Bantu Education made you stupid. Why don't our people realize what these maBhunu are doing? If you close the door to education, you kill the nation.''

He saved his money and bought a knitting machine for nine hundred rand. It was obviously a prodigious purchase for someone of his income. He took a course in Johannesburg to learn how to operate it, then he returned to Tshaneni and taught his wife. They now run a modest business from their home, which together with what they produce on their small plot of land enables them to survive without the join.

In Tshaneni, he joined the congregation of the Church of Christ that Ezekiel Njongwe had started. It is a radical denomination, which meets in each other's homes and has no formal clergy. Shad Mkele is hostile to the local ''churchmen,'' who are all blacks. ''We have read our Bibles,'' he explained. ''It says there that Jesus was a working man, a carpenter. The churchmen here don't want to remember that. They give the service, then they ask for money. They are the only fat ones here.''

Shad strictly observes his religion's prohibition of alcohol. ''My late mother never let me drink,'' he said with a fond smile, ''and I stick straight to what she said.'' His voice took on a serious tone. ''There's no future in a beer. The maBhunu use beer to keep you from thinking about your life, to keep ideas out of your head.''

Shad Mkele is an avid, energetic member of the farmers association. He has a sense of history about farming in the region, part of which he acquired during the six-week ''initiation school'' he attended, like the village's other young men, when he was twenty. ''You go and stay up, up, up in the mountains, in a cave there. Each day, an old man comes to teach you. He takes you up even higher. You sit in a circle, and he teaches you about our customs, our history. We learned that our ancestors had much more land than we do. We learned they grew big crops.

''Now we are all pushed together here like sheep in a kraal. We lucky ones have one half-hectare of land. Others have nothing. Over in the Free State, just there, one iBhunu can have a farm as big as four thousand hectares. To live, we must leave here on the join. So we can no more look after our land properly.

''The farmer's association is trying to teach people better farming. My uncle; he's old, but he's learning. He built a dam to stop the rain carrying away the soil. He's growing more vegetables. He's making his own fertilizer. When he was on join in Joburg he had no time for such things. Think if he was still a young man, with all his strength—think what he could have done!''

The history Shadrach Mkele learned at initiation school is accurate. His observation that the area once prospered agriculturally has been amply confirmed by more formal historical research. A missionary who visited the Herschel District in 1869 reported that the flourishing black farmers produced enough grain both to supply their own needs and to export the surplus to surrounding areas. The missionary described Herschel as "the granary of both the [Cape's] northern districts and the Free State too."

Then, the South African regime started to apply the pressure to force some of these independent farmers into the mines or onto the big white-owned farms. The merciless taxation and land policies begin to bite; within twenty years, the value of Herschel's grain exports had dropped by half. By the late 1920s, another observer reported that the area was no longer self-sufficient; it had started importing some of its foods. Today, agriculture has almost completely collapsed, and the district survives only by exporting its people.

Despite the valiant efforts of groups like the Tshaneni farmer's association, the situation can only get worse. The resettlement policy has been grinding along; the district population, 75,000 in 1970, had jumped to 104,000 ten years later. The deportees are dumped into vast rural ghettos, some of them near Tshaneni, where they are not permitted to own either land or stock.

Those slums, euphemistically called closer settlements, already constitute one-third of the population in all the Bantustans. Their desperate residents naturally yearn for the cities, where in the past they had at least a hope of finding work, however badly paid. Their passes prevented them from moving to town officially, but they slipped in as "illegals," living in constant fear of police raids. Even if they were caught and arrested, breaking the law still made economic sense. They would still improve their standard of living over what it would have been had they not left the Bantustan. Dr. Jan Lange of the University of South Africa has made a remarkable set of revealing calculations. A man from Lebowa, in the north, who worked six months illegally in Johannesburg and was caught and imprisoned the other six months still boosted his living standard 170 percent over what it would have been if he had remained, law-abiding, in Lebowa. A Ciskeian who did three months in jail and nine months in Pietermaritzburg was *703* percent better off.

As an adequate safety outlet, illegal migration may be coming to an end. The great increase in prospective fines, from one hundred rand to five hundred rand with further hikes envisioned, is deterring employers from continuing to hire illegals. In any case, the total number of jobs in South Africa is insufficient; black unemployment had reached three mil-

lion by the end of 1982. It is hard to see how truly a monumental disaster in the Bantustans, a widespread famine, can continue to be staved
off.

The South African government says it is promoting "decentraliza-
tion," encouraging businesses to establish "border industries" just outside the Bantustans to provide convenient, accessible jobs. The policy
has basically come to nothing. On the contrary, the relocations have tended
to move people even further away from their work. Hundreds of workers who have been dumped in KwaNdebele, in the eastern Transvaal,
have to start rising at 2:00 A.M. in order to get to Pretoria or the Rand
on time.

About the only commercial development of any significance has been
the establishment of gambling casinos in several Bantustans. Each year,
mostly white tourists sidestepping South Africa's puritanical laws gamble about 350 million rand. They win back 280 million. One modest
jackpot on a slot machine is nearly equal to the yearly per capita income
in the apartheid archipelago.

There is no such glitter in Tshaneni; there are in fact few artifacts of
the twentieth century. Small boys, like elsewhere in southern Africa, build
intricate models of automobiles from pieces of wire, often complete with
sophisticated steering mechanisms and rubber-band suspensions. But there
are only three actual vehicles in the whole village. None of the roads
there or anywhere else in the Herschel District are paved. There is no
electricity. There is no sewage system, or piped water.

In one sense, Tshaneni is even worse off than before. The older stone
huts with thatched roofs, a few of which remain standing, are sturdy,
warm in winter and cool in summer. The mud, cement, and tin buildings that have replaced them are inferior in nearly every respect. But
stone masonry takes time and energy, and the men are away on their
joins. The art is in danger of dying out.

About the only signs of progress in Tshaneni are cheap transistor radios, and the occasional military jet, probably on patrol from the air base
up in Bloemfontein, droning overhead in a silver mockery of the village's backwardness.

Advanced technology is by no means unknown to the people of Tshaneni. They, and their ancestors, are longtime workers in the modern industrial world. On their joins, they fix heavy machinery, drive long-
distance trucks, use sophisticated equipment to mine gold and diamonds; they perform the host of complex tasks essential to the South
African mining and industrial sector. They—and their parents and their
grandparents before them—pushed "white" South Africa into the late

twentieth century, and they live worse than their ancestors did in the nineteenth.

In the outside world, the Bantustan policy has been strongly criticized for its effect on the "urban blacks," the approximately 25 percent who live semipermanently in the cities. As soon as "their" Bantustan becomes "independent," they are stripped of their South African citizenship, and directed to exercise their political rights in the far-off territories. The ultimate goal, as stated explicitly by cabinet ministers, is "no black South Africans." This policy, which has been compared to the Nuremburg Laws that denationalized Jews in Nazi Germany, has rightly aroused worldwide condemnation.

But the Bantustan program's effect in the actual territories themselves is even more wicked. It has caused massive suffering for more than half of all black South Africans. And the apartheid regime has no intention of backing away from the policy, even slightly. Central to the government's "reform" proposals of the early eighties is that the Bantustans remain unchanged. It is readying more of them for "independence."

It has been widely suggested that the Bantustan policy amounts to genocide. The word ought to be used with great caution, in respect for those people who have been victims. Genocide, according to the 1951 United Nations Convention, is "the intent to destroy, in whole or in part, a national, ethnical, racial or religious group." The Convention continues that in addition to outright mass killing, genocide is also "deliberately inflicting on the group conditions of life calculated to bring about its physical destruction in whole or in part."

Black South Africans in the towns, on the mines, or remaining on the white farms are not in the greatest danger. Their continued relative well-being is essential to the nation's economic growth and prosperity. It is the "surplus" black people, those who are not needed in the economy, who are the major victims. Already, the rates of disease and infant mortality are huge.

The excuse that South Africa is still on balance a poor country, unable yet to provide for all its people, is an obscene lie. Of the sixty-six countries in the world for which statistics are available, South Africa has the most unequal rate of income distribution of all. About 73 percent of all national income goes to whites, who are only 17 percent of the population. Blacks (Africans), who constitute about 70 percent, get 23 percent of the income. Even a small improvement in this grotesquely lopsided ratio could mean, quite literally, the difference between life and death for hundreds and thousands of people.

The regime will continue the Bantustan policy. It talks of spending one *billion* rand to consolidate the territories into slightly more coherent entities. Another one million black people are slated to be forcibly moved. The new deportations will only increase the danger of collapse in the fragile territories. The regime's policy already constitutes murder of some degree. As government leaders push the scheme relentlessly forward, they will certainly raise the amount of suffering, disease and death, if they have not already, to a level that can only be defined as genocide.

10

Namibia: The Last Colony

THE BENGUELA CURRENT flows up the southwest coast of Africa, churning up icy Antarctic water from the lower depths of the ocean. Despite the tropical latitudes, the air above the surface therefore remains cool. Offshore, a steady high pressure zone forces warmer air downward toward the coast. The warm air traps the cooler air beneath it, preventing rain clouds from gathering. The result is one of the world's most barren deserts, the Namib, which stretches along the coast for several hundred miles. The desert is an eerie curiosity. Interaction among the cold water and the warm and cool air creates clouds of mist, a blanket of salty moisture that envelopes the burnt orange sand dunes. The air feels wet, but it never rains.

South Africa, which controls the territory, calls it South West Africa. But the men and women who are fighting for independence call it Namibia. Naming the country for a desert is poetically appropriate. Aside from the barren Namib, the territory also includes a huge portion of the Kalahari Desert. In a total area twice the size of California just over one million people are scattered. Half of them are concentrated in the far north, in a narrow band along the Angolan border that is the only region in the country with enough rainfall to raise crops. The territory has a population density lower than anywhere else in the world except Mongolia.

The emptiness of Namibia is overwhelming on the 200-mile drive east from the coastal town of Swakopmund to Windhoek, the capital. You pass through Usakos and Okahandja, lonesome, raw, dusty frontier dorps. In between the towns, the countryside is desolate. At the coast there is no vegetation, only the stretches of white-and-orange sand, molded constantly into rivulets and dunes by the cool, salty winds. Further inland, you start to see tenacious scrubby plants, which increase in frequency until the landscape is an undulating sea of thornbushes, of marginal value only as grazing land. A range of blue-gray mountains is jaggedly visible on the northern horizon. Road signs warn of kudu crossings; the huge antelopes have been known to panic and leap straight for oncoming cars, causing fatal wrecks. An occasional jackal darts into the road. Otherwise there is no sign of life. Windhoek appears unexpectedly, a large town carved out of the brown hills under a cloudless sky.

Nearly a century ago, a German colonial force followed approximately the same route into the interior. Germany entered the scramble for Africa late, but its conquest imitated the pattern of brutality and deceit already set in the subcontinent by Boers, British, and Portuguese. In nearly all cases, the black Africans at first welcomed the colonizing forces, eager to trade with the newcomers and even willing to share the use of their lands. In nearly every instance, European greed, together at times with genuine misunderstanding regarding matters like the "purchase" of land, caused armed conflict. Black Africans defended their territories with enormous courage, but they always lost due to inferior technology and tribal divisions. In the end, the Europeans crushed the defenders, took most of their land, and started to force them to work on the mines and the newly formed white farms.

In Namibia, German investors searching mainly for lucrative mineral deposits used trickery to start acquiring territory. In one case, one black group "sold" the Germans a strip along the coast twenty "geographical miles" wide, in the belief that the agreement meant the familiar English miles rather than a German measure five times as great. The Namibians started to see through such guile, and resisted further German efforts to establish "protection" over them. Hendrik Witbooi, the leader of the Nama people, warned another chief to reject agreements with the colonizers. "This giving of yourself into the hands of the whites will become a burden as if you were carrying the sun on your back," he said. The Germans had to resort to naked force, dispatching troops trying to provoke conflict and create a pretext to conquer the territory outright.

Of the eight or so Namibian ethnic groups, two, the Herero and the Nama, were the most directly in the line of the colonial advance. The two groups had fought each other intermittently during the late nineteenth century; their warfare had helped the German occupation. In early 1904, the Herero people decided on a full-scale revolt against the colonizers. Samuel Maharero, their leader, sent a famous letter to the Nama chief Witbooi requesting an alliance. "All our obedience and patience with the Germans is of little avail," Maharero wrote. "Each day they shoot someone dead for no reason at all. Let us die fighting rather than as a result of maltreatment, imprisonment or some other calamity."

The letter never arrived. Even if it had, Witbooi had already decided not to join with the Herero; he even sent a small contingent to fight on the German side. Nine months later, when the Nama also saw no alternative but armed rebellion, the Herero had already been crushed.

The German commander, General Lothar von Trotha, did not hide his frank intention to put down the Herero uprising with a policy of genocide. "That nation must vanish from the face of the earth," he wrote. He promised to employ "unmitigated terrorism and even cruelty. I shall destroy the rebellious tribes by shedding rivers of blood and money." Von Trotha issued a proclamation: "Within the German boundaries, every Herero, whether found armed or unarmed, with or without cattle, will be shot."

In the German Reichstag, the great Socialist opposition leader August Bebel protested vigorously against the colonial policy. But he was unable to halt von Trotha's plans for mass murder. The German general could not defeat the Herero decisively in battle, so his troops forced them into the Omaheke Desert and drove them away from the water holes. They died by the thousands. Other Hereros were treacherously killed when they tried to negotiate during a truce. The German army, by now fifteen-thousand strong, then turned toward the Nama in the south. Hendrik Witbooi's people fought a stubborn guerrilla campaign, delaying the final German triumph by more than two years.

In 1904, there had been an estimated 60,000 to 80,000 Herero people in the territory. About 2,000 escaped across the Kalahari desert to neighboring Botswana. Of the rest, only 15,000 were still living at the end of the uprising. Of the 20,000 Nama people, only about half survived the war of extermination. By the mid-1970s, the Herero population had still not recovered to its level of 1904.

The German influence is still very much present in Namibia. One-quarter to one-third of the white population of about seventy-five thousand is German-speaking. Germans are well represented in commerce and the professions. Windhoek and the other towns have beer gardens, Wiener schnitzel, and clandestine remnants of the Nazi party. The main thoroughfare in Windhoek is still called Kaiser Street. The older buildings, with their steep roofs originally designed to shed the northern hemisphere snows, are incongruous in the dry desert air.

But the majority of Namibian whites are Afrikaners, who started migrating to the territory after South Africa conquered it in World War I. South Africa wanted to annex it immediately, but U.S. President Woodrow Wilson blocked the move because it would have denied the people in the territory the right to choose their own government. Instead, South Africa would administer the territory under a mandate from the new League of Nations. Pretoria was enjoined to prepare South West Africa for eventual self-rule.

After World War II, several Third World countries argued that the United Nations, as the successor to the League, had inherited the responsibility for the territory. Pretoria heatedly disagreed, and took the first steps toward absorbing South West. After interminable and inconclusive wrangling in the World Court, the U.N. General Assembly in 1966 stepped in, revoked South Africa's mandate, and placed Namibia, at least in theory, under direct U.N. control. South Africa's continued occupation since then is illegal.

The United Nations maintained that South Africa had betrayed the "sacred trust" of the original mandate. Instead of guiding the territory to independence, Pretoria had installed a system of white supremacy modelled after apartheid, with Bantustans, migratory labor, and a powerful secret police. South Africa neglected the genuine needs of the Namibian people; as late as 1960, only two out of every ten black children were in school.

In the late 1950s, black Namibians formed the South West Africa People's Organization (SWAPO), which sought independence by peaceful means. SWAPO and other nationalist groups patiently petitioned the United Nations to intervene. In 1959, police opened fire on a crowd of black protesters in Windhoek who had refused to be forced out to live in a new segregated township. Thirteen people died in the Namibian version of the Sharpeville Massacre.

On January 26, 1968, Herman Toivo ya Toivo rose to address a packed courtroom in Pretoria. He, like the thirty-six other Namibians alongside him in the defendant's dock, had just been convicted of "terrorism" and other offenses. The others had selected Toivo to speak on their behalf before the judge sentenced them. Most of the men in the dock, including Toivo, conceivably faced the death penalty.

Toivo spoke boldly, "We find ourselves here in a foreign country, convicted under laws made by people who we have always considered as foreigners. We find ourselves tried by a judge who is not our countryman and who has not shared our background.''

The courtroom, as in other major political trials, was jammed with spectators—newspaper people, representatives of embassies and international bodies, swaggering security policemen. But one group of people who are usually well represented in such courtrooms was not present. Toivo explained, ''We are far away from our homes; not a single member of our families has come to visit us, never mind be present at our trial.''

Toivo then pointed out that the South African government had designed the broad, vague, and retroactive Terrorism Act of 1967 with the thirty-seven Namibians in mind. ''It has even chosen an ugly name to call us by,'' he went on. ''One's own are called patriots, or at least rebels; your opponents are called terrorists.''

Then Toivo outlined some of the reasons Namibians had formed SWAPO. He himself was one of the organization's cofounders. ''Many of our people, through no fault of their own, have had no education at all. This does not mean that they do not know what they want. A man does not have to be formally educated to know that he wants to live with his family where he wants to live, and not where an official chooses to tell him to live; to move about freely and not require a pass; to earn a decent wage; to be free to work for the person of his choice as long as he wants; and finally to be ruled by the people that he wants to be ruled by, and not by those who rule him because they have more guns than he has.''

In 1958, Toivo had hidden a taped plea for Namibian independence inside a copy of *Treasure Island* and mailed it to United Nations headquarters in New York. After his speech was read out to the General Assembly, he was banished to Ovamboland, in far northern Namibia, and placed under house arrest. Toivo told the court that despite his suffering he had never abandoned SWAPO's belief in a nonracial society. ''I do not claim that it is easy for men of different races to live at peace with one another. I myself had no experience of this in my youth, and at first it surprised me that men of different races could live together in peace. But now I know it to be true and to be something for which we must strive. The South African government creates hostility by separating people and emphasizing their differences. We believe that by living together, people will learn to lose their fear of each other. We also believe that this fear which some of the whites have of Africans is based on their desire to be superior and privileged and that when whites see themselves as part of South West Africa, sharing with us all its hopes and troubles, then that fear will disappear. Separation is said to be a natural process. But then why is it imposed by force, and why is it that whites have the superiority?''

Toivo explained that SWAPO had only chosen armed struggle with reluctance. "I am not by nature a man of violence and I believe that violence is a sin against God and my fellow men." But, he asked, "Is it surprising that in such times my countrymen have taken up arms? Violence is truly fearsome but who would not defend his property and himself against a robber? And we believe that South Africa has robbed us of our country."

In the trial, Toivo had been charged with supplying food to the first small band of SWAPO guerrillas. The judge had mocked him, suggesting he was too much a coward to actually take up arms himself. Toivo, with patient dignity, denied the charge. Instead, he explained he had felt SWAPO was still far too weak to challenge South Africa militarily. But once the first guerrillas had gone into the bush, he had acted. "I am a loyal Namibian and I could not betray my people to their enemies. I admit that I decided to assist those who had taken up arms. I know that the struggle will be long and bitter. I also know that my people will wage that struggle, whatever the cost."

Toivo's fellow accused sat to one side, listening intently. They wore demeaning numbers around their necks so the judge and the prosecution could distinguish among them. They were exhilarated by Toivo's firmness and eloquence. Some months before, they had feared he was losing his mind. The security police had kept him for three hundred days in solitary confinement, and hung him from a pipe for four consecutive days to try to get him to confess. Another accused, John Ya-Otto, wrote later, "Nine months of torture and complete isolation had wrapped him in a cloud of despair."

But Herman Toivo, with the help of the others, had willed himself back to health. Now, with the threat of the gallows still before him, he completed his speech from the dock. "My co-accused and I have suffered. We are not looking forward to our imprisonment. We do not, however, feel that our efforts and sacrifice have been wasted. We believe that human suffering has its effect even on those who impose it. We hope that what has happened will persuade the whites of South Africa that we and the world may be right and they may be wrong. Only when white South Africans realize this and act on it, will it be possible for us to stop our struggle for freedom and justice in the land of our birth."

In the end, the high level of international concern ensured that none of the thirty-seven got the death penalty. Several were sentenced to life. Herman Toivo got twenty years.

In the early 1970s, burly South African Prime Minister John Vorster was at the height of his powers. He had temporarily crushed the resistance movement inside South Africa, leaving the anti-apartheid forces in a sullen, demoralized calm. His country was still surrounded by a ring of apparently impregnable white-ruled states. Vorster was eager to reduce world criticism of South Africa, which posed a nagging threat to the continued high levels of foreign investment. Pretoria was most vulnerable over its occupation of Namibia, which even the more sympathetic Western governments now regarded as illegal.

Vorster had reason to believe he could negotiate with the United Nations over Namibia. He felt he could install a government of pawns in Windhoek, and then grant the territory the formal independence that would satisfy the overseas critics but not menace South Africa's strategic and economic interests there. Vorster sensed little danger from SWAPO. The movement had managed only a few feeble landmine explosions since launching guerrilla warfare. Vorster regarded it as an insignificant matter for the police, no threat to his negotiating plans. He was about to make his biggest blunder.

A decade later, all had changed. The Portuguese military overthrew the dictatorship in Lisbon in 1974, and granted independence to Angola and Mozambique. The new revolutionary government in Angola immediately offered SWAPO base camps and a long border to infiltrate across. Through a fortuitous twist of geography, the strip of territory just south of the Angolan border is the most thickly settled section in Namibia, with about half the territory's population; the guerrillas would not lack for people to feed and hide them. By the late seventies, a SWAPO military force of up to eight thousand was fighting a full-scale guerrilla war in northern Namibia. In response, South Africa, which had once handled the insurgency with only its police, had dispatched a giant expeditionary force of one hundred thousand soldiers. If the United States Army had been as large a percentage of the Vietnamese population, it would have numbered 2.5 million, or five times its actual peak size.

It was no surprise that black Namibians were giving SWAPO strong support. Pretoria had installed a system of apartheid in the territory that was even harsher than the version in South Africa itself. The government had set up nine Bantustans, with separate islands of territory for nine black ethnic groups. The nine form an inverted horseshoe, with its base on the northern border. As in South Africa, most blacks are allowed to leave the Bantustans only as single migrants, after signing contracts, generally for a year, to work in the diamond and uranium mines or on the sheep ranches further south. An estimated two-thirds of all

Namibian workers are migrants, which is a proportion higher than in even South Africa and probably unequalled anywhere in the world.

South Africa produced a bizarre and unwieldy governmental contraption in order to remain faithful to this Bantustan system. Each ethnic group had its own "political party," which were linked in something called the Democratic Turnhalle Alliance (DTA). The little ethnic parties, which in the main consisted of coteries of prospective embezzlers, won "elections" to "legislatures" in each individual Bantustan. Their assignment was to manage "internal affairs" in each island. At the same time, each of the parties in the DTA sent representatives to a "legislative assembly," which was to oversee the territory as a whole. Possibly never before in history had one and one-quarter million people been governed by so complex a political system. Local wags amended the expression "one man, one vote" to "one man, one government."

In practice, the arrangement allowed whites to maintain most aspects of segregation, on the grounds that all-white schools and hospitals were not at all discriminatory, just facilities for the white "nation." But the majority of whites turned against the Alliance because they found its modest desegregation of restaurants and some other amenities dangerously reformist; they continued to vote for parties further to the right. At the same time, the DTA failed to win support among blacks to the extent where South Africa believed it could challenge SWAPO in an internationally supervised election. Pretoria's doubts increased greatly after the 1980 vote in neighboring Zimbabwe, where to its astonishment another "terrorist" movement won a sweeping victory. In early 1983, South Africa dumped the Alliance's first leader, a wealthy white farmer named Dirk Mudge, and kept on searching for more lifelike puppets.

By then, South Africa found itself in an agonizing dilemma. It was still trapped in a negotiating process it had entered ten years earlier, at a more propitious time. The United Nations, in an effort to be accommodating, had delegated its bargaining authority in 1977 to a "contact group" consisting of the United States, Britain, West Germany, France, and Canada. Even if the "Western Five" were more congenial to Pretoria than a group of Third World countries might have been, they did not change the underlying truth: South Africa is convinced SWAPO would win any internationally supervised election. Pretoria has therefore continued to stall. Whenever the negotiations have seemed to come dangerously close to success, as in 1978 and again in 1982, South Africa has created new obstacles.

Meanwhile, the apartheid army sweeps through the north from its huge bases at Ondangwa and Oshakati, and launches regular invasions into southern Angola. Access to the "operational area" is severely restricted. Military checkpoints prevent unwanted visitors from even entering the far north. The press, whether South African or foreign, is only occasionally allowed to accompany the army on carefully guided tours. Casualty lists and news of large-scale operations are released weeks later, and they are often suspiciously vague.

Hannes Smith, the crusading editor of the *Windhoek Observer*, found a way to hint at the real nature of the war. The law requires that under certain circumstances judicial hearings be held into deaths by violence. Smith's newspaper, by zealously covering these occasional inquests in detail, is able to give a glimpse into life in the war zone. Black civilians risk their lives if they break the dusk-to-dawn curfew. In a case that Smith reported in July 1982, thirty South African soldiers opened fire after dark on two innocent black farmers, killing them instantly; one of the soldiers tossed a grenade afterward for good measure. In another instance, two mothers with infants strapped to their backs died in a similar furious ambush after sundown. In both inquests, and in other similar cases, the magistrate exonerated the South African soldiers, finding that they had acted "in a bona fide manner in campaigning against terrorism."

The man responsible for these reports is universally called Smittie. A frontier society like Namibia almost requires among its cast of leading characters a swashbuckling newspaper editor, and forty-nine-year-old Hannes Smith fills the role to perfection. The mere mention of his name brings a delighted, knowing grin to the face of anyone who has ever spent more than a few hours in Windhoek.

His nickname is "Mal," which means "mad" in Afrikaans, his first language. He says he dislikes the name, but his behavior is certainly highly eccentric. You see him often on the streets and in the pubs of Windhoek, unkempt, florid, his arms spinning like propellers, shouting in his peculiar Afrikaans-accented English overlaid with what sounds like an Irish brogue, wild-eyed, sputtering about the latest plot his "enemies" have concocted to bring about his downfall and possibly his physical demise.

His journalistic feats are legendary. There was the time before the war that he raced the opposition out to a farmhouse where a gruesome murder had occurred, only to run out of gas and arrive after the corpse, and his chance for some splendid yellow-journalism photographs, had been taken away. No matter. Smittie racked his brain, then got into the bed in which the victim, a woman, had been surprised, drew up the covers, and imagined and subsequently described how she must have felt as the murder weapon, an axe, descended on her. The gory pictures in the rival papers were tame by contrast with the brutal, lurid power of Smittie's description.

The *Observer* is the opposite of restrained and neutral. Over reports of positions adopted by his political enemies—and he does not lack for adversaries—he puts headlines like: "Absurd Little Propaganda Trick," or "The Latest Twaddle." He previewed a congress of the Republican party—he found its leader, Dirk Mudge, particularly malodorous—as a "Tedious Song in Store."

Smittie also publishes a gossip column. Some of it is fairly standard innuendo: "The pretty young girl who waits in a powerful six-cylinder car just off the road, near the service station of the Safari Motel, for her important lover, is cautioned that the advice of a private eye has been sought and given."

Other items are less obvious: "A Tupelov aircraft will take off from Rome airport between July 20 and July 25 for Luanda, and on board will be an assortment of very interesting men, some of them dressed in field grey uniforms and others in the powdery blue of the Warsaw Pact powers and there is every likelihood that a Windhoek resident will also be on board."

The "Windhoek resident" is of course Smittie. He was not on the Russian plane. He is fond of throwing his "enemies" off the scent by spreading the word that he is off on mysterious missions to meet SWAPO, Russians, and East Germans—and then holing up over a long weekend on a farm within shouting distance of Windhoek.

In fairness, he has in the past left Namibia to interview SWAPO first-hand—or at least he did on one occasion produce "Special Pages" he said were based on such direct contacts. The authorities hastened to ban them, despite his lengthy fulminations. One alleged trophy of that trip is a photograph of himself, wearing a combat helmet, riding in what appeared to be a mysterious military aircraft, and reading a copy of *Pravda*!

Smittie, not surprisingly, ran into trouble with the regime by 1982. He regularly publishes photographs of topless models, more to irritate the authorities than to increase his circulation, which is already at probably its natural limits. In late March that year, the police raided him and confiscated some of the photos. He fought back in his April 1 edition, which included eight pages of nudes, more than his usual quota, and also advised readers they could acquire sex aids and blue movies at the *Observer* office. The police missed his April Fool's Day joke, and added further charges. Smittie promptly reprinted the first batch of nudes—in case some readers had missed them. He also published an inconsequential blurred photo of a military installation—to bait the army by challenging the restrictive Defense Act. I met him one evening declaiming on a street corner about his upcoming trial. He thundered, "We expect to lose. But we will turn that courtroom into a forum." (His statement, amplified later in his paper, earned him even further charges—for impeaching the integrity of the justice system by suggesting his fate was already decided.)

Smittie's multitude of idiosyncracies can obscure the simple fact that he is an outstanding journalist with keen political insight who is not afraid to publish what he finds out. It is he who pioneered the reports on inquest courts in the far north. He regularly exposes the awful conditions in the single-sex hostels and gritty townships where black Namibians live. He refuses to call SWAPO "the enemy," or refer to its guerrillas as "terrorists." He, with more sensitivity than most Western journalists, has discarded the word "tribe," which is offensive to many blacks, and now uses the preferred expressions "Owambo-speaking" or "Herero-speaking." (Blacks throughout southern Africa ask why two hundred thousand Icelanders are a "nation" or "people," while four million Zulu-speakers are a "tribe," with its primitive connotations.)

Smittie has sources, who must number in the thousands, in place in every hamlet in the huge desert territory. He also travels hundreds of miles weekly, often to the northern combat zones. His journeys over roads that are possibly mined permit him to ruminate in print on one of his favorite themes—the nearness of his demise—but he also gets stories no one else does. He disdains the idea of an office-bound editor, and insists on calling himself the Reporter-in-Chief. Other Windhoek newspapermen, both local and South African, sprint every Thursday afternoon to the printer as Smittie's paper churns out so they can immediately start to follow up on his scoops.

His editorials (which do at times masquerade as news stories) vigorously demand that South Africa grant Namibian independence, and end its complicity in draining the territory of its mineral wealth. One sample of his fireworks appeared in July 1982 under the headline "Extreme Cynicism."

"South Africa's utter contempt for the welfare of South West Africa is reaching new proportions daily. Her past deceit as far as her control of South West Africa is concerned taught her that she could get away with murder in the literal sense of the word. The fraying out process is happily observed from the vantage points created by the massive tentacles of the Pretoria system. . . .

"She is deceiving the emissaries of Western powers. She is getting away with it because she uses her pawns, Dirk Mudge and company, and of course the fictitious Red Bear to convey to those Western emissaries her difficulties in reaching a South West Africa settlement. . . .

"Cynical in the extreme. . .

"Does she care about the tens of thousands of children rummaging in dirt heaps for scraps of food? Do her foreign companies who belong to other multinationals abroad care about the plundering of the land, a plundering protected by the South African bayonet?"

Smittie's rambling, at times disjointed style—his opening paragraphs can be sixty to seventy words long, twice the customary limit—is due to his peculiar mode of writing. He strides back and forth in his small office, dictating at the top of his voice, working himself into a frenzy, while a member of his staff rushes to get it all down on paper. He jerks about like a large mechanical toy as new clauses dripping with abuse for his enemies bubble up in his imagination.

What characterizes much of his verbal composition is his intense nationalism, his unabashed patriotism for his bewitching desert country. His is not a love merely for landscapes and wildlife, like much of what passes for patriotism among whites in southern Africa. Smittie is devoted to his "countrymen," the name he uses to beseech them in the *Observer,* to all of them. He says his own impoverished childhood enables him to understand what many poorer black Namibians are experiencing now.

Smith is from the northern town of Grootfontein. On his mother's side, he is descended from the Thirstlanders, a legendary band of Afrikaners who late in the last century trekked 2,000 miles in search of a place to build their Calvinist utopia. Over five years, they journeyed through the Kalahari Desert, into Namibia, and beyond, to southern Angola.

His parents were poor farmers. He was only able to complete elementary school, after which he worked as a laborer on the railroads for a spell. He arrived in Windhoek, learned to repair fuel pumps and studied for his high school equivalency in his spare time. Smittie claims he had to work for several years before he could afford a pair of socks; he is probably exaggerating, but he must have been very poor in those days. "My experience embittered me," he told me in his office one afternoon, during one of his rare free moments. "I had a better brain than my contemporaries who went on in school, but no chance. Poverty and destitution shaped my ideas."

"But," he cautioned, starting to wave his arms theatrically, his fingers trembling, "my countrymen are now worse off than they were when I was a boy. Then, there was at least enough to eat in the rural areas.

They could hunt. They could grow their own food. Now, the overwhelming majority of them live below the breadline.''

Smittie joined an Afrikaans newspaper at the age of twenty-three, and moved to the English-language *Windhoek Advertiser* some years later. It was a remarkable shift, given that he had only learned English as an adolescent. He spent seventeen years at the *Advertiser*, the last seven of them as editor.

In 1978, a mysterious consortium bought the *Advertiser*, and started to turn it into a mouthpiece for the Democratic Turnhalle Alliance, South Africa's stand-in political movement. Smittie resigned in a firestorm of publicity. Six days later, he brought out the first edition of the *Observer*. He delivered the early issues on a bicycle.

He employs a hard-working staff of twelve, including two other reporters. The division of labor is blurred; the receptionist also writes the women's column. (One of which, an attack on obscene male telephone callers, was headlined in typical *Observer*-ese: "Telephone Thugs—Dirty Anonymous Cowards.'') Smith says the paper gets by financially, "despite the total onslaught against me.''

Not unexpectedly, he warmed to the topic: "We exist on a shoestring which can be snapped at any time. We have additional costs compared to the other papers. The other tenants in our building were uneasy about being near us, so we had to appoint two security guards. Our insurance premiums are high. . . .''

By now, Smittie was stalking to and fro in a towering rage, giving full cry in his resonant brogue: "They say the Communists give us money. I can tell you, I would accept a check from the Communists with deep-felt gratitude. I am fighting for my country, and I don't care who is aiding me. I would be happy to acknowledge their support on the front page. . . .''

Smittie is understandably discreet on the SWAPO question. Certainly, the movement's advocacy of a single, unified nation appeals to him. He must also be attracted to its promises to rein in the foreign-owned mining corporations. But whatever his sympathies, he would unquestionably fight to maintain his editorial independence if a SWAPO government came to power.

What worries Smith the most in the meantime is the war. He has done more than anyone else to bring its atrocities into public view. He has risked his life to do so (even if probably not with weekly regularity, as he has suggested in his paper). And he is extremely pessimistic. "The war is progressively escalating,'' he warned. "It may still become one of the wars of the world, one of the wars of this century.''

Smittie sometimes talks of going into exile. You find it hard to imagine him outside Namibia. Especially if the war continues, he will want to be around to chronicle it as best he can.

His endurance prompts a certain wonder among his admirers. Any other newspaper in either South Africa or its colony with a similar content would be closed down after one issue. There is suspicion his "madness" could be at least partly artifice, some protective coloration for himself and his beloved newspaper. Also, although he gives the impression of never listening, reams of information, a great deal of it accurate, appear in each week's *Observer*. As he bellows along—he gleefully describes his verbal style as "making their teeth rattle"—he may also be surreptitiously listening and weighing the responses his tirades provoke. He could be laughing inwardly at the de facto immunity from both prosecution and public censure he enjoys as an eccentric "mad" man.

In August 1982, Smittie went on trial for the pornography and Defense Act charges. He conducted his own defense, before a courtroom jammed with his supporters, two-thirds of whom were black. His argument was characteristically bizarre; he said he was the victim of a "witch-hunt" and he even claimed the South African military was plotting to kill him. At the same time, he said he had published the photograph of the army installation to reassure the public the military was extremely well prepared for attack!

Smith was predictably convicted. He faced a potentially stiff sentence. In mitigation, he pleaded that a criminal record endangered his career in journalism and was itself sufficient punishment. The magistrate nearly agreed, fining Smittie about 1,150 rand. Supporters collected pledges for the money within minutes. The sentence was universally regarded as surprisingly mild. Hannes Smith, keeping his innermost thoughts to himself, returned to his newspaper office to publish that week's edition.

My visit to Namibia in July 1982 coincided with another flurry of optimism about progress toward a settlement. Steady leaks about an imminent cease-fire followed by an election had started to emanate from several capitals, principally Washington and Pretoria. None of these sunny feelings were shared in Windhoek. Hannes Smith voiced the widespread sentiment that the positive noises were "a hoodwinking, a political trick of such magnitude that one can only describe it as the most cold-blooded deceit yet launched by the cynical masters in control of the country."

Smittie was proven right again. Within months, the optimistic predictions faded away. In retrospect, the whole episode looked like an effort in contrived optimism, another attempt by South Africa to appear accommodating and hope that SWAPO broke off the negotiations. This time,

Pretoria said its excuse for balking was the continued presence in Angola of about twenty thousand Cuban troops.

The Cubans had no bearing at all on Pretoria's continued illegal occupation of Namibia. South African sanctimony about foreign troops in Angola was darkly ironic, given that its own army had been the first to invade that country in force. A South African column pushed north in October 1975 after the Portuguese departed in an effort to install Pretoria's favorite Jonas Savimbi and his UNITA movement in power. The fledgling Angolan government of Dr. Agostinho Neto was well within its rights in requesting Cuban assistance to repel the South African invasion. Since then, the Cubans have been restrained and unprovocative; they have almost never, for instance, come forward to defend southern Angola against the regular South African incursions.

Even so, the Reagan administration has gone along with the South African case. Reagan himself said in 1981 of Angola, "It would seem to me that, if they really want to be a nation in the community of African nations, they ought to get rid of the outside forces." In fact, Angola's standing in the African community is unquestioned, and its right to host Cuban troops and receive Soviet aid is supported fully by even the more conservative states in the region. As moderate president Kenneth Kaunda of Zambia has said, "Britain and the United States joined forces with the Soviet Union to defeat Hitler during World War II. What is wrong now that our countries receive similar help as we confront another version of Hitler here in southern Africa?"

The Reagan administration issued an even more grotesque statement after the August 1981 South African invasion, in which up to forty-five thousand troops drove 150 miles into southern Angola and killed five hundred or more people. A State Department spokesman said, "In this context, we naturally deplore these actions just as we deplore any escalation of violence from whatever quarter." The Reagan administration was thus clumsily trying to distribute blame equally among SWAPO, which fights to liberate its country; Angola, which fights to protect its fragile independence; and South Africa, which illegally occupies the first and invades the second.

The administration's lack of fairness can only have served to encouraged Pretoria to continue its invasions. In January 1984, the South African generals once again sent several thousand troops 200 miles into Angola, killing between three hundred and five hundred of "the enemy."

After that invasion, Pretoria announced it would agree to a cease-fire and "disengagement" with Angolan forces. As Angolan troops had never been inside Namibia, the euphemism really meant South Africa agreed to stop invading northward for at least the time being. Pretoria simultaneously said solemnly it was ready to negotiate once again toward a comprehensive settlement in Namibia. It even released SWAPO leader Herman Toivo four years before the end of his long prison sentence. (There was some speculation that Toivo was ill, and South Africa did not want him to die on Robben Island.) Yet again, the United States accepted Pretoria's conciliatory noises as genuine, and even agreed to help supervise the "disengagement" agreement.

Throughout the lengthy negotiations, SWAPO and its supporters in the frontline states had actually been quite flexible. They long ago agreed, for instance, to defer discussion of Walvis Bay, the territory's only deepwater port, until after independence. The apartheid regime controls the port and a surrounding enclave because it inherited a nineteenth-century British claim. SWAPO has thus, however reluctantly, conceded South Africa a stranglehold over an independent Namibia.

Outside forces dominate other sections of the Namibian economy. South Africa owns key elements of the territory's infrastructure, such as the electric utility and the railroad network. The huge uranium and diamond mines—the two largest account for fully half the territory's gross domestic product—are owned by powerful multinational corporations. Political uncertainty has not halted the mineowners from plundering the territory. Consolidated Diamond Mines, a subsidiary of Harry Oppenheimer's Anglo-American Corporation, has reportedly been sifting the sands day and night at Oranjemund on the southern coast, even though the world diamond price has been at rock bottom. As a resource that could be exported to benefit the Namibian people, diamonds are not forever—there have been estimates those deposits might be exhausted by 1990. In theory, the mining enterprises are violating United Nations restrictions on exports from the territory and are liable for huge reparations. In practice, the mines have embedded themselves so deeply in the Namibian economy that any SWAPO government, however radical, would find it nearly impossible to discipline them.

South Africa does not fear an independent Namibia as a serious economic or military threat to its own existence. Pretoria's major worry is, rather, the domestic political reaction among white South Africans. The National Party is already under fierce attack from its right. Any hint at transferring power to SWAPO would generate a militant and probably violent resistance among right-wing whites in Namibia, just as French *colons* in Algeria created the underground OAS in the early 1960s to fight against independence there. The right in the territory would immediately conspire with their allies in South Africa in a serious, probably violent challenge to the National Party government. Only an even worse alternative, some kind of economic sanctions, could force the Nationalists in Pretoria to give in over Namibia. Unless the Reagan administration and other Western governments are privately making convincing threats, the 1984 effort toward settlement will be no more successful than its predecessors.

The South African casualties in the war have made its withdrawal even more unthinkable in domestic terms. By early 1984, an estimated three hundred South African soldiers had already been killed in action. That figure, as a percentage of the white South African population, would be roughly proportional to fifteen thousand dead Americans. The actual death toll may be even higher, as the statistics grow increasingly fuzzier; some combat deaths are probably relabelled "accidents." Nearly all white South Africans have by now lost an acquaintance if not a closer friend in the fighting. They will naturally be bitterly opposed to seeing SWAPO, the "Communist terrorists" they are warned against every day, taking power in Windhoek.

The South African Army has been unable to defeat SWAPO on the battlefield. Successive generals regularly declare the movement on the verge of extinction, in an eerie reprise of Vietnam. But within months, they are forced to justify yet another invasion of southern Angola to prevent a SWAPO resurgence.

There is one ominous way out of this stalemate. South Africa could simply kill or expel enough people in the north, primarily civilians, to force SWAPO to disintegrate. In a country with a larger population base, such a campaign of extermination would necessarily be on a large enough scale to attract world attention and condemnation. In sparsely populated Namibia, the South African military, which is already operating in remote semisecrecy, might have a chance to carry out mass killings and dispersals quickly and then declare the ensuing calm the result of a military "victory" against a minority of "terrorists."

This horrendous scheme has been at least discussed in the regime's higher circles. There is the precedent of the German genocide against the 1904–07 uprising, and there are already signs of similar barbarism in the present war. An estimated sixty thousand people have already fled north into Angola. The army has already declared the northern border a no-man's land, and forced residents to leave or be shot. A new elite unit, chillingly called only *Koevoet,* Afrikaans for "crowbar," has been charged with widespread torture and murder.

Most sinister, South Africa apparently takes no prisoners. The army claimed by 1984 it had caused about six thousand "SWAPO deaths." But a number of people I had met in the Windhoek legal community in 1982 estimated there were only perhaps two hundred people in prison or detention camps in the entire territory. An International Red Cross representative named Peter Lutorf who inspected some of the camps in 1981 said he was bewildered by Pretoria's official communiqués on war casualties. Lutorf cited one typical release as he told the press, "It simply does not happen in any conflict or battle that you have a clash with 200 or so people in which 45 are killed and no prisoners or wounded taken."

Another of the many interesting features of Namibian life is the intensely religious belief of the majority of the people. Some 90 percent of the black population are practicing Christians, most commonly Lutherans, Catholics, and Anglicans. Many blacks in their precolonial religions already believed in a deity and in a form of resurrection, so the coming of Christianity was not an abrupt change. Also, South Africa neglected the territory, so whatever schools and clinics exist were built and staffed by missionaries.

SWAPO has incorporated this religious side of Namibian culture. Chaplains conduct prayer meetings for the guerrilla soldiers before they head south, over the border, into a war where they will be outnumbered by more than ten to one. It would be a final bitter epitaph to the Namibian tragedy if they and the brave people who hide and support them were to be exterminated by a regime that piously represents itself as the Christian light at the tip of a dark and barbaric continent.

PART TWO

From Rhodesia to Zimbabwe

11

The Year of the People's Storm

THE RESTAURANT, just off Salisbury's First Street Mall, was nearly empty when I took a seat there one balmy spring evening in November 1979. I had just arrived on the all-day train from Bulawayo, in the southwest. A black waiter in a brown jacket came to take my order. After the pleasantries, I asked: "If there's another election, who will win?"

"Bishop Muzorewa, of course."

I put as strong a twang into my American accent as possible. "I'm new in Zimbabwe, but I hear most people really prefer the Patriotic Front and the guerrillas, but they're afraid to talk."

He walked away with a slight smile. Moments later, he returned with a bottle of Lion Lager and said: "If we put Bishop in, we can at least take him out sometime. With those others, we don't know." He watched my reaction, with a teasing hint of insincerity in his eyes. That day's editorial in the conservative *Herald* had made the same point. Then, he shrugged nonchalantly, "Of course, no one denies that those boys in the bush are the ones who are bringing this change about."

We met the next afternoon, in a nearby hotel bar that had been desegregated recently. Our arrival provoked stares from a raucous party of white soldiers in green camouflage uniforms who sat two tables away, amid piles of beer bottles.

The waiter's name was Lawrence Hodza. He was thirty-five years old, and he had worked in restaurants for the past ten years. He worked six days a week, and earned fourteen Rhodesian dollars, which was equivalent to about twenty-five American dollars. He had six children. One of his sons, he told me with a smile, was named for the American soul singer Percy Sledge.

It did not take Lawrence long to tell me that he did in fact support the Patriotic Front guerrilla alliance. He particularly preferred ZANU, the wing headed by former schoolteacher Robert Mugabe. In common with other black Zimbabweans, he referred to Mugabe as "Rob" or "Bob" and to Joshua Nkomo, the leader of ZAPU, the Front's other wing, as "Josh." "Most of us blacks support Rob and Josh," he said in a low voice. "But we have to play this cat-and-mouse game with the white people."

Some weeks later, after we had become closer friends, I asked why he had risked confiding in me. He said only, "We Africans can tell if a man's smile is sincere or not."

I had arrived in Rhodesia a few days earlier, to find the seven-year guerrilla war at its peak. More than a hundred people were dying every twenty-four hours. I had flown up from South Africa at night to Bulawayo, the second city. The Viscount airliner had extinguished all its lights and spiralled tightly down to the airport; the maneuver was a defensive precaution against ZAPU guerrillas, who had already used heat-seeking missiles to shoot down two of the passenger planes up at Kariba. All the people on one Viscount had been killed. On the other, eighteen had survived the emergency crash landing in the bush, but ZAPU guerrillas had killed ten of them.

In Bulawayo, young off-duty white soldiers walked boldly about in the dry heat wearing T-shirts that said "The Rhodesians are Coming" and showed a mob of goggle-eyed black caricatures running for their lives as Rhodesian air force helicopters landed in the background. An effluence of racist terminology flowed freely in the bars and restaurants, as the young "troopies" talked with some indiscretion about the brutal rural war. To the inevitable "kaffirs," and its long-standing Rhodesian counterpart, "munts," the whites had added "gooks," apparently imported by American mercenaries, and "floppies," a hideous term said to have originated in the observation that blacks "flop" when they are shot to death.

During occasional lapses into coherence, the whites endlessly repeated their central axiom—that blacks were too stupid, inefficient, and corrupt to run the country. Quite a number of white Rhodesians had left Kenya, Zambia, and other former colonies after independence and they were full of apocalyptic tales of decline and disintegration. These when-we's, so called because they started a good proportion of their sentences with, "When we were in Kenya . . . ," promised with grim determination that they would make their last stand for civilization in Rhodesia. Some of the people who loudly associated themselves with this noble endeavor were being less than honest. Some 40 percent of the whites had arrived in Rhodesia within the past fifteen years, attracted by the already high standard of suburban living rather than by any heroic desire to bring civilization into the bush.

From Bulawayo, I had then taken the train up to Salisbury. Along the 300-mile Rhodesia Railways line soldiers were posted behind sandbagged fortifications at major bridges and crossings. Guerrillas based in the thick surrounding bush had derailed trains several times. In the club car, a white woman made some reference to "the kaffirs" within earshot of the tall black waiter. Her companion retorted in a tone of mincing insincerity, "You can't use that word anymore. This is Zimbabwe now."

The actual official name at that stage was a monstrosity: Zimbabwe-Rhodesia. The ostensible prime minister was a black man, Abel Muzorewa, a bishop in the Methodist Church whose UANC party had won elections held the previous April. The Patriotic Front leaders—Mugabe, in exile in Maputo, Mozambique, and Nkomo, based up in Lusaka, Zambia—had denounced Muzorewa and the "internal settlement" that brought him to power as fraudulent, a sellout agreement that left real power with the white minority. They promised that their twenty-five thousand guerrilla soldiers would keep fighting until they achieved genuine independence. Mugabe's ZANU, in a sign of its determination, had declared 1979 the "Year of Gukurahundi," an expression in the Shona language that translates approximately as "The People's Storm."

Black Zimbabweans had similar grievances as blacks in South Africa. The major issue was the land. The white settlers who started arriving in the 1890s seized, literally, half the country. By the 1970s, a mere six thousand white farmers presided over huge estates of tobacco, maize, tea, cattle, and other products. They employed several hundred thousand landless black farm laborers, who worked for incredibly low wages. Meanwhile, the settler regime designated the other, generally poorer half of the country as Tribal Trust Lands, which were modelled after the South African Bantustans. There, about four million black people tried to survive on small plots. Even Western conservatives who argue piously that some inequality is necessary to stimulate initiative would be hard-pressed to justify the state of affairs in rural Zimbabwe.

Most families in the TTLs, aside from the few government-appointed chiefs, were not able to survive from their plots alone. So they were forced to send family members to the mines, which are scattered across the country, or to the towns. Zimbabwe therefore developed the same painful oscillating migratory labor pattern that prevails in South Africa. Segregation and profound inequalities persisted on the job, in education and health, in all realms of national life.

The huge discrepancies were instantly visible in Salisbury, a spacious city of 650,000. Salisbury has perhaps half a dozen ten-story buildings in its center; beyond, it is a true garden city, with large homes for whites drowning in bougainvillea and a technicolor of other flowers. The quiet suburban streets are lined with trees; the powder blue jacarandas bloom in October, the bright orange flamboyants burst forth the next month. Swimming pools, tennis courts, and bowling greens are everywhere. To the southwest, in contrast, are the crowded dusty black townships, High-fields, Harare, and Glen Norah, with the familiar, tiny standardized rectangular homes, here sometimes called shoeboxes.

The first nationalist movement arose in the 1950s, led by Joshua Nkomo. It was first called the African National Congress, later ZAPU, and it agitated peacefully for change. The white electorate, after flirting briefly with moderation, moved to the right as black demands grew more insistent. Whites voted in the Rhodesia Front, led by an undistinguished farmer named Ian Smith, who promised no majority rule in his lifetime and later, apparently unconscious of whom he was echoing, extended his promise to "a thousand years." Blacks nicknamed Smith "Chimuti," or "Tree" because of his intransigence.

Some black nationalists, generally younger people like a teacher named Robert Mugabe, grew increasingly disturbed at what they considered Nkomo's overly moderate, temporizing stance. They broke away in 1963 to form ZANU, and they started to prepare for guerrilla warfare. In 1965, the white parliament voted the Unilateral Declaration of Independence, breaking away from Britain in order to preserve the system of white supremacy. In response, both ZANU and ZAPU staged commando raids with small bands of armed men, hoping the resulting chaos would force Britain to send troops and depose Smith. The Rhodesian police crushed these attacks and detained their leaders. Britain did nothing, providing an interesting contrast to its quick military response in Guyana, Malaya, and other colonies where its black subjects had risen against the Crown. Blacks remained resentful but powerless into the early seventies.

In 1896–7, blacks in the newly declared colony had revolted and sought to drive out the first settlers. The second Chimurenga, or war of national liberation, began in earnest in late 1972, in the Centenary district to the northeast. A small band of guerrillas had spent two years reconnoitering the area, conducting lengthy, patient political meetings with the local people before launching the first attacks. Mayor Urimbo, one of these early guerrilla commanders, told me his band had spent an entire year taking political soundings along the Zambian border to the west, pretending to be fishermen, before deciding conditions there were not propitious.

That kind of patience succeeded. The guerrillas started to gain the support and protection of the rural poor. The war spread slowly at first; by early 1976, the conflict was still confined to the northeast and the death toll amounted to only several hundred at most. That year, the newly independent Republica Popular de Mozambique observed United Nations sanctions and closed its long border with Rhodesia; it also provided camps for refugees and for guerrillas, primarily those of ZANU's military wing, the Zimbabwean African National Liberation Army (ZANLA). The war now escalated rapidly. Volunteers, many of them young secondary school students, poured into Mozambique for military training and then infiltrated back, penetrating ever deeper into Rhodesian territory. Meanwhile, Nkomo's military wing, ZIPRA, which was based up in Zambia, was starting to infiltrate into the western part of the country. By late 1979, the maps at the Smith regime's Combined Operations headquarters in Salisbury showed that the entire countryside now constituted "hot areas." Comops, in an effort to evoke the spirit of World War II among the whites, had divided the country into operational zones with names like Repulse, Thrasher, and Hurricane. The death toll, already established at more than twenty-five thousand, continued to increase rapidly.

In the rural areas, life was transformed brutally and totally. The regime did not welcome press inquiries. But an independent agency, the Catholic Church's Commission for Justice and Peace, monitored rural conditions as best it could through the network of church mission stations. The Commission—its stalwarts included a brave middle-aged white couple, John and Pat Deary, whose concern for human rights earned them a right-wing gasoline bomb attack—reported that the regime had herded up to 750,000 people into crowded "Protected Villages," a traditional strategy designed to sever the ties between guerrillas and the people who support them. The government implemented a strict curfew to stop the clandestine night political meetings with the *vakomana* (the boys), as the rural people came to call the guerrillas. It also instituted harsh penalties for feeding or refusing to report the presence of guerrilla soldiers. Some 250,000 rural people fled the battlefield for the relative safety of the cities, while an equal number left the country entirely.

There were steady reports of atrocities, particularly as the minority regime declared martial law over wider tracts of countryside. Secret trials were conducted for captured guerrillas and their sympathizers, after which some, at least several hundred, were hanged, also in secret. Mrs. Deary, who often had to struggle to maintain her normally jolly demeanor, told me with horror one day the Commission had heard that a fourteen-year-old child was under the sentence of death. She was unable to confirm the story.

The brutality was by no means totally one-sided. Some of the widely publicized atrocities that the Smith regime attributed to ZANU and ZAPU were actually the work of its own forces. Others were committed by bandits, or deserters from the two guerrilla armies. Just as certainly, though, other killings of some missionaries and other civilians were carried out by genuine guerrillas.

Such attacks were never ZANU or ZAPU policy. But the guerrillas were at the very distant end of a tenuous chain of command from outside the country. The government's statistics indicate that about one of four guerrillas were killed in action. Even if you assume the regime was classifying some dead civilians as "terrorists," the casualty rate must have still been appallingly high. The young twenty-year-olds, on their own with automatic weapons, frightened—both of their prospects in actual combat and their fate if captured—exhausted, sometimes inflamed by drink, did commit some of the horrible massacres. As the level of violence spiralled upward, the bush fighters also killed civilians they suspected of informing for the regime. Almost certainly there were innocent people wrongly denounced by their neighbors, possibly on the basis of ancient grudges, who died in that way during the war.

The situation in the countryside was complicated further by the ambiguous status of the white farmers. They were in one sense civilians, who lived with their families. They were in another sense part of the regime's rural militia; they fortified their farms, armed themselves heavily, and went on regular military patrols. The guerrillas wanted to drive the farmers off the land, thereby breaking the backbone of the economy, weakening the regime, and hastening independence. If farmers did not heed warnings to leave, ZANU and ZAPU regarded them as legitimate military targets and did not hesitate to attack them; a clear majority of the approximately 450 white civilians who died during the war were farmers.

Even in the cities, the ugliness of war was apparent. Hotels and bars matter-of-factly posted signs directing white patrons toward gun racks where they could check their weapons. Ominous bizarre-looking armored vehicles rumbled through the streets. Due to sanctions, they were jerry-built in the country, and given names like "kudus," "leopards," or "rhinos." Some were filled with the all-white Rhodesian Light Infantry, others with black troops under white officers. Security guards outside major buildings searched everyone entering for bombs or weapons. Squads of soldiers and police regularly sealed off sections of the main streets to check identity documents and the contents of parcels. One young father told me he had learned with horror that his daughter and her elementary school friends had a new hobby; they collected and traded bullets of different sizes and shapes, just as they had once trafficked in marbles.

As the war widened, Britain and the United States took interest. Both nations had been rather more complacent about Rhodesia while Smith's authority remained unchallenged on the battlefield. The two countries did have genuine humanitarian concerns, no doubt, that induced them to try to mediate. In legal terms, Britain also remained responsible for the breakaway colony. The two also said they worried that continued turbulence in the region could somehow benefit the Soviet Union and Cuba. They were less open about their other fears. A prolonged war might well result eventually in a more radical government coming to power in Salisbury, a government that might, for instance, pose a threat to foreign investments in the country. In any case, Ian Smith was to Britain and America a harmful anachronism, who stubbornly stood in the way of an orderly transition to moderate black rule.

South Africa also wanted to dispense with Smith and end the chaos on its northern border. Pretoria had never sought to export apartheid, arguing that the policy was a specific solution to the country's own, unique mix of peoples. South Africa also sought larger regional markets for its manufacturing and agricultural surpluses. Then-Prime Minister John Vorster had pursued policies of "dialogue" and "détente" with his moderate black neighbors, including flying to Zambia for a highly publicized 1974 summit meeting with President Kenneth Kaunda.

During those talks, Kaunda told Vorster a now-famous joke that naturally involved Van der Merwe, the Afrikaner Everyman. This particular Van is one of the white maize farmers who trekked up to Zambia and remained there after independence. Years pass. Van prospers. He returns to South Africa to his high school reunion. There he meets his old classmate—John Vorster. Van, uninterested in current events, learns to his surprise that his old chum has become prime minister of South Africa. He is unimpressed. "Ach, man, John," he says. "In my country we let the bleddy kaffirs have that job long ago!" The real Vorster is said to have laughed heartily, without any discomfort. He never minded black governments in the region, as long as they remained under South Africa's political influence and its economic dominance.

Late in 1976, South Africa, Britain, and America pushed Smith toward the bargaining table. They had already forced him to release leading nationalists, including Robert Mugabe and Joshua Nkomo, from decade-long stretches in detention. But ZANU and ZAPU, which joined in an uneasy alliance that year as the Patriotic Front, refused to consider any settlement that did not guarantee sweeping land reforms and other changes. As their guerrillas spread across the country, they anticipated winning the war and marching into Salisbury. Smith also refused to negotiate in good faith: his military launched murderous raids into Mozambique, hitting ZANU camps there and slaughtering thousands of refugees and guerrillas indiscriminately.

Bishop Abel Muzorewa then came to Smith's aid. The little bishop had achieved genuine stature as a nationalist in the early '70s. But his prominence came largely by default; the major ZANU and ZAPU leaders had long been silenced, in detention or in exile. In the mid-70s, after Smith had released Mugabe, Nkomo, and other leaders, they immediately started to reestablish contact with their organizations, and with the people at large. As the bishop and another largely discredited nationalist, the Rev. Ndabaningi Sithole, slipped in esteem, they reached out—to Smith and the whites. In March 1978, they signed the "internal settlement" agreement, which gave them the trappings of political power, while reserving its substance—control over the army, the police, and most of the civil service—to the white minority. The bishop's government did abolish some remaining petty apartheid restrictions, but made no significant advances toward land reform, a minimum wage, or other substantial changes. Muzorewa had pleaded during the campaign that the guerrillas would stop fighting as soon as a black government took power. He broadcast pleas for an amnesty, and got no response at all.

As the war continued to escalate, the new British Foreign Secretary, Lord Carrington, convened yet another peace conference, at Lancaster House in London. Muzorewa and Smith attended in a joint delegation. They had no choice but to come; the war had not stopped and the West was not going to lift sanctions or recognize their hyphenated regime. The Patriotic Front, particularly ZANU, arrived with even more reluctance. They had been pressured by their allies, the "frontline" states. Rhodesia was now striking regularly into Zambia and Mozambique, and no longer aiming at only camps of Zimbabwean refugees and guerrillas. Commandos had destroyed all but one of Lusaka's road links to the outside, and hit deeply into Gaza province, Mozambique's breadbasket just north of Maputo. Britain was conspicuously silent about these raids, arousing suspicions that the Foreign Office actually welcomed the increased pressure on the Patriotic Front's allies.

This then, was the situation when I arrived in November; the talks in London went on, reported in touching one-sided fashion by the *Salisbury Herald* and the Rhodesian Broadcasting Company, both incapable of referring to ZANU and ZAPU as other than "external terrorists." At the same time, the war continued everywhere. All newscasts included a dry bulletin from military headquarters reporting the deaths of "35 terrorists, 17 terrorist collaborators and four stock thieves. Six civilians were also killed in crossfire. In addition, Sergeant——— and Trooper——— also died in action. Next of kin have been notified."

Among most whites, it was still axiomatic that "the terrorists" were a small minority of young blacks who were brainwashed outside the country by mysterious Cubans, Russians, and Chinese and who then returned to intimidate the rural majority. Whites took the turnout at the elections earlier that year, which the regime estimated at more than 60 percent, as proof that the majority supported Muzorewa and the internal settlement. This cheerful outlook was bolstered by quick interrogations of maids, gardeners, and other black dependents. The Rhodesians, therefore, saw no reason to abandon their most treasured cliché—"In this country, race relations are excellent."

Lawrence Hodza's elderly uncle seemed to personify the contented black man. Moses Hodza had been a waiter at the Hanover Hotel for the previous thirty-five years. He was the model of polite deference on the job. He grinned frequently at his mostly white customers, revealing an ill-fitted set of false teeth. He endured the rudeness, the frequent insults, and the occasional physical cuffs with the dignified stoic bearing of a church deacon. Certain of his older white customers were so fond of him they would only patronize the Hanover's lounge if he were on duty.

In truth, Uncle Moses Hodza was a lifelong nationalist. He had belonged to ZAPU in the 1950s, and then transferred his allegiance to ZANU after the 1963 split. Lawrence remembered living with his uncle two decades previously. "Every weekend, early in the morning he banged on my door. 'Son, it's time for the meeting. Those political people are standing up for our rights.' " Uncle Hodza's son-in-law, a bank teller, had left in 1972 for exile and the ZANU army. The family had heard through the "bush telegraph" that he had been seen in Mozambique a few years earlier, as a guerrilla instructor. They did not know whether he was still alive. While they waited, Uncle supported his daughter and grandchild.

Uncle Hodza and his nephew greeted each other in traditional Shona fashion; a slight bow, a single handclap, and a verbal greeting that differed depending on the time of day. Lawrence spoke softly to him in Shona, explaining my presence. The uncle nodded and said "Hmmm," glancing about the lounge cautiously. He held his waiter's tray and his waiter's smile in readiness for customers as he started talking in musical Shona. Lawrence translated. "Bishop Muzorewa is leading the people astray. Our true leader is Robert Mugabe. I would like to meet him, and thank him, as one man to another, for bringing about the return of the land of our fathers, Zimbabwe. The white man said we must not fight, that violence is wrong. But the white man went overseas to his war in 1939. When he returned, the government gave him a farm, or money to start a business. I've worked since I was fifteen years old, and I still have nothing. I never had schooling. I had to use my own brains to teach myself to read and write. If war was not wrong for the white man, why is it wrong for us?"

Uncle left to serve a customer, a florid, white-haired man who greeted him with a tone of hearty condescension. "Howzit, Moses," the man called out. Lawrence was explaining; "In our African custom, he is the same as my father. I address him as 'Baba,' which means 'father.' He paid for my school fees because my own father, his brother, was too poor. He bought me my first suit."

Uncle Hodza returned. "We want peace. We want the peace talks in London to succeed. In our African custom, we believe it is wrong to hate. After the war, we will say to the whites, 'You have fought hard, but now you have lost. But we must put the past behind us. We have been enemies, but we should now be friends.' "

Lawrence Hodza and I continued to meet regularly. We frequented the Msasa beer hall, a cavernous noisy establishment with a totally black clientele. Posters of Muhammad Ali were on the wall. The place was often filled with a pulsating reggae beat, interrupted by news bulletins on the radio to which the patrons paid close attention. One day, we heard that President Carter had refused to lift sanctions against the Smith-Muzorewa regime, despite strong pressure from right-wingers in Congress. Lawrence's friends congratulated me warmly and raised their beer bottles to America.

Lawrence told me about the white couple who owned the restaurant where he worked. "We call him Paul, even though it's not his real name. He has a very quick temper, and he gets angry several times a day. In the New Testament, the Apostle Paul sent his epistles to the Romans, Greeks, Corinthians . . . just like our Paul gets angry at anyone, Africans, Europeans, men, or women. His wife is 'grandmother,' because she's always trying to comfort people. Especially him.'' Lawrence said ten of the eleven restaurant workers supported ZANU; only the head-waiter was a Bishop Muzorewa loyalist. ''He wears a bow tie, he thinks he's better than the rest of us,'' Lawrence explained, making a gesture of dismissal.

He disclosed gradually he had not always been a waiter. He had worked as an elementary school teacher for nine years, until 1970, when he had been blacklisted for political reasons. ''I didn't tell you because I didn't want to burden you with my own problems,'' he said simply. The police had detained him and ten other teachers on suspicion that they had in-stigated students to destroy tobacco plants on white farms near his rural school. ''We were inside for only three weeks. They weren't quite so harsh back then. It was before vakomana, our boys, were in the bush. Also, if you were educated, if you could speak English properly, they didn't do the things they do to the others. There were quite a lot of evils in the educational system, and in our country. We all felt the injustice, but there was no way to get a redress. I knew they could sack me, but I couldn't condone that system. I don't take myself as a hero, but it was the right thing to do. I stood there as a man anyway.''

Lawrence Hodza was out of work for a year and a half, aside from a short stint as an agricultural laborer at nine Rhodesian dollars a month (about five U.S. dollars). His wife, nervous about how they would sup-port their growing family, quarreled with him. (Uncle Hodza mediated successfully.) Lawrence said that during the crisis he had returned to traditional Shona religious beliefs. He had consulted spirit mediums, people who went into trances to intercede with his ancestors. He left out pots of home-brewed beer and took other measures to propitiate the forefathers. Then, he got work down in Bulawayo for a time, as a waiter. There, a little white girl had politely asked him if he had a tail. He re-turned to Salisbury, still at a fraction of his former salary. He said he was too poor to even take his family on an outing into town.

Lawrence had not even bothered to reapply to teach after Bishop Mu-zorewa came to office. ''That ministry didn't change hands, so I'm still blacklisted,'' he said. He had longed to return to teaching. He talked proudly of his former students, some of whom he had heard were now guerrilla commanders. He said he was sometimes embarrassed when his former classmates at the teacher training college entered his restaurant and saw him on duty, in his brown jacket.

The Rhodesian Broadcasting Corporation continued with its regular war communiqués. Guerrillas ambushed a train in the south, near the Beit Bridge crossing over the Limpopo River. Others attacked a farm at

Hartley, killing Walter Brown, his wife, and seventy-four-year-old John Gilbert. The RBC had hired a couple of token black newscasters when Muzorewa took office; they adopted appropriately stern looks as they announced the deaths of dozens of nameless "terrorists, terrorist collaborators, and stock thieves."

The reports from Lancaster House in London were on balance positive. The British foreign secretary, whom the Patriotic Front occasionally inadvertently called Comrade Lord Carrington, had decided to reach agreement from all parties on a new constitution before turning to the even more sticky transitional and electoral arrangements. Muzorewa and Smith agreed readily to a constitution that favored them in a number of respects. The PF objected, especially to reserving 20 (out of 100) seats in the new Parliament for whites, to be elected by whites, who constituted only 3 or 4 percent of the population. But the PF's allies, particularly Mozambique and Zambia, were now the victims of continual, ruinous Rhodesian raids. They pressured the guerrilla alliance into accepting. The news bulletin came on a dry, hot afternoon. An older black barman congratulated me with a solemn handshake.

"The bush" is an all-purpose term in southern Africa. It applies to any generally uncultivated rural area, ranging from nearly treeless grasslands, almost like parks, to areas dense with thornbushes and msasa trees. In the northeast, on the road past Bindura, the bush is medium-density—thick enough to cut visibility, but not so thick as to impede movement. "You could lose a regiment in there within fifty meters of the road," said Dick Watson as we raced through the hot afternoon toward his farm. There were no speed limits in rural Rhodesia. Occasional black people, women, children, and older men, trudged expressionlessly along the edge of the narrow highway. "There's one of the gooks' favorite spots," he said, as we were forced to slow through a sharp bend in the road. "Couple of my neighbors got 'bushed just here. One of them, well, he's history now."

Dick Watson's tobacco farm was in one of the major "hot areas." All his neighbors but one had been attacked. He, like them, had turned his farm house and adjacent labor compound into a fortress, surrounded by walls, barbed wire fencing, and mesh netting to intercept grenades. (Companies in Salisbury advertised on television they could erect security fences in a matter of hours.) A hair-trigger alarm system connected his house with the watch tower down in the compound, which was heavily sandbagged and manned continually by his black hired guards. He kept seven guard dogs, including five Dobermans. Inside his house was a large collection of weapons and an Agric-alert radio that linked him with his neighbors and a nearby army camp. He moved everywhere with a pistol strapped to the belt of his shorts.

Watson was a hospitable, tanned blond in his late thirties. He was almost childishly proud of his large collection of tropical fish, which he imported from "down south," meaning South Africa. His wife and infant daughter lived with him. His younger brother Clive, who was on military call-up for half the year, spent the other half helping out on the farm. Over in the labor compound, a jumble of huts and shacks, were some three hundred black people. The seventy or so able-bodied men were the core of Watson's work force, but he also employed the others, including the children. He called them picannins, or pics for short. He apparently paid more than the national average, which was less than twenty Rhodesian dollars (twelve dollars U.S.) per month for adults, plus some rations. The children earned less.

After dinner, Watson and his brother sat back distractedly, drinking cold Castle beer and half-watching the television. The guard dogs scampered in and out of the house. The Agric-alert radio crackled from time to time: routine, regular checks. Clive, who was nineteen, described his latest tour of duty in the east. He had seen heavy fighting. "The gooks now move in sections of up to a hundred. We cull a few, but more keep coming over from Mozambique. They've started to stand and fight; we were having contacts that lasted for hours. They've even taken out some of our copters. You could actually say . . ." He paused, as if startled by his own realization. "You could actually say that some of them are soldiers now."

A news bulletin flashed suddenly on the television screen. President Kaunda of Zambia, after yet another punishing Rhodesian raid, had put his army on full alert and called up his reserves. The Watson brothers speculated earnestly. Would Kaunda invade across the Zambezi? Would the Cubans and Soviets join him? "We'll sort them all out," they said, with some forced boldness. "We'll have some *mushi* culls." Mushi is the Shona word for beautiful.

The Watsons obviously had been misled by years of Rhodesian propaganda. Kaunda, a moderate, somewhat bumbling figure rather than the cold-eyed Muscovite of their imagination, had neither the will, nor the means, nor the Cuban and Soviet troops to invade. His call-up was purely defensive. But the propagandists in Salisbury had long concocted vast external conspiracies that menaced the minority regime; "race relations" within Rhodesia, still good, would have remained excellent without the external meddling.

As we retired for the night, Watson handed me a shotgun from his arsenal. I was to keep it next to my bed. The floodlights outside threw up garish shadows in the surrounding bush.

The next morning, we set out for the fields in Watson's mineproof vehicle, a dark blue Land Rover that had been strengthened with armor plate. On both sides, racks fastened to the roof held six separate shotgun barrels, jutting skyward. As we lurched along the dirt track, passing women and children dressed in tattered clothes, Watson gestured toward two cords inside the vehicle, running along the seam between the windshield and the roof. "If I pull those, the shotguns lower and fire in series," he explained. "They'll take out anybody up to fifty, seventy-five meters away from the vehicle."

We went on a quick circuit of the farm. Columns of black children moved to and fro, singing as they carried tins of water mixed with fertilizer for the young tobacco plants. Watson used the first person with seigneurial grandeur: "I'm planting barley here," "I'm fixing the curing shed back there." He showed me the compound where his laborers lived. "There are a few switched-on chaps with kept-up places here," he said, "but most of them sit around drinking beer when they're off. They'll go through three big barrels at the weekend." He helps maintain a small school, with three grades. "But I have to force them to go," he said mechanically. He had discovered that several of his laborers had been in contact with the guerrillas. "We sorted them out," he said cryptically.

During the war, Watson, like a remarkable number of white Rhodesians, had turned toward fundamentalist Christianity, even though he had been raised as a Catholic. He mentioned several times he had achieved an inner peace since he "became a Christian." He added, with a beatific smile, "I could die tomorrow. I'm ready to go. But I feel . . . the Lord will protect me and my family."

He gestured toward a remote section of the farm, an unplowed corner next to the bush. "The gooks use that section as a travel route. We went after them once, past those rock outcroppings. I came through the grass. . . . Then I saw one, right next to me, a couple of meters away. I turned. . . ." He demonstrated, holding an imaginary rifle. "There's the adrenalin, everything happens in slow motion. . . . You don't get scared until afterwards." He paused, without saying what had happened. Then, in a burst of words: "It's wrong, I know. But I like it." He shrugged sort of helplessly.

Back in Salisbury, I tried to arrange to meet ZANU guerrillas in a rural area. I learned my aim was probably impossible; whoever guided me would be put in an ambiguous and possibly dangerous position. My presence, which would be communicated quickly through the legendary "bush telegraph," would arouse the suspicions of both the guerrillas and the "security forces."

I did manage to talk with an elementary school teacher, a shy, pretty woman with a Mona Lisa smile who came from a rural village fifty miles to the east. We met in the Norfolk Hotel's Jacaranda Bar, a racially mixed establishment where we were unlikely to attract much attention. Formal segregation in restaurants and bars had been abolished, but most all-white places had retained their old character, due to informal pressure exerted by trigger-happy young white troopies. She told me softly the vakomana had arrived in her village of about a hundred people a year earlier. The regime had quickly declared a 6:00 P.M. to 6:00 A.M. curfew, during which the villagers were forbidden to be more than fifty meters from their homes. Government soldiers, who she called the Green Arrows, had killed several children from neighboring villages who had strayed outside the invisible boundaries.

Nonetheless, "the boys" still came to her village after dark to hold *pungwes,* or political meetings. They talked about land reform and other aspects of ZANU policy. They were predominantly in their early twenties, former secondary school students. She said they were very polite. They forced no one to attend their meetings. In time, they did force the tribal council, an unpopular group of government appointees, to disband, thus putting a stop to the collection of taxes and the hated school fees and thereby gaining even more approval in the village. Small boys, called *mujibahs,* were in regular contact with the guerrillas out in the bush, keeping them informed about developments in the village and the movements of the soldiers. She gestured toward her own seven-year-old, who had accompanied her to town to help carry the shopping. "He's a mujibah," she said.

The Green Arrows, by contrast, were often drunk and brutal. Most were black, although white officers commanded them. One black soldier had hit her because she failed to speak to him in Ndebele, although she lived in a Shona-speaking region. In the elections the previous April, which Bishop Muzorewa had hailed as his mandate, the soldiers had forced her and her neighbors to vote at gunpoint. "The boys told us to try and boycott," she remembered. "But they said, 'If you have to vote so they don't hurt you, don't worry.' " Then she said sharply, "One boy can fight off ten Green Arrows."

She confirmed what I had heard elsewhere, that the attacks on white farms were to at least some degree selective. The guerrillas, she said, inquired first about the labor practices of the nearby farmers. She laughed briefly. "One white man, he doesn't report them. He gives them meat and *sadza* [the Shona word for maize meal]. He's never been attacked. When he goes on his call-ups, he leaves his farm—but the boys stay there to look after it for him. No one takes anything while he's away."

I also made contact with a member of the ZANU urban underground, a high school headmaster named Henry Shoniwa who lived in one of Salisbury's black townships. He was a bulky man in his mid-forties with a boyish face and an enthusiastic temperament. He had spent years collecting money and clothing for the guerrillas, and getting new recruits from among his older students. "You learn which students are honest after teaching them for some time," he said with a modest grin. "Those are the ones I picked." As the London peace talks moved along, Shoniwa and his cohorts had started planning for the election campaign. He produced a huge, rolled map of the country, wrestled it flat on his desk, and zestfully predicted ZANU's support in each of the eight electoral districts. Shoniwa, sounding like a veteran election strategist rather than a man who would be voting for the first time in his life, based his forecasts on the detailed, complicated political and social history of each region. He laid particular emphasis on how effectively the ZANU army had operated in the respective zones. "We won't have to do all that much campaigning in the places where our boys have been operating longest," he said. "We don't want to mess up the good work they've done already."

Shoniwa predicted that ZANU would win more than fifty of the eighty black seats, which the party would need to control the new Parliament because the twenty seats had been reserved for whites. His speculations were totally at odds with figures the Rhodesian whites and certain old Africa hands had started to bandy about, which gave ZANU fifteen to twenty seats at most.

As Shoniwa rolled up his map, I raised a potentially raw subject, the political infighting within ZANU. Some 70 or more "dissidents," including former party leaders, had been imprisoned by the Mozambiquan government at ZANU's instigation. Earlier, in 1975, Herbert Chitepo, the nation's first black lawyer and then ZANU's de facto leader in exile, had been killed by a bomb in Lusaka, Zambia. Among those implicated in the murder was Josiah Tongogara, the ZANU military commander, who was held in Zambian prisons for the next year and a half. There was never any conclusive proof against Tongogara and the others, but the suspicions lingered. The official ZANU party line was that Rhodesian agents had been behind Chitepo's assassination, but there has never been any convincing evidence to substantiate the charge.

Shoniwa did not hesitate to dismiss the official explanation. He said he was almost certain that some other ZANU leaders had ordered Chitepo's death, although he was not sure which people were responsible. As he spoke, he had a certain set to his jaw, as if he were performing an unpleasant task that he was nonetheless determined not to avoid. "Herbert Chitepo was a close friend of mine. He was a guest of honor at my wedding. My wife and I still keep a certain chair he used to like to sit in when he visited us at home. We've kept it over the years because it reminds us of Herbert.

"Am I still angry? Well, yes. I do bear some grudges against certain people in the party. I think Herbert was the victim of a tribal, or regional dispute. There were misunderstandings and mistakes. . . ."

Shoniwa paused for an instant. "We must try to put all that behind us now. ZANU is much more than only those people. Getting back our country is more important."

The Rhodesian Central Intelligence Organization was strained increasingly in prosecuting the full-scale war against more than twenty-five thousand guerrilla fighters; it could no longer effectively monitor relatively trivial matters, such as the lyrics to locally produced recordings. A number of songs in Shona with thinly hidden meanings started to appear on jukeboxes in the beer halls and around the townships. One such tune was called, "The Crow Lives by Hooks and Crooks." Some of its words were: "The farmer plants, the maize grows. But then the crow comes by night to steal the grain. How do you feel now, after your hard work? The crow is feeding while you are sleeping." The southern African crow is black, but with a ring of white around its neck—much like the clerical collar favored by Bishop Abel Muzorewa. "The farmers" whom the song encouraged to protect their gains were naturally the Zimbabwean people, particularly the guerrillas and their supporters.

Dr. Ahrn Palley, a short, rotund white man with a fringe of gray hair, followed the progress of the London peace talks with mounting excitement. He crisscrossed central Salisbury at what was a rapid pace for a man in his sixties, with a bundle of newspapers under his arm, in continual consultation with his wide range of friends and connections. He tried stoutly to play the hard-boiled, tough-minded politician, but his almost adolescent happiness at the turn of events kept showing through.

Fourteen years earlier, Dr. Palley had been the only white member of the Rhodesian Parliament who opposed Ian Smith and the Unilateral Declaration of Independence (UDI) from Britain. He had come to politics indirectly, working as a medical doctor until his mid-thirties. "Then, I got bored," he explained. He studied law, practiced, and entered liberal politics just as the nearly all-white electorate was moving to the right.

The Rhodesian Parliament brought UDI to a vote on November 11, in a deliberate effort to use Armistice Day to evoke a spirit of solidarity with Western values. Dr. Palley vigorously denounced the vote in Parliament as treason to the Crown. He refused to stop speaking. The sergeant-at-arms ejected him from the chamber at the point of a ceremonial sword. Dr. Palley marched out, singing "God Save the Queen" at the top of his voice.

The Rhodesian Front changed the election laws, he told me proudly, to remove him from Parliament. He ran again under the new, more exacting rules in 1974, and lost by only three votes. Dr. Palley had remained friends with the nationalist leaders during their decade-long stretches in detention. Now, Dr. Palley sensed ZANU and ZAPU were about to win political power—and he was elated. His Rhodesian Front enemies were nearing their downfall. "Most of the RF politicians are preposterous, deceitful caricatures," he said, with a rise of anger. "Smith said Rhodesia would have no majority rule for a thousand years. They all said they would never negotiate with the 'terrorists'; they would rather blow up bridges and burn down their farms. As they talk in London, where are their brave words now?"

On November 30, 1979, a fifty-five-year-old man named Maurice Nyagumbo was released from prison. The event was unnoticed by white Rhodesians, or by the world press, but it signalled a happy end to one man's heroic saga of resistance. Nyagumbo, a moon-faced, warm, and humorous man, had originally been attracted to politics back in the early 1940s when he was a migrant worker in Cape Town. He had enjoyed going to ballroom dances sponsored by the Communist party, which had still been legal in South Africa. But soon he got more deeply involved and he was deported back to Rhodesia. He was detained for the first time in February 1959 when the African National Congress, the first nationalist organization, was banned. He was released four years later. In 1964, now a founder-member of ZANU, he was sentenced to three years for making a "subversive" statement. He appealed, and was set free a year later, only to be detained again after the UDI in November 1965. He was released ten years later, during the brief "détente" period. He went straight back to underground political work. He was arrested four months later, and faced the death penalty. He got ten years in prison.

At the time of his final release, Maurice Nyagumbo had spent only two and one-half of the previous twenty years as a free man. He had never been outside a jail for more than twelve consecutive months. He flew immediately to London, to be present with his fellow members of the ZANU Central Committee at the signing of the peace agreement that had been finally reached at Lancaster House. Then he returned to Zimbabwe-Rhodesia, to start campaigning for the elections.

12

The Land of Our Fathers

MUCH HAD CHANGED when I returned to the country only two months later, at the beginning of February 1980. The arrangements for holding the election, which was scheduled for the 27th, 28th, and 29th of the month, were well under way. The British government, in the person of Governor Lord Christopher Soames, had taken official control of the breakaway colony in mid-December. Soames had declared the cease-fire would take effect on December 27. He ordered the Rhodesian Army, which he now in theory commanded, to pull back to its bases. At the same time, the soldiers in the two guerrilla armies were also to stop fighting, and report to eighteen "Assembly Points" scattered around the country's periphery, where they would be "monitored" by small contingents of troops from certain Commonwealth countries. The guerrillas, at first suspicious of a trap, trickled in slowly. As their confidence increased, they rushed to report. By January 12, there were twenty-two thousand men and women in the APs, which had been given military-type names like Alpha, Echo, and Hotel. Scattered episodes of violence continued to take place in the countryside, but the overall death rate dropped dramatically to less than 5 percent of its former level.

To assist in the cease-fire, eighty-two senior guerrilla commanders from both ZANU and ZAPU had flown into Salisbury airport, where they were greeted by tens of thousands of cheering people. Among the eighty-two, to the particular and great joy of the Hodza family, was their long-lost relative; the former bank teller was now the equivalent of a colonel in the ZANU army. Joshua Nkomo returned in mid-January to be met by an even bigger crowd. Robert Mugabe's homecoming two weeks later attracted what was judged the largest single gathering of people in the country's history. Both parties opened campaign offices in Salisbury, Bulawayo, and the smaller towns. Thousands of volunteers began spreading literature, placards, T-shirts, and other election paraphernalia across the country.

White Rhodesians were shocked at the increasingly visible and vocal evidence of support for the "terrorists." The British authorities were also frightened, particularly at the display of support for ZANU, which they regarded as the more radical party. Both the British and the white Rhodesians started to plan to keep Robert Mugabe from power.

If the two wings of the Patriotic Front had run together, they would have won. By now it seemed clear, even to the obdurate, that jointly the two could handily out-distance Bishop Muzorewa. The Bishop was starting to show panic and petulance as attendance dropped at his rallies, despite massive secret funding.

Joshua Nkomo had pleaded with ZANU to maintain the Patriotic Front wartime alliance into the elections. But the ZANU Central Committee, after spirited debate, turned Nkomo down. Robert Mugabe promised the two parties would form a governing coalition after the vote, but insisted politely ZANU would field its own candidates in every electoral district.

The whites, along with most of the Western press, attributed this split wholly to "tribalism." Nkomo, they said, "represented" the Ndebele-speaking people, the twenty percent of the population concentrated in the western third of the country around the city of Bulawayo. Mugabe and ZANU were contending with Bishop Muzorewa for the Shona vote in the rest of the country. People would simply vote like automatons for their respective "tribal leaders."

This was a serious misreading of a much more complicated reality. ZANU had split off in 1963 for reasons that were political rather than tribal. Its generally younger leaders advocated a more militant, eventually Socialist, position. They admired the Chinese revolution, and China aided them with arms and training. They distrusted the old guard, particularly Nkomo, who they feared would make unacceptable, self-serving compromises with the minority regime. Ethnic distinctions never mattered much in the leaderships of either party. An Ndebele-speaker, the irrepressible Enos Nkala, was a senior figure in ZANU from the start. Many Shona-speakers remained on Nkomo's executive even after the ZANU breakaway.

Fifteen years later, the patterns of support for the two parties looked deceptively tribal, in part due purely to circumstance. ZANU, the more avowedly radical organization, had established itself in revolutionary Mozambique, which by geographical coincidence, bordered the Shona-speaking areas. The bases of the more moderate ZAPU remained up in more moderate Zambia, which was just across the Zambezi River from the Ndebele-speaking territory. In both instances, people, especially the eighty percent in the rural areas, planned to support with their votes the guerrilla movements they had fed, sheltered, and protected during the war. There was certainly some ethnic consciousness, though it was in part a simple and understandable loyalty to friends and neighbors. But ethnicity was not—then—a paramount factor.

Nkomo, who was being eclipsed in the late sixties and early seventies by the younger, more combative ZANU, might have been expected to fade away. But he is a cunning man, with an admirable sort of tenacity. He is well in excess of three hundred pounds, with a hoarse, unexpectedly high-pitched voice. He is an actor, alternately beguiling and hectoring, who can feign a burst of temper followed by an angelic smile and a self-deprecating wisecrack. He maintained himself at the head of ZAPU during his ten years in detention and afterwards, in exile in Zambia. He endorsed the turn toward armed struggle and even procured for himself a flamboyant general's uniform. He strengthened his party's ties with the USSR, which aided his army with weapons and some training.

Throughout, Joshua Nkomo remained in essence a moderate. ZANU seethed as he continued his vacillating ways; he and Ian Smith made serious efforts during the fighting at negotiating a settlement that would have fallen well short of genuine majority rule. Even worse from the ZANU point of view, he seemed to be holding back part of his growing, more conventionally trained army in Zambia. The ZANU leadership suspected he was waiting for their more lightly equipped bush fighters to weaken Smith, while suffering heavy casualties of their own, before he sent his own fresh troops into Salisbury to install him in power. ZANU cooperated with Nkomo grudgingly, in the Patriotic Front alliance, but a majority distrusted him deeply enough to balk at collaborating in the election. ZANU was determined to demonstrate it was the stronger party in the elections before making any governing coalitions.

This division gave the British authorities and the Rhodesian whites their chance. The rumors were thick in the air. The basic scenario was simple. It conceded ZANU would probably emerge as the largest party, with thirty-five to forty seats. But the schemers expected Nkomo would win twenty to twenty-five seats, and Bishop Muzorewa about the same number. The whites would have their twenty reserved seats. Lord Soames would then stitch together a coalition among Nkomo, Muzorewa, and Smith, with Nkomo as prime minister. ZANU would be shut out, even if it were the largest single party. Nkomo had clearly originally preferred to run jointly as half of the Patriotic Front. Once that option was denied him, he coyly refused to rule out his participation in the stop-Mugabe alliance.

The injustice of the proposed deal would have been compounded by the racial division in the electorate. In winning 40 or more of the 80 black seats, ZANU would have been getting half the popular vote, as the 20 white seats only represented 3 percent of the population. They could win not just a plurality, but an actual majority, and still be shut out. To be safe, the party had to win 50 of 80, in order to control the 100-seat Parliament on its own.

The proposed stop-Mugabe effort would require an effort of willed forgetfulness on the part of the whites. It had been Nkomo's troops who had shot down the two Viscount airliners, and who had killed ten survivors after the first one crash-landed. A number of white people had pledged personally to assassinate him. The white electorate (which included the country's few thousand colored and Indian people) voted two weeks before the rest of the country, and as expected, picked Rhodesia Fronters for all twenty seats.

I went around that evening to RF headquarters on Fourth Street for the victory party. The atmosphere was subdued and tense. Most of the celebrants left early. The only person showing much enthusiasm was James Thrush, a very tall, elegant former member of Parliament with a full head of snow white hair. Thrush was a sports broadcaster who also did volunteer press relations for the party. He told me right away that the Nkomo-led coalition was a definite possibility. "I believe Nkomo is a politician," he said with zest. "He wants power; he's for capitalism. I believe that in 1978 he and Ian Douglas Smith, who's a very far-sighted man, had come to a private agreement. And then there was the Viscount. I lost a very dear friend on the second Viscount. It's hard for us to forget." He paused, with a theatrical sigh. "But that's politics."

In the late 1960s, Britain had offered rebel white Rhodesia an agreement that would have provided a leisurely transition to majority rule, taking the rest of the century. Ian Smith had refused. Now, Smith was the signatory to an agreement that brought majority rule immediately—after white Rhodesia had suffered through years of sanctions and guerrilla war. Had Smith's refusal, with hindsight, been wise? "Of course," Thrush answered without hesitation. "Our African leaders now, Nkomo, Muzorewa, have before them the sad example of the other independent

African states, these countries to the north of us, where communism has not worked, where it has brought near-total collapse. They can see they mustn't try to install the same system here.''

Thrush smiled in an oddly conspiratorial way. ''Also, Ian Smith was unable to move back then because of his own right wing. Between us, I can tell you there were some real crazies in the Rhodesia Front back then. But what's happening now is inevitable; the black man should be my equal, he deserves the same things I have. . . .

''But if Mugabe wins. . . .'' He took on a somber expression. ''I was on that death list of his. After one of the massacres at a rural mission station, I said, in the House, that he and the rest of ZANU should be shot if they ever came back to the country. So they put me on the list. His victory would mean the end of southern Africa as we know it.

''But he doesn't have a chance. I was doing a football match recently, and I was just about the only white chap there. The Rhodesia Front colors came out, at the start of the match. The black people sitting near the broadcaster's booth turned toward me and shouted, with genuine happiness. 'Look. Those are Baas Jim's colors!' So, you can see that race relations here in Rhodesia remain excellent.''

Prodigious efforts were underway to block ZANU and Robert Mugabe. Millions of mysterious dollars poured into Bishop Muzorewa's campaign, from South Africa and elsewhere. His smirking face was everywhere, in full-color posters and newspaper advertisements, promising a pork-barrel of free schools, medical care, everything. He had somehow also acquired three helicopters, vital in a large country with terrible back roads. Nkomo's campaign was also well funded; only ZANU seemed short of money.

Muzorewa also enjoyed the more vital and ominous support of a force of twenty-three thousand armed men. He had originally created these brown-shirted ''auxiliaries'' as a private army, lured from among the unemployed by the prospect of a job. They had ostensibly been transferred to the state's control some months earlier, but they remained under the command of white officers and loyal to Muzorewa. They—and the rest of the ''security forces''—should have been confined to base under the cease-fire agreement. But Lord Soames disingenuously cited the continuing low level of violence, blamed it on some five thousand to seven thousand ZANU guerrillas he said had not reported to the Assembly Points, and redeployed the ''security forces,'' including these already notorious auxiliaries. There was an immediate rush of reports that Muzorewa's brownshirts were robbing, raping, and electioneering at gunpoint throughout the rural areas.

Soames and his small team of British assistants undoubtedly were handicapped at having to administer the colony through the existing Rhodesian government apparatus. But he still was surprisingly tolerant of questionable Rhodesian practices. The 250,000 refugees outside the country, nearly all of them supporters of ZANU or ZAPU, were supposed to be repatriated in time to vote; the Rhodesian officials used delaying tactics to keep almost all of them outside. Soames was also relatively unperturbed about right-wing violence, including the three attempts on Robert Mugabe's life that forced him to stop campaigning in person.

The British instead hammered at a single theme, the ZANU guerrillas they said had remained in the bush to "intimidate" rural people. The Rhodesian media contributed by dwelling at morbid length on incidents of violence, all attributed to ZANU, in order to create the false impression the ceasefire had broken down. Soames then threatened to throw out election results from areas in which he judged ZANU "intimidation" was high.

Joe Jokonya was an intense young history lecturer, a serious, rapid-fire speaker. During the month of February 1980, he had a permanently hoarse voice due to his constant campaign speeches for ZANU. He lived in Salisbury, near the university, but electioneered in his home area, the Charter District about 100 miles due south of Salisbury on the Fort Victoria road. He had been a student leader in the early 1960s and a ZANU activist. After the UDI, the regime served him with a five-year detention order. Six months later, he and other detainees overpowered their guards and escaped to Botswana and freedom. He had gone to Britain to continue his studies and to promote ZANU in Western Europe. He had returned the previous year to teach and to work in the ZANU urban underground.

Joe invited me and a photographer friend to accompany the campaign in Charter. We rode down there one warm evening in a ZANU car, a beat-up Peugeot driven by a young bodyguard who disarmingly opened bottles of cold drink with his teeth. With Joe was another youngish, cheerful, and unassuming man, who had a cracked front tooth that gave him a certain innocent look. He introduced himself simply by saying, "Call me Ernest." Only from others did I learn that he was Ernest Kadungure, the legendary military commander who had led the very first group of ZANU guerrillas into the country. He was presently the party's secretary for finance, and one of the most influential members of the Central Committee. Kadungure was also from Charter. He had left there in the early 1960s, to work as a schoolteacher in Salisbury before heading into exile. He was about to see his mother and father again for the first time in fifteen years.

We arrived that night in the little town of Enkeldoorn, the district's unofficial capital. We went directly to Chivu township, which was separated from the "white" town by the requisite half-mile-wide sanitary cordon. The political nerve center in the township was the multipurpose store and eating place owned by Mr. Philemon Mabika, the ZANU local branch chairman.

Mabika was sitting in the corner next to his old-fashioned crank telephone when we arrived, talking to, or more accurately, bellowing at, the party's Midlands office over in Gwelo. He was a big man, over six feet, dressed in a white shirt and an improbably narrow tie. He came over immediately and fidgeted nervously as he reported on stepped-up military patrols, arrests of ZANU supporters, and auxiliaries terrorizing the area around Sadza, out in the Tribal Trust Lands. He was clearly worried. "If Bob doesn't come into power," he said with feeling, "we'll all die of being poor." He pointed proudly to the Mugabe poster he had just put up next to pictures of the Dynamos soccer team and a faded advertisement for Captain Kleen soap powder.

We sent out the next morning toward the east, to the Narira and Sabi North Tribal Trust Lands. The local party office had obtained the necessary police permits for two three-hour election rallies, at Chisangano in the morning and at Zheke in the afternoon. Two messengers had been dispatched, one to each village, the day before. In two battered cars, we soon left behind the sprawling cattle ranches and entered the TTLs. The party drivers, two youths called Comrade Gringo and Comrade Clever, swerved to avoid land mine craters and the occasional wide ditch that the vakomana had dug to trap Rhodesian military vehicles. There was no other traffic on the narrow dirt road. Utility poles tilted at crazy angles, their lines dangling below. Joe Jokonya mused aloud: "It was fine to cut the wires, but our boys should have left the poles alone. That's another item in the cost of reconstruction."

All along the way, some of the small villages were gutted and abandoned. In many cases, stores and other buildings were without roofs, a bizarre sight. Ernest Kadungure explained: "The Rhodesian Army ordered our people to take the roofs off so that their helicopters and planes could see from the air if our boys were hiding inside. Or the people sometimes removed the roofs to prevent the army from staying in buildings near them."

At Masasa, one of the ghost villages, Jokonya looked at an abandoned store and permitted himself a quick smile. "The guy who owned this place had two beautiful daughters. They were the target of aspiring bachelors from all around. We used to make special trips here to buy cold drinks and chat up the daughters." He laughed. "It's been twenty years now."

Groups of people trudging toward Chisangano began to appear a good five miles short of the town. They waved happily when they recognized the ZANU campaigners. Some saluted with raised clenched fists. "The bush telegraph is working properly," Jokonya said. "Some of these people will have walked twenty miles by the time they get to the rally." Kadungure added, "The committee will have swept the road for mines in case the security forces planned anything."

Our cars splashed through a shallow stream and climbed the last hill toward the village. Three thousand people were already waiting. Hundreds of them surged forward, screaming joyously, and formed a human corridor as the ZANU vehicles entered. The local committee, led by a dignified older man, stepped forward solemnly to greet the visitors. An older woman shyly spoke to Ernest Kadungure and handed him a basket of ears of maize. She was his aunt, and she had not seen him since 1965. She thought the campaigners might be hungry after their journey from town. Women ululated loudly, wailing through rapidly moving tongues in a piercing high-pitched sound of joy and approval.

The crowd gathered in the shade of a grove of trees, waiting expectantly. Men and women sat separately, in line with rural custom. They glanced at a knot of policemen armed with FN automatic rifles who had arrived earlier in an armored vehicle called a kudu to monitor the rally. The five black policemen and their young white commander remained nearby throughout, moving at times to within ten yards of the speakers.

It was a crowd of the rural poor, such as you see in the South African Bantustans, elsewhere in Africa, and, with alterations of race and dress, elsewhere in the Third World. It was a crowd that must somehow survive on a per capita income of just over two hundred dollars a year. Probably never before in history has such a degree of inequality existed in the world, especially in terms of access to existing levels of technology. In Salisbury, Johannesburg, London, and New York, people were using personal computers, travelling about in jet planes, and talking by telephone over oceans. Here, in the village of Chisangano in February 1980, there was no electricity, no running water, and no proper sewage system. People lived in the mud-walled, thatched-roof huts and tried to cultivate maize with oxen and hand tools. People died from diseases that have all but disappeared in the West, like cholera and tuberculosis.

They wore faded, shabby clothes, patched many times over. Quite a number were barefoot. The married women covered their heads, with kerchiefs or stocking caps, as a sign of their status. Many adjusted the infants strapped to their backs. A few, on the fringes of the crowd, opened umbrellas to protect them from the midday sun. Older men rolled cigarettes from bits of newspaper. Lean pariah dogs of an indeterminate muddy brown hue circled warily, snapping at flies.

One of the young ZANU aides stepped forward, raised a clenched fist, and said calmly, *"Pamberi ne* ZANU. Forward with ZANU.''

Three thousand people thrust their fists into the air and answered, *"Pamberi."*

"Pamberi na Comrade President Robert Mugabe.''

"Pamberi."

Ernest Kadungure stepped forward. "Thank you," he said quietly. "Thank you for giving us your sons and your daughters to fight for our Zimbabwe. Let us now remember those who died in the struggle.''

The crowd prayed in traditional fashion. They clapped quietly, at the same cadence as thousands of marching feet, relentless and overpowering. Kadungure spoke quietly and somberly. The women ululated now and then.

Then the mood brightened. A young woman on the campaign team, Sharlome Chabayah, sang, in a throaty voice, the first line of a battle song:

"There is much suffering in our country.''

The crowd joined in immediately. Hundreds of women jumped up and started to dance.

"The white soldiers are running away.'' The women snake-danced through the crowd, passing insouciantly in front of the group of camouflaged police.

"Zimbabwe is the land of our fathers.'' Everyone sang loudly. One old man stood on his head with excitement.

"We will celebrate when we get our Zimbabwe back.'' The wave of sound rose to a roaring crescendo, peaked, and then dropped away. The crowd sat down. A couple of infants, possibly startled by the noise, started to cry. Their mothers comforted them.

Jokonya stepped forward. A young aide whispered a translation for me and the photographer. "We have two comrade journalists from overseas with us today.'' The crowd looked warmly in our direction. "In town, people tell them you are intimidated into supporting us.''

A chorus of angry nos swept through the crowd.

"People tell them we of ZANU are terrorists, killers, *magadanga*.''

"N-o-o-o-o.'' The people shook their heads vigorously. "Down with these people.''

"Next week, in the elections, we will show these people who is master in Zimbabwe.''

There was a prolonged burst of gleeful applause. The next song, a fast number paced by rapid clapping, simply repeated the words, "Be Brave."

Ernest Kadungure spoke next. He smiled and winked as he talked to the crowd, pivoting to address everyone, projecting warmth and good humor. He started by talking about the land. "The settlers took half of our country," he said. "They left us with bad land. It is covered with anthills. It is sandy. We will divide up many of the big white farms, and everyone can have land. Then those who want to remain in the sand, well, they can."

The crowd clapped and laughed.

"School fees," he continued. There were loud sounds of disapproval. "School uniforms. Text books. We pay twenty-five dollars per child each year. We will make these things free to all."

Laughter and more applause.

"Muzorewa says we have our own government now. But have any of you ever seen a black police commissioner?"

"N-o-o-o."

"Look at these police here." He smiled and gestured toward the six. "Is a black man in charge?"

The crowd laughed. The white police commander shifted nervously and whispered to one of his underlings. "Is he talking about me?"

"Muzorewa says we are Communists who don't believe in God. He says we will turn all the churches into beer halls."

Laughter.

"That is nonsense. You can pray to God, or to the African spirits."

"He also says our fighters are still out here. But the British say there are twenty-two thousand in the Assembly Points. Or are those not people there?"

Kadungure closed with a few lines of "*Pamberi ne ZANU*," adding the "General Staff," "the High Command," and "the Central Committee." The crowd responded excitedly.

The next song was another fast, driving number. "The gun has freed our country. The gun is supporting us. The gun is the backbone of our struggle."

Joe Jokonya stepped forward. "Let us not forget the help of our comrades in Africa, especially Tanzania and Mozambique. *Pamberi na* Comrade President Julius Nyerere of Tanzania!"

"*Pamberi!*"

"*Pamberi na* Comrade President Samora Machel!"

"*Pamberi!*"

He then unfurled a ZANU flag. The people stared with almost mystical intensity, and murmured approvingly. The flag had a black rectangle at the center, surrounded by bands of red, gold, and green.

Joe paced about, speaking hoarsely. "Black is for the people of our country. But our struggle is not between black and white. There are white people who support us. Some are here. Some are overseas. And Muzorewa is black—but he has ordered the Rhodesian soldiers to continue killing our children. The red in our flag stands for the bloodshed which has been necessary to win our freedom. Since Muzorewa became prime minister he is responsible for that bloodshed."

He paused. Several men on the edge of the crowd angrily shooed away one of the pariah dogs without shifting their gazes away from Jokonya and the bright flag.

"*Pas pasi na* Muzorewa," he said. "Down with Muzorewa."

Three thousand thumbs jutted toward the reddish ground. A rumble of noise. *"Pas pasi."*

Joe gestured toward the flag again. "Gold is for the mineral wealth of our country. Our men work in the mines for twenty dollars a month. They dig up the wealth, but most of that wealth goes out of the country—to South Africa, Britain, and overseas. Muzorewa wears a clerical collar. He is keeping the wealth of Zimbabwe inside that collar, away from us. But the collar is open at the back. That's where the wealth can flow away, to overseas. We will keep the wealth of Zimbabwe in Zimbabwe."

A burst of cheering.

"Muzorewa says we are Communists. Britain and America have free education for all. That is what we want. Are they Communists in Britain and America?"

Laughter turned to applause.

"Green in our flag is for the land. We will get our land back, and distribute it to our people."

More applause.

"This is the land of our fathers. But nothing in our country belongs to us. There is Barclay's Bank, from overseas. But where is the bank of the people of Zimbabwe?"

Cheering.

"We have no money for helicopters and airplanes, like Muzorewa does, that drop papers telling the people to vote for him. But we have something better. We have the people. ZANU is the people. The people are ZANU."

A roar of agreement.

"We will win the election. If they try to cheat us, well, we don't like war. But if they want it to start again, we are not afraid to fight back."

The crowd rose to its feet with an explosion of noise. Three thousand people proudly and defiantly raised their fists once again.

The younger ZANU aides closed the rally with more songs, including a new favorite called "Vhoterayi Jongwe"—"Vote for the Rooster." The British had required ZANU to replace its old emblem, the AK-47 rifle, only a few weeks before, but the new symbol was already sweeping the country. Hundreds of screaming people, flapping their arms like ecstatic roosters and crowing at an ear-splitting level, escorted the ZANU cars out of Chisangano, and some gaily paraded alongside us for half a mile.

The police followed behind in their armored kudu. "They think we know by some kind of instinct where the mines are buried," Ernest Kadungure chuckled. "They'd rather be safe back there, behind us."

A little later we stopped, and Ernest Kadungure walked through a small maize field toward a cluster of huts. He returned fifteen minutes later smiling, half to himself. "My mother and father are fine," he said. "But some of my other relatives had forgotten me." He laughed.

That evening, the ZANU campaign team stopped to have a few beers on the verandah of the Enkeldoorn Hotel. "They used to segregate us in a little room in the back," Jokonya remembered. "But that, at least, has already changed."

People of all races and political persuasions chuckle at the mere mention of Enkeldoorn. The little town is the archetypal sleepy conservative dorp, Zimbabwe's Podunk or Dogpatch. The name is Afrikaans— it means "Single Thorn"—and perhaps three-quarters of the whites in town and the surrounding cattle country are Afrikaners, who have trekked up from South Africa over the years. The population is about three hundred. There are two main streets, four general stores, a half dozen shops, four gas stations, and one post office. The town's central institution is the Enkeldoorn Hotel. A few military vehicles were parked outside.

A large, middle-aged white man appeared from the bar inside, stared, and then said with theatrical dismay, "Oh no, it's ZANU."

The group laughed. "Come and join us," Kadungure offered.

"Just a minute." He returned with a younger white man, a burly farmer named Du Plessis, who looked our group over warily before sitting down. The older man turned out to be Colin Thorpe, a garage owner and prominent Enkeldoorn booster.

"I'm an African," Thorpe began immediately. "I was born in Africa before any of you were. Why do you want to push me out?"

"Who wants you to leave?" Jokonya asked. "We want you to stay and be part of the new Zimbabwe. There's enough room here for all of us."

"What about me?" Du Plessis ventured. "Are you going to take over my farm? I'm not interested in politics—I just want to farm."

Kadungure and Jokonya assured him ZANU planned no wholesale, indiscriminate nationalization of farms. Kadungure explained politely, "We will acquire unutilized or underutilized land at first. We will pay compensation. If your farm is fully productive, you shouldn't worry. But you'll have to pay your laborers more." He grinned.

Thorpe turned toward Jokonya. "What's your profession?"

"I'm an historian."

Thorpe registered his surprise—and doubt. "When was the battle of Waterloo?"

"That's ridiculous. What's your profession?"

"I'm an accountant."

"Hmmm, how do you make a trial balance?"

Other curious whites, including the policeman from the rally, now out of uniform, emerged from the bar. They paired off with the ZANU people, and three or four simultaneous arguments started. Du Plessis and an equally hefty friend, facing Jokonya, put forward the familiar proposition that the whites had brought "civilization" to southern Africa. "You were running around in animal skins when we got here," Du Plessis said, not intending any malice.

Jokonya responded in his hoarse whisper. "Civilization! Machine guns? Bombs? Exploitation?" Kadungure meanwhile expanded more dispassionately on ZANU's land reform proposals. Sharlome Chabayah talked about how the inadequate educational system had induced her to choose exile in Mozambique. Voices rose and fell in the general hubbub.

One hour and several rounds of drink later, the whites drifted away. "I respect them," Jokonya said. "They weren't afraid to confront us."

Kadungure chuckled. "When we were growing up here they never asked our opinion about anything. They never even noticed us. Now that we look as though we might win the election they suddenly discover they can talk to us. Ahhh, they've definitely got to change. But maybe they will."

The bus back to Salisbury was no longer labeled "African," but all the other passengers were black nonetheless. The Muzorewa regime had removed most of the remaining vestiges of official segregation, except in the schools, but little had actually changed. Whites owned cars, blacks did not, so blacks continued to travel in battered buses trailed by foul oily smoke.

A police roadblock stopped all traffic on the southern outskirts of Salisbury. All of us alighted, grumbling, to be searched. Then we reboarded the bus. A black policeman, stern, erect, and proper in his khaki uniform, beckoned the vehicle forward. After it had moved enough to block the view of his white superior officers, he relaxed, grinned from ear to ear, and flapped his arms wildly.

The passengers roared. Even the police were supporting jongwe.

In Salisbury, the pre-election tension continued to rise as the depth of support for ZANU became even more apparent. The frightened *Sunday Mail* published an editorial headed, "Free—or cogs in a Marxist machine?" The paper asked, "Is Zimbabwe to become a Godless country? . . . There can be no unity with Marxism, and any attempt to sup with the devil can lead only to anarchy and a type of suppression which will make colonialism look angelic." Bombs exploded in two Salisbury churches, and the media rushed to blame "the terrorists." The strategy backfired when the bombers blew themselves up accidentally near a third church. They were identified from their remains as black members of the notorious Selous Scouts, an elite military unit that frequently had been blamed for carrying out massacres while disguised as guerrillas. The destabilizers also attacked the Catholic weekly newspaper *Moto*, the only publication that treated ZANU with balance. First a mysterious fake edition of the paper appeared on the streets, filled with vicious, unprintable slurs about Robert Mugabe. A few days later, bomb explosions destroyed the newspaper's press.

Whites were nervously strident. Lawrence Hodza told me the customers at his restaurant regularly lectured him and his coworkers on how to vote. "They say we'll starve in a month if Rob gets in," he said in disgust. "But I argue with them. I tell them straight—no more cat-and-mouse game. Those people are chaff anyway."

Rhodesian whites felt a particular hostility to the thousands from overseas who had descended on Salisbury for the vote: the press, diplomats, and members of various commissions, official and unofficial, who planned to monitor the fairness of the elections. Even Americans, who hardly enjoy a left-wing image elsewhere in the world, were not exempt from the abuse. On a half dozen separate occasions, white Rhodesians threatened me with violence wholly on the basis of my accent. Tensed-up drunks informed me repeatedly Americans were "white kaffirs" and "nigger-lovers" who had "sold out to the Communists."

Bishop Muzorewa also got increasingly snappish as his campaign stumbled along. He even rudely refused at one of his press conferences to take questions from any journalists from Africa, on the grounds they were all biased; it was an odd stand for a man who presumably hoped to lead his country into the Organization of African Unity after the election. Joshua Nkomo continued to slyly sidestep questions as to whether he would accept the postelection pact Mugabe still offered. The British continued to denounce ZANU "intimidation," barred the party from campaigning in certain areas, and repeated their threat to invalidate the results from some districts.

The ultimate strategy to stop ZANU, a military coup, was talked of openly. It was probably no coincidence that all-white units, whose loyalty would be unquestioned, started to take over the armored patrols through Salisbury. Troops spoke hopefully about surrounding and bombing the Assembly Points, perhaps in collaboration with the up to six thousand South African troops who were already in the country. Lord Soames, in violation of the Lancaster House agreement, had allowed the South Africans to stay on the grounds they were "protecting" the Beit Bridge link with their own country.

Stirrings and military clankings could be heard from down inside South Africa. Even the normally moderate Johannesburg *Financial Mail* warned: "The Marxist ring of iron that will encircle us, should Rhodesia follow Mozambique and Angola, will also be a ring of violence, bloodshed and anarchy. It must not be allowed to happen." If ZANU had, as the British charged, really left five thousand troops out in the bush, the move looked increasingly like a sensible and necessary precaution.

Assembly Point Delta was located 150 miles east of Salisbury, near the Mozambique border. Just before the voting started, two friends and I, a photographer and another journalist, paid Delta a visit. We caught a lift with a black lawyer named Godfrey Chidyausiku, a large bearded man with black glasses. As we rode along, passing towering formations of balancing rocks, he explained he was visiting his younger brother, a guerrilla at Delta, whom he had not seen in years.

The Assembly Point was in a rugged bush area, near a small lake. A range of bluish hills shimmered off to the east. The sentries at the gate, dressed in an unmatching assortment of uniforms, checked our credentials and then half-extorted our cigarettes before they passed us through. About twenty-seven hundred guerrillas, including six hundred women, had set up a sprawling bivouac amid the ruins of an abandoned Methodist mission station. They seemed to have established good relations with the thirty-seven Commonwealth monitors, who were lightly armed Australian and British troops.

The guerrillas carried their AK-47 rifles, with the distinctive curved clips shaped like bananas, with them at all times. Many also had ammunition belts slung over one shoulder. They had set up kitchens, in which women stirred at enormous pots of sadza, or maize meal, and a rudimentary hospital. Groups of fifty guerrillas marched back and forth, chanting political slogans as they drilled. Others squatted in small groups, using their weapons as precarious, makeshift stools. When an officer passed, they jumped to attention and saluted by snapping their clenched fists diagonally across their chests and saying, *"Pamberi!"*

Godfrey Chidyausiku had spotted his brother, also a big man, just inside the entrance. The two embraced clumsily. There was a sudden noise, like a short peal of nearby thunder. "Land mines," the brother said as he saw our surprise. "The security forces put them around us here. But we know where they are. Stray animals set them off. There's nothing to worry about."

We left the two brothers to catch up on family news while we made a quick circuit of the Assembly Point. I noticed one guerrilla, who looked slightly older than the average. He was wearing a red beret and sitting quietly on his rifle. His name was Comrade Bernard and he was twenty-seven years old. I told him I was the same age. He smiled with a hint of complicity and lit a Madison cigarette. We talked for a while. Another land mine went off with a muffled crump.

Bernard had left high school back in 1972 for guerrilla training in Tanzania. He was presently a deputy detachment commander, the equivalent of a major or a lieutenant colonel in a more conventional army. He asked me informed questions about the American presidential primaries, which had just gotten underway. "George Bush—wasn't he the CIA director?" he wanted to know. "I don't think I trust him."

I asked him about the war. He hesitated, then said, "A few months ago, we were in a battle near the Mozambique border. Three of my men were wounded. They couldn't crawl away. We had to leave them. We came back the next day. We found them hanging from trees." He looked straight at me, with a drawn expression. "War is a terrible thing." He shook his head slowly.

Then he burst out, in an imploring, almost pleading tone, with the same pained look on his face. "The outside world thinks we're barbarians. But we are human beings. We had to fight. We fought because of the suffering of our people, especially in the rural areas. We had no choice. They don't have land. There aren't enough jobs. . . . We're not against white people. We're against discrimination."

He wanted to know what I had seen of ZANU's electoral prospects elsewhere in the country. He asked gingerly if I thought the election would be stolen. I said it was certainly possible. He shook his head decisively and took a ferocious drag on his cigarette. "Then we'll just keep fighting until we get it." I said I understood. I added I had never fired a weapon in my life. He looked at me with real surprise—and a kind of envy. We wished each other good luck, shook hands, and parted.

In Salisbury, Lawrence Hodza had interesting news. He and his fellow workers had persuaded the head waiter to stop backing Muzorewa. All eleven now intended to vote for ZANU. Other Bishop supporters also were switching, despite his last-minute propaganda blitz that included a four-day festival at which he provided free food and drink. The warm nights resounded with the piercing cries of happy, tipsy adults imitating roosters.

The election was scheduled to last three days so that people deep in the rural areas would have time to reach a voting place. Lines more than a mile long formed at some polling stations the very first day. To prevent duplicate balloting, each voter had to dip their hand into a chemical solution that could be checked under an ultraviolet light. The rumor started immediately that the solution could be washed off by Coca-Cola. It was not true.

In Charter, Mabika and the local ZANU committee had rented a bus to ferry old and infirm voters to and from the polling stations. Brown-shirted auxiliaries and Rhodesian black Special Branch men arrested the middle-aged driver on specious grounds. A friend and I misrepresented ourselves as "observers" and obtained his release. In Mabika's establishment that evening he thanked us lavishly for saving him from a certain beating. An old man interjected angrily, "Muzorewa has airplanes to drop papers for him. We are barefoot. Where does a black man get airplanes?" Military vehicles rolled through the township outside regularly.

A bus stopped, and disgorged passengers from humid Victoria province in the southeast. That area had long been regarded a ZANU stronghold; the sugarcane cutters on the big plantations at Chiredzi and Triangle, who did some of the roughest, most wretched work in the country, needed little persuasion to support radical change.

As Mabika's wife, daughter, and other relatives served the passengers, I asked one of them, a young man, how the election was going in Victoria. He took on a mystical, reverent air, as if he had seen something holy. "They all voted the first day. At one place, the security forces had nailed a dead jongwe outside the polling station, but they were not afraid. Now, they're just marching along the roads, back and forth, many,

many kilometers, hundreds, no, thousands of them, singing, chanting. It's like . . .'' He fumbled for the superlative. ''It's like the marches of Martin Luther King in your country.''

The stunning election results were broadcast simultaneously over radio and television at 9:00 A.M. on March 4. The entire nation listened. Eric Pope Simonds, the election registrar, read the amazing results in a deadpan, bureaucratic voice. Twenty seats for ZAPU and Joshua Nkomo. Three seats for Bishop Abel Muzorewa. And a phenomenal fifty-seven seats for ZANU and Robert Mugabe. The crushing finality of the result, validated by the imprimatur of Britain and the international community, would forestall any coup attempt.

The sound of roosters crowing reverberated through Salisbury. Car horns blared. Arms flapped wildly all over town. People festooned themselves with flags, pictures of Mugabe, purple-and-white stickers that read, ''ZANU and the People are One.'' In none of the controlled ecstasy was there any hostility toward white people.

On the contrary, Lawrence Hodza and his friends, with whom I celebrated that afternoon in the noisy Msasa beer hall, were genuinely hurt at the negative reactions of whites. Some were threatening to leave the country immediately. A teacher said he had heard luggage sales over at Greaterman's were on the rise. Others described how their superiors had rushed off to apply for passports. One younger man, a waiter at the nearby Meikles Hotel, told our gathering his white general manager had acted strangely. ''He said 'good morning' to us. He's been there for twenty-five years and this is the first time he's ever said 'good morning' to an African.''

Lawrence reported the owners of his restaurant had also threatened to leave before the inevitable disintegration. ''Grandmother'' had been particularly biting in her comments. Over the years, he had developed a theory to explain her conduct. ''According to the information we got, she comes from a very poor family. She even used to cook for herself.'' He looked around, to make sure his listeners were duly impressed at this revelation. ''It's people like her that become bullies. They want to make their presence *known* to an African.'' He sighed.

A very fat, very drunk woman staggered into the beer hall and started dancing to the Bob Marley and the Wailers record playing loudly on the phonograph. An office worker in our group recited a humorous little formulation that alluded to Muzorewa's alleged extramarital activities. ''Bishop,'' he said, forcing a straight face. ''Three helicopters. Three women. And. . . .'' He laughed in anticipation of his own punch line. ''Three seats in Parliament.''

Lord Soames had no choice. He responded immediately to the sweeping mandate by asking Robert Mugabe to form the first government of Zimbabwe. The prime minister–designate held a press conference on the lawn of his rented home in northern Salisbury, at which he issued the first of many repeated calls for national reconciliation. As his delicate, regal wife Sally moved quietly among the hundreds of journalists, offering them homemade snacks, Mugabe assured whites and others that ZANU would not "victimize the minority." He added, "There should be a sense of security on the part of everybody—winners and losers." Just as he had promised, he offered Joshua Nkomo a place in the new government. As he spoke, he pressed his fingertips together, a characteristically pensive gesture. He is a serious, cerebral man—"Rob" is somehow inappropriate—who is not given to emotional outbursts. But there was no mistaking the joy he felt that day in his garden.

It had been a long journey for Robert Mugabe, who was then nearly fifty-six years old. He was himself a child of the rural poor, who had studied to be a teacher at a church mission; he remained a practicing Catholic. As a young man, he had worked in Ghana, attracted by Kwame Nkrumah's anticolonial leadership. He met his wife there. In 1960, he returned home to join Joshua Nkomo's National Democratic Party, later ZAPU. He joined the 1963 walkout that formed ZANU, and served as secretary-general of the new organization.

The Rhodesian regime detained him along with the other leaders of both movements when it issued the Unilateral Declaration of Independence. He remained imprisoned for the next ten years. In addition to the three college degrees he already had, he earned four more through correspondence courses. He was released during the brief détente period in the mid-1970s. He escaped to Mozambique, crossing the border on foot. After a confusing interregnum he was confirmed as ZANU's president. He led the party unswervingly through the torturous prolonged negotiations, refusing to settle for anything less than genuine independence.

During Robert Mugabe's decade in detention, his only child, a small son, had died. He had asked Ian Smith for a brief parole so he could attend the funeral. Smith had refused. Now, Robert and Sally Mugabe were too old to have children of their own. As the votes in the historic election were being counted, rumors of the ZANU landslide had started to trickle out. A worried Ian Smith had appeared in person one night at the Mugabe home. Mugabe had greeted him courteously and reassured him ZANU would not seek vengeance. Robert Mugabe, with this superhuman act of personal forgiveness, was setting the example of reconciliation in the new nation that had chosen him as its leader.

13

Independence and Reconciliation

WHEN I RETURNED to Enkeldoorn a year later, the central institution in the little town was still the dimly lit barroom of the single hotel. Suspended over the bar itself is a canopy made of grass thatching, meant to resemble the roof of a hut. The walls are covered with typical barroom knickknacks, including the inevitable placards with messages like: "Marriage has a ring to it. Engagement Ring. Wedding Ring. Suffering." To one side of the bar is a gun rack. During the war, whites left their weapons there. Now, a year after the independence elections, the rack was empty.

During the hot afternoon, the proprietor, Brian Field, originally of London, tended bar for the occasional traveller on the Salisbury–Fort Victoria highway. He sipped his own beer out of a silver mug he won in some high school competition back in 1933; he "came out" to Rhodesia three years later to join the police force. He was dapper in his safari suit and customary ascot. His accent was still syrupy and English; it had not transmogrified into flat, nasal Rhodesian English. He said "well done" a lot.

Promptly at 5:30 P.M., in walked Colin Thorpe, the garage owner. He headed directly for his usual barstool. Field quietly set the first of several Castle Pilsener beers in front of him. Field and Thorpe smiled at each other with the peculiar familiarity of men who had seen each other nearly every day for the previous thirty years. The two quickly reviewed the day's novelties—there are few in Enkeldoorn—and then started to discuss "the situation."

Other people, most of them black men, began streaming in. Field, assisted by a black bartender, moved to serve them. One contingent of young men entered in a rush of noise. A short, well-dressed one, quite obviously the leader, said, "Hello, Mr. Thorpe."

"Hi, Mike," the garage owner responded wryly. The young men were all ex-guerrillas, former members of ZANLA, the Zimbabwe African National Liberation Army, the military wing of ZANU. Until a year before, they and Thorpe, who had served in the police reserve, were trying to kill each other.

Blacks rarely entered the bar then, even though the official discriminatory laws had already been repealed. They apparently felt ill at ease breaking old taboos; moreover, the place was frequented by young white troopies, chronically tense because of the constant danger of ambush.

Now the bar had changed character. Whites, except for Colin Thorpe and a few of his friends, had abandoned the place. They were now drinking up at the private Enkeldoorn Club. Blacks, emboldened by the change in government and the appearance in their midst of the former guerrillas, and also enjoying appreciable pay increases, had flocked into the bar.

Thorpe had observed the change with equanimity, and gotten to know the new clientele. He acknowledged his own attitudes had changed, though he stubbornly continued to insist the war had been necessary. He was a very fit, big man, who only showed his fifty-eight years in his creased face. He spoke emphatically, in bursts of words.

"We were surprised after independence," he said. "We didn't know there were all these capable blacks, Ph.D.'s, around. Of course, they were overseas, in exile. Now they're back, as cabinet ministers, officials.

"But if they'd been handed independence twenty years ago? They'd have mucked it up, just like in the countries to the north of us. The war delayed the change here, for everyone's benefit. They can see the chaos in these other places, Zambia, Mozambique, caused by inefficiency, bad policies, socialism. They know they have to keep the white man here, to help build up the country. Mugabe is showing himself to be very intelligent, statesmanlike.

"I'm an optimist. I'll stay as long as there is law and order and an independent judiciary."

Thorpe took a visible, perverse delight in stressing to me that he had become no liberal. He described himself as "sensible" and "middle-of-the-road." He said he still opposed allowing everyone the vote; he favored limiting the franchise to people of education and property. "The electorate would still be majority black," he explained. "And some of these local Afrikaners who can't even write their own names wouldn't be allowed to vote."

Brian Field, the bar owner, had also modified his views. Amid the clutter of memorabilia on his walls was a yellowing clipping of a letter he had sent to the Salisbury *Herald* back in 1974.

He had written, "The indigenous African in the present Parliament [Smith's legislature had fifty whites and sixteen token blacks] is automatically in opposition to any white person for anthropological reasons.

"An increase in seats for the African means an increase in opposition of the wrong sort. We should be working with them, not against them.

"If an African government runs the country there will be a rapid exodus of whites and an immediate deterioration of conditions for the poorer black Africans. Therefore the white man must continue to run the country for the benefit of all."

Now, seven years later and one year after a black government had come to power, Field planned to sell the hotel and retire, but not to leave Zimbabwe. "We'll move to Salisbury," he said. "Buy a plot on the outskirts. Breed cattle. Raise a few vegetables. I'll keep busy and ride horses."

Field had no intention of returning to England. "Too cold," he explained. "Too expensive. I'd retire there only if I had more money and a faster rate of blood circulation." He had been back only four times in fifty years, most recently to attend the Grand National steeplechase. "Had to stay fourteen days because of the air ticket," he said. "Would have come back right after the race otherwise."

He was unhesitatingly critical of his previous racial attitudes. "I was like Ian Smith, you know. Said I'd never have a black barman. Couldn't trust them to do the job properly. Had to do it all myself. Well, I have one now. Sam. Wish I'd trained him years ago. First-rate chap."

The most widely used expression in independent Zimbabwe was surely "reconciliation." Whites had been amazed from the start as Robert Mugabe, who their own propagandists had told them was a diseased man with a pathological hatred of whites, delivered calm, soothing, eloquent speeches. He had promptly appointed two whites to his first Cabinet, including David Smith, who had served in the minority regime as deputy prime minister. Joshua Nkomo and three other ZAPU ministers also entered the cabinet, giving the government a broad base.

Mugabe declared repeatedly there would be no sweeping nationalization of white-owned land or businesses, no precipitate purge of the white-dominated civil service apparatus, no reprisals against senior white commanders for their conduct during the war. The prime minister insisted color should start ceasing to be a factor in national life. White people who had in some cases already literally packed their bags decided to wait and see. Out-migration that first year was only about 20,000, leaving the overall white population at about 215,000. Some better-off blacks started to move into Mount Pleasant, Borrowdale, and Salisbury's other lush suburbs, but the areas remained the same, sleepy and filled with flowers. During that first year, the Zimbabwe's women's hockey team, once again eligible for international competition, won the gold medal at the Moscow Olympics. The all-white team spoke by long-distance telephone to their prime minister. *"Pamberi ne* Zimbabwe,'' they told him joyfully.

The most pressing task at independence was to reconcile the three separate armies. Mugabe, working with some senior white officers, disbanded certain of the Rhodesian army's most notorious units, then carried through a delicate three-way merger among some remaining units, ZANLA forces loyal to him, and Joshua Nkomo's ZIPRA. The integration process had broken down tragically in November 1980, when an uprising of certain ZIPRA elements near Bulawayo was quelled at the cost of at least three hundred dead. But now, the integration into a National Army of sixty thousand was back on course, with the assistance of British military instructors. Violence in the countryside had nearly disappeared. There were no more convoys, armored vehicles, full gun racks.

ZANU promoted reconciliation not only because it was a generous and morally right policy. Whites nearly monopolized the skilled technical and managerial positions in the economy, and a white exodus would have created instant chaos. In nearby Mozambique and Angola, the sudden departure of more than 90 percent of the Portuguese settlers after independence in 1975 had left the two desperately poor countries short of people with even basic skills, such as the ability to drive automobiles. The ZANU leaders had been based in Maputo, Mozambique, during the war and they had observed the disruption there close at hand. If they had come to power through military victory, and if most of the settlers had fled, they could have started immediately to rebuild the country along Socialist lines. Instead, they inherited a functioning economy, and they decided to transform it gradually and with minimal disruption. They really had little choice. There were serious predictions at the time of independence that a famine could strike later that first year.

The party achieved its first objective immediately. The economy, aided by a bumper maize crop that ended the pressing danger of mass starvation, had jumped 8 percent in 1980; it would grow another 5 percent in

1981. By 1982, when the world recession and a continent-wide drought started to overtake Zimbabwe, the economy would be strong enough to survive the crisis.

This economic stability and growth meant that ZANU was able to start carrying out some of the reforms it had promised voters; "reconciliation" certainly did not mean no change at all. The government abolished school fees, provided increased facilities for secondary schooling, and, working closely with committees of parents, rebuilt the rural schools that had been destroyed in the war. In the first year alone, the number of children in school jumped from 800,000 to 1.3 million, and further increases to more than 2 million were expected. The government also abolished fees for health care for the very poor.

The government also implemented a minimum wage. The wage levels were still appallingly low, but some poor people found their incomes nonetheless doubled or tripled. You could see the change. In other parts of the world, poor people with a little extra money tend to spend it on clothing. In Zimbabwe, men developed a taste for suits; people all over the country started wearing them on many occasions, even during long, dusty bus trips.

These reform measures provoked some displeasure among whites. They grumbled about the minimum wage. They complained about health and education, even though the government had mainly just removed de facto segregation instead of aggressively attempting to integrate.

Whites also objected to the change in the press, especially the broadcast media. The ZANU government had simply inherited control over the television and radio network. Programming did not change all that much—*Dallas* and *Rich Man, Poor Man* continued to be aired—but whites objected to Mugabe and other leaders being described as "Comrade," to South Africa being described in newscasts as "racist" and to other changes in emphasis. (There was a story, almost certainly apocryphal, that a weather report had included an item about "heavy rains in racist South Africa.") The newspapers, which had been bought by a government-sponsored trust, were at first less controversial.

Another long-overdue change took place with the appearance of a new guidebook to the spectacular thirteenth-century ruins at Great Zimbabwe, the nation's symbol and the source of its name. Even though every trained archaeologist from 1905 onward who excavated at the site confirmed that it had been constructed by Africans, the white settlers continued to insist its builders were mysterious outsiders, possibly Phoenicians, or extraterrestrials. The minority regime had actually forced previous guidebooks to include exotic origin as a plausible hypothesis. The new, accurate booklet was written by Peter Garlake, a white archaeologist who had once left the country rather than acquiesce in the restriction to his integrity.

In Enkeldoorn, a major local issue was the government's attempt to abolish the racial restriction over at the Enkeldoorn Club. Mike Mushonga, the local ex-guerrilla leader, had raised the issue in high government circles. Thorpe, the most accessible of the club's leading members, found himself in negotiations with the man he had first met on the hotel verandah during the election—Ernest Kadungure, now the minister of youth.

Thorpe probably secretly favored desegregating the place. But he resisted due to his belief in "individual property rights" and his pronounced streak of simple obstinacy. He told Ernest Kadungure the government would have to pass legislation to require the club to open its doors.

"Stupid," was Brian Field's view. "They should open the place right now to what we might call 'upper-class blacks.' Then *they* can keep the riff-raff out."

As Thorpe, Field, and I talked, Mike Mushonga and his colleagues were animatedly discussing politics in the Shona language further down the bar. A stack of newspapers were brought in; they had just arrived on the late bus from Salisbury. A half dozen of the young men bought copies and opened them eagerly, in synchrony, to the sports page. The Dynamos were off to a fast start in the national soccer league.

Mike Mushonga—Comrade Mike—is from the Range, a hamlet ten miles to the east. The party had assigned him and other ex-guerrillas to Enkeldoorn to do both political organizing and more mundane chores, such as arranging the visits of high officials to the district.

Quite a number of guerrillas chose special names during the war, partly to protect their families at home from possible reprisals, and partly to help them make the psychological jump from high school student to soldier. The names some of Mike Mushonga's friends picked seemed appropriate. Comrade Blessing was a peaceful, soft-spoken man, quiet behind his aviator glasses. Comrade Ranger wore his black cap pulled over one eye at a rakish angle. Another friend, Comrade Advance, was tall, with a lengthy forward stride.

Mike Mushonga was a poised, serious, sometimes aggressive man of twenty-five, slightly older than his colleagues. He had worked as a clerk in several small enterprises, losing his job in each case after a clash with white superiors. As soon as revolutionary war came to Charter, he joined ZANLA.

He takes snuff, which is an unusual habit for a young man. He pours it out from his little leather pouch with no apparent joy, with rather a mild distaste. People expect him, as a "spirit medium," to use it.

As a child of six or seven, Mike started to act strangely. At times, he went into trances. The elders conferred, and decided that the spirit of his great-grandfather, who also had been a spirit medium, was occasionally taking possession of him.

In Shona religion, spirit mediums are the link between the world of the living and the world of the dead. The living, through the entranced medium, approach the ancestors for advice, or ask them to intercede with the divinity. In the first Chimurenga in 1896–97, the spirit mediums had also encouraged the resistance to colonialism. One, a woman called Nehanda, was captured after the uprising failed and hanged. She became a national hero.

Mike Mushonga performed "cultural duty" during the war in addition to reconnaissance and courier work and actual fighting. It would not be too far-fetched to regard him as a sort of military chaplain. Some of the guerrillas held fervently to the beliefs of their ancestors through the pressures of the war. They believed that they would be protected from their enemies if they comported themselves properly, by not stealing or brutalizing the local people. There were even tales of bush fighters who had escaped death by becoming invisible, or who had covered many miles in short split seconds. These stories, while not necessarily widely believed in a literal sense, symbolically embodied the central truth of the war—the guerrillas could never have survived without the support of the local people.

In the bar late one afternoon, Mike, Ranger, and Blessing explained ZANLA's war strategy to me at length. They said the High Command in Mozambique first sent a small advance party into a selected area, with strict instructions not to disclose their presence. The unit travelled light, intentionally, which forced it to rely on the goodwill of the local people for food and blankets. The three ex-guerrillas used the word *povo*, Portuguese for "people," an import from Mozambique. The reconnaissance team moved through the area, took the political pulse in each village and then "footed it" back to Mozambique to report. It is one week to the border from Enkeldoorn; some units walked more than twice as far.

The High Command studied and weighed the reports, then flooded the most promising areas with large detachments of fighters. "At our first meetings," Mike explained, "the povo would first say to us that the white man had invented the gun, so only the white man could use it. They didn't believe we could use it against the soldiers. So we had to show them." Often, six months had elapsed between the appearance of the guerrillas and the first order to "open fire."

The three men were reluctant to discuss the actual fighting. There was no boasting about specific engagements or battlefield feats, no overall glorification of the war, no fond reminiscences. They did say friends of theirs had been captured and hanged. They said they had attacked some farms and left others alone, based on the local reputation of the individual farmer.

Mike downed another beer quickly and launched into a garbled but still intelligible story about a certain black informer. The man, an overseer at a white farm, had tipped off the regime's forces about the location of ZANLA units. Mike's tone grew aggressive, with a strong defensive undercurrent. "We went into BF [battle formation] and attacked that farm. We surrounded his house. We set it on fire. It burned down. He was inside." Mike glared. "He was a traitor. He caused the deaths of many of our people."

In Shona religion, a dead man's spirit will return to haunt his killer. "That was suspended during the war," Mike said quickly. But he did not seem entirely certain.

The ex-guerrillas said again and again that their fight had been against "the system," not white people as such. To underscore their point, they encouraged me to accompany them to the outdoor beer garden up in Chivu township. They wanted to publicly demonstrate the friendship between former guerrillas and a white man.

Chivu—the name means simply "soil"—was a half mile out of town at the end of a bumpy dirt road. In addition to ZANU branch chairman Philemon Mabika's multipurpose institution, there were a cluster of other shops, several dozen tiny cement houses, people milling about, the odor of dust mixed with wood smoke from the stoves, and the blare of driving guitar and drum music from antediluvian phonographs. At the marketplace, Mike showed me some metal hand axes. "Our ancestors tried to fight the invaders with these in the first Chimurenga," he chuckled.

We sat in the warm evening around a table, intentionally in full view of a hundred other people elsewhere in the ugly concrete beer garden. The ex-guerrillas greeted passersby and played clumsily but affectionately with a couple of small children. I asked the men about the increasingly menacing noises South Africa had been making toward independent Zimbabwe. Blessing answered: "Any child in Zimbabwe knows we can fight. They have seen it. If the South Africans come, even our smallest children won't be afraid to fire a gun."

Mabika's establishment was still the informal political headquarters for the area. Prospective customers approaching the place were greeted by a huge sign, with flamboyant lettering: "Mabika Eating Place." Underneath were smaller signs: "Mabika General Dealer," "Mabika Store," "Record Bar." Guitar music issued from the phonograph in the rear; brownish ugly dogs sprawled sleepily on the verandah.

Inside, members of Mabika's large family were stationed behind two counters. There was still a paucity of items on the shelves: orange juice, candles (the township is only partly electrified), biscuits, sweets, and an inexplicably prodigious number of boxes of detergent, faded and gathering dust. (Mabika regularly wailed about the low stock; he said he needed a bank loan to put the store "up to date." He said he has been stymied in the past by discriminatory banking practices.) In the back, two of his daughters labored over a hot, smoky, wood-burning stove. Customers could either take their meals in a tiny back room, or in the front at a yellow, formica-topped table. The store was decorated lavishly with posters of Prime Minister Mugabe and other news clippings.

The big man himself conducted business from a corner, next to his crank telephone, with a sheaf of papers spread in front of him. Before he had saved enough to buy the store, he had worked as a truck driver, a traffic policeman, and as a cook at Uncle Willie's Steakhouse down in Johannesburg. He was very busy as the ZANU branch chairman, actually preferring politics to his business. He had a rather whimsical attitude about charging his customers.

"Politics" is really too stingy a word to describe Mabika's function in his community. One morning, as he was characteristically bellowing over his telephone, an elderly man wearing a shabby jacket rode a rickety bicycle up to the shop and entered solemnly. Mabika banged the phone down, and the two conducted a conversation in Shona. One of Mabika's sons whispered a translation to me: "This man says his wife goes with other men. She has become a prostitute, he says. He is going to tell her to pack her things and go. He is informing Mr. Mabika."

The branch chairman listened, and gravely nodded that he had understood. The aged visitor walked out with dignity, got back on his bicycle, and set off down the road toward town.

Mabika had gained greatly in self-assurance during the first year of Zimbabwe's independence. His prominence had in fact earned him some resentment locally; he had apparently been defeated in his efforts to win a post in the municipal government. But he was undaunted in his political involvement. One of his first tasks was to monitor the implementation of the new minimum wage rate for laborers on the surrounding cattle ranches. Wages used to be five or ten Zimbabwean dollars a month (plus some food rations); now they had to be at least fifty dollars.

One morning, he showed me a complaint he was sending to ZANU national headquarters in Salisbury. He had printed it in large letters on a sheet of foolscap. A certain local white farmer, he wrote, "dispises the ZANU (PF) government and the prime minister, Comrade Mugabe." This farmer "calls his workers kaffirs and says the government is for them, not the whites." He attacks them physically and he even beat one older man "unconsciously." He only pays them ten dollars a month. The laborers have appealed to the police, but nothing has happened. Mabika wanted action.

The branch chairman's activities were one small part of a vast nationwide undertaking. ZANU had declared 1981 the "Year of Consolidating the People's Power." Among the vices of the colonial period was the sheer lack of organization. The settlers had crushed or undermined the traditional political structures, but replaced them with essentially only a police system to preserve order and protect white property. There were no legitimate structures for popular democratic participation, a situation that had contributed to a sense of apathy that was shaken only by the coming of the war. ZANU was creating village and branch committees all over Charter, relying heavily on the previously underground support organizations. A district-wide body had just been elected.

Leading government and party officials regularly came out from Salisbury for mass meetings. One delegation, led by Simon Muzenda, the deputy prime minister, visited Charter one weekend while I was there. As we travelled on to the rally, to be held at Manyeni, there were many signs of reconstruction. Schools and trading stores had been rebuilt; the land mine pits and vehicle traps filled in; the utility poles and lines set up again. The thousands of small farmers, who had rebuilt their homesteads, were about to harvest their big maize crop.

At Manyeni, a town of ten or so buildings in bright blue and green pastels, the local committee was behind schedule in preparing the mass meeting. The embarrassed chairman scolded his helpers, spurring them on. He was blind in one eye, and wore a red beret tilted at a preposterous angle.

In the doorway of one of the trading stores, I encountered Comrade Advance, who was on a weekend pass from his army base. He was drinking a bottle of beer. Even though he is well over six feet, which is quite tall by Zimbabwean standards, he was wearing platform shoes. He agreed happily to be my translator.

Advance—his original name was Elliot—was after several years in ZANLA a communications specialist in the new, unified National Army. He told me several times he was prepared to remain a soldier "for the next thirty years." He had picked up military jargon; he was fond of saying "negative" instead of "no," and he described any kind of sustained activity as "a mission."

The rally finally began. The crowd of about three thousand, separated as usual into men and women, had gathered in the shade. Contingents of children from four local schools marched up in orderly fashion, singing and brandishing placards welcoming the guests.

The children stopped. Mayor Urimbo, the young, good-looking national political commissar, sauntered forward. "Why aren't you singing?" he teased the crowd. "Aren't you free?"

The multitude roared happily. Someone started singing a revolutionary song, and everyone else joined in. Women rose to their feet and started dancing.

After the singing died down, the deputy prime minister, Simon Muzenda, a pleasant, grandfatherly man who had once been a carpenter, approached the makeshift podium. He edged into his informal, rambling speech. As he talked, members of the village committee who were seated nearby intently and laboriously scribbled notes on soiled bits of scrap paper.

Muzenda, who himself comes from the southernmost part of Charter, only briefly mentioned the government's achievements. The main thrust of his talk was to encourage people to continue organizing themselves, rather than expecting the government to do everything for them. "You must have your own meetings," he said. "You must deal with your own problems, instead of coming to knock on my door."

He talked frankly about the difference between political and economic power. "We—that means you—are now the government," he said. "But many things in the towns are still owned by just a few people. We have not yet started on this problem." He stressed "reconciliation." "It is not good to say a person is Shona, Ndebele, colored, or white. You should just say 'Zimbabwean.' Our ancestors gave food to any travellers who passed through our land. They didn't care who these people were, where they came from. We want to follow that custom again."

Muzenda warned the crowd against falsely accusing their neighbors of rebelling against the government, of witchcraft, or of other crimes. "Those who tell such lies cannot succeed. They are like the fool who chases the shadows of the clouds all day, and never catches up." He presented a detailed review of other aspects of government policy, answered a number of questions, then raised his clenched fist. "*Pamberi ne* ZANU."

Mayor Urimbo jauntily stepped forward. He looked slyly toward the women. "You must form more women's groups, meet together," he said. "I know your husbands resist this. They say you pretend to go to meetings at night in order to meet other men, or to drink beer."

Some of the women giggled.

He spun toward the men, his eyes bulging, a mock glare darkening his face. "You must stop this," he shouted. "You are suppressing your wives!"

The women broke into loud cheering and applause. The men eyed each other, discomfited.

Urimbo grinned at the men, sympathetic but still firm. Then he sat down. Advance whispered, "That one—he's one of our best. He used to come into the battle zones many times during the war. My detachment met him once in the south, near Chipinga Pools."

The mayor's exhortation highlighted a sensitive issue. The Zimbabwean revolutionaries were concerned not only with ending foreign domination but also with transforming certain aspects of "tradition," such as the second-class status of women. At the top level, the record of both ZANU and ZAPU was respectable; nine of their seventy-seven members of Parliament were women, including several cabinet members. But the traditional pattern of women deferring to men still held at the grass roots— only 22 of the 1,204 district councillors elected in rural areas were women. A higher percentage of men were enrolled in school. Half of all men could read and write, contrasted with only 31 percent of women. Only in 1983 did the government repeal laws under which black women had been regarded as perpetual minors, legally under the guardianship of first their parents and then their husbands. Some women had fought as guerrillas during the war, which had started to modify the old views. But the task ahead remained enormous and delicate.

As the rally broke up, there was a commotion at the other end of the village. A black man passing by in an automobile had apparently shouted "Down with ZANU." Some of the young people in the crowd had rushed him, pulled him from his vehicle, and were about to beat him senseless. The bodyguards in the ZANU entourage, all ex-ZANLA men, leaped forward, rescuing the victim and slowly restoring order.

Back in town, I joined Colin Thorpe at the hotel bar. The garage owner was deep in discussion with a rancher named Visser, a middle-aged Afrikaner with sparkling blue eyes and a friendly smile. The rancher had been accusing Thorpe of being an "optimist" about Zimbabwe's future. "Things are already going down, Colin man," he said with a strong Afrikaner accent. "After only one year. Man, the schools and hospitals are buggered. We used to learn about George Washington at school. Now I suppose they'll be learning about blokes like old Karl Marx, man, and the sheets at the hospital are dirty. . . ."

Thorpe commiserated as the Afrikaner sadly talked of heading for South Africa. "Man, I'll miss this place," Visser said. "Sometimes, when the sun's going down, I walk out on my farm. I sit out there on an anthill. I look out at the nature, the trees, the birds. I think 'Man, this didn't just happen. What's it all for?' "

Thorpe and I later headed up to the Mabika emporium. The garage owner had long felt a begrudging admiration for the energetic branch chairman, who he described as "always in the forecourt." (Mabika, a soccer fan, would probably fail to understand the metaphor.)

The two big men eased themselves into small chairs, leaned across the yellow plastic-topped table, and took each other's measure. The store's lighting gave the scene a garish quality. "It's been some time since you were here, Mr. Thorpe," Mabika observed.

"Yeah, last year we stopped in once or twice on police patrols." The garage owner was plainly somewhat ill at ease. The trickle of black customers registered some surprise at seeing him there.

Mabika pushed across the little table a cardboard carton of Shake sorghum beer, a gooey, cheap, mildly alcoholic substance popular among many blacks. Thorpe eyed the beer with some reluctance, but he still downed a couple of glasses.

His host inquired after Mrs. Thorpe, and lauded her efficiency at the Enkeldoorn Bank, where she worked as a teller. Thorpe was wary, and still slightly uncomfortable. When Mabika got up to answer his old-fashioned telephone, Thorpe whispered to me: "Africans always carry on with this praise—they don't always mean it."

The entrepreneur returned. Thorpe teased him about the dozen of unsold boxes of Surf detergent on his shelves. Mabika responded with his familiar litany about his problems in getting bank loans.

An ancient black man with a single tooth approached, and began speaking Afrikaans to Thorpe. All three men laughed loudly. "He's going back thirty years," the garage owner explained to me. "When I first came up from South Africa in '48, as an English-speaking bloke I used to have a little trouble with some of these Afrikaners."

He shrugged happily. "So I got into a few scrapes. These two remember. Seems I have quite a reputation."

Thorpe was now visibly more expansive. He raised his glass of sorghum beer and offered a toast to Prime Minister Mugabe. Mabika and the old man joined in eagerly. They continued reminiscing in Afrikaans. One of Mabika's teenage relatives, eavesdropping from behind the counter, muttered under his breath, "He's changed. If it weren't for reconciliation, all the whites could have been killed."

A slightly intoxicated young man entered the Mabika establishment. "I know it's late, but is sadza possible?"

One of Mabika's daughters nodded and went into the kitchen. The newcomer smiled. He approached the yellow table. "Anything is possible," he said to us. "They say you can't carry water in a sieve. But think of this: what if the water is frozen?" He saluted with a little flourish and ambled happily into the back room for his sadza.

The ZANU government, despite its success at reconciling black and white, still faced enormous problems. By 1982, two full years after independence, its land reform program was in trouble. Both ZANU and ZAPU had vowed during the war they would drive the Smith regime from power, expropriate the white-owned land, which would be largely abandoned by that stage, and simply hand it over to the rural poor. That policy was certainly morally defensible, as the settlers themselves had simply taken the land by force, in some instances within the living memory of older Zimbabweans. But ZANU and ZAPU had been required at Lancaster House to agree to pay fair compensation for any land taken. What's more, "white" agriculture was providing roughly 40 percent of export earnings, over and above all of Zimbabwe's own needs; any disruption in the rural areas that caused production to drop would be disastrous to the country.

The government had resolved to buy up white farms, starting with un- or underutilized lands, and then resettle people from the overcrowded black rural zones. It was to be a monumental undertaking. A 1981 Commission of Inquiry, headed by a brilliant, hard-working economist named Roger Riddell, estimated the black former Tribal Trust Lands could only support about 325,000 families—which meant that another 455,000 families presently living there would have to leave. Of these, some 235,000 families already had their principal wage-earner living away as migrants in the towns or on the mines. The Commission reckoned that the sharp increases in wage levels, together with a crash housing program, could within five years enable all the migrants to bring their families to live permanently with them. After nearly a century, Zimbabwe would be able to largely abolish the hated oscillating labor system.

But the remaining 185,500 families—nearly one million people, or about one-seventh the country's entire population—would still need to be resettled. To find room for them, the government would eventually have to purchase up to three-quarters of the white land; it would have to, in other words, buy back nearly 40 percent of the territory in its own country. In American terms, this task would be roughly equivalent to purchasing most of the Great Plains and Pacific Coast states at prevailing market prices and then, in a few short years, resettling more than thirty million people from New England and the Southeast. In Zimbabwe, estimates for the cost of resettlement ranged from a bare minimum of $750 million up to $2 billion. Britain had off-handedly mentioned financial aid at the Lancaster House peace conference, but specified no figures. Now that Britain had finally freed itself of responsibility for the country, it seemed unlikely to grant anywhere near the required amount.

By 1982 only about ten thousand families had been resettled. Lack of money was not even yet the major obstacle. The bureaucratic snarls were inevitable, especially with holdover white civil servants who were sometimes not particularly energetic. The rural poor themselves sometimes insisted on moving to the nearest white farms, remaining close to the graves of their ancestors, rather than resettling in more distant available lands.

Impatience mounted. In the east, more than seventy thousand people took direct action by occupying white farms illegally. In most cases, the government persuaded them peacefully to move back. But the number of squatters increased even further the next growing season, placing ZANU in the agonizing position of contemplating the use of force against those who had been among its most fervent supporters.

Events far more disheartening than the slow progress in land reform began to take place in 1982, and independent Zimbabwe was soon in a major crisis. In February, Robert Mugabe announced dramatically on television that his government had uncovered huge caches of arms buried on farms that belonged to Joshua Nkomo's ZAPU. Mugabe bitterly accused Nkomo and some other ZAPU leaders of planning to overthrow the government. He dismissed Nkomo from his cabinet and detained two popular ZAPU ex-military commanders, Dumiso Dabengwa and Lookout Masuku.

Immediately, some former ZAPU guerrillas began to desert from the now unified National Army. They apparently returned to the familiar bush areas in southwestern Matabeleland where they had been based during the war. Sporadic attacks started to take place in the area, including the ambushes and murders of several white farmers and black civilians. Six young foreign tourists, including two Americans, were kidnapped in July by an armed band that forwarded a ransom note demanding the release of the two ex-ZAPU guerrilla commanders. (More than two years later, the six were never found and were presumed dead.) The National Army started to move through the area in force, detaining up to several thousand people suspected of being either "dissidents" or their supporters. There were disturbing reports that prisoners were being beaten, and that some had died.

Joshua Nkomo and other ZAPU leaders acknowledged having the arms caches, but insisted that they had been buried in self-defense, in case they were needed in the turbulent period during and after the election. They heatedly denied any plot to overthrow the government. Nkomo denounced the dissidents publicly and asked them to stop their murderous attacks. But Mugabe continued to claim some of the ZAPU leadership was behind the violence, and only pretending to disavow it.

After the dissidents committed several more vicious murders over Christmas 1982, the government evidently decided on even more drastic action. It ordered the Fifth Brigade, a special five-thousand-strong elite army unit on whose loyalty it could depend, on a major sweep through the southwest. Quickly, there were widespread reports the Fifth Brigade was carrying out beatings, atrocities, and summary executions. Nkomo dramatically fled the country in March 1983, claiming his own life was in danger. Accurate casualty figures were not available. But a mass of evidence from independent sources started to accumulate, confirming that the brigade had killed hundreds and very possibly several thousand people in the area. Survivors, some of whom fled to exile in neighboring Botswana, described an indiscriminate reign of terror and murder.

The ZANU government's response was ambiguous. Robert Mugabe privately told horrified church groups he was reigning in the brigade. But publicly the government dismissed a measured statement by the Catholic bishops criticizing the atrocities as "utterly one-sided" and "propagandistic." In the end, the brigade was withdrawn from the southwest, and the reports of killings dropped off. Joshua Nkomo returned from his exile in London after six months, stressing the need for peaceful reconciliation.

But the conflict continued to smolder. The dissidents continued their campaign of violence, killing some seventy-five more civilians, both black and white, in the last six months of 1983. Reports persisted that government troops continued to retaliate with brutality. In early 1984, there were further allegations that the army had delayed or cut off emergency shipments of food to the drought-stricken southwest. The move, apparently intended to starve out the rebels, also threatened the civilians in the area. Even if settlement is somehow reached, the bitterness in Matabeleland is likely to linger on for years.

Even if Nkomo or other ZAPU leaders had in fact conspired against the government, ZANU had unquestionably inflamed the danger with its harsh talk and brutal action. The ZANU political program of land reform and social welfare was also relevant to the rural poor in Matabeleland. A judicious appeal to ZAPU supporters could have isolated any plotters and left them without popular support. Instead, there was from the start a strong propensity in the ZANU leadership to widen the differences between the two parties, even when they were ostensibly co-operating in a coalition government. There were combative speeches and spiteful acts of partisanship. For instance, the government compiled and released the official list of ZANU war dead first, with the ZAPU casualties following separately, almost as an afterthought. The national media, increasingly controlled by ZANU party-liners, disparaged ZAPU endlessly, suggesting that those who continued to support it were almost traitors to Zimbabwe. None of this excuses the ZAPU dissidents, who after all did kidnap and murder innocent people. But the ZANU government had contributed to a climate of hostility in which the rebels could survive.

One clue to understanding ZANU's combativeness lies in the character of its leadership. Enos Nkala, a stocky, exuberant man, was one of the party's four most senior officials. He was himself from the southwest, the stronghold of rival ZAPU, and his outbursts against the smaller party, including a threat to "crush" Joshua Nkomo, had been widely quoted.

In the middle seventies, Enos Nkala had been released during the brief period of détente after ten years in detention. He went straight out into the country to promote ZANU. One of Philemon Mabika's sons told me what happened when he showed up to give a political speech in Enkeldoorn.

The police had arrived to monitor the rally. Enos Nkala refused to accept their presence as an uncomfortable but necessary given. He challenged them immediately. "Why are you here?" he asked, to the amazed delight of the crowd. The astonished white commander answered, "To maintain order." Nkala riposted immediately. "Why do you come here, to town, to keep the peace? Our boys are out there, in the bush, fighting your racist regime and winning. Go there if you want to 'preserve order.' In the meantime—leave us to have our meeting!"

To the enormous astonishment of everyone, including possibly the police themselves, they actually did leave. Soon, though, Enos Nkala's outspokenness led inevitably to another conviction on political charges. He served three more years in prison, and was freed only just before the election. He was not a raw, impetuous youth when he made those fiery speeches, but a mature man in his middle forties.

Enos Nkala is a hard man. This does not mean he is either unfriendly or unkind. The circumstances called for extraordinary stubbornness, reckless courage, and sacrifice. He never flinched. But over the years of suffering he has come to feel an almost religious sense of loyalty to his political party and its destiny, and a corresponding feeling of anathema toward those he thinks stand in its way. There are many like him in the Zimbabwean government.

These men and women also know from personal experience the effectiveness of violence. They know that when they agitated peacefully for an end to minority rule, using the conciliatory language and tactics of Western democracy that they had been taught in their colonial schools, they achieved nothing except lengthy terms in prison. Ian Smith and the whites simply declared illegal independence. Britain had sent soldiers to its other colonies to put down rebellions by darker-skinned colonial subjects. But no paratroops arrived in Salisbury to topple Smith. Only when the ZANU leaders formed their own army and fought for seven bitter years did they compel both Smith and the British government to take them in earnest.

What's more, violence against the young government had continued even after independence. Joe Gqabi, the representative in Salisbury of the African National Congress of South Africa, was assassinated one night outside his home. A powerful bomb had ripped through ZANU's Salisbury headquarters in December 1981; the explosion had been timed to occur when Central Committee meetings were usually held. In July 1982, saboteurs somehow penetrated the Thornhill air base and destroyed onefourth of the country's air force. There was strong evidence the apartheid regime was training former Bishop Muzorewa auxiliaries across the border, and three white South African soldiers were intercepted and killed inside Zimbabwe in 1982. Even governments long at peace would find it trying to maintain restraint in the face of such provocations.

So when the several thousand dissidents started their campaign of assassination and disruption in Matabeleland, the ZANU leaders were not in a compromising temperament. They were familiar from their own long and tragic experience with the effectiveness of force, and they must have reacted almost instinctually with counterforce. Robert Mugabe and the others probably never told the Fifth Brigade to brutalize people in the southwest. But they were at least partly responsible for the combative atmosphere that made widespread murder possible.

The catastrophe was also poisoning the relations between the Shonaand the Ndebele-speaking people. Until a few years ago the differences between the Ndebele, who are one-fifth of the population living mainly in the southwest, and the Shona majority in the rest of the country had been an insignificant factor in Zimbabwean politics. The latest dispute began as a political conflict between ZANU and ZAPU. Many Zimbabweans, however strong their feelings, still regard ethnicity as wholly irrelevant. But the political division, due mainly to accidents of history, coincided with the ethnic regions. In the atmosphere of tension, ethnic labels started to take on increased significance. You started to hear ugly comments like, "The Shonas want to dominate us and force us to speak their language," or, "The Ndebeles drink too much; they are violent by nature."

The crisis in the southwest was accompanied by a hardening of ZANU authoritarianism. During the war, a hierarchical command structure had been to some extent inevitable; a widespread degree of internal democracy was unlikely with leaders separated by prison and exile and supporters underground in village committees and urban cells. After independence, ZANU could come out of hiding. The party opened its ranks to everyone, including whites, quite a few of whom joined. Cabinet Minister Eddison Zvobgo said the intention was to build ZANU into "a gigantic mammoth." Membership skyrocketed, to more than four million.

But this expansion did not lead to the growth of inner party democracy. ZANU waited until August 1984 to schedule the party congress it had been informally promising since 1980. The thirty-two-member Central Committee continued to make major decisions largely on its own. The armed threat in the southwest had reinforced the tendency to authoritarianism. The government attempted to dominate the emerging trade union movement, and it crushed some strikes with a haughty lack of explanation. After a near perfect human rights record during its first two years in office, it started to use legislation inherited from the minority rule period to detain suspected dissidents and others without trial. There were reports government agents had tortured some detainees. The government asserted increasing control over the media, which parroted its line ever more faithfully.

Almost none of this tension existed outside the southwest. Across most of the country, peace prevailed. Reconciliation was catching on between black and white. In Salisbury, total strangers greeted each other on the street. The sidewalk café in the First Street mall, once the bailiwick of nervous, uniformed white troopies, had now acquired a multiracial collection of amiable "punks" in bizarre clothing. On one of the streets bordering Cecil Square, I even saw two young boys, one black, the other white, intently using a flat piece of metal in an integrated attempt to rifle a parking meter.

Reconciliation was also gaining ground in the new Parliament. It embraced what was arguably the broadest spectrum of opinion in any legislative body in the world. The Rhodesia Front's collection of landowners, air force wing commanders and colonels sat across from the black teachers and workers that they personally had imprisoned or forced into exile. Yet there was little bitterness on the black side. Dr. Ahrn Palley, who was now conducting training sessions for novice civil servants, contrasted reconciliation with the treatment he had received as an opposition MP in a Parliament dominated by the Rhodesia Front. "I got telephone threats from whites, promises that I would be killed. On several occasions the police had to guard my home. I've seen literally dozens of black people around who were in detention back then. Many of them are now in Parliament. You don't see them banging on Ian Smith's door, threatening him."

Some of the Rhodesia Fronters sniped steadily as the ruling party piloted its reform legislation through Parliament. On one day that I visited, RF Senator Air Marshal Wilson, speaking against the government's economic policy document over the sounds of his supporters and opponents telling each other to "shut your face," suggested the time had come to end "the tedious game of knocking colonialism." Instead, the government had to build on its "very real benefits." Black Senator Joseph Culverwell responded sharply, "Shame. You mention a couple. Rubbish."

But not all the Rhodesia Front legislators were taking such an unreconstructed approach. James Thrush, the robust, white-haired party publicist I had met at the postelection celebration, was back in Parliament as an MP. I visited him at the Salisbury recording studio in which he was a part owner, just before the first anniversary of independence in 1981.

He was unabashedly enthusiastic about the ZANU government. "I'm staggered, absolutely shattered at the achievements of the past year," he said. "I had argued, you'll remember, that the prime minister should be shot. They could have chopped our heads off on Day Two. They could have stopped me from broadcasting. Well, there's been nothing of the kind. When I went back into Parliament, it inspired me immensely. There were handshakes everywhere, good humor, bonhomie. I enjoy Parliament now; it used to be rather boring.

"I'm in Parliament not as opposition, but just to point out where I see problems. Whites can no longer shape the political destiny of this country; the twenty white seats are only a transitory safeguard. I hope that the whites will meld more and more with the government in power."

In 1982, after the passing of another year, James Thrush flashed briefly into the world news. Nine of the twenty white MPs resigned from the RF and announced they would stay in Parliament as "independents," giving measured support to the ZANU government. Thrush was their first spokesman. Ian Smith had bitterly denounced the nine. Thrush, in a tone of sadness mixed with some condescension, told me that Smith had been even more harsh when the rebels made their intentions known in a private party caucus. "It just shattered the old man. With obvious contempt for us, he claimed Churchill had said that the trouble with the extension of democracy is that you had to be careful not to stumble over all the dogs that would now be running around on the rugby field."

Thrush shook his head. After the breakaway, Smith had left on a visit down to South Africa. "IDS must still be down there," Thrush said with a short laugh, "because there have been no insulting comments in the newspapers to herald his return."

I asked him his present view of the 1965 Unilateral Declaration of Independence. I reminded him that two years earlier he had justified the UDI as having extended the period of white stewardship, during which blacks in Rhodesia had supposedly been able to draw vital lessons from the purported chaos in other black-ruled countries. He smiled with a trace of self-consciousness as he readily agreed he had changed his mind. He slowly composed his new answer. "It's easy to be wise after the event. . . . I suppose UDI had to happen. The whites were in power, and they felt badly treated by the British. But there should have been a settlement long before 1980, before the war really escalated in the middle seventies. We did have the opportunities. . . . And one didn't have to be a military genius to see that defeat was inevitable."

He grew more decisive. "But what has happened since independence has been nothing less than a miracle. Who would have believed that people like IDS, all of us, would be walking around unmolested? I think it's the greatest achievement in the continent of Africa. Now that some of us in the House are starting to be more positive about the government and the prime minister, I think that some of the whites who left in disgust at the negative approach of IDS and the others will return, and make their homes here.

"Whites will be in Zimbabwe as a minority group. We will be like the Jews, Greeks, and Lebanese in some other societies, with our own culture, our own schools perhaps. But we will also belong to the country. We will look on ourselves as Africans, as white Africans.

"People have got to change. Even IDS has changed; he once said he would never accept African rule in a thousand years. One has got to change with the times. It's not too big an exaggeration to say that I'm a right-wing Socialist now. It's not all that different from a moderate, a left-wing conservative." Thrush smiled broadly. "I've never been a Fascist. If you like people, you can't be a Fascist."

A middle-aged black man stuck his head in the office door, excused himself, and with obvious warmth confirmed a luncheon engagement with Thrush. After he left, the white-haired MP said: "He's one of our directors. I'm the only white of seven. You see, it *can* be done.

"You know, people had too many of the wrong attitudes. I walked past a swimming pool, right here in town, the other day. The little girls of all colors were standing there, laughing and playing. . . . If you'd predicted that scene ten years ago you would have been called a madman!"

As he spoke, he was getting steadily more excited and visibly moved. He made a sweeping gesture. "You go into the supermarket now. You watch the old black guy there walk out with an overflowing shopping basket. All along, he wanted to eat what we eat. Not just sadza. And now he has the money!"

James Thrush is a courageous man. Not all white Zimbabweans have been brave enough to reexamine the racial dogma for which they once fought. Some left the country, often for the more congenial ambience in South Africa. Others remained behind, mainly for financial reasons, taking a perverse delight in the new government's troubles. They retained their inventiveness in devising racial insults. Robert Mugabe, in a heated 1981 speech, had told black Zimbabweans they had a right to strike out physically at whites who called them kaffirs. Some whites promptly started to use the word *stills*. The new term, they would confide with a childish smirk, was short for "still kaffirs."

But this sort of racism was no longer a near unanimous sentiment among whites. Thrush and his fellow independents attracted growing support. By April 1983, they had won their first Parliamentary by-election. "Good old Smithy," once a national white hero, was now increasingly regarded as a tiresome anachronism.

The change in white attitudes would probably not have taken place without either war or some other form of strong, assertive collective action by black people. There had been articulate and patient black spokesmen all through the fifties and sixties, but few whites had listened back then. Sadly, reason alone may not be enough to change deeply embedded white feelings. In part, as Lewis Nkosi, an exiled black South African author, once wrote, "It is not so much because they have 'a different smell' or because their cultures are different that black people are frequently beaten over the head by marauding gangs of white men, notwithstanding assertions to the contrary by social scientists and social workers, but simply because powerless people invite contempt and deserve being beaten over the head."

Nkosi may be exaggerating, but his cold observation did have some relevance in Zimbabwe. It was only after black Zimbabweans formed a political movement, fought their way to power, and started to govern the country, in the main with intelligence and understanding, that whites felt compelled to think deeply about their old racist doctrines. This does not of course mean that the vicious seven-year war in which twenty-five thousand people died was the indispensable price for improved race relations. It does mean that blacks, by being unafraid to assert their own demands for dignity and power, and by struggling for those demands through years of suffering, in the end won respect from enough whites so that there is a chance to build a genuine, stable nonracial society in Zimbabwe. In a country that a few short years ago seemed on the verge of a racial apocalypse, that is a considerable achievement.

Three years after independence, Uncle Moses Hodza had a new properly fitting set of false teeth. He had accidentally stepped on his old crudely made teeth in the middle of the night. With the general rise in income levels, he had no problem purchasing a better set.

The hotel where he had been working when I first met him closed down. After being out of work for a year, he had finally found another waiter's job at a Greek restaurant.

He and another waiter, who was also in his middle sixties, joined his nephew Lawrence and me at a pub during their break after serving lunch. The talk turned to pensions. The old men were worried. Lawrence's father, who had retired some years back after thirty-five years as a laborer, had received only a lump sum of one hundred Zimbabwean dollars. Uncle had done slightly better, getting fifteen hundred dollars. He estimated he could get by with that money for two years at most. As he planned to live longer, he had no choice but to continue working. The hotel owners had also given him a watch on his retirement. On the back was stamped: "Moses. 35 years." They had evidently thought his last name superfluous, or perhaps they had not known it. He showed me the watch with a dignified gesture of contempt.

Lawrence spent some time reassuring the two elderly waiters they could depend on their offspring for support in their old age. He said to me in an aside, "That's one of the reasons we have so many children. Your children are your pension." He turned back to the men to encourage them to solicit help from the local ZANU office about their grievances at their present place of work. "The owner should pay you more than the minimum wage," Lawrence said. "He shouldn't call you always by your first names. You should get redress."

The two men had to return to work to wait on the dinner customers. Lawrence and I adjourned to one of our old haunts, the spacious lounge at the Meikles Hotel. From time to time, he pointed out black passersby and proudly described their achievements since independence. "This one's now at Foreign Affairs," he would say. "That one's a supervisor at a hospital. They were qualified before, but they were not allowed into those posts."

Lawrence grinned as he told me about a new postindependence euphemism. During the minority-rule era, the black urban areas like the one where his family lives were called, as in South Africa, townships; the white areas were suburbs. Now, township was frowned upon due to its association with the segregation of the past. But people still found it necessary at times to make the distinction. So all residential areas are now suburbs. Some are "high-density," and some are "low-density."

Lawrence himself did not stay with his family in their suburb during the week. He had fulfilled his nine-year dream by returning to teaching. The Ministry of Education had naturally removed him from the blacklist. He had told them he would go anywhere they needed him. They posted him to a rural area in the northeast, out past Bindura, to the very primary school he had himself attended as a child. He lived out there alone, returning to Harare, as Salisbury had been renamed, every other weekend to be with his family.

He was very happy to be back teaching. He was bemused by the comportment of some of the more pretentious of his colleagues. "Everywhere they go, they carry a newspaper and a rolled up umbrella. They want you to *know* they're teachers."

He was enthusiastic about the changes in education the new government was carrying through. Now that fees had been abolished, many more children were in school. The teachers were no longer afraid to speak out in the classroom. The schools now invited outsiders to visit, mineworkers, for example, or policemen, who spoke to the children about their work. Lawrence was quick to assure me that many problems remained; the system was still far too rigid and hierarchical, and there were unfair salary discrepancies. But on balance the trend was positive.

I asked him for a more general summary of the change during the first years of independence. He grinned with anticipation at the chance to indulge his fondness for picturesque language. "Before," he began, "we were like caged animals. Now, we're suddenly free. We start to explore, slowly, tentatively." He made the appropriate swiveling gestures, and then abruptly switched metaphors. "Before, we lived on one side of an impenetrable wall." His eyes brightened as the image formed in his head. "Now, the wall is still there. But there's a door as well. We knock "—he smiled with further joy at his originality—" we knock, and sometimes, *sometimes,* we hear someone on the other side, running to open.''

Evil governments reveal themselves vividly in their specific sins. There are plenty of appalling general statistics about life in minority-rule Rhodesia, including the grotesquely lopsided inequalities in land ownership, in wages, in the incidences of disease, and in the numbers of political prisoners and executions. But the Rhodesian government's barbarism is also shown strikingly by its treatment of my friend Lawrence Hodza. It punished him for a minor, never proven infraction by keeping him from teaching for an entire decade, in a country where 40 percent of the people could not read and write. That he is now happily back in the classroom is in its own way as valid a measure of the reforms the new government is carrying through as the arithmetic of minimum wages and land reform.

Zimbabwe's success has aroused the fear and wrath of South Africa. The new government's success at reconciling black and white has posed a compelling challenge to the practitioners of apartheid. Zimbabwe still has far to go before it is a genuinely nonracial country, a place where color is no longer a factor in national life. But it has already demonstrated, just across the Limpopo River, that liberation is not inevitably accompanied by economic collapse and an apocalyptic racial bloodbath. That is why Pretoria is determined to sabotage the new government. The tragedy is that the menace from South Africa strengthens the authoritarian strain in Zimbabwe that is already so troubling.

But there is good reason to hope that despite the danger a democratic way of life will win out. A central feature of the war for national liberation was that it drew thousands upon thousands of poor people into political activity who had previously been silent and afraid. That kind of massive and vocal popular participation has if anything increased since independence. There have been the formal elections to newly created institutions, from the village committees on up. There have been informal assertive actions, the land occupations and the frequent protest marches in both city and countryside. The poor in Zimbabwe had little chance until recently to practice democracy; for them, the vaunted theoretical system of British constitutionality meant in practice the theft of their land and the lengthy detention without trial of their leaders. That these people, some of the poorest in the whole world, are now in a position where they have a chance to create their own democracy may in the end be the best justification for the long and terrible war that they had no other choice but to fight.

PART THREE

South Africa's Long Walk to Freedom

14

Peaceful Defiance Fails

In 1912, three years after Americans established the NAACP, a young black lawyer decided South Africa needed a similar organization to campaign for black rights. Pixley ka Seme, who had studied law at Columbia University in New York and at Oxford, returned to his homeland to set up practice in the booming mining center of Johannesburg. He was shocked to encounter discrimination again after he had gotten used to the relative openness overseas. He was required to carry his pass everywhere, to travel fourth class, even to step into the street to allow a white person the run of the sidewalk.

Seme and several other young black lawyers who had also studied overseas decided to take action. They invited black leaders from all over the country to a big meeting in Bloemfontein. Some of the arrivals were the traditional chiefs, while others, like the organizers, were from the small emerging class of black professionals. "We have discovered," Seme told the assembly, "that in the land of their birth Africans are treated as hewers of wood and drawers of water. The white people of this country have formed what is known as the Union of South Africa—a union in which we have no voice in the making of laws and no part in their administration. We have called you, therefore, to this conference so that we can together devise ways and means of forming our national unity and defending our rights and privileges." The gathering enthusiastically voted to form the organization that would come to be called the African

National Congress. "We felt wonderfully optimistic," one delegate said. "To us freedom was only round the corner."

The ANC, like the NAACP, its American equivalent, was during its first three decades a restrained and moderate organization. Its leaders, mainly dignified professionals, sought to win improved conditions for blacks through patient petition and lobbying campaigns. ANC delegations travelled to Britain and to the post-World War I peace conference at Versailles to try to win international support. The organization held itself aloof from the black mass actions like the 1919 antipass campaign, the 1943 bus boycott in Johannesburg's Alexandra township, or the big 1946 mineworkers' strike.

In 1944, a new generation of young men, many recently arrived in Johannesburg, founded the ANC's Youth League. Nelson Mandela, who belonged to a branch of Xhosa royalty, was a tall, athletic, young lawyer. Oliver Tambo, a high school science teacher, was later to also take up law and set up practice in partnership with Mandela. Walter Sisulu, at thirty, some five years older than the others, had worked in the mines, as a kitchen servant, and in factories; he was a proud, independent man who clashed so often with his white superiors that he preferred eventually to work on his own, trying to sell real estate. The band's unofficial leader was a driven, incandescent intellectual named Anton Lembede, the son of farm laborers, who eventually worked himself to death at the age of thirty-three.

The Youth Leaguers argued that the ANC had to become more militant, more involved in nationwide mass protest. They charged the organization with "regarding itself as a body of gentlemen with clean hands." They demanded a more vigorous movement to resist the National Party, which came to power in 1948 promising to reinforce the existing system of racial domination with the even more stern and comprehensive policy of apartheid.

In 1949, the Youth Leaguers persuaded the ANC convention to approve their Program of Action, which called for strikes, civil disobedience and noncooperation with any of the regime's institutions. The younger members also replaced the organization's president-general with a more activist candidate, a Free State doctor named James Moroka, and they elected one of their own, Walter Sisulu, as secretary-general. The ANC moved toward closer alliances with other groups menaced by the stream of apartheid legislation issuing forth from the Nationalist-dominated Parliament. It cooperated with the Indian Congresses and with sympathetic whites, including some who had belonged to the Communist party before the regime outlawed it in 1950.

As mass support for the ANC grew, the movement decided to conduct a Defiance Campaign during the year 1952. All over the country, blacks, Indians, and some whites promised to openly and deliberately break certain apartheid statutes. The program of massive, nonviolent civil disobedience was clearly in the Gandhian tradition; the Mahatma's own son, Manilal, who had remained behind in South Africa after his father returned to India, was one of the defiers. Dr. James Njongwe, an ANC leader in the Eastern Cape, where Defiance was due to begin on June 26, emphasized that only disciplined volunteers who had been enrolled by volunteer-in-chief Nelson Mandela or others should participate in the campaign. Dr. Njongwe asked for people who would "submit to arrest willingly and with gladness in their hearts, knowing that ours is a fight against malnutrition, high infantile mortality, landlessness, deprivation, humiliation, oppression, and against destruction of family life and faith in Christianity as a way of life."

So, years before the American civil rights movement was in full swing, defiers across South Africa deliberately used the "Europeans Only" facilities, remained in center cities after the evening curfew for blacks, and entered "Group Areas" reserved for other "population groups." The world watched as the singing volunteers bravely walked to the jails. By the year's end, some eighty-five hundred people had submitted to arrest. The ANC's membership soared to one hundred thousand.

The government struck back harshly. It used the elastic definition of communism in its Suppression of Communism Act to ban fifty-two ANC leaders, including Nelson Mandela. Even more importantly, it passed new legislation sharply increasing the penalties for defiance. Now civil disobedience, even for trivial offenses, was punishable by up to three or five years imprisonment. In 1956, there was a further crackdown; the regime arrested 156 leaders of the ANC and other resistance organizations and put them on trial for treason. The prosecution's case was so comically inept and flimsy that all the defendants were eventually either released or acquitted. But the treason trial dragged on for five years, diverting the energies of key ANC leaders and draining the organization's meager resources.

The movement's president-general was by now a deeply religious teacher in his fifties named Albert John Lutuli. He was a hereditary chief of the Zulu, but the government had already deposed him as punishment for leading the Natal ANC into the Defiance Campaign. Lutuli was an imposing, moon-faced man, endlessly patient, tolerant even of his adversaries. In 1961, in recognition of his humanity and courage and that of the organization he led, he was to be awarded the Nobel Prize for Peace, the first man of Africa who would be so honored.

During the 1950s, the ANC continued the spirit of Defiance by working steadily more closely with the Indian Congresses, the Colored People's Congress, and the Congress of Democrats, a small but vigorous group of white radicals. It was a time when people formed deep and lasting friendships across racial lines, in direct contradiction to the philosophy of apartheid.

Lutuli was sometimes asked how he, as a devout Christian, could countenance the presence of Communists in this Congress Alliance. The South African Communist party had been founded in 1921, and it had over the years attracted a modest but dedicated membership, including black leaders like Moses Kotane and J. B. Marks, Indians like Dr. Yusuf Dadoo, and whites such as Michael Harmel. The party had been declared illegal, but it was assumed, accurately, that its members had reconstituted it in clandestinity. Lutuli explained in his autobiography, "The Congress stand is this: our primary concern is liberation and we are not going to be side-tracked by ideological clashes and witch hunts." He added, "Communists are people, they are among the number of my neighbors, and I will not regard them as less. . . . I am confident enough in my Christian faith to believe that I can serve my neighbor best by remaining in his company."

In 1955, the Congress Alliance met at Kliptown, a slum area outside Johannesburg, to draw up a declaration of their principles. Some three thousand delegates from all races met to discuss the short document called the Freedom Charter. It is not at all an inflammatory manifesto. Its very first line says clearly, "South Africa belongs to all who live in it, black and white." It promises to repeal all apartheid legislation and replace it with one man, one vote and guaranteed human rights for all. The Charter also calls for various social welfare measures in education, housing and the like. The only conceivably radical section is a pledge to nationalize the mineral wealth, the banks, and "monopoly industry." But these measures, together with a promised land reform, are mentioned in only vague terms.

One faction within the ANC, known as the Africanists, heatedly disputed the Charter's first sentence. In their view, it accelerated the drift toward multiracialism that they already opposed. To them, South Africa "belonged" to "Africans," who had to "go it alone" in the struggle for liberation. The man who became their leader, a brilliant academic named Robert Sobukwe, once defined an African as anyone "who owes his loyalty to Africa, who is prepared to accept the democratic rule of an African majority." In practice though, the proselytizers in Africanist strongholds, which included parts of Soweto and the Western Cape, tended to describe whites, Indians, and Communists as "foreigners," who, whether by design or by chance, were weakening the authentically African nationalist struggle with alien ideologies that had limited appeal to the black masses.

The dissidents, who finally broke away in 1959 and set up the Pan-Africanist Congress, also blasted the ANC for being overly timid. The older organization had in fact lost numerous battles with the regime during the 1950s. It had been unable to prevent the introduction of Bantu Education or to save Sophiatown, the black community in western Johannesburg, from being levelled. Some twenty thousand ANC women had marched on Pretoria in 1956, but the regime had been able to disdainfully ignore their petitions and extend the pass laws to women. The newer PAC may have been quicker to realize that the masses of people, disappointed in the failure of moderate tactics and encouraged by the heady news of decolonization further north in Africa, may have been already prepared for more militant action. Unrest had in fact by the late fifties spread from the urban areas into three Bantustans, forcing the regime to call in the army.

In 1960, both organizations, which were by now competing for support, declared war on the pass laws. Despite the PAC's militant tone, it still declared it would adhere to nonviolence. PAC followers congregated in several urban centers to destroy their passes. At Sharpeville, one of the townships outside the steel town of Vereeniging, the police unexpectedly opened fire. Most of the sixty-nine people killed were shot in the back as they ran for safety. A horrified reaction against the massacre spread across the country; in Cape Town, thirty thousand people marched from the black townships in protest. The nation seemed in a mood of insurrection. The panicked government outlawed both the ANC and the PAC two weeks later. Chief Lutuli was banned and restricted to his home in rural Natal. The nonviolent phase of resistance, which South Africans had patiently carried out for fifty years, was about to come to an end.

Chief Lutuli's widow, Nokukanya, still lives in the family home in Groutville, a 'black spot' in the muggy sugarcane country north of Durban along the coast of the Indian Ocean. I found her there one afternoon in 1979, in her garden pruning rosebushes. She was seventy-six years old, with eyes that sparkled behind her bifocals and a musical laugh.

She and the other twenty-five thousand black residents of Groutville had just won a reprieve from the latest of the regime's efforts to deport them westward, into the Kwa–Zulu Bantustan. "We've been living here, with permission to own our land, since 1856, since Queen Victoria's time," she told me as she clipped her rosebushes. "They want us to move up there to the mountains. They say we are baboons. Even though we are the higher level of baboons, we still must be up there with the others.''

She paused with a friendly smile, and gestured with her clippers across the green-gray sugar fields toward the ocean. ''This is the place of our ancestors. Our King Shaka is buried over that side. How would the British like it if they had to move from the place where King George is buried?''

Chief Lutuli's final ban had lasted from 1959 until he died in a train accident nearby in 1967. Mrs. Lutuli remembered, ''He couldn't even go to church. He was told he could petition the minister of justice to have the banning order relaxed, but he refused. He said he wasn't going to ask anyone for permission to worship *his* God.''

She laughed as she remembered. ''So he held prayer meetings here at home after the rest of us had returned from church. He read from the Bible. He gave a sermon. Then we would sing hymns together. The children would be so tired they would start to fall asleep, but he would carry on.''

Chief Lutuli had worked managing a small shop in Groutville. ''He went down there every day,'' she said. ''He sat by himself in a mud-walled hut next to the shop. He wasn't allowed in the shop itself, with the other people. That would have been a violation of the banning order. At the end of the day he counted the money. He always trusted the people in the shop not to steal.''

Then, in a sudden, slight change of tone, she added, ''That was Lutuli's great gift—he had complete faith in others. Sometimes people took advantage of him, but he never lost that gift.''

The chief's banning order had been lifted briefly in December 1961 to allow him to travel to Oslo, Norway, to receive the Nobel Prize. ''Those five days were the happiest of my life,'' his widow said. ''For a short time, the apartheid disappeared. People would see you on the street there and they would come over and greet you with that full love— not like here, where people will often pass you by.

''But then, as soon as we got off the airplane in Johannesburg, two white men, giants, large, healthy men, came up to him. They gave him a piece of paper reminding him he was back in South Africa, that he was a banned person again. Freedom was over. We said it was very kind of them to come and remind him.''

She laughed. ''I still have the photograph,'' she said. ''I keep it in the bank with his Nobel Prize and his other awards. It will be safe there.''

After Chief Lutuli was restricted to Groutville, the bold and charismatic Nelson Mandela became the ANC's de facto leader. There seemed no alternative now but violence. Still, the organization hesitated. Mandela moved secretly around the country, organizing a peaceful nationwide stay-at-home for May 1961. The regime mobilized all its forces to threaten and intimidate workers, making the strike effort only partly successful.

The rival PAC, with its most capable leadership already in prison following the antipass law campaign, collapsed into a state of confusion. Certain of its supporters in the Cape staged a few random attacks on white civilians; they were captured, and imprisoned or hanged. The ANC was much more scrupulous. Mandela had left the country secretly and toured Africa and Britain to present the organization's case. He returned, fully aware he was the most wanted man in South Africa. He and others established the guerrilla organization they called *Umkhonto we Sizwe,* the Spear of the Nation. It was to commit specific, limited acts of sabotage against targets such as remote electrical pylons, where the danger to human life would be low. Umkhonto's aim was to shock the regime into negotiating. It opened its offensive a week after Chief Lutuli received his peace prize. Somewhat later a different group, composed primarily of young whites, formed another commando organization called the African Resistance Movement that was similarly intended to induce the government to talk.

The minister of justice, John Vorster, guided detention without trial legislation through Parliament. The security police began to torture the political detainees. In September 1963, Bellington Mampe and Looksmart Ngudle were the first of more than fifty who would die mysteriously while in custody in the next two decades. The security police arrogantly offered only the most transparent excuses. The Imam Abdul Haron, a Cape Town religious leader, "fell down a flight of stairs." Ahmed Timol, a geography teacher, "fell out of a tenth floor window." Others allegedly committed "suicide by hanging." One man, Nichodimus Kgoathe, even supposedly died "following head injuries sustained in a shower."

Those who belonged to the underground Spear of the Nation soon developed a number of freedom songs. "We are the soldiers of Lutuli," was one refrain. "Mandela is our leader." One of the first soldiers was a tall, good-looking man from the Eastern Cape named Ronald Sandile, who was then in his early twenties. Ron has a deep voice and a warm laugh, which he sometimes uses to try and take the edge off his more harrowing reminiscences.

Ron had been raised in a rural area outside the industrial city of Port Elizabeth. "My mother was a half-caste. My maternal grandfather suffered the ignominy of having his wife impregnated by his German boss. The German paid one pound in damages, and so my mother was named Noponti, which means 'one pound.' Of course, she was brought up as a true Xhosa girl, completely steeped in the traditions of our people. The question of her bastard birth was never talked about. She was very beautiful, tall, and always elegant in her bearing.''

Ron Sandile's father had worked as a sharecropper on the surrounding white farms. As the farmers mechanized, they cancelled their agreements with the older Sandile. He had to now work as a low-paid laborer. ''My father had been a very proud man, earning an independent living. He now had to work all day with a spade, from 7:00 A.M. to 5:00 P.M. Before, he could be with us any time he chose.''

The elder Sandile had been the patriarch of a large clan. ''It was to him that the others brought children who needed money for school fees. It was to him that they appealed for an ox to slaughter, or an ox to sell in order to pay debts somewhere or another. But after my father went to work as a laborer, I then realized that the big household had thinned out. My father had to send many of his relatives away. And I realized that it was because he could no more shoulder the responsibilities which he had once held.''

Ron also moved away during his teenage years, to stay with relatives in Port Elizabeth's New Brighton township. He remembered one painful episode that took place when he returned to visit his father, who was working for a white farmer named Clark. ''I was walking along on the farm, and I picked up some oranges. They were not good enough for export. They were in a heap, to be collected by a truck and dumped in a nearby game reserve for the elephants. I picked up about five of them. As I walked, I passed Clark. I greeted him nicely. He didn't respond, and I went past. But before I could reach my father's place, his son came running after me, wanting to know why I had stolen oranges. He was the same age as myself. I said I had taken them from the heap for the game reserve. He insisted I had stolen, and he delivered a big blow. Of course a fight ensued. He had to run away in the end.

''That afternoon I was collected by the police, and I slept in a police cell. The following day, my father and Clark came for me. Clark had very hard words both for me and my father. He was bent on seeing to it that I was tried and jailed. My father employed a lawyer for me and I won the case. But it left a bitterness that, well, from that moment I knew that the white people in South Africa were very unjust. And from that moment, my interest in the African National Congress, which preached justice, came to be very strong. I began to be an active member of the ANC, to correct this wrong imbalance in our social, economic, and political life. I could not have put it like this in those days, but I know that these were exactly my feelings.''

Ron started distributing leaflets for the ANC in the Port Elizabeth townships. He also attended informal history courses taught by adult ANC Volunteers. He was a student at Newell High School, a rough urban institution, during the 1952 Defiance Campaign. "People were pouring out of the trains at the stations, and many of them were getting arrested, because they had been sitting in the carriages for the white people. Even as some were getting arrested, others were taking their places in the carriages. Still others were moving to sit on the benches reserved for white people at the station. They were also being arrested. Big trucks were being used to haul the people away. In fact the police stations were full by that time, and the people were being hauled straight to jail.''

At Newell High, Ron excelled both as a student and in rugby. (The Eastern Cape is the only region of South Africa where the sport is also popular among blacks.) In his final year he was made the school's chief prefect, or head of the student body. He was also by then a member of the ANC Youth League. "One of our jobs was to cyclostile [mimeograph] ANC material right in our school. Every night, each one of us would come out of the gates carrying a bundle for his area.''

He was the first in his family to complete high school. He planned to continue on to Fort Hare, located in the region, which is the oldest of the black colleges. To earn money for tuition, he worked for several years as a clerk in a dairy and then as a driver at the General Motors plant in Port Elizabeth. Because certain of his high school friends had already entered the college, they were able to save him from embarrassment when he finally enrolled. "As a fresher, you sometimes got a typed letter, with a college stamp, inviting you to tea with the vice chancellor, or to dinner at the principal's place. I took these letters, innocently and excitedly, to my friends. And they of course warned me that these were pranks!''

While Ron Sandile was at Fort Hare, Bantu Education went into effect at the university level. The college, once largely autonomous, was placed under the control of a restrictive government department. Many faculty members, blacks and English-speaking whites, resigned in protest; they were replaced with conservative Afrikaners. The students staged big demonstrations, and many of them were expelled. Ron Sandile was himself thrown out for publicly insulting Kaizer Matanzima, later the "president" of the Transkei Bantustan; he had called Matanzima an *inwyagi*, or sell-out, in front of a group of students. The students boycotted classes for three days, which forced the administration to readmit Ron Sandile.

Ron graduated from Fort Hare in 1961, the year after the Sharpeville Massacre and the bannings of the ANC and the PAC. He had qualified as a teacher, but he did not look for work. "I made it very clear that I could not teach in a system calculated to enslave our people mentally." He started to train as an attorney. But he was spending most of his time in underground political action, as a member of the Spear of the Nation.

"Sabotage was of course a change in the method of struggle. In the past, the ANC had firmly believed in passive resistance, in peaceful struggle, and many, many people had come to believe that this was the way to bring human rights, to bring freedom, to South Africa. So when the decision was taken to go underground and to change to violence, it was a very difficult moment.

"The ANC, true to its democratic principles, did make it possible for people to make known their views and to take a decision whether they agreed or not. It was a very emotional moment. For my part, I had no problem; we in the Youth had always felt that the method of nonviolence would never carry us to our desired end. I attended one such clandestine meeting, which was addressed by Nelson Mandela himself, who was moving underground around the country. It was sad to see people making known their feelings; how they had spent all their lives in the ANC, because of its peaceful policies, and how they could not now reconcile themselves to a new ANC which was now adopting the principles of violence. These people were very Christian in their beliefs, and they said these beliefs would not permit them to remain in an organization that does violence. And so, at the end of that meeting, we had to say, 'Farewell, dear colleagues' to people who had struggled for a long time, all their lives. We told each other that we would meet again on the other side of freedom."

Ron Sandile's underground work ended with his arrest at four one morning in 1963. He was detained without trial for the next eighteen months. Most of the time, he did not even know where he was being held. "I saw nobody outside of warders and police for eighteen months. Nobody at all. They wanted me to give information about my underground activities. They said, 'M—— told us all about your role in the underground. Now, with whom were you in your unit?' I refused. Only if I had informed could there have been a trial. They would have unearthed them, broken them, and either used me as a witness against them or they would have put me back in the group and selected who they would have used as witnesses against us. And all of us would have gone to Robben Island for many years.

"But the police interrogators couldn't get to that point, because it was my word against that of M——. I tried to make him out to be the biggest liar. I even challenged them to bring M—— to me. They never did. But he was dead right! [Ron burst out laughing.] I was indeed the leader of an underground ANC cell.''

Ron, like other political detainees, explained that solitary confinement was terribly punishing and demoralizing. ''You are left alone in this irreal atmosphere. In Port Elizabeth they have underground basement cells. You soon lose touch with the time, and the day. In the ceiling of the cell is one single bulb, yellow, which is lit for twenty-four hours. You will sometimes fall asleep during the day, and soon you are going to be unable to tell whether it's daytime or night because there's no change in the lighting system. When the clock from the Town Hall strikes twelve you can't tell whether it's twelve midday or twelve midnight.

''Then they've got other, little things, which ultimately do get you. You are deprived of your cigarettes if you're a smoker. You are deprived of your comb, you are deprived of your toothbrush. What was also very bad was that they didn't leave you with a water container. I was forced to drink from the toilet basin. I would flush it and catch the fresh water as it is running there. That wasn't easy for me, but what could I do?

''The other thing that gets you is the loneliness. You're all by yourself, all the time. At one time I did begin to suffer a bit of hallucinations. The warders rushed into my cell, wanting to know with whom was I speaking. I must have been speaking my thoughts aloud.''

In that crisis, Ron remembered what he had been advised by his political mentor, the ANC leader Govan Mbeki, who has been serving a life sentence on Robben Island for the past twenty years. ''I started to exercise. Ordinarily I hate physical exercise, but I can tell you that when you're detained you can go a long way if you keep fit. I also know that prior to starting to exercise I had started to feel some pity for myself. When that happens, you're approaching a dangerous moment. If the police knew, if they could get you at that stage, then they can break you within no time. But they didn't break me. But I suppose I could say that I was quite lucky, because I was never beaten by the police. Subsequent to my time, people were beaten up very, very badly by the police.''

Ron Sandile only discovered the actual date on the way to his trial. ''The police joked with me. Some said it's Tuesday, others said it's March. Finally, I learned from other prisoners. I was surprised. I knew I had been inside longer than a year, but I thought it was only something like fourteen months instead of eighteen months.'' He laughed uproariously.

Ron expected a five-year sentence. He was pleasantly surprised to get only one year; the judge took into account the time he had spent already in detention. He, along with others convicted of political offenses, was shipped to the Fort Glamorgan prison in East London, a notorious institution for hard-core criminals. "They had hoped perhaps that we politicals would get it from the criminals, that they would ill-treat us. But our going there was to serve, in many ways, a good role.

"South African prisons are very violent, dehumanizing places. People group themselves into gangs, with numbers. I remember number twenty-eight was the gang of the country bumpkins, while the tsotsis, the town boys, belonged to gang five. These gangs smuggle a sharpened implement into the jail, and then you've got hell that night. Because there are strange rules about these things, that once a knife has been brought into a cell it cannot return without blood. It's a creed, a ritual.

"It became one of our duties to separate, to mediate between these people. We did this via our political experience. We were sixteen politicals, including four PAC men. (We cooperated with the PAC men without any problem.) We started to show the gang members that their quarrels lie far deeper than what appear to be their differences there in jail. We distributed ourselves throughout the prison, and we talked with each individual, starting with the leaders. We were gradually able to stop gang warfare there. We became accepted as leaders by the gangs; we were very respected."

By some lucky quirk of fate, Ron Sandile was due for release on December 16, 1965. That date is celebrated each year as the Day of the Covenant, marking the triumph of the Afrikaner voortrekkers over the Zulu in a bloody battle in 1838. Prisoners are released a day early. But the dispensation is not supposed to apply to politicals. The chief warden blundered, and let Ron free. He expected to find the security police waiting to rearrest him on further and more serious charges. He quickly asked a friend to drive him back home. "I subsequently got to know that as we were going toward Port Elizabeth, the security police were driving the other way, toward East London, to collect me the following morning. We must have passed each other on the highway!"

His family staged a huge celebration the next day, which included the slaughter of two sheep and the consumption of much alcohol. But Ron was uneasy during the festivities. He posted sentries, and then he left early, refusing to remain at home. "As sure as fate, the security police surrounded my home again at four A.M. They found a lot of drunken, sleeping people." Ron laughed. "I'm told it was very interesting how those people were waking up and running away into the darkness."

Ron's chances to evade the security police were lessened because his pass was not in order. During his imprisonment, he had been "endorsed out" of Port Elizabeth into the Transkei Bantustan. "I had never been a member of any Bantustan; I had no links there. I was now asking myself, 'Where can I go?' I was illegal! I was illegal; I had nowhere; I did not belong to any place, in my own country!"

He also found that the regime had crushed the ANC underground and ended its sabotage campaign. Members who were not already imprisoned were demoralized and afraid. Ron decided that exile was his only choice. "I informed my mother, and my younger brother and sister. But not my father. Or my older brother. They would not have approved. Yes, it was the last time I ever saw my father."

He journeyed up to Natal, where his fiancée was training as a nurse. They married quietly, and then he headed further north, to Swaziland and exile. "I arrived there with thirty-six cents. I had to protect my bride, who was finishing her studies, by sending her a telegram purporting that she didn't know about my going to Swaziland. So I was left with five cents. I had to think very hard, whether to buy food, or to buy a newspaper. Ultimately I settled for the *Daily Mail,* no [laughing], it wasn't the *Mail,* it was the *Post.* I read in there headlines that said I had been released, gotten married, and run away!" He laughed.

By the middle 1960s, the regime had completely crushed all armed resistance. The security police swooped on a farm in Rivonia, in the outskirts of Johannesburg, and captured much of the leadership of Umkhonto we Sizwe, including Walter Sisulu; a young white engineer named Denis Goldberg; Govan Mbeki, the Eastern Cape leader who had been Ron Sandile's mentor; and Ahmed Kathrada, an Indian South African once active in Gandhian passive resistance. They, along with Nelson Mandela, who was already in prison on a lesser charge, were all sentenced to life. Kathrada refused to appeal against his sentence despite good legal prospects because he did not want to break the solidarity with his fellow prisoners. Two years later, their attorney, Bram Fischer, of a distinguished Afrikaner family, was also convicted for his underground activities and sentenced to life. There is no parole in political cases. Other ANC people got jail terms of ten, fifteen, and twenty years. Dorothy Nyembe, released after a three-year sentence for "furthering the aims of a banned organization," went straight back to the underground; her next sentence was for fifteen years.

The security police suppressed the other resistance movements as well. The PAC's Robert Sobukwe, who had originally been sentenced to only three years, was kept on Robben Island indefinitely under special legislation designed solely for him. Another outstanding PAC leader, Zephania Mothopeng, was at one stage tortured so badly with electric shocks that when he reached for a metal cup in his cell afterwards sparks leaped from his fingers. The regime also imprisoned many of the leaders of the African Resistance Movement, the group made up primarily of young whites. A white ARM member, John Harris, panicked after his companions were arrested. In an act of individual desperation, Harris set off a bomb in a Johannesburg train station that killed a woman passerby. He was sentenced to death and hanged in 1965. He walked to the gallows singing "We Shall Overcome."

By then hundreds of people were serving prison terms. Nearly all of them had gone to jail with calm defiance, standing in the courtroom docks before uncomprehending white judges and explaining politely but firmly that they did not repent of their beliefs or their acts. Nelson Mandela told the court, "I have fought against white domination and I have fought against black domination. I have cherished the ideal of a democratic and free society in which all persons live together in harmony, and with equal opportunities. It is an ideal which I hope to live for and to achieve. But, if needs be, it is an ideal for which I am prepared to die."

Bram Fischer also spoke for other whites when he told the court, "All the conduct with which I have been charged has been directed toward maintaining contact and understanding between the races of this country. If one day it may help to establish a bridge across which white leaders and the real leaders of the non-whites can meet to settle the destinies of all of us by negotiation and not by force of arms, I shall be able to bear with fortitude any sentence which this Court may impose on me." Bram Fischer did not live to see such negotiations. He died, still in custody, in 1975.

The white politicals were held at Pretoria Local Prison in conditions of appalling isolation. They were forbidden newspapers from outside, and allowed to receive only one five-hundred-word letter and one half-hour visit every six months. They slept on floor mats, had no toilets or running water in their cells, and spent their days in the windy exercise yard sewing damaged mailbags. One of them, Hugh Lewin, later wrote a powerful description of life inside called *Bandiet: Seven Years in a South African Prison*. He emphasized that life for black prisoners was even worse.

Hugh was working as a journalist in independent Zimbabwe when I met him in the early 1980s. In person, he is like his book, understated and generous. I asked him if he was bitter about the lost years in prison. "No, no," he rushed to reassure me. "I had a totally rewarding experience. There was the personal aspect, getting to know people like Bram Fischer, his quality of greatness. He was old; he was under stress; his eyes were failing; and one night they told him his son had died and then they locked him in his cell for the next fourteen hours to be alone with the news. But he was always kind and humble. He even spent hours advising one of the warders on water law; the guy had a stream on his property and he was in some dispute with his neighbor. There was John Mathews; he never had the chance to finish high school, but in the seven years I knew him and in the eight more years he did after that he never once complained about himself. Or there's Denis Goldberg, who I think about every single day of my life. He's still there. He was always contributing, helping people. . . .

"No, no, it was a great experience." Hugh paused, and smiled slightly to himself. "I wouldn't have chosen it, and it did go on a little bit too long, but it was very rewarding."

In the world outside, the African National Congress had directed a reluctant Oliver Tambo to flee the country as the crackdown after Sharpeville got underway. He started the laborious task of establishing the movement in exile and lobbying for international support. Certain PAC leaders did the same. Both organizations trained small numbers of guerrillas, but the young fighters found it impossible to penetrate the protective ring of white-ruled states. The two movements clung to life in exile. The later 1960s, a period engraved in Western consciousness as a time of political and cultural upheaval, was in South Africa the precise opposite, a stretch of sullen, uneasy, fearful calm.

15

The Movement Turns to Fighting

BLACK AMERICA has long exercised a noticeable influence among black people half a world away in southern Africa. In the late nineteenth century, missionaries from the African Methodist Episcopal Church, the large black American denomination, helped to establish congregations in South Africa. This connection between the A.M.E. churches on two continents persists to the present day. A number of early African National Congress leaders had studied in America; the wife of Dr. A. B. Xuma, the ANC president in the 1940s, was actually a black American, Madie B. Hall, of Winston-Salem, North Carolina. Over the years, black South Africans have maintained an abiding interest in black American political leaders, sports figures, music, and slang. In South Africa, you have no trouble encountering Muhammad Ali T-shirts, jazz records by Duke Ellington, or books by Dr. Martin Luther King, Jr.

In the late 1960s, black South Africans followed the U.S. civil rights movement with sympathy and great interest. One of these observers was a black medical student just twenty years old named Steve Biko. As Biko surveyed the depressing and demoralized state of affairs among black South Africans, he used language strikingly similar to the way black Americans were talking about their situation. Biko wrote, "The type of black man we have today has lost his manhood. . . . He looks with awe at the white power structure and accepts what he regards as the 'inevitable position.' . . . All in all the black man has become a shell, a shadow of man, completely defeated, drowning in his own misery, a slave and ox bearing the yoke of oppression with sheepish timidity.''

At the time, Biko belonged to the National Union of South African Students, a multiracial organization based mainly on the five English-speaking white campuses that also had branches at the black colleges. NUSAS was the only organization with any claim to radicalism that remained aboveground after the crackdown in the middle sixties. So it was at first somewhat surprising that Biko led a walkout of black students in 1968. They set up the South African Students Organization (SASO), a group for blacks only.

Some white liberals were shocked by the secession, seeing it as a perverse black acquiescence in the philosophy of apartheid. But Biko explained patiently that racism had triumphed so overwhelmingly in South Africa that it had distorted the thinking of both white people and black people to such a degree that for the time being at least they could not work together in the same organizations. ''The integration they talk about is . . . artificial,'' Biko explained. ''The people forming the integrated complex have been extracted from various segregated societies with their built-in complexes of superiority and inferiority and these continue to manifest themselves even in the 'non-racial' set-up of the integrated complex. As a result the integration so achieved is a one-way course, with the whites doing all the talking and the blacks listening.'' Biko and his growing band of young supporters politely encouraged whites to fight racism in their own communities rather than trying to preach to blacks.

There was much in this message that is reminiscent of the similar insistence on black exclusivity that came to characterize a part of the American civil rights movement. But Steve Biko rightly resented the occasional suggestion that he had merely copied a philosophy from across the sea. Black consciousness was above all a defiant answer to the South African reality at a dismal time when resistance had seemed hopeless.

Biko and other black consciousness leaders like A. O. R. Tiro and Barney Pityana boldly exhorted blacks to shed this sense of inferiority and despair and to start again to organize for liberation. They discarded the insulting term *non-white* and extended the definition of black. Indian and colored people like Peter Jones, Saths Cooper, and Strini Moodley became prominent black consciousness advocates.

The young leaders urged total black boycotts of the Bantustan system and other government-sponsored institutions. They directly attacked figures like Chief Gatsha Buthelezi of Kwa-Zulu, who had achieved a certain popularity partly due to the absence of more radical alternatives. They revived a word the PAC had first used for ''South Africa'' and counterposed to the divisive purposes of the apartheid system the unifying slogan, "One Azania, One Nation." They praised both the ANC and the PAC, but stressed they represented an entirely new force. They founded an organization called the Black People's Convention that enlarged their following; they established vigorous self-help projects in health and education in the shabby townships. They boldly staged rallies to celebrate the fall of Portuguese colonialism in nearby Mozambique and Angola.

The apartheid regime had at first regarded black consciousness with some approval, as an apparent echo of its own separatist philosophy. Soon, the government recognized that black consciousness was dangerously successful in stirring black political activism once again. Even though Biko and the others had always insisted on nonviolence, the security police went into action. Tiro was killed by a parcel bomb; Biko and others were banned; still others were convicted of "terrorism" and imprisoned on Robben Island.

In August 1977, Steve Biko, then just thirty-one years old, was detained near King William's Town in the Eastern Cape. Within weeks, he was dead—the forty-sixth victim of the detention-without-trial system. Inside South Africa, those who knew him surmise that he resisted when the security police started to torture him and they then beat him to the point of death. He had once described how he handled an earlier stint in detention, "We had a boxing match the first day I was arrested. Some guy tried to clout me with a club. I went into him like a bull. . . . And of course he said . . . , 'I will kill you.' He meant to intimidate. And my answer was, 'How long is it going to take you?' "

A month later, on October 19, 1977, the government responded to the furious outcry over Biko's death by banning all the remaining black consciousness organizations. But the crackdown had come too late. Black consciousness had already achieved its immediate goal, to dispel the fear, shame, and impotence that had existed among blacks. The courageous young students who marched through Soweto in June 1976 and their counterparts in the other urban areas had demanded an end to an educational system designed to maintain them in ignorance. An organization of high school students strongly influenced by black consciousness, the South African Students Movement, had been an important part of the upheaval. The quest for simple dignity had ignited the largest uprising in South African history.

The October 1977 repression left a temporary political vacuum inside the country. It appeared that the apartheid regime would no longer tolerate even the most peaceful forms of opposition. Even older, more moderate leaders suffered. Dr. Nthato Motlana was arrested and Bishop

Desmond Tutu harassed. The Riotous Assemblies Act, now in effect continually, outlawed all open-air gatherings. The police continued to fire into crowds and to detain hundreds of people. Many of the students and others had no choice now but exile. Several thousand crossed the borders illegally and entered the surrounding independent countries of Lesotho, Botswana, and Swaziland.

There, they mainly encountered the African National Congress. In exile, the Pan-Africanist Congress had been torn by violent internal disputes. Robert Sobukwe had died, still under restrictions, in 1978. The rest of the PAC's leadership was simply not up to his caliber. The ANC had held itself together during the long hard years in exile. The organization's representatives began to recruit guerrillas for the Spear of the Nation from among the young exiles.

A few scattered guerrilla incidents occurred inside South Africa during 1977 and 1978. In 1979, small bands of three or four Umkhonto soldiers attacked police stations in Soweto, killing several black policemen. On June 4, 1980, the guerrillas struck with explosives simultaneously at three separate targets hundreds of miles apart. No one was killed. The most spectacular attacks took place just south of Johannesburg, at one of the three Sasol refineries at which South Africa converts coal into precious oil. In predawn explosions, the saboteurs sent smoke billowing miles into the air and destroyed about $7.2 million in supplies. War was now very definitely underway.

By then, Ronald Sandile's friends in neighboring Swaziland were already starting to regard him as a man under a sentence of death. As one of the leading ANC representatives in the country, he was an obvious target for South African bombing and assassination attempts, which were starting to happen more frequently throughout the region. It was unnerving; there he was before you, bidding you good-bye with his familiar laugh and his firm handshake, and it flashed through your mind that you might never see him alive again.

Ron had a truly enormous set of keys to the range of hideouts among which he moved randomly. He carried a revolver and was often accompanied by young ANC bodyguards. He had sent his wife and children to live in another, more distant country. Still, the tension gnawed at him. But the only time I ever heard him complain over the years was when he observed off-handedly one evening, "It's not very pleasant . . . to know that you can just get blown away on the street at any time."

Soon after he had arrived in Swaziland in the middle sixties with thirty-six cents, he had started teaching English at a Catholic high school. He had remained there for a decade, until ANC business required his full-time attention. At first, he and the other refugees had been mainly concerned with keeping the organization alive. He still had enough spare time to reduce his golf handicap to five.

But after 1976 he had to leave the fairways for good. Young people started pouring into Swaziland, adding to the several hundred refugees who were already settled there semipermanently. Some of the youths, bitter at seeing friends and relatives shot by the police, wanted simply to obtain weapons and return home for revenge. Ron explained, "We had to cool them. We told them, 'Look, you don't just pick up a gun and go use it. We need engineers, doctors—perhaps you should rather continue your schooling. In any case, you wait to be taught about a gun. And to be taught the politics of South Africa. We will give you the guns eventually.' "

In exile, the ANC had forged a closer alliance with the small, multiracial Communist Party of South Africa. A few ANC leaders were also openly Communist. Other ANC members probably kept their party membership secret. The relationship between the party and the much larger ANC has prompted criticism in the West that the liberation movement is Communist-dominated. Ron Sandile's answer is heated: "We in South Africa have never been oppressed by the Communists. It is the Western powers that support the Pretoria regime with their big investments. It is also said that the Communist party is dominated by whites. This is not true. It has always been a majority black organization. For many years, the party secretary was Moses Kotane. Now, it is another black man, Moses Mabhida. One thing we do know—those white people in the party have been together with us for many years. They do not have the superior attitude that many of the other white people have. They work alongside us. They suffer as we suffer. They also go to prison.

"It is true that we are getting support from the Soviet Union and the Socialist countries in Eastern Europe. That aid has been very valuable to us. But the trade union movement in Britain also supports us. The Scandinavian countries are also helping us. Many individuals in those anti-apartheid movements in the West are giving us very important support."

In talking with the young prospective guerrilla recruits, Ron found some suspicion about the ANC for having white members, and objections to its insistence, as in the first line of the Freedom Charter, that whites have a right to remain in the country after liberation. He confronts those fears head on, without any hesitation. "In fact, I sometimes think that nonracialism is our strongest point as an organization; we do use it to convince those young people. We tell them that we are against racism, and if we engage in that type of politics it will be racism in reverse. As far as the ANC is concerned, the most important factor is that a person is a human being. These white people have been there for over three hundred years, and you cannot try to say that they no more belong to South Africa. Where do they belong? You can't try and push them to Holland—they didn't come only from Holland; they came from all over those European countries. Where do you push them to? And remember, they are human beings, who are only following a wrong philosophical line.''

Early in 1982, the ANC leadership decided the danger to Ronald Sandile had become too great. The South African security police were apparently sending special assassination teams into Swaziland with instructions to kill him. He was surprised at the individual attention; he continued to regard himself as a "small fry." Against his desire, the ANC high command removed him from Swaziland, and posted him to a safer spot, farther away from the front line. On his way to his new assignment, he did get a chance to stop off and visit with his family. He would not be able to see them again for nearly a year.

Inside South Africa, the role of white people in the movement against apartheid was changing once again. After Steve Biko and the other black students had walked out of NUSAS, the more radical whites who remained had followed his suggestion and reexamined their racial attitudes. They came to recognize the truth of much of Biko's charge that whites could be paternal in multiracial settings. The young whites also rebuked themselves for their lack of knowledge of their own country. They needed to learn about South Africa instead of Europe and America if they wanted to contribute to the welfare of their countrymen rather than emigrate. "You are part of Africa," one student newspaper told its readers. "Your challenge lies here and you must be prepared to stay and face it.''

A growing number of whites, mainly but not only the young, started to accept that challenge in the course of the 1970s. Lawyers set up legal aid centers for black people who ran afoul of the pervasive apartheid statutes. Energetic scholars began to reexamine the South African past, coming up with bold new interpretations that showed how the Bantustan system and migrant labor were central and enduring features in the region's history, rather than, as in the prevailing conventional wisdom, bizarre aberrations that were somehow bound to disappear. Newly trained agricultural experts established pilot projects in remote rural areas to try and learn how to reverse the terrible deterioration there.

In these efforts the whites were usually careful to handle themselves as partners with black people rather than as arrogant do-gooders, to listen and to learn about black life and culture. This new attitude was perhaps best symbolized by the musical group Juluka, in which Jonathan Clegg, a young white man, and Sipho Mchunu, his black friend, produced a string of popular hits in so flawless a Zulu that many black listeners refused to believe Clegg was an *umlungu*.

The vast majority of whites continued to support apartheid. But by the end of the seventies, there was a visible group of some thousands of whites, which easily constituted the largest number who had ever worked toward a genuine radical alternative to white supremacy.

By now, black people were far more tolerant of working together with whites. Efforts to revive organizations that stood explicitly for black consciousness had only limited success. There was certainly still some evidence that blacks in South Africa continued to suffer psychologically from racism. The extremely high rate of murder, assault, and rape in the townships, which had been cited as an indication that some blacks were internalizing the racist view of black inferiority and turning their rage, shame, and hatred against other blacks, showed no sign of decline. But many of the more politically minded black people, who had never in any case made a practice of robbing their neighbors, had moved on to multiracialism.

The parallel with black America had never been exact. As Ezekiel Mphahlele, the novelist who had lived in both countries, explained to me one day, "Black people there are a minority. They are cut off from their African roots. They are in a state of siege. White culture is impinging on them all the time. In Black Power and similar movements, they therefore felt the need to be more outspoken and assertive.

"Here, *we* are the majority. We are still on African soil. We have retained our own languages and our own culture. We certainly know that a white power *out there* oppresses us, but we don't feel it as directly, as internally. At deeper levels, we have maintained our identity."

There was a growing view that black consciousness had served its purpose. The Soweto uprising and the continuing steady drumbeat of guerrilla, trade union, and community actions had largely destroyed the sense of black impotence and inferiority. There was no longer the need to insist so heatedly on black exclusivity.

After the October 1977 crackdown, the pace of activity slackened for a time. Then, late in 1979, a new organization called the Port Elizabeth Black Civic Association burst on the scene in the Eastern Cape's large motor industry. Some seven hundred Pebco members who worked at Ford carried out a series of wildcat strikes, first to demand the reinstatement of their leader, Thozamile Botha, whom they said Ford had fired for his political activities, and then to demand improved conditions at their plant. Ford fired all the striking workers, but then had to rescind the move after the outcry in South Africa and overseas started to corrode the company's carefully burnished image as a progressive employer.

Black people all over the country listened eagerly to the live radio announcement of the Patriotic Front's stunning election victory in Zimbabwe in March 1980. The celebrations in the townships started immediately. A mood of optimism and renewed determination swept across the country. In Cape Town, black and colored schoolchildren began boycotting their classes, protesting that the 1976 upheaval had brought no improvement to their "gutter education." The boycotts spread everywhere, to the Eastern Cape, Johannesburg, even Bloemfontein, the heart of the conservative Free State. In Durban, the first major crack in Bantustan leader Gatsha Buthelezi's support among blacks there opened as students defied him and joined in the boycott. In total, some one hundred thousand children stayed away from their segregated schools, in some cases setting up their own "awareness programs" instead. One of their theme songs was black American Michael Jackson's "Don't Stop 'Til You Get Enough." Some white students at the English-speaking universities joined in the protest.

Black political and religious leaders pointed out that a long and bitter war had not prevented a Patriotic Front victory in Zimbabwe; they urged the South African government to negotiate before the fighting increased even further. Within weeks, petitions asking for freedom for ANC leader Nelson Mandela had collected fifty thousand signatures. Even the more moderate white press joined in urging the government to release Mandela and start talking with him.

The unrest continued, with workers staging an unprecedented wave of strikes. The government declared the Eastern Cape industrial town of Uitenhage a military "operational area," in what may have been an ominous portent for the future. As police pressure increased nationwide, there were scattered incidents of blacks stoning white motorists and burning buildings. Then, during the successful stay-away from work in mid-June to mark the anniversary of the 1976 uprising, the police in Cape Town opened fire, killing an estimated forty-two people in the ghetto of Elsie's River. The death toll, nearly comparable to the Sharpeville Massacre two decades earlier, no longer aroused similar surprise and shock. There was by now a grim air of inevitability to it all.

Among those most active in the 1980 upheaval were black workers. Blacks had organized themselves in the past, as far back as the 1920s, but only a very few unions had survived the repression of the middle sixties. Then in 1973 a wave of strikes shook Durban, as more than a hundred thousand workers at some 150 different enterprises walked out to demand higher wages. Activists across the country started energetically to try to convert that kind of renewed spontaneous militance into strong, organized unions.

By 1980, a half dozen new labor federations had emerged in an alphabet soup of acronyms. There were some differences among SAAWU, FOSATU, CUSA, GAWU, GWU, and the rest, but they shared a determination to strike if necessary to support their demands for recognition and improvement in wages and working conditions. The new unions also tended to be fiercely democratic. Workers who were often voting for the first time in their lives elected officials and stewards and jointly formulated their grievances. Black trade union membership grew from a small number in the mid-seventies to three hundred thousand by 1982. That year alone, there were four hundred strikes in South Africa, contrasted with a mere seventy or so annually into the early seventies. In several cases, there were nationwide boycotts of certain products to support striking workers.

The South African government was at first tolerant of the new unions. It feared the repercussions overseas if it tried to suppress the fledgling organizations, particularly those that were organizing in subsidiaries of American or European enterprises. Also, some government officials, along with certain leading businessmen, realized that moderate unions could be a force for stability, guiding the discontent on the factory floors into safe, institutionalized channels.

To keep the new unions sufficiently tame, the regime expected them to "register," or submit to a set of legal controls. The most significant restriction barred them from participating in "politics." But "politics" was precisely what motivated the organizers of the new unions. Some were veterans, like the septuagenarian Oscar Mpetha, who was later imprisoned even though he was terminally ill. Others, younger blacks, were people who had participated in the 1976 uprising and remained active in their workplaces and communities; the apartheid system prevented them from participating in formal politics, so the new unions were one of the only outlets for their energies.

Also active in the new unions were some of the younger whites. Their participation in leadership positions in almost totally black unions would have been unthinkable during the heyday of black consciousness. The whites, many of whom had once been radical students and younger faculty members, had started in an auxiliary fashion, conducting economic and legal studies and opening advice offices for the neophyte unions. Over time, their energy and dedication had won them genuine and enthusiastic support among many black union members, who did not hesitate to elect them to leadership posts.

The growing militance was not at all what the South African government had in mind when it had decided to permit the unions to function. The security police began to detain quite a number of leaders. Thozi Gqweta, whom I had visited in his East London office in 1981, was locked up a total of eight times by mid-1983. That year, he appeared as a witness in an insurrection case. He boldly told the court that during one of his spells in detention the police had handcuffed him and hung him from window bars, tortured him with electric currents, and tightened a wet canvas bag around his neck until he had passed out from the lack of air. He testified fearlessly right in front of the security police who waited in the courtroom to take him straight back to detention.

Another unionist, a white medical doctor named Neil Aggett, did not survive his time in detention. He was found hanging in his cell in police headquarters in the early hours of February 5, 1982. There were only a few photographs of Neil Aggett readily available after he died. He was a quiet and unassuming young man, not the sort who often thrust himself in front of a camera. The organizers for his funeral did manage to find a group photo from which they could crop and enlarge his individual portrait. It showed a young, bearded white man in his late twenties, ruggedly good-looking. There was a set to his jaw and a slight, serious narrowing of his eyes. At the same time, there was also the suggestion of a twitch at the corners of his mouth and the hint of a twinkle in his eye, as though he were about to burst into a grin after the camera clicked. The organizers distributed thousands of copies of the funeral program with this photo on the cover to the mourners entering St. Mary's Cathedral, in central Johannesburg, early in the hot afternoon of February 13, 1982. Over the photo, the program read: "NEIL AGGETT—DIED IN DETENTION." Underneath: "AN INJURY TO ONE IS AN INJURY TO ALL."

Inside, the large cathedral echoed with the steady wailing of women's voices. Hundreds of black nurses in crisp white uniforms were scattered about in the nave, or leaning from high, overhanging balconies. They were only the most distinctive of the thousands of black people and the hundreds of white people who filled the cathedral. The wailing oscillated in pitch; there was an undertone of anger when it rose, a disbelieving anguish when it dropped off. Through the hymns, the prayers and the eulogies, the wailing continued unceasingly.

After the service, we spilled out into De Villiers Street to begin the long funeral march to West Park Cemetery, a burial ground for white people only. The only form of outdoor gatherings the regime still permitted were funerals. One group of mourners, including a black man in a wheelchair, formed the vanguard, in front of the hearse, and unfurled the green, black, and gold flag of the outlawed African National Congress. Others, clutching Neil Aggett's photograph like a talisman, poured into the dozens of hired buses, open-backed trucks, vans, and autos.

Many of the vehicles had come from all over South Africa. There were metalworkers from the foundries and mills along the East Rand, dockworkers from Durban, auto workers from the big plants down in the Port Elizabeth area. From Cape Town, fifteen hundred miles away, where Dr. Neil Aggett had completed his medical studies, there was busload after busload of black, white, and colored people, including cannery workers who belonged to Neil Aggett's union. They marched with a huge red banner: "Our Brave Hero."

Our cavalcade started westward at no faster than a walking pace, bringing central Johannesburg to a standstill. We could see the security police photographers five stories overhead, light glinting briefly off their cameras. The buses rocked with impassioned chants.

"Botha is a TERRORIST—Aggett is a HERO."

"*Amandla*—Power. *Awethu*—To the People."

The stream of vehicles passed the flats and the small shops of Braamfontein. Passersby, at first astonished and wary, soon started saluting the hearse with clenched fists. Black street cleaners in their dirty blue overalls gathered in a knot, bowed their heads slightly, as if in brief, silent prayer, and raised their fists. Further along, young whites, probably students at nearby Wits University, did likewise. Gas station attendants came to the curb to salute. Further up, black laborers at the gasworks saluted from behind the massive barred gates. A black maid in her pink uniform at first raised her fist shyly and tentatively, and then more firmly.

The mood in the huge caravan, now fifteen-thousand strong, changed by the moment. There was a grim, shared joy at seeing the enormous crowd, at seeing the overwhelming sympathy from the bystanders; there was pride in noting that the police had backed off for once, clearly afraid of the international reaction if they were to open fire on such a gigantic and visible gathering. There was also pride in the true nonracialism of the event; there were Indians, whites, so-called coloreds along with blacks, mixing unselfconsciously, everyone together, catching a brief glimpse of the South Africa for which they were fighting. There were all these reasons for genuine joy—and then, up at the front, you glimpsed the black hearse, moving along at a crawl, bearing the broken body of a twenty-eight-year-old man. You saw the man's picture, with that twinkle in his eye, brandished everywhere. You realized that there would be more, many more, funerals to come before South Africa became like that procession.

The long line of vehicles slowed even further on entering the quiet, well-off white suburbs of Auckland Park and Melville. Large homes, many with swimming pools, were set well back from the tree-lined side streets.

Many of us disembarked from the buses and walked the last few miles, swinging through the usually quiet streets chanting: *"Amandla—Awethu."* An older black man, dressed in overalls, strode along with dogged determination just in front of me, clutching a little bouquet of yellow flowers he had plucked somewhere along the way. Other marchers imitated him, grabbing sprigs of greenery to lay on Neil Aggett's grave.

The police were waiting near the edge of West Park cemetery. Several hundred of them lounged about smirking on the streetcorners, while more were visible up the side streets. Most were white, though there were a few blacks. They were dressed in camouflage riot gear, with revolvers strapped to their belts; the bigger weapons were out of sight. Some twiddled whips of hardened rubber or plastic. Aside from a few sidelong glances, the marchers paid them no attention.

As the crowd approached the cemetery, the hearse stopped. The pallbearers, mostly young black and white union officials, removed the wooden coffin and carried it slowly toward the grave. Hundreds of people lined up in advance, forming a somber arch of raised clenched fists.

There was a brief religious ceremony at the graveside. Neil Aggett's parents sat slumped and dazed, pale in the heat. A minister intoned, "Man that is born of woman hath but a short time to live, and is full of trouble. He cometh up, and is cut down, like a flower; he fleeth as if it were a shadow, and never continueth in one stay."

Neil Aggett's coffin was then lowered into the ground. A middle-aged black woman turned her head away, sobbing softly. The pallbearers, and others, came forward and with drawn looks started to slowly and deliberately shovel the red African earth over the coffin.

The thousands spread out in the grass in a huge semicircle, facing a makeshift dais. An older black man, one of Neil Aggett's fellow officials in the Food and Canning Workers Union, moved to the microphone. He glanced helplessly over at the grave and burst out, "He was not a terrorist. He was a hero." There was a loud, rolling cheer of agreement.

Then, more slowly, the man continued, "When did he sleep? Some nights, he worked in the emergency room at Baragwanath hospital in Soweto. Other nights he was at union meetings. Other nights, he was treating union members; he never charged us any money. Every day, he was working at union headquarters. He never slept. He was too busy helping people to sleep.''

There was a song, in the long, mournful vowel sounds of the Zulu language:

> *Lihambile*
> He has left
> *Ighawe lama ghawe*
> Hero of the heroes
> *Hamba kahle, Nkukeli ya basebenzi*
> Go well, Fighter for Freedom
> *Unyana we Afrika*
> Son of Africa

Others spoke. It was noted that the security police were still holding Dr. Liz Floyd, Neil Aggett's companion for many years; they refused her request to attend his funeral. Samson Ndou, the black president of the General and Allied Workers Union who was also in detention, had managed to smuggle out a spirited message of condolence; people in the big crowd winced as they imagined how the security police, who were certainly present, would quickly relay the news to wherever Ndou was presently being held. A number of speakers referred with pride to the successful protest two days earlier, during which a hundred thousand workers across the entire nation had stopped work for one-half hour to honor Neil Aggett.

David Lewis, the white union leader from the Cape who had been Neil Aggett's longtime friend, said boldly, ''Economic sanctions will not come from the British and American governments. They will come, one day, from British and American workers, when they refuse to deal with South African goods.'' Then, the slight, deceptively frail-looking Lewis, himself a former detainee, added: ''For every Neil they kill, there will be a thousand to take his place.''

There was loud cheering, reinforced moments later when the translation into Zulu reached those in the audience with an imperfect command of English.

After further speeches, including admonitions to us to stay together and to avoid the inevitable police provocations on leaving the cemetery, the huge gathering ended Dr. Neil Aggett's funeral with *''Nkosi Sikelel' iAfrika''*—''God Bless Africa,'' the anthem of national liberation, a song written back at the end of the nineteenth century. The slow, inspiring cadences of the song echoed, in harmony, across West Park cemetery.

> *Nkosi Sikelel' iAfrika*
> God bless Africa

Maluphakanyisw' Uphondo Lwayo
Raise up her spirit
Yiva imithandazo yethu
Hear our prayers
Usi-sikelele
And bless us

Sikelel' amadol' asizwe
Bless the leaders of the nation
Sikelela kwa nomlisela
Bless also the young
Ulitwal' ilizwe ngomonde
That they may carry the land with patience
Uwusikilele
And that you may bless them

Sikelel' amalinga etu
Bless our efforts
Awonanyana nokuzaka
To unite and lift ourselves up
Awemfundo nemvisiswano
Through learning and understanding
Uwasikelele
And bless them

Woza Moya! Woza Moya!
Come Spirit! Come Spirit!
Woza Moya Oyingcwele!
Come, Holy Spirit!

In the months that followed, Dr. Neil Aggett's parents used most of their life savings to finance an effort to discover how their son died. They retained George Bizos, a lawyer known as a devastating cross-examiner, to represent them at the official magistrate's inquest. At the start, Bizos acknowledged that Neil Aggett had in fact hanged himself from the bars on his cell window, as the regime claimed. But Bizos said he would show that the harsh and disorienting experience of detention had driven the young man to suicide.

Other detainees, blacks, whites, and Indians, some of them only just released, testified fearlessly about their treatment. They named individual members of the security police who had prevented them from sleeping, handcuffed them in painful positions, forced them through hours of vigorous physical exercises, required them to stand aching and motionless, beaten them viciously, and tortured them with high-voltage electric shocks—all the while joking about people who had previously died in detention. Morris Smithers testified he had glimpsed the security police putting Neil Aggett through some of these tortures. Other testimony showed that Neil Aggett had been kept awake and tortured intermittently for sixty-two continuous hours before his death. Another ex-detainee, Auret van Heerden, testified how he and Aggett, escorted by police, had passed each other in a corridor four days before Aggett's death. Aggett had been a broken man, he said.

The security police denied every charge. They said they had established a warm and friendly relationship with Neil Aggett; they had even discussed sporting events with him. They had been as shocked as anyone else by his death.

After eight months of testimony and deliberation, magistrate Petrus Kotze released his findings. Neil Aggett had committed suicide. There was no reason to assume any security policemen had induced him to kill himself. They were all blameless. But the magistrate did have harsh words for ex-prisoner Auret van Heerden. He should have informed the authorities immediately about Neil Aggett's condition after seeing Aggett stumble through the corridor. If informed, the warders and police might have been able to help Neil Aggett. Van Heerden's silence was therefore partly to blame for Aggett's death.

The guerrilla soldiers of the ANC continued their sabotage campaign into the early eighties. There were some fifty-five separate attacks in 1981, including a daring rocket assault against the big Voortrekkerhoogte army base near Pretoria. The guerrilla strikes continued at the same level through 1982 and 1983, although there was suspicion the regime was suppressing news of some raids. Most of the attacks continued to be directed against military targets: oil refineries, rail lines, electric generating plants, and police stations. Very few civilians were being killed or injured.

In response to the attacks and to the escalating war in Namibia, the government continued to increase its military budget dramatically. The appropriation for 1981–82 was about 2.5 billion rand, a 30 percent increase over the previous year and a huge 860 percent hike in the past decade. As the army increased its influence in the high councils of government, it was able to win approval for a strategic military answer to the ANC guerrilla campaign.

In January 1981, South African commandos struck into the outskirts of Maputo, Mozambique, attacking three residences that Pretoria claimed housed ANC guerrillas. They killed twelve people. Two South African soldiers also died; one had a swastika marked on his helmet. In July that year, assassins shot Joe Gqabi, the ANC's first representative in Salisbury, Zimbabwe. Later in 1981, the government winked as a band of mercenaries led by the infamous Colonel Michael "Mad Mike" Hoare, a self-styled swashbuckler who is in real life an accountant, caught a commercial airliner to the Seychelles, an island country in the Indian Ocean, in an unsuccessful effort to overthrow its government. In August 1982, a parcel bomb killed Ruth First, a highly respected white journalist and academic who lived in exile in Maputo. That December, the army simply crossed the Caledon River and invaded the Lesotho capital of Maseru, killing another forty-two people. South Africa raided Mozambique again with warplanes and helicopters several times during 1983.

In addition to these direct attacks, the army used surrogate forces to help "destabilize" the neighboring countries. It had learned well from its experience in Angola, where its support for Jonas Savimbi's dissident UNITA movement had caused major problems for the fledgling government. In Mozambique, South Africa bankrolled and supplied the National Resistance Movement, a band of up to several thousand in which collaborators with the former Portuguese colonial regime were prominent in the leadership. Pretoria's ally in tiny Lesotho was called the Lesotho Liberation Army.

These attacks across the border were putting the moderate white opposition in South Africa in a steadily more irrelevant position. All indications were that an overwhelming majority of the whites, both Afrikaans- and English-speaking, endorsed the raids. To the horror of blacks, the Progressive Federal Party joined in this support, thus reducing even further its potential ability to serve as some kind of bridge between black and white.

In the short term, Pretoria's aggressive strategy of striking at its neighbors won some apparent success. In early 1984, Mozambique was forced to sign a nonaggression pact with South Africa. The Mozambiquan government pledged not to allow the ANC to launch attacks from its territory. Pretoria agreed in turn to end supporting its surrogate, the Resistance Movement. Mozambique had no choice but to agree to what became known as the Nkomati Accord. It was already one of the world's twenty-five poorest countries, and it had suffered terribly from the 1983 drought, after which the Resistance had not hesitated to block the emergency food shipments to tens of thousands of starving Mozambiquans. At the same time, South Africa's other neighbors also bowed to the military pressure and promised to increase their efforts to prevent ANC guerrillas from using their territory as a springboard.

But South Africa's success may have come too late. The ANC's military wing was now firmly established inside the country, and capable of sustaining the guerrilla attacks at a steady level without much help from outside. Over its seventy year history, the ANC had learned to be patient; the Nkomati Accord represented only a temporary setback. The raids had already won the ANC increasing support among blacks, and raised morale tremendously.

Opinion polls, though admittedly inexact when conducted under police-state conditions, did show the ANC to be easily the most popular movement in the major urban areas. Even when black civilians died in ANC raids, as in the car bomb attack in May 1983 at a Pretoria military headquarters, many blacks said they regarded the casualties as a tragic but inevitable consequence of a necessarily violent struggle.

The security police went after the anti-apartheid movement with methodical fury. Beside Neil Aggett, other people started to die in detention again, after a several-years hiatus following the worldwide protest at Steve Biko's murder. Young guerrillas who were captured were tried and sentenced to death, while others were routinely sent to prison for twenty and twenty-five years.

Even those who had not participated in violent acts were sentenced to long prison terms. Renfrew Christie, a white academic, got ten years for researching the regime's frightening nuclear program on behalf of the ANC. A cheerful, thirty-year-old white woman named Barbara Hogan was tricked by security police who posed as ANC members into writing innocent reports on the political scene in Johannesburg, information that was basically common knowledge. She bravely told the court she supported the ANC despite her own personal commitment to nonviolence. "The ANC does not believe in unnecessary violence and it is not committed to a policy of terrorism," she said. "It has not killed for the sake of killing and it conserves life as much as possible." Barbara Hogan was convicted of high treason and sentenced to ten years.

Ronald Sandile's successor as one of the leading ANC representatives in Swaziland, Petrus Nzima, was the opposite of elegant. He was short, fat, and always sloppily dressed, with his shirttails flapping about. His real last name was Nyawose, but everyone called him Nzima, the Zulu word for "large."

Petrus was a trade unionist. This was not just his work; it was his heritage and his very existence. His father had been a stalwart in the Industrial and Commercial Workers Union, which had flourished across the country in the 1920s. He himself had been a garment worker in the Durban area until he had to flee in the late seventies. He had an easy, informal way about him, emphasized by his earnest, two-handed handshake, and he won many friends, even among the Swazi Special Branchmen who were assigned to watch him. He so charmed them that he became privy to many of their secrets. When South African agents entered the country, Petrus often learned right away.

He and Ron had made an extraordinarily compatible partnership despite their differences; one tall and graceful, the other short and tubby; one an articulate college graduate, the other quieter, with probably no more than five years of schooling. They shared an indefatigable dedication to their work. They also had in common a prodigious sense of humor, as I learned one afternoon when they stopped to give me a lift in one of their cars.

"We have problems," Ron said. Petrus was silent. "One of our people reported to me that Nzima had been seen in the streets of Manzini talking to a Boer."

Petrus looked somber and somewhat contrite.

"He said Nzima was friendly with this Boer. He was smiling, and talking nicely to him. Our man is worried Nzima may be a spy or a sellout."

Petrus was even more downcast.

"So I asked this comrade, 'Was this Boer very tall?' 'Yes.' 'Was he wearing spectacles?' 'Yes.' "

Petrus shot me a glance and guffawed. Soon they were both gulping with laughter, barely paying attention as they steered the car on the long descent through the hills into Manzini. It took me a little longer to realize that this suspicious South African agent was me.

One morning, Petrus dropped by my place with bad news. A refugee, an Indian South African, had been kidnapped late the night before by what were certainly agents of Pretoria. The refugee, a schoolteacher, was only a slight acquaintance of his, but he still felt he had to do something. He placed emergency telephone calls to relevant Swazi officials and drove off to meet them, leaving me to contact the press. Though we said nothing, we both felt that the teacher's life might be at stake.

Petrus spent the next two days without sleep, rushing from meeting to meeting. I saw him next out on the road, his tubby figure wedged behind the steering wheel. "He's safe," he said with a huge smile. "Local police caught some of the kidnappers. All that noise we made will force the Boers to make an exchange. They can't kill him now." He reached over to give me one of his characteristic two-handed handshakes. I had never seen him in a better mood.

Petrus was very happily married. His wife, Jabu, was taller then he was, with a winning smile. Inside South Africa, he had at first kept his ANC connection a secret even from her. He had eventually told her, and she insisted on participating as well. She had also been a garment worker, and she eventually became a ranking official in SACTU, the ANC's trade union wing. She insisted on remaining in Swaziland despite the danger in order to carry on her work.

After Ron had left the country in 1982, Petrus started to be more expansive. Ron had never tried to stifle him, but he had clearly felt the older man's commanding presence. Now, he allowed himself to range more widely in conversation over South African and world affairs. He seemed to be really coming into his own. He even started to wax his mustache, in a modest move toward rakishness.

By now, I was from time to time doing various minor tasks for the movement, like carrying messages to and from people inside South Africa. One time, Petrus asked me to take a car over a certain border. The vehicle was for some reason a Mercedes-Benz. He and I went to pick it up. We approached the car, which was a gleaming silver. Simultaneously, we glanced from the car to ourselves, with our customary irregular attire, and we burst out laughing with telepathic understanding. When I drove off later, he nodded with approval at my borrowed blazer and tie, suitable camouflage for the luxury car. *"Hamba kahle,"* he said. "Go well."

That episode took place in March or April. In late May, I invited Petrus and his wife to a party. He wanted to know how many guests would be present. After I told him more than a hundred he nodded and said, "Fine. I don't think they'll try and kill us with so many people around."

Petrus and Jabu did not make it to the party. Early in the morning of June 4, 1982, they left one of their hideouts together. Petrus insisted on driving. Jabu got in next to him. They may have been distracted; perhaps one of their children was having problems at school. In any case, they failed to see the land mines that had been hidden under their car. They were both killed instantly.

They left four children. The oldest, Precious, was a poised young woman of twelve. She said dully that day, "They always wanted to kill my parents. And now they have."

The ANC and SACTU sent a high-ranking delegation to the double funeral. Moses Mabhida, one of the representatives, said just before the coffins were lowered side by side into the ground, "He could talk to the grass. He could convince a stone that it absolutely must give forth water." Then Jabu's father, a thin, wiry man, gestured toward the two coffins and the freshly dug red soil of Africa. In a voice choked with tortured confusion, he asked, "How can three million people rule over twenty million people? Are we not all equal? How long can this go on?"

In 1948, Alan Paton published his novel *Cry, the Beloved Country*. At the end of the book, the gentle old black preacher Stephen Kumalo awakens before dawn on the morning that his son, who has been a casualty of the oppressive and disorderly life in a Johannesburg township, is to be hanged for killing a white man during a robbery. Kumalo prays. He prays for the soul of his wayward son, for his wife, and for his young daughter-in-law, soon to be a widow. He prays for the white man's family, whom he has befriended. And he prays for the future of his suffering beloved country. "I have one great fear in my heart," the old preacher reflects, "that one day when they turn to loving they will find we are turned to hating."

My friend Petrus Nzima, who, like the preacher Kumalo, was from the beautiful hill country of Natal, more than three decades later could have given an answer. Nzima did make war. But he did not do it gladly. He had an understanding for his enemies, even for the very people who killed him, that would have astonished them if they had ever listened to the garment worker who once lived among them. He never denied their humanity, or their right to live in the beloved country. Petrus Nzima was turned to fighting, but never to hating.

16

Hope Rising

AMERICANS IN SOUTH AFRICA discover that there are many familiar names around to relieve any pangs of homesickness. Right in central Johannesburg facing on Joubert Park is an outpost of Colonel Sanders Kentucky Fried Chicken. There are Holiday Inns scattered across the country, even in remote Ulundi, the "capital" of the Kwa–Zulu Bantustan. (A week at the Inn costs roughly the same as the yearly per capita income in the Bantustan.) John Deere tractors are common on the large white farms. One American car has become so much a part of the culture that it has even inspired a little jingle: South Africa is said to be characterized by "sunny skies, *braaivleis* [Afrikaans for barbecue], and Chevrolet."

Certain other American products, more vital to the South African economy, are not quite so visible. A powerful Control Data Cyber 170 computer is functioning at a government research institute that has ties to both the military and the atomic energy agency. Another large computer, this one a Sperry Univac, has been sold to Atlas Aircraft, a subsidiary of the regime's armaments corporation. In all, American businesses, with IBM in first place, control an estimated 70 percent of the high technology computer market in South Africa.

Still other U.S. corporations, including Westinghouse, have bid on the contract to maintain the new Koeberg nuclear power plant near Cape Town. In this and certain other sensitive transactions, the Reagan administration has justified its approval because the companies involved had assured that their products and services would be used for "peaceful" purposes. Such U.S. government oversight seemed less convincing after April 1982, when the Commerce Department inexplicably authorized the sale of twenty-five hundred shock batons to South Africa. The crowd control devices are reminiscent of the cattle prods once used against civil rights marchers in the American south. Officials later excused the sale as "an honest mistake" and "a simple, unfortunate screw-up."

By mid-1983, direct U.S. investment in South Africa was valued at $2.3 billion. American banks had made another $1.1 billion in loans. Annual trade between the two countries was estimated at about $6 billion. Visitors from other Western countries and Japan are also surrounded by familiar products; British investment is even higher, at about $6 billion.

Such economic links are highly lucrative. Foreign companies have reported profit margins as high as 30 percent in some years. In 1979, Joel Stern, the president of the financial policy division of the Chase Manhattan Bank, admitted to an audience in Durban that U.S. enterprises were "very embarrassed" at the high returns on their South African investments.

It is an old truism that to define the terms of a debate is to powerfully guide its outcome. Those who defend continued U.S. investment often frame their arguments narrowly, trying to restrict the discussion to the approximately seventy thousand blacks who work for the 350 American companies that operate in South Africa. There is much stated concern over the loss of those jobs if the American firms were to pull out. There is the further argument that those enterprises serve a positive good. They supposedly pay more than the national average; some of them have desegregated their workplaces; they have better job training programs. The American companies are therefore an inspiring example, leading the way toward enlightenment. Above all, the defenders of investment argue sadly that U.S. business influence, however positive, is unfortunately limited; American firms constitute only a small segment of the South African economy, employing a paltry 2 percent of the black work force.

The South African government certainly does not act as if American and other foreign investment were such a peripheral matter. In the late 1970s, the country had its own variant of the Watergate scandal, which was called either Infogate or Muldergate. Certain high officials in the Ministry of Information, including the Minister, Cornelius P. "Connie" Mulder, misused millions of rand and then tried to cover up. Mulder and others had to resign in disgrace. The trail of evidence eventually led up to John Vorster, the state President and former prime minister, and forced him from office. The case, complete with a crusty jurist heading a special investigating commission and a press rendezvous with a key figure in the scandal who was hiding in South America, stayed in the headlines for months.

Prime Minister P. W. Botha cleverly used the scandal to destroy some of his rivals within the National Party. But in the process, certain revelations about the Information Ministry came to light. Only part of the $74 million that was not satisfactorily accounted for had been diverted to the private use of the culprits. Other millions went to establish the *Citizen,* the egregious right-wing tabloid designed to draw readers away from the more moderate English-language press.

But part of the rest of the huge slush fund was used to try to extend South Africa's influence overseas, in countries with vital economic links. Some went to help right-wing American publisher John McGoff's 1974 effort to buy the *Washington Star.* Other money was allegedly used in the 1978 Iowa Senate campaign to help defeat the Democratic incumbent, Dick Clark, an outspoken opponent of apartheid. One Infogate figure suggested South Africa had secretly funnelled several hundred thousand dollars to Clark's opponent, a figure that could have been decisive in a race in which each candidate spent about $1 million. (There is no evidence that the winner, Roger Jepsen, was aware of Pretoria's help.)

It is likely that these secret efforts have continued, although with more circumspection. It is, however, certain that the South African regime is openly concerned about the climate of opinion in the United States. When Connecticut was considering whether to order its pension funds to divest their holdings in companies that do business there, the South African ambassador sent the governor a telegram that was eighteen feet long.

Pretoria's deep concern about foreign investment is not new. In the uncertain year after the 1960 Sharpeville Massacre, foreign capital flowed out of the country at a rate of about $17 million every month, causing a serious economic recession. Stronger financial controls, together with the crushing of the liberation movements, brought that hemorrhaging to a halt, but not before it had underscored South Africa's dependence on the West.

Foreign investment and trade is critical partly because it often includes the transfer of high technology. There are simply not enough trained experts in South Africa with enough resources to develop all the technology that is necessary to the advanced mining, manufacturing, and military economy. It is true that the arms embargo the United Nations voted in 1977 has reduced South Africa's ability to acquire military

technology directly, although there have been some celebrated viola-
tions of the boycott. But the proponents of "total strategy" who guide
the apartheid regime recognize that the preservation of white power is
more than a narrow military question. Neither the nuclear reactor at
Koeberg nor the Sasol oil-from-coal plants, which Fluor, another American corporation, is helping to build, are "military" in the limited sense.
But they help to reduce South Africa's dependence on imported oil, which
is one of its major strategic weaknesses.

The foreign bank loans are also an important part of Pretoria's total
strategy. Under pressure, some U.S. banks have promised they will not
lend directly to the government or its agencies. This distinction is largely
irrelevant. The loans help strengthen the overall economy, which gen-
erates more than enough profit to then finance the police and the army
lavishly.

There is also the less tangible but no less significant fact that the visible Western presence is strongly reassuring to most white South Africans. They may express irritation at the occasional verbal criticisms from
some of the less conservative Western governments. But all around them
is vivid evidence of the Western stake in their system, from Kellogg's
Corn Flakes to mainframe computers. It all only stiffens their resolve to
fight to keep the "Communist terrorists" out of their portion of the "Free
World."

There is another, more sophisticated pro-investment argument, which
goes beyond simply justifying foreign economic involvement for its alleged benefits to a small number of black workers. Its advocates, who
include businessmen like Harry Oppenheimer and the Progressive Federal Party leaders, frankly recognize that foreign investment is essential
to the continued growth of the economy. But they argue that growth is
precisely what is needed to end apartheid. An expanding economy will
require an increasingly skilled work force. Growth will therefore inevitably raise educational levels and living standards for blacks.

Time has proven that argument to be mainly wrong. The South African economy grew by 6 percent annually through the 1960s, a high rate
in comparison with other countries at similar levels of development. But
apartheid only grew more intense. More recently, growth has continued:
8 percent in the 1980 boom, another 5 percent the next year. The fruits
of that spurt were not used to start reforming the migrant labor system,
or to improve the appalling conditions in the Bantustans, or even to up-
grade the urban townships in any sweeping way. Instead, the windfall
went to the military and the police, or enabled the white population to
go on a buying spree for luxury goods. Over the years, economic growth

has only served to entrench the most fundamental features of apartheid. Black people recognize they are being counselled to pursue a mirage, which will always shimmer just a few years in the future.

The anti-apartheid movements in the West have won some significant victories. But they are still a long way from forcing their governments to implement comprehensive sanctions. In the meantime, though, the protesters overseas still have a positive influence on events inside South Africa.

In September 1981, a black man named M. X. Bhengu wrote a letter to the *Rand Daily Mail*. He explained that he had decided to watch the telecast of the final match the rugby Springboks were playing in New Zealand even though he was not a fan of the sport. "My main purpose," Bhengu wrote, "was to watch the Springboks being beaten, like any average black."

The Springbok tour of New Zealand had been disrupted by huge demonstrations, which would continue in the United States when the team moved on to play there. The protesters pleased Bhengu enormously. "I couldn't help wondering why whites, like the demonstrators, were thinking black like us. We are thousands of miles apart but they have something in common with us."

He closed his letter by describing the match as "a great game." (The Springboks lost.) And he added, "As much as South African whites have their friends over there, we also have ours."

To boost the morale of Bhengu and millions of other blacks is a considerable and worthy achievement. But overseas protest has also caused more concrete changes. In 1974, the United Mine Workers of America protested to the U.S. Commission of Customs that coal in South Africa was produced by "slave labor" and should not be imported; at the same time, dockworkers in Mobile, Alabama, refused to unload South African coal. The frightened apartheid regime moved with unusual speed, repealing legislation under which black workers who quit their jobs without permission could be tried as criminals. There had been seventeen thousand prosecutions under the laws the previous year. South African workers continued to suffer under government repression, but their friends overseas had lightened their burden.

More recently, in July 1983, the apartheid government allowed all but eleven of its banning orders to lapse. Fatima Meer, the Indian woman sociologist I had met in Durban, was one of those who were now unexpectedly free to lead more normal lives. The concession left the police state basically intact. But even such a limited change would have been impossible without the unremitting protest from overseas. The international attention also certainly contributed to the regime's decision in 1984 to free Herman Toivo, the Namibian leader, before the end of his twenty-year sentence.

That foreign vigilance is also one of the reasons that a little political space remains open inside South Africa. The regime would surely prefer to dispense altogether with the remnants of the judicial system and to crush all the trade unions, the English-language press, and other organizations that even mildly oppose apartheid. But the world outcry that always follows the regime's crackdowns restrains it by reminding it of its vulnerability to foreign economic pressure. In August 1983, some fifteen thousand people from all races met in Cape Town, indoors, to form the United Democratic Front, an organization clearly sympathetic with the outlawed African National Congress. The UDF was a coalition of some four hundred community, labor, religious, youth, and other organizations of all races, representing an estimated 1 to 1.5 million people. It was a promising indication that at least some aboveground political activity is still possible. The security police harassed the gathering, but they did not dare to break it up.

International attention has helped restrain the regime in even more critical ways. By the end of 1983, judges had sentenced eleven captured ANC guerrillas to death. But only four had been executed. Solomon Mahlangu was hanged in 1979. Simon Mogoerane, Jerry Mosololi, and Marcus Motaung went to the gallows together in June 1983. All four brave young men should properly have been treated as prisoners of war, just as their organization will treat the South African soldiers and police who will certainly be captured in the coming struggle. But world pressure had at least induced the regime to commute the sentences of the other guerrillas to imprisonment. Parts of the South African press gave prominence to the campaign for clemency conducted by Amnesty International and other groups, printing letters from all over the world.

But there is an even more compelling reason to keep up the pressure. In February 1982, Prime Minister P. W. Botha opened the parliamentary session with an ominous warning to the national liberation movement. "Something will happen in South Africa that the proponents of violence cannot even dream of," he said somberly. "I am trying to avoid this. They don't know what they are going to reap." Later in his speech, he added even more chillingly, "A big silence and desolation will come over many parts of South Africa."

The temperamental and impetuous Botha was apparently carried away by the parliamentary debate. He probably had not planned to threaten the use of nuclear weapons or something similarly cataclysmic. There has been much speculation about whether South Africa has been able to build a bomb. The evidence has continued to mount, particularly after a U.S. satellite detected a mysterious flash over the South Atlantic in September 1979. A lackadaisical Western policy on the proliferation of nuclear technology over the years had made a South African–built weapon feasible. If an apartheid bomb does not already exist, it cannot be far off.

South Africa is now in a position that is in many ways analogous to Nazi Germany during the 1930s—a regime that is already evil but that may still not have committed its greatest crimes. South Africa is arming steadily, and putting its economy on a war footing. It is already responsible for thousands of deaths, in its colony Namibia, in the other surrounding nations it raids at will, and in its Bantustans, where it has created conditions that are approximating genocide. Pretoria has or will have a monstrous weapon that Adolf Hitler never acquired, and its prime minister has openly threatened its people with some kind of holocaust. As the exiled journalist Donald Woods has pointed out, advocating continued economic links with such an outlaw government is like endorsing investment in Nazi Germany because it provided some employment for Jewish people.

Meanwhile, those who are in exile wait. In Harare, Lusaka, Dar es Salaam, and dozens of other cities and towns of independent Africa; in London, Stockholm, Paris, and New York; in Moscow and Prague, they wait, piecing together the reports from "home," their joy at each fragment of positive news tempered by a patience instilled by decades of waiting. When they meet, they bubble over with excited shared memories of the majesty of Cape Town, the deep blue of a Transvaal winter sky, the cacophony of colors in Durban's bustling Indian market. Dennis Brutus, the black poet, wrote:

> Exile
> is the reproach
> of beauty
> in a foreign landscape
> vaguely familiar
> because it echoes
> remembered beauty.

When I returned from southern Africa in 1983, I reestablished contact with Dennis Brutus, who was teaching at Northwestern University. Five years earlier, Dennis had been one of the people who had stimulated my interest in his part of the world. He had encouraged me to travel there and see for myself and to write about what I had seen.

During 1983, Dennis Brutus had become better known in America for his fight against the Reagan administration's shameful effort to take advantage of a legal technicality and deport him. The administration arrogantly dismissed his plea that he would be in danger back in southern Africa, even though in the early 1960s he had been arrested there, shot down in the street in central Johannesburg while trying to escape, and then imprisoned on Robben Island, where he had been beaten to a degree unusual even by the brutal standards prevailing there. In exile, he, more than anyone else, had brought about South Africa's isolation from international sports. He was hated by white South Africa, and his life certainly would have been in jeopardy in Zimbabwe, his theoretical destination.

The Reagan administration was not plotting his actual death. They must have assumed he would be granted asylum in Britain or elsewhere. They wanted to deprive the growing American anti-apartheid movement of his enormous energy and eloquence. He and other critics have embarrassed the U.S. government by pointing to the failure of its "constructive engagement" policy, which has in practice meant American appeasement of Pretoria on a number of issues in return for nothing—no moves toward genuine reform in South Africa or independence for Namibia.

In person, Dennis's unruly mane of hair gives him a bohemian appearance, which is undercut somewhat by his cultured, precise manner of speaking. The most appropriate word for his demeanor is "patient." I have seen him time and again talk to people about the most elementary aspects of South African life, always with an earnest and engaging manner that suggests he is speaking on the subject for the first time. I dropped in to see him after the U.S. immigration judge had thrown out the Reagan administration's case and granted him asylum. He told me that his immediate plans were to "step up" his speaking engagements across the country now that the case no longer took up his time; I would have thought it humanly impossible to be more active.

Exiles like Dennis Brutus are driven people. They are obsessed by the memory of those who remain in South Africa trying to live under apartheid. Dennis and other former prisoners are particularly haunted by the men and women who are still locked up in the regime's prisons, especially those with life sentences. Nelson Mandela is sixty-five years old. Walter Sisulu is seventy-one. Denis Goldberg, a young engineer of thirty-one when he was imprisoned, is now over fifty. In 1979, Zephania Mothopeng, who had already served time, was at the age of sixty-six sentenced to another fifteen years.

Dennis Brutus wrote:

This night
in the endless light
of Robben Island
the men lie
with lidless eyes
and stare down the glaring corridor of time
with an open coffin at its end
and frantically scrape
at the bare smooth walls of unyielding knowledge
seeking some moss of comfort
some lichen-particle of hope
that shows there will be some change
some hint that freedom will arrive,
break through these walls of life-in-death
life-till-death
How will they forgive us?

Dennis Brutus served eighteen months on the Island. He is convinced the world attention to his case prevented a longer sentence. "There was a great deal of publicity," he said. "Amnesty International and other observers were right there in the courtroom. Without them, I would have gotten eighteen years."

With a fond smile, he sketched a diagram of his section of the prison. "Nelson was here, in the first cell," he remembered. "I was further along, in the eighth. Our work was breaking stones, just there in the central sort of courtyard. As we worked, we could talk with each other off and on. But we had to be careful. If the warders caught you, they gave you no food for that day."

During Dennis Brutus's last weeks on the Island, the other prisoners gave him verbal messages for their families and friends outside. "Each of them had to think what was most important to them," he explained. "They might only have a few moments to speak freely to me. They might, for example, surreptitiously whisper when we were gathered around the tap at the end of the day, washing off the rock dust."

Nelson Mandela carefully composed his parting words, back then in 1966. "We must ask ourselves how we got here, to this prison," Mandela said. "A system put us here, a system with a chain of command. Those overseas corporations are a vital link in that system. We've got to get those corporations off our backs."

If we in America and in the West generally were asked to identify our greatest privileges, we might point to our extensive systems of education, or our technological amenities, like autos or washing machines.

These are indeed luxuries contrasted with southern Africa, where most people fetch their water in buckets and live by candlelight. But there is an even greater privilege we enjoy, usually without realizing it; we are not forced to make painful choices among terrible alternatives.

In southern Africa, black men and women in the rural Bantustans must decide whether to watch their children starve or to leave their families as migrants for most of their lives. Black people in the towns have to choose between enduring the oppressive and humiliating treatment every day, such as carrying their passes, or risking imprisonment. Journalists have to decide whether to tone down their work or have it censored. Teachers must choose between spreading untruths or risking the loss of their jobs.

As war comes, the decisions are even more agonizing. Young whites must decide between the apartheid army and exile. Young blacks must choose whether to do open political work or join the underground; either way, they risk their liberty and often their lives. Older black people, together with sympathetic whites, have to decide the kind of support they can give to the national liberation movement, knowing that a single mistake, trusting the wrong person, even for a moment, can mean years in prison. In the end, there is the most terrible dilemma of all; my friends, many of them, are deciding whether to kill.

South Africans will face these tormenting choices again and again in the years to come. There are really only two predictions that can be made with any confidence. There will be increasing violence. The violence will last for a long time. Even the unlikely event of a settlement in Namibia would not address the major source of conflict in the region, which is apartheid in South Africa itself. We may well admire the heroes of southern Africa as they fight to create a nation in which no one must make such terrible choices. But it is within our power to help them shorten the time of bloodshed.

Economic sanctions are also in the interest of the people, most of them white, who fight on the other side. They fight partly due to their mistaken view that nonracial, democratic rule will mean the end of their culture and their expulsion from Africa. As long as they remain strong and resolute, they, like their counterparts in Rhodesia before them, will have no inducement to reexamine their wrong beliefs. But economic sanctions will weaken their war machine, undermine their smug feelings that the West will stand by them, moderate their intransigence, and force their leaders to negotiate. Sanctions will help them learn to live as equals with their fellow Africans.

It will not be easy to persuade those in the West to act in larger numbers on behalf of people they have never even seen, who live on the other side of the world. But in moments of doubt, I prefer to remember an old bus I used to often see chugging along one of the byways of rural southern Africa. The bus was usually overflowing with migrant workers and their belongings, off to the mines and towns on another join, and with women bringing sacks of grain and ancient hens to market. The radio blasted out raucous guitar music; the bus swayed under the weight of the battered suitcases and sacks piled on the roof; a cloud of reddish dust trailed behind. Inside, as the driver peered out intently in case cattle strayed into the road, there were conversations—the latest village gossip, talk of sports, or, more guardedly, politics. As the bus lurched along, there was a sense of spirit, of endurance, of smiling optimism. The driver had named his vehicle, in big gaudy letters painted along the side: "Hope Does Not Kill."

People sometimes ask me to summarize what I learned during my time in southern Africa. My answer is simple. From afar, apartheid seems like a monstrous wickedness, a convincing proof of the evil in mankind. And at first hand, the apartheid system is in some ways even worse than can be imagined. But there is much more than mere evil. There are people, black and white, who fight bravely, who are not afraid to be kind, to believe in and trust each other, who do not become cynical, and who will go to jail and even die without denying their beliefs. It is likely that they face many more years of violence. But hope does not kill. We can help them.

Epilogue

LATE IN 1985, after the first edition of this book appeared, I returned to southern Africa. After debating some of the representatives of apartheid in America, I did not waste time applying to go back into South Africa itself. I went instead to Zimbabwe and certain other neighboring countries, and from there tried to get a better sense of the changes that had taken place since I left two years before.

Back in the middle of 1984, Prime Minister P. W. Botha had apparently achieved some major breakthroughs. His military raids had forced the surrounding states to reduce their already-limited support for the African National Congress. The U.S. State Department boasted that its "constructive engagement" policy was nudging South Africa toward internal reform and a negotiated settlement in Namibia. Botha went off on a triumphal tour of Europe, meeting leaders like British Prime Minister Margaret Thatcher and Pope John Paul II. Most white South Africans were euphoric as the pressure from Western governments relaxed.

P. W. Botha returned home, about to exchange the title of Prime Minister for that of State President. He would preside over the new three-chamber parliament he anticipated would win over significant numbers of colored and Indian people. But his plans went immediately awry. More than 80 percent in each group boycotted "elections" to the new, segregated chambers. At the same time, an uprising began among blacks in the Vaal triangle, an industrial region south of Johannesburg. P. W. Botha's inauguration coincided with the start of the greatest upheaval in modern South African history.

In October 1984, Bishop Desmond Tutu was awarded the Nobel Peace Prize. Tutu moved courageously and skillfully to use his newfound prominence to expose the sham reforms to an increasingly concerned world. (The new parliament's true nature was comically underscored soon after it opened, when colored and Indian delegates were refused admittance when they tried to join colleagues from the white chamber in a parliamentary canteen.) Tutu's arguments that blacks forcefully rejected the new arrangement were convincingly supported in early November, when the still-growing union movement called the biggest strike in the nation's history. Some 300,000 workers closed down the Johannesburg area for two days. Another 400,000 students joined in the boycott.

In 1985, the urban unrest continued and spread—to the Eastern Cape, to Durban, the Western Cape, even to smaller towns in the Northern Cape and the Free State that had never rebelled before. The death toll, which was almost certainly understated by the police, was represented to have reached two hundred in March, six hundred by August, and neared one thousand toward the year end. The police alone were unable to maintain control. For the first time, the army had to enter the townships in force.

The government tried to defuse the protest wave with vaguely conciliatory talk. Early in the year, Botha suggested that at least some of the "urban blacks," the approximately one-quarter of the black population who live in the townships, could be granted the right to remain there permanently. The government also abolished the notorious Immorality Act, which had outlawed interracial sex. (The law, which had brought grief to more than one Afrikaner *dominee*, had not been rigorously enforced for some years.)

But the nationwide rebellion continued. The turnouts at funerals, the only form of public gatherings that the regime permitted, grew in number and intensity. There were highly successful consumer boycotts of white-owned stores in some areas, particularly the Eastern Cape. On July 21, Botha declared a State of Emergency. Over the next few months, some five thousand people were arrested. Many of them were active in the United Democratic Front (UDF), the coalition of six hundred labor, community, and religious groups that advanced views similar to those of the outlawed African National Congress. A thousand people were still being held without trial later in the year. A brave young white doctor, Wendy Orr, revealed that large numbers of the detainees were being tortured, and several had died.

Despite the State of Emergency, the level of violence only increased. The apartheid government and its apologists tried to portray the upheaval as a senseless, criminal outburst, a case of "blacks killing blacks." Film footage of angry crowds killing black people they suspected of being informers was shown repeatedly on South African television. But independent agencies, such as the Institute of Race Relations, while not denying that black police and others suspected of collaborating had been attacked, confirmed that the overwhelming majority of the victims were people shot or beaten by the police and the army. There was further evidence that government assassination teams secretly carried out other killings to promote strife between the UDF and the Azanian People's Organization (AZAPO), an heir to the black consciousness philosophy.

As the violence spread across the townships, their residents tried to keep a sense of humor. There were reports that Sowetans had nicknamed swift little police vans "Mary Deckers" and "Zola Budds," after the American middle-distance runner and her South African-born rival. The Kaizer Chiefs, in a slight slump, drew 1-1 with Pretoria Callies; one of the Callie strikers was called Edward "Teargas" Tsie.

But the humor was becoming more strained. In 1984, a parcel bomb sent to Angola murdered a white teacher and activist named Jeanette Schoon and her small daughter, Katryn. Inside South Africa, death squads increased their night-riding.

One of their victims was a black, middle-aged Durban civil rights lawyer named Victoria Mxenge. She had replaced her husband, Griffiths, also a lawyer, after he was murdered in 1981. I learned from mutual friends how the Mxenges, who had been sweethearts since university, had during the 1970s matter-of-factly discussed how she should complete her law degree so that she could take over the practice—they used the term *when* rather than *if*—anything befell him. The killers trapped this fearless woman on a darkened street, shot her, and then buried an axe in her skull.

Such brutality helped the protest overseas grow at an astonishing rate. In America, there were daily arrests outside the South African embassy, and demonstrations and sit-ins on dozens of college campuses. Disinvestment legislation moved forward at local, state, and national levels. Groups, including the United Mine Workers, started legal action to block further imports of South African coal and steel. The Reverend Leon Sullivan, whose Sullivan Principles mandating workplace desegregation and better training for blacks had been signed by about one-third of U.S. companies doing business in South Africa, said that he questioned whether his measures went far enough.

The growing sense of outrage had an important bipartisan aspect.

Thomas Kean, the Republican governor of New Jersey, signed the strongest disinvestment legislation of any state, and Republicans in both houses of Congress joined Democrats to pass limited sanctions measures with crushing majorities.

The Reagan administration's allies were dwindling down to people like fundamentalist preacher Jerry Falwell, who after a brief visit to South Africa announced he had learned that Bishop Tutu was "a phony." The administration eagerly predicted that a speech P. W. Botha planned to deliver on August 15 would be a major departure, during which South Africa would boldly cross "a Rubicon" toward far-reaching reform. Instead, Botha was his familiar combative self, claiming reform meant leading the country down "a road to abdication and suicide."

The apartheid government has always boasted of its economic strength and self-sufficiency. Pretoria has repeatedly hinted that under pressure it could readily pull into a *laager,* the circle of covered wagons the voortrekkers had used in their nineteenth-century wars against blacks. But the regime's vulnerability one hundred years later was about to be proven beyond all doubt.

In late July, the Chase Manhattan bank decided quietly to stop all lending to South Africa. Dozens of other American banks, which were similarly disturbed at the rising protests against their policies and which were also concerned at the deteriorating economy in South Africa itself, rushed to follow after Botha's intransigent speech. The banks started to refuse to automatically roll over some $10 billion in short-term loans. A humiliated South Africa was forced to declare a moratorium on repayment, and the head of the national bank took off for Europe and America to plead for forbearance.

Almost immediately, a group of leading South African businessmen flew up to Zambia to meet with the exiled leadership of the African National Congress. The group, which included Gavin Relly, who had succeeded Harry Oppenheimer as head of the huge Anglo-American Corporation, issued calls for reform. Their sincerity was at least open to question. Earlier in the year, Anglo had let one of its holdings, the *Rand Daily Mail,* die because of relatively small financial losses, even though the *Mail* had at times been a voice for genuine reform. But even if the business leaders were motivated by expediency, they at least had the good sense to recognize that apartheid could no longer function in the old way, and they were willing to recognize the leading opposition force.

Another unusual group wanted to meet with the ANC—a delegation of students from Stellenbosch, the oldest Afrikaans university in the country. The government withdrew their passports to prevent them from making the journey. But this overture by the next generation of Afrikaner leadership suggested that the world protest campaign was starting to encourage some whites, particularly among the young, to question the regime as their country slid toward war. The economic sanctions that Ronald Reagan ordered in September to preempt stronger congressional action were mild; the measures included a ban on importing the gold coins called *krugerrands,* and an end to exporting computers to the government. (The Common Market countries and the British Commonwealth followed with similarly weak sanctions. France had already approved more forceful measures, including a ban on all new investment.) But the tremendous publicity the overseas protest campaigns had generated had started, however slowly, to erode white South African assurance that Western support was unconditional. The number of young white men who refused to report for compulsory military service increased fivefold, and thousands attended rallies of the End Conscription Campaign.

Throughout the year, the world's attention had remained concentrated on the carnage in the urban black ghettoes. But out in the rural Bantustans, where more than one-half of black South Africans continue to live, the terrible poverty and overcrowding stayed unchanged. In early 1985, relief workers estimated that 2.9 million black children under fifteen suffered from clinically diagnosable malnutrition. From 35,000 to 50,000 children die every year of illnesses related to or made worse by hunger.

On February 1, the government had announced that it was suspending the forced resettlement program, under which another one million people were scheduled to be deported to the Bantustans to join the 3.5 million who had already been dumped there since 1960. Later in the year, after world pressure had increased even further, P. W. Botha said that South African citizenship could be restored to black people who had been stripped of it when their Bantustans became "independent."

It was too early to tell how significant these concessions would prove. There was immediate talk of relying on apartheid's old weapon of euphemism—making some sort of distinction between "citizenship" and "nationality" to maintain the system intact with new terminology. Nor was there any effort to improve the lives of people already in the Bantustans. Neither did the government (or the businessmen) take any serious action to start to move away from the migrant labor system.

With respect to Namibia, South Africa had dropped nearly all pretense that it meant to go forward to United Nations-supervised elections. While international television crews stayed in South Africa, the apartheid army continued to battle SWAPO guerrillas in northern Namibia, regularly invading and bombing neighboring Angola. The Reagan administration, which had promised for five years that "constructive engagement" would bring a settlement, was particularly embarrassed when Angola captured a team of South African saboteurs in its northern enclave of Cabinda, on their way toward the drilling rigs of America's Gulf Oil Corporation.

South Africa further clamped down in March on travel to northern Namibia. But observers in Windhoek were estimating that the number of dead in the territory had already climbed to 10,000, and another 100,000 had been forced to flee the war zones. In other terms, 1 percent of the population had died, and 10 percent had become refugees. It would be the equivalent of 2.3 million dead Americans.

The apartheid government's ability to wage war throughout southern Africa showed clearly that it was still strong. P. W. Botha had stumbled so badly that he may be replaced from within the National Party, but apartheid is not a one-man dictatorship. Despite the signs of stirrings in the white community, most whites continue to support the system. Pretoria still has room to maneuver politically; there were early signs of overtures to Chief Gatsha Buthelezi, the Kwa-Zulu Bantustan leader, whose popularity among blacks in the Natal region, though declining, was still a reality.

Most important, the government and its supporters are still in complete control of an advanced industrial, and increasingly militarized state. The limited sanctions approved so far have not fundamentally weakened that war economy. The year 1985 may turn out to have been the end of the beginning in the effort to overthrow apartheid. But it was not the beginning of the end.

As the rebellion flamed across South Africa, one man increasingly came to symbolize the spirit of resistance. Aside from a single blurred image in the foreground of a bleak stone prison yard, there have been no photographs of Nelson Mandela taken since the early 1960s. Only rarely have his views been publicized, either. Yet, from inside the prison walls, he has earned the support of millions of his countrymen.

It is now twenty-three years since Nelson Mandela went to jail—in 1962, when John Kennedy was president and the first astronauts were circling the globe. His wife, Winnie, an outspoken activist in her own right, was later banished from her Soweto home to the dusty town of Brandfort, in the middle of the Free State. She and their two daughters can only infrequently travel down to visit him in Cape Town's Pollsmoor prison, where he was transferred after nearly twenty years on Robben Island.

In early 1985, P. W. Botha publicly offered to release Nelson Mandela on condition that he "renounce violence." Nelson Mandela smuggled his answer out from Pollsmoor; his daughter Zinzi read it out to a cheering crowd in Soweto:

> I am surprised [he began], at the conditions that the government wants to impose on me. I am not a violent man. [He went on to list the peaceful efforts the African National Congress made during the 1950s to negotiate with the government, efforts that ended with the banning of the ANC in 1960:]
>
> It was only then, when all other forms of resistance were no longer open to us, that we turned to armed struggle. Let Botha show that he is different . . . Let *him* renounce violence. Let him say that he will dismantle apartheid. Let him unban the people's organization, the African National Congress. Let him free all who have been imprisoned, banished or exiled for their opposition to apartheid. Let him guarantee free political activity so that people may decide who will govern them.
>
> I cherish my own freedom dearly, but I care even more for your freedom. Too many have died since I went to prison. Too many have suffered for the love of freedom. I owe it to their widows, to their orphans, to their mothers and to their fathers who have grieved and wept for them. Not only I have suffered during these long, lonely, wasted years. I am not less life-loving than you are. But I cannot sell my birthright, nor am I prepared to sell the birthright of the people to be free.

Toward the end of the year, the worldwide pressure for Nelson Mandela's release increased even further. There were signs that the apartheid government was considering putting him on an airplane and forcing him into exile. Mandela himself apparently continued to insist on his unconditional release inside South Africa. Freedom for Nelson Mandela, even if he were forced out of his country, would represent a tremendous victory. But it would not be a fundamental change in the apartheid system itself, nor would it alter the status of the hundreds of other political prisoners and the thousands of detainees who would be left behind.

In mid-1985, the African National Congress held a national consultative conference up in Zambia. About 250 delegates attended, including some who arrived clandestinely from inside South Africa. The ANC voted overwhelmingly to reaffirm its commitment to non-racialism, to the view, expressed in the first line of the Freedom Charter, that "South Africa belongs to all who live in it, black and white." The organization elected the first white man, a longtime activist named Joe Slovo, to the National Executive Committee.

The conflict in South Africa is sometimes called a "race war." This is only half true. Certainly the apartheid government regards its enemy as blacks, and its police and soldiers open fire indiscriminately in black areas. But the African National Congress has refused to respond in kind. Toward the end of the 1985, there were starting to be instances in which blacks lashed out at whites; after black ANC man Benjamin Moloise was hanged in October, some black people leaving a memorial service attacked white passersby in central Johannesburg. As the conflict grows even more bitter, this kind of incident will probably become more common.

But the African National Congress does not endorse such attacks. It opposes anti-white "terrorism," whether airplane hijackings, bombs in white-only buses or clubs, or sending its guerrillas to open fire at random in white neighborhoods. The ANC approach is by all accounts completely and enthusiastically endorsed by Nelson Mandela, who has spent one-third of his sixty-seven years in prison, confined there by white people. In this principled refusal to answer racial hatred with more racial hatred, the national liberation movement continues to uphold values that the Western world sometimes claims as its own unique heritage.

If we in America and in the West generally were asked to identify our greatest privileges, we might point to our extensive systems of education, or our technological amenities, like autos or washing machines. These are indeed luxuries contrasted with southern Africa, where most people fetch their water in buckets and live by candlelight. But there is an even greater privilege we enjoy, usually without realizing it; we are not forced to make painful choices among terrible alternatives.

In southern Africa, black men and women in the rural Bantustans must decide whether to watch their children starve or to leave their families as migrants for most of their lives. Black people in the towns have to choose between enduring the oppressive and humiliating treatment every day, such as carrying their passes, or risking imprisonment. Journalists have to decide whether to tone down their work or have it censored. Teachers must choose between spreading untruths or risking the loss of their jobs.

As war comes, the decisions are even more agonizing. Young whites must decide between the apartheid army and exile. Young blacks must choose whether to do open political work or join the underground; either way, they risk their liberty and often their lives. Older black people, together with sympathetic whites, have to decide the kind of support they can give to the national liberation movement, knowing that a single mistake, trusting the wrong person, even for a moment, can mean years in prison. In the end, there is the most terrible dilemma of all; my friends, many of them, are deciding whether to kill.

South Africans will face these tormenting choices again and again in the years to come. There are really only two predictions that can be made with any confidence. There will be increasing violence. The violence will last for a long time. Even the unlikely event of a settlement in Namibia would not address the major source of conflict in the region, which is apartheid in South Africa itself. We may well admire the heroes of southern Africa as they fight to create a nation in which no one must make such terrible choices. But it is within our power to help them shorten the time of bloodshed.

Economic sanctions are also in the interest of the people, most of them white, who fight on the other side. They fight partly due to their mistaken view that nonracial, democratic rule will mean the end of their culture and their expulsion from Africa. As long as they remain strong and resolute, they, like their counterparts in Rhodesia before them, will have no inducement to reexamine their wrong beliefs. But economic sanctions will weaken their war machine, undermine their smug feelings that the West will stand by them, moderate their intransigence, and force their leaders to negotiate. Sanctions will help them learn to live as equals with their fellow Africans.

It will not be easy to persuade those in the West to act in larger numbers on behalf of people they have never even seen, who live on the other side of the world. But in moments of doubt, I prefer to remember an old bus I used to often see chugging along one of the byways of rural southern Africa. The bus was usually overflowing with migrant workers and their belongings, off to the mines and towns on another join, and with women bringing sacks of grain and ancient hens to market. The radio blasted out raucous guitar music; the bus swayed under the weight of the battered suitcases and sacks piled on the roof; a cloud of reddish dust trailed behind. Inside, as the driver peered out intently in case cattle strayed into the road, there were conversations—the latest village gossip, talk of sports, or, more guardedly, politics. As the bus lurched along, there was a sense of spirit, of endurance, of smiling optimism. The driver had named his vehicle, in big gaudy letters painted along the side: "Hope Does Not Kill."

People sometimes ask me to summarize what I learned during my time in southern Africa. My answer is simple. From afar, apartheid seems like a monstrous wickedness, a convincing proof of the evil in mankind. And at first hand, the apartheid system is in some ways even worse than can be imagined. But there is much more than mere evil. There are people, black and white, who fight bravely, who are not afraid to be kind, to believe in and trust each other, who do not become cynical, and who will go to jail and even die without denying their beliefs. It is likely that they face many more years of violence. But hope does not kill. We can help them.

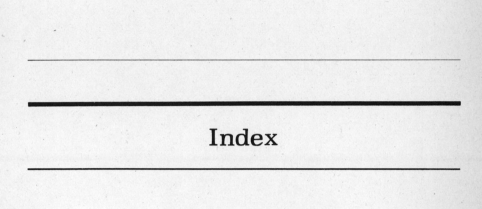

Index

Index